D1523897

Twelve Smooth Stones

By
Wanda MacAvoy

Twelve Smooth Stones
Copyright 2013 Wanda MacAvoy.
You may use brief quotations from this novel in reviews, presentations,
articles, and books. For all other uses, please contact Wanda at
wandamcavoy.com for permission. Or email me at wmacavoy@gmail.com
Scripture quotations from the King James Version (KJV).

ISBN-13:978-1493707645
ISBN-10: 143707647

"And the stones were according to the names of the children of Israel, twelve, according to their names,
like the engravings of a signet, every one with his name, according to the twelve tribes."
Exodus 39:14

I dedicate this book to my gracious Heavenly Father,
who gave me the idea in the first place
and then led me every step of the way.

Contents

Prologue

*"For if thou altogether holdest thy peace at this time, then shall there enlargement and deliverance arise to the Jews from another place; but thou and thy father's house shall be destroyed: and who knoweth whether thou art come to the kingdom **for such a time as this**?"*
Esther 4:14

May 24, 2018

The auditorium was quickly filling with family and friends of the graduates. Because of the significance of the occasion, Esther and her family had been able to get good seats—front and center. As she looked down the row, Esther couldn't help but smile. What an occasion! What a wonderful time to celebrate. As her mind thought back over the years, she was overwhelmed with emotions. Jehovah had certainly blessed her family beyond her wildest dreams.

They couldn't all be there. Many were scattered across the nation; some had even migrated back to Amsterdam. As she gazed into the sweet face of her dear husband beside her, Esther could only lift her heart in praise for the miracles that God had done in each of their hearts and lives. Her husband looked down at her and took her hand.

"And what is my precious Esther thinking?" he asked.

She smiled up into his still handsome face, gently tilting her head to one side. "I was just wondering at God's goodness to us."

He squeezed her hand and shook his head. "Who would have thought that our grandson would graduate from this university? And now this!"

"Yes, and who would have thought that our God would have chosen him for such a task?"

"For such a time as this?" He smiled. The phrase had become a reoccurring theme of their families.

Esther's face glowed, "Yes, for such a time as this."

She looked down the row at her namesake and oldest great-granddaughter. She would be turning sixteen this fall. The thought made Esther's mind whirl back to another time, another life—her own sixteenth birthday. Oh, how times had changed! She marveled at all the wonders that God had wrought in her own life—*for such a time as this!*

5

Part One
The Netherlands

Chapter One

*"They have said, Come, and let us cut them off from being a nation;
that the name of Israel may be no more in remembrance."*

Psalm 83:4

April 10, 1944

It was a day she would later look back upon with both fondness and heartache: her sixteenth birthday. The year was 1944.

"*Fijne verjaardag*, Esther," her family sang with cheerful voices and happy smiles, each face glowing in the candlelight. She looked fondly upon her dear parents and brothers. They had made quite an effort to make this day so special.

"Blow out the candles, Esther, before they drip all over the cake," her bother Daan said with mock anxiety. At seventeen, he was still the boy at heart he had always been—the sunshine in their rather stark and straightforward family.

As Esther paused for just a moment to imprint this memory into her mind, she had no way of knowing it would be her last birthday with her family. Surveying the circle of candles, she methodically blew each one out.

Mother whisked away her favorite chocolate cake, which rested upon the beautiful heirloom cake plate. Traditions—birthday cakes and candles, family feasts. Even the cake plate spoke of tradition. Given to Mother from her grandmother, the plate served as a reminder of who they were: *Maarssen Sephardim*, or Spanish Jews. Their ancestors had migrated to the Netherlands in the late 1500s to fashion their place in the great city of Amsterdam. Although her father's brothers had all made their mark in society as professors at the university, David Raul chose the family business of manufacturing stained glass.

As a young child, Esther had loved to watch her father as he inspected the creations of colored glass that would be used in lamps, windows, and jewelry. She had loved to see the colors flash as the rays of sunshine shone through. When her family had decided to build a new home, it was her father's idea to use the stained glass in the upstairs hallway to catch the late afternoon sun, as well as in the east-facing dining room to brighten their morning breakfast table. It seemed that their lives were touched with color from dawn to dusk.

"Mmm, Mother," exclaimed Ad. "You've outdone yourself this time!"

While Daan's intent was to bring laughter to the home, Ad was the official taste tester. His ambition was to become a chef, and he was already well on his way, studying the culinary arts at the university and assisting the main chef at one of Amsterdam's finest restaurants.

"If my son, the soon-to-be greatest chef in all the Netherlands, says so, I am flattered," Mother said genuinely. She knew her skills were adequate, even excellent in the eyes of friends and neighbors; but their opinions certainly held little weight against her own son's.

After the dishes were washed, dried, and put back in their places, the normal chain of events would have led to the excitement of opening packages, marking the most special time of the day. But these were not normal times.

In these difficult days, who would expect any birthday gifts? Truly, Esther's gift was that her family still lived together in their own home. Home and family had created the only stability in Esther's young life during the dark and uncertain times of 1944. Already, Esther's father had been forced to give over the ownership of his glass company to a Gentile vice-president. During this dreadful time of living under German occupation, so much seemed unfair and confusing to a sixteen-year-old mind.

But Esther and her family did not talk about these things. The family followed the German regulations as best they could: wearing the hateful yellow Star of David, keeping curfew, speaking only when spoken to, and most of all, keeping their opinions to themselves. At times, it seemed as though the air would explode with cries of indignation against the unfairness of it all. Mother especially found it difficult to accept their lot in life. She was from a rich Dutch Jewish ancestry. Was it not her mother's lineage that bore Isaac Aboab da Fonseca, the first appointed rabbi of the Americas? Was it not her relatives who founded New York City? And now this Hitler thought he owned the world, even the Netherlands!

Esther was shook from her reverie as Father and Mother came toward her with an air of expectation. Their faces were strange—filled

9

with calm excitement. Father tenderly looked into Mother's eyes. An understanding passed between them, a harmony rarely seen these days. Then, at Father's nod, Mother pulled her hands slowly from behind her back. She held an exquisite wooden box of detailed design. Esther had never seen it before. Made of rosewood and intricately carved, the box was beyond beautiful, and above that, it was old—ancient.

"What is it, Mother?" Esther barely whispered.

Her mother's eyes were shining. Hands trembled. Her voice sweet, simple, yet charged with intensity. "This belonged to your great-great-grandmother. It was given to her on her sixteenth birthday, and so each generation has passed it on to the oldest daughter on her sixteenth birthday." With that, she slowly opened the box. Within the folds of blue velvet lay a locket—*the* locket.

Esther had not seen it since she was a young girl, but now she remembered her mother wearing the exquisite piece of jewelry. It was oval and made of gold. Around its edges were set twelve stones of various colors. The intricate etchings were deep and of expert quality, made to last for many generations. It hung from a heavy chain, strong yet delicate.

Father was speaking. "For generations, your mother's family has cherished this treasure, not only because of its worth, but because of the message it carries. The jewels symbolize the twelve tribes of Israel. The high priest wore these same colors upon his breastplate as he entered the holy of holies. He bore the children of Israel upon his heart and truly *in* his heart."

Her usually gentle father continued, his eyes flashing as Esther had never seen them before. "We are God's chosen people! We are the children of Abraham, Isaac, and Jacob! '*The angel of the* LORD *hath said, I made you to go up out of Egypt, and have brought you unto the land which I sware unto your fathers; and I said, I will never break my covenant with you.*' Jehovah brought an end to our bondage in Egypt, and He will break the bonds of Hitler as well."

As he turned to her, Father took the locket from its ancient home and snapped it open. The right side was ornately engraved with three letters, all interwoven: *ERR*—her initials, as well as her great-great-grandmother's. He reverently placed it about her neck. As if reciting a benediction, he continued, "Oh Jehovah God, care for the bearer of this family treasure. She is the greater treasure, and as she

10

wears the chain about her neck, may You break the chains of bondage that would seek to enslave her. May these twelve stones continue to remind her of who she is, and may You build a wall of protection about her as precious as the jewels around her neck. May it always be near her, reminding her of Your never-ending presence no matter where she goes."

A peaceful silence lay upon each heart. No one dared to move—fearing to break the holy sense of God's presence. And then, as if summoned from somewhere deep inside of each of them, they began to sing the songs of Zion.

When the room fell into silence once more, Esther reverently asked, "Father, is it safe for me to wear this?" She lovingly fingered the locket.

"You will need to be careful who you let see it. Be wise, Esther. These are difficult days, and we can trust no one." Father's shoulders drooped as he said these dark words; his character was to trust and love everyone.

***

The room was brilliant white with the light from a single-bulb lamp only an inch from his face. He could feel the heat of it on his cheek— the only warm spot in the otherwise frigid room.

"Your name!" shouted the officer in front of him, standing to the left of the lamp.

"Kurt Gerstein, sir," he replied.

"What? I can't hear you!" the voice commanded.

"Kurt Gerstein, sir!" he shouted back.

"Louder!"

"Kurt Gerstein, sir!"

Over and over the shouting match continued.

"Who is our leader?"

"Adolf Hitler, sir!"

"Is he ever wrong?"

Kurt hesitated, earning a blow to the head. He already felt weak and confused by the lack of sleep and food.

Again, the officer shouted, "Is he ever wrong?"

"No, sir," Kurt managed to reply, but not with enough enthusiasm for the Nazi fanatic.

"I can't hear you, Gerstein."

11

"No, sir!" he shouted

"Louder!"

"No, no, no ..."

Kurt woke from another nightmare with perspiration beading on his forehead. He couldn't remember having a dreamless night in the past three years.

As a reinstated SS officer of the Nazi Party and an engineer, his duties had taken him to some of the worst camps in Germany and Poland.

At first he had joined the Third Reich thinking that it was for the good of his nation. His love for country was only second in his heart to God and family. Kurt Gerstein also knew that by joining the Nazis, he would be able to use his engineering degree. Never in his wildest imagination would he have dreamed that his knowledge and hard work would be used to destroy an entire race of people—God's chosen ones, at that.

After his own time in a concentration camp for speaking out against the Nazi reign of terror, he was encouraged to rethink his loyalties; but the internment had only hardened his resolve against the Goliath nemesis. Now, as part of the SS, he looked for any opportunity that would aid him in fighting his own personal war against the enemy from within.

He wiped the cold sweat from his brow as he remembered the unexpected meeting on the train with the secretary to the Swedish legation in Berlin. Baron Göran von Otter had given him the opportunity he had been seeking. He was certain that the man thought he was mad, for as he listened to his own account of the atrocities that he had personally witnessed, he too thought they sounded beyond anything possible. If he hadn't seen it with his own eyes, he wouldn't have believed it either.

Now, here it was, two years later, and still no word from Göran von Otter. It seemed that no one would listen to him, not even his own church leaders. Disappointment and nightly images of horror were driving him mad. What could he do? He had to find a plan. Even if it meant saving only a few, it would be better than nothing.

There was a knock at his door. Again, his fiendish nightmare and cries had disturbed someone's sleep. To his chagrin, it was Elizabeth, his dear niece. Her room was next to the well-appointed guest room that was his when he came for a visit. Truly, his sister's house was the only place that felt like home to him. Too many years of war and too much destruction had taken its toll on the very fiber of his core. Oh, how he longed for the simple days of his childhood! Even with the disappointments of the Great War, he had had the security of home and God on which to anchor his soul. But now, even God seemed to mock his very existence. Most nights, his Bible lay unopened on the nightstand beside his bed.

"Uncle Kurt, are you alright?" came the sweet innocent voice from the other side of the door.

He instinctively reached for his housecoat and went to the door, taking a deep breath to still his shaking hands. As he opened the door, he cleared his throat and tried to place a convincing smile across his face.

There she stood, looking up into his face, eyes as big as saucers ready to run over at the brim with fearful tears. "You were shouting again," she said, her voice trembling with emotion.

Feeling deep regret, he pulled her into his arms—as much for himself as for her. "I'm sorry, pumpkin. It was just another bad dream."

"Did the monster have you again?" came her innocent reply.

How many times had he covered his tracks with a lie? She need not know the truth about her uncle; it would break her adoring heart. They all thought that he was doing some heroic deed for the German nation, and indeed, he was trying to, but the way seemed dark and foreboding.

"Yes, little one, but I'm feeling better now. I'm sorry I woke you and worried you." He pulled her closer and patted her head. She was the dearest one on earth to him. The youngest daughter of his only sister, Elizabeth and her family were safely tucked away in the family estate in Münster.

"That's alright, Uncle. You know I don't mind. I'm just glad you are here. I only wish you could stay longer." That was always her reply; there was never enough time for either Elizabeth Steinmeyer or Kurt Gerstein. He would be leaving again in the morning for Belzec.

Chapter Two

"For thou art an holy people unto the Lord *thy God,*
and the Lord *hath chosen thee to be a peculiar people unto himself,*
above all the nations that are upon the earth."

Deuteronomy 14:2

June 3, 1944

"Ah, the last day of school," sighed Silla. "I won't miss it one bit!"

Esther's mood was more sober than that of her dearest friend, Silla. "I will."

"But think about it, Esther. I can come over every day, and we can read and bake and lounge in the sun!"

"Aren't you the least bit afraid about what might happen—what *is* happening?" Esther retorted rather sharply. She envied Silla's carefree ways. Nothing seemed to ruffle her—except maybe a broken fingernail.

"Ach! This mess will all be over soon. It won't reach us." She toyed with the strap of her book bag, a frequent habit. "We obey the rules, and we are not in Germany. They'll leave us alone. Our families are different. We are too important to the Netherlands. They won't let anything happen to us."

Silla's air of confidence managed to lift Esther's somber attitude for the moment. As they began to leave the confines of their Jewish school, Esther's hand automatically moved to hide the locket beneath her blouse. She had lovingly cut out the faces of her family from an old photo and placed them inside. She wore it proudly every day while at home, at school, or in the synagogue—secretly when walking the streets. The looks on the faces of the German soldiers who were standing at the upcoming corner made her feel that they could see right through her blouse to the hidden treasure. They leered openly at her. She knew it was not the locket that attracted their attention.

Esther was attractive, even to the Jew-hating soldier. Her dark hair and deep brown eyes fringed with unusually long lashes set her apart from other girls her age. Some would even call her beautiful. It was one thing for her mother and father to say it, but when her friends at school made comments about her beauty and when she looked at her reflection in the hall mirror, she knew it was true. *You can have any boy you want,* Silla had told her one day. That was the first time she had noticed Gabriel watching her.

Gabriel Bachman was the smartest boy in the class ahead of hers. Bright and talented as well as strong and handsome, every girl's dream was for Gabriel to notice her, but it was in Esther's direction that he set his cap. Nothing had been said as of yet, but with him heading off to the university next year, she hoped he would at least give her some token of intent. However, with tensions mounting daily, who even knew what tomorrow would bring, much less next fall? It was just another rent in their fiber of life caused by this wretched war.

As Silla and Esther crossed the street to avoid the soldiers, Esther heard steps approaching quickly from behind them. When someone tapped on her shoulder, she nearly jumped out of her skin, and a little gasp escaped from her lips.

"I'm sorry, I didn't mean to startle you, Esther," came the rich low voice she loved to hear.

"Gabriel!" *What would he think if he knew I was just daydreaming about him?* "I ... I guess it's just the soldiers," she replied, casting a sideways glance their way.

Gabriel's brow furrowed as he looked across the street. The soldiers had been watching the whole scene with amusement. He turned his attention back to the one he had been seeking. All semester he had looked for an opportunity to talk to this beautiful young lady.

He wondered, at times, if he was only drawn to her good looks. Yet after many sleepless nights with thoughts only of Esther, he realized that she was not only beautiful and bright, but her heart was genuinely beautiful as well. He watched her devotion to her father and mother, her kind yet sparking exchange with her older brothers, and her gentle, respectful ways toward her elders. He often referred to her in his mind as his Queen Esther. Surely the captive maiden of long ago couldn't have been any lovelier. And even though he was by no means a king, he would choose her and spend his days lovingly providing for her.

15

"Are you looking forward to the summer?" he asked.

"Well, I really haven't given it much thought," Esther replied. *Did that sound as ridiculous to him as it did to me?* She didn't want to make a fool of herself. "Do you have any plans?" she finished lamely.

"Yes, I'm planning to go to America," he responded. He could see the shock in her eyes and quickly went on. "My father has an uncle there that needs help in his New York City business. I plan to assist him and then attend the university there in the city."

"Oh, your mother must have a heavy heart," Silla gushed. She knew that his attraction was to Esther, but she didn't want to stand idly by like a dunce.

"Yes and no," Gabriel replied, noticing Silla for the first time. "She knows that it is for the best."

"Then you will be safe," Esther said almost as if to herself. She sighed.

"Yes, I feel it is the best thing to do under the circumstances, but it will make things difficult."

"What things?" Esther asked innocently.

His eyes seemed to swallow her up. At that moment, there were no soldiers, no war. There was just Gabriel.

"I know these times are so uncertain, but we are all hoping that the war will end soon. It's really not fair of me to ask this, but I'm leaving next week." He hesitated.

Esther's heart raced. She clutched the locket through her blouse, and it seemed to give her strength. Then he was speaking again.

"May I write to you?" There! It was out! How many times had he rehearsed that simple sentence?

Esther's mind was in a fog. Was this really happening? Was he really asking her? "Yes," came her simple whisper of an answer. "I would be glad if you would." She feared that she sounded too unemotional, mechanical, and stiff, but it was all she could afford. If she said more, she would embarrass them both.

Relief washed over Gabriel's face. It was a lot to ask, and he knew he would need to speak to her father, but she had said yes. His street was just coming into view. Now what was he to say? He had never gotten further than the question in his rehearsals. How could a straight A student and head of the debate team be so tongue-tied?

"Good, good," he managed. "I will talk with your father on the Shabbat."

They said their goodbyes at the corner. Esther walked numbly ahead as Gabriel turned and crossed the street.

Silla let out a long sigh. "I told you," was all she said.

Esther was glad to have reached her door—if only to escape the inevitable discussion of the scene in detail with Silla. She felt as though she had somehow aged several years in that single moment. It seemed too sacred to share, and Silla sensed it as well.

Thankfully, Mother was in the kitchen preparing dinner. Esther tossed a greeting her way and went to her room. She looked in the mirror: cheeks flushed, eyes sparkling—she wouldn't have been able to hide them from Mother. Part of her wanted to shout from the roof top, *Gabriel Bachman asked me to write to him!*

She thought of telling her mother. Maybe then she would keep from bursting. But she decided otherwise. *He needs to talk to Father first, and then Father will tell Mother … What if Father says no?* The thought of it drained her face of its flush. No, Father liked Gabriel and his family. They were well respected in their community.

Oh, maybe Silla would be right and this war would be over soon. After all, America *had* entered the war. That brought a light of hope into Esther's heart.

That evening at sunset, the Shabbat began. Esther and her mother stayed home making preparations for the Shabbat meal while the men went to the synagogue. *Maybe Gabriel will even talk to Father tonight!* Esther thought as she set out the special dishes.

As soon as Father entered the dining room, Esther knew that he had. He looked tenderly at her, his smile sweet yet shadowed. Was there pity in his eyes? A sense of foreboding fell upon her heart. Father had said no! She didn't dare ask any questions until the evening ritual was finished.

This was usually Esther's favorite time of the week, but this Friday evening, Shabbat preparations seemed to last forever. She chided and rebuked herself. *Look at you, you silly school girl. Who is your God, Jehovah or Gabriel?* Esther managed to keep her thoughts on Father's words and even kept up with the conversation during the meal.

She didn't have to wait long for Father's attention. Directly following the evening prayers, he called her to the library. Mother

17

looked up with raised eyebrows but knew she should say nothing. She would know later, so she set about clearing the table.

He went to one of the overstuffed chairs beside the fireplace and motioned to the other. "Have a seat, Esther. There is something I need to talk to you about." His eyes were full of meaning, but she could not read the message.

"Someone talked to me tonight concerning you." There was a hint of a smile about his lips.

"Yes, Father?" Esther replied. She could feel the color rising in her cheeks.

"Gabriel Bachman." Just at the sound of his name, Esther's heart flipped. "He asked permission to write to you." Father was always straightforward, getting right to the point, and Esther loved him for it.

"Yes, Father. He spoke to me on the way home from school today."

"Would you like to do this?"

"Oh, yes, Father—if you have no objections." She held her breath, waiting for his response.

"I love Gabriel as my own son, Esther. There is no one I would rather see join my daughter in marriage, but ..." He hesitated. Esther waited. She knew she should not speak, but the few minutes of waiting seemed like hours. "Under the circumstances, do you think it is wise? Our lives are so uncertain. Should such hopes and promises be made?"

He finished with such a loving look of pity that it brought tears to her eyes.

"I know the times are volatile, Father, but we can't put our lives on hold forever, can we? I am of age, and he will be leaving for America next week. We would just be writing, and perhaps before we got too serious, this war would be over." Her little speech had accelerated as she plunged forward, leaving her breathless.

Another pause, another sigh. Father stretched his long legs out in front of him, rubbing the back of his neck. "You're right. I wish we could somehow send you off to America—perhaps we should all go."

But even as he spoke the words, David Raul knew he could never leave his homeland. And to ask such a thing of his wife would break her heart.

"Father, with America now in the war, do you think it may end soon?"

18

"It is everyone's hope, child. We can only pray that it is so."

"Then I can write to Gabriel?" It seemed so serious when she spoke his name—her Gabriel!

"Yes, dear daughter. But I don't understand," Father said with a frown.

Esther's pulse quickened again. "What, Father?"

"When did my little girl grow into such a beautiful young lady?"

He smiled and reached for her hand. She instinctively went to him and sat at his feet. She had often sat there as a child while he read and stroked her hair. He did so now, and her tears marked his trousers—tears of joy, yet tears of sadness.

***

The morning Shabbat dawned bright and beautiful; the leaves on the avenue trees rustled softly with a gentle summer breeze. Window boxes displayed splashes of colors: red geraniums, white narcissus, and sunshiny marigolds. Everything seemed brighter to Esther. A smile played on her lips, and Mother didn't need to ask why.

Father had told her of the young Bachman boy's request. She thought it was a bit premature—they were so young.

Of course, engagement and marriage had happened later in life for her. Another war had caused her own delays. *They were different times,* she thought. How many young men had sought her hand in marriage? How many had she refused, keeping her heart open and eyes upon David Raul? True, he was much older than her, and he didn't move too fast when it came to romance, but he had been worth the wait.

Ten years her senior, she had watched him build his father's business and climb to the top. She knew he needed to feel secure before he would approach her father. *Oh how intimidating Father could be,* she remembered. After all, she was his little girl—his only daughter as well as the youngest, like Esther. Anna Aboad hadn't minded her father's selectiveness. It made her allusiveness easier. She instinctively squeezed her husband's arm, and he cast a loving smile her way.

As they approached the synagogue, Esther sensed eyes upon her. As she looked to her left, Gabriel and his family were coming up the walk. Their eyes met. He smiled. She smiled. Their parents called

19

greetings to each other. Everyone had an air of happiness—and it didn't all have to do with the Shabbat.

Esther was glad to head toward the women's balcony with her mother. From there, she could see Gabriel seated with the men. He slipped a glance her way and caught her staring at him, causing her to blush. He gave her a slight smile just as the elders were starting the service.

Esther was never so proud to be of Jewish descent than when she was at Shabbat services. The singing was her favorite part. Oh, how her people loved to sing! Her spirit rose and fell with each cadence, and for those sacred moments, she was able to forget Hitler and the atrocities that were happening. She felt safe in the hands of her God, Jehovah, God of Israel. He was her high tower and her rock. Her life was in His hands, and He would guide her and care for her wherever she would go.

A peace settled over Esther's whole being. Only God knew her future. He knew whom she would marry, where she would live, even how long she would live. Somehow the thought brought comfort and strength to sixteen-year-old Esther Ruth Raul.

Chapter Three

"How long wilt thou forget me, O LORD?
for ever? how long wilt thou hide thy face from me?"

Psalm 13:1

Summer of 1944

The summer passed slowly. Gabriel had left in June. Esther had managed to see him the day before he left; he had come to her house, and she was the one who answered the door. Before he even spoke, her eyes threatened to tear.

"Esther," he said as he nervously placed his hands into his pockets. *Why does she have such an effect on me?* Clearing his throat, he continued. "May I come in for a moment?"

"Why, yes," she answered, stepping back to allow him to enter the foyer. She had never entertained male guests before, but she knew enough to invite him into the parlor. Her father and brothers were at work, and her mother had just stepped across the street to visit with a neighbor. She had hoped—even dreamed—of a moment alone with Gabriel, and it seemed as though she would have her wish. "Please, have a seat. Would you like something cool to drink?" Esther motioned to a chair and graciously awaited his answer.

In a way, Gabriel amused her. He had always seemed so sure of himself at school. Perhaps it was the setting and the circumstances that made his hands shake and his brow glisten. He seemed relieved to be able to focus on something as sure and solid as a chair.

"No, thank you," he managed to say after clearing his throat. "I just wanted to stop by and ... say goodbye," he faltered to a stop. His eyes mirrored his heavy heart, and Esther could not hold back the tears. She tried to hide her face, but he was there, standing close to her, lifting her chin. Her tears had the opposite effect on him than he would have thought: They broke his heart, but at the same time, they gave him strength. How he desired to protect her! Gently, he took her hands and pulled her close. "There, there, Esther. It won't be forever."

"But how do you know?" she sobbed, barely recognizing that she was in his arms. She didn't mean to be so forceful, but the strain of the past few weeks crumbled her resolve to be strong. How badly she wanted to escape with him to America. She felt completely protected in his arms.

He held her close for a moment. As much as he enjoyed her nearness, he didn't want to cast a shadow upon their relationship before it was even established. What would her father or mother think if they saw him holding their daughter? He gently pushed her back to arm's length, knowing the memory of that moment would strengthen him in the days to come. "I don't know, but even if it is—I will wait for you, Esther." His deep voice and penetrating eyes melted her heart.

"I will wait for you too, Gabriel," she whispered.

There was one more hug—gentle yet firm. She felt him sweetly kiss her hair, and he was gone. She caught just a glimpse of wetness on his cheek as he turned to leave.

That seemed like ages ago. She tenaciously held on to the memory. At times, it brought her great joy, at other times, only torment. Her heart ached for him as she daily checked the mailbox. His first letter seemed to take forever to arrive. She knew her brothers would have loved to tease her, but they seemed to sense her struggle.

In the quietness of her room, she poured over each letter. Now there was quite a stack of them in her desk. As soon as one came, she sent her own epistle back across the ocean to the man with whom she was falling in love.

Throughout the summer, tension continued to mount in every country, including the Netherlands. News was never good in 1944. How long? Was there not an end to this wretched war? Could no one stop Hitler's long arm of destruction and the mayhem he was causing?

All over Europe, Jews were continually rounded up and sent away, never to be seen again. Every family who had any family or business connections across Europe knew of someone who was now missing. Could the rumors of the atrocities be true? Esther, whose heart was kind and good, could not comprehend such cruelties—her mind refused to register such inhumanity. Were not all men made in the image of God? She knew many did not believe as she did, or the horrors would not be happening.

Meanwhile, each of Gabriel's letters signaled a continual mounting of his anxiety. The earlier missives of news and affection contained slight traces of concern, but now each letter begged and pleaded for her to come to America. It had not been easy for him to be smuggled out of the country, and as news of Hitler's tight hold reached his ears, his nightmares grew in enormity—he became desperate for the woman he loved. How could little Netherlands protect her Jewish population against such a foe? Would the Netherlands protect them even if she could? People's minds were being poisoned against God's chosen race even across the ocean. Surely his Esther would be swallowed up by this engine of destruction if she stayed anywhere in Europe, and he would lose her forever.

One night, Esther approached her mother about his pleas. She knew Mother was worried. Her usual no-nonsense approach to life was shadowed by doubts. Although her hands kept busy with all her daily tasks, her brow was often furrowed, and even an unbidden tear would make its way down the now well-worn trail. Tears had always been so foreign to Mother's face. The sight nearly melted Esther's resolve to speak, but she pressed on.

"Mother, I got another letter from Gabriel today."

The words brought a tight smile to Mother's lips as she swatted away the tears. "And how is our dear Gabriel?" she asked. Her heart wanted to sarcastically say, "Safe Gabriel," but she bit her tongue.

"He will be starting classes at the university soon," Esther replied. She hesitated. "He has been mentioning an idea of his for the last few weeks." She breathed deeply, slowly, and then drove on. "He wants me to come to America. His uncle has many good friends there and knows that one of them would take me in, and that I could find work easily. There are many jobs in America, Mama." She didn't often call her mother by that name anymore, and she saw its effect as another tear gave way.

"Oh, Esther, it has been discussed."

"It has?" Mother's response surprised Esther.

Turning from the counter, Mother continued, "Yes. Father and I have talked about it, even to Gabriel's family. We can all see the seriousness of your growing relationship, and the danger of staying here continues to worsen. Would you be willing to go?"

The question ran deep in her mother's eyes. Esther could see the conflict clearly: If she went, her mother may never see her again. But if she stayed ... God only knew what danger may sweep her away.

"I—I don't know. I've thought about it but never really considered it a possibility." Her thoughts were in a whirl. "Then Father has thought about this too?"

"Yes—it was actually his idea." Mother left the counter where she had been cutting vegetables and pulled out a kitchen chair. Esther put the kettle to boil, sensing her mother's need for a cup of tea, and then sat opposite her.

Her mother spoke wearily, tension fringing every word. Her hands traced the edge of the table. "We think that it could be arranged. With your father's business connections, we believe we can get you safely to England and then to America. It would be a difficult journey. Most of the ports have been closed, and you would often be traveling with complete strangers. Who knows what you might have to face? But then, who knows what anyone faces who stays here." The bitterness in her voice tainted the air.

Esther rose to get the tea ready, and when she returned, Mother's head was on her arms across the tabletop—her shoulders heaving as a silent sob caught in her throat. Esther's heart ached to the point of breaking.

"Oh, Mama, please, don't cry!"

The tears were now flowing freely. Mother reached out and enveloped Esther in her arms. Together, they found comfort. The pain seemed to lessen when held by two together instead of two alone.

"I'm sorry, sweet girl. I just can't bear the thought of losing you—losing all that is dear to me. Will we lose our home? Our own lives? It's so frightening." She stopped long enough to dab the tears with the ever-present handkerchief before continuing. "I've always thought of myself as a strong woman, but then I realize that my life has been so carefree and easy. We've never wanted for anything! Our lives have been the same as those of most of our dear ancestors before us! We've kept the traditions of our fathers and dutifully passed them on to the next generation. It was all that was expected of us, and we did it willingly, happily." She paused. "But this! How do you prepare for such madness?"

Her face distorted with indignation, her words spewing forth like venom. "These horrid soldiers! They've taken over our streets as if they were their streets! I don't doubt that they will take our homes as if they worked a lifetime and more to earn them. Was it their ancestors who built this beautiful city? No! And now ..."

But she could not finish. She wept against Esther as though she were the ill-tempered child and Esther the mother. As her forehead touched the smoothness of the locket, she looked up and gingerly reached for it. "Oh, Esther—your beautiful locket! What will become of it?" Her voice was strange, like that of a deranged woman. Esther felt pity. She needed to be strong for her mother, the one who had always been strong for her.

"I will always keep it close, Mother. Even now, I wear it all the time, hidden when in public." The statement seemed to satisfy Mother, as a child who has been let in on a good secret.

"Good, good. They will never know."

And with that, she returned to her task at hand as if the conversation had never taken place. "Look at the time! Father will think we've sat and sipped tea all afternoon instead of getting his supper."

To Esther's surprise, Mother was humming. She wondered just how stable her mother really was, but she dismissed the awful thought from her mind.

Chapter Four

"Behold, he taketh away, who can hinder him?
Who will say unto him, What doest thou?"

Job 9:12

August 14, 1944

Father came home with unexpected good news. His face lit up like the great North Star as soon as he saw Esther. "I have something very important to talk to you about. Please, go into the library."

Before following her there, he dutifully yet lovingly went to his wife with a tender embrace. They talked in excited hushed tones for a moment, casting furtive glances her way. He squeezed Mother's hand and headed to the library. Wasn't it just yesterday that he had taken her there to speak about Gabriel? No, that was surely a thousand years ago.

He gently pulled a chair closer to Esther's and sat down. Clearing his throat, he began. "Mother says that you two talked this afternoon about our plan."

"Yes," was the only reply she could give. It seemed to Esther as though everyone had a plan for her life.

Father seemed to want more. "And … what do you think?"

She sighed deeply. "I don't know. One moment, it seems like a wonderful dream come true; at other times, it seems like a nightmare. I can't even imagine leaving you and Mother and Ad and Daan, much less Amsterdam and all that I have ever known." Now she was sounding like a woman on the verge of hysteria.

Father's strong hands were there to steady her. He gently touched her shoulder. "I think it is the best thing, considering our uncertain future. I sense that something is brewing."

Esther looked alarmed.

"I want to shield you from it, Esther! I wish I could protect us all, but the boys are determined to stay, and Mother …" He didn't need to finish. Esther knew that Mother would never leave. Father looked so old tonight. The laugh lines that always crinkled his face in such a special way—the face she loved so much—now looked old and worn out. His tender eyes were full of burdens he shouldn't have to bear.

"I will do whatever you think is best, Father."

She determined then and there not to add to his already heavy load of care, and with her words, his face brightened.

"I think I have it all arranged." He went on excitedly, "You will be traveling with a business associate of mine as far as England. He thinks that he can pass you off as his secretary. From there, we've made arrangements with another company with which we do much business. They have already booked passage for you with one of the vice-presidents' wives. They are very sympathetic to our plight and were more than happy to help."

"It's already arranged?" she asked incredulously.

"Yes." He hesitated for a moment, knowing she would be overwhelmed. "You will leave next Friday." He leaned forward, as though ready to catch her.

Indeed, she was shocked. Next Friday was only nine days away. Sensing her father's fear for her reaction, she simply said, "That will work out just fine, Father." She rose to rush to her room, but before she could escape, he had her in a papa-hug, and all her resolve to be the strong one dissolved into a fountain of tears. How good it felt to nestle against her rock and cry away the pool of mixed emotions.

"There, there, puppet." The use of her childhood name only brought more tears. "You will be safe in America with that wonderful man of yours. And who knows—maybe this will all blow over and your mother and I will take a much-needed vacation to the USA. I've wanted to see that country for a long time. What better reason to go than to check on my little girl?"

He was soothingly stroking her hair with one hand and holding her steady with the other. Soon, the tears subsided, and she felt ready to stand on her own—something she would be doing more and more as time marched on.

***

That had been on Wednesday. The next frantic days were filled with preparations for her departure. She wouldn't be taking much, since it

27

was to look as though she was on a business trip, and the task of choosing which items to take seemed impossible. Over and over again she sorted and tossed aside garments and treasures. What if I never come back? Can I leave *this?* And on and on it went until she felt she would explode with frustration. Only six days left until her August eighteenth departure. How would she ever be ready?

Monday morning, August 14th, dawned dreary. The sun would not shine today. Esther looked out her window as the trees dripped from the evening's thunderstorm. The air felt fresh and clean, and the colors in Mother's garden glistened vibrantly even without the sun. But in spite of all this, there was heaviness in the air. All seemed strangely quiet.

Esther would often look back and wonder if nature had a premonition about the day's agenda. Even the birds were not singing their usual morning canticle of praise to their Creator. She dressed quickly, putting the degrading yellow star on her sleeve. Today it seemed to mock her, as if to say, "Here I am, come and kill me!" Last, as always, the locket was placed around her neck and tucked underneath her blouse.

As she descended the stairs, the sweet aroma of Mother's morning scones tantalized her stomach. She was hungry. When everyone was assembled, Father bowed his head for prayer, and Mother poured the rich brown coffee. Scones and coffee were Esther's favorite.

It was a usual morning—the usual amount of banter, the usual clinking of silver and china, the usual sweet fellowship, the usual tasty morsels. All that was missing were the beautiful splashes of color that would adorn their table as the sun's rays washed in through the stained glass window.

Esther instinctively looked up at the window to admire its glowing translucent colors when suddenly, every shred of normalcy was shattered by a rock crashing through the colored glass. Mother screamed.

"What—" was all Father had time to say before the pounding of the front door brought him to his feet.

Ad and Daan were close behind their father as he went to the door. The sense of foreboding seemed to blanket Esther's world. They were here—shouting and pushing into their privacy, their sweet, tranquil home. At first she thought that they only wanted the men, but two soldiers were heading for her and Mother, shouting, pushing, and cursing. Before she knew what was happening, Esther was outside on the front sidewalk, and Mother was behind her. Her precious father and brothers could only watch as their women were herded like cattle out into the street. It was then that she heard her mother's voice speak such angry forbidden words.

"How dare you come into our home like this?" her mother shrieked. "Who do you think you are? You are no better than us! In fact, you are less than the lowest of God's creation. Snakes! All of you—snakes! Barbarians! Murderers!"

As if signaled by the last insult, with half a sneer and half an air of total indifference, the soldier standing behind her pulled his revolver from its holster and shot her in the back. Mother seemed to stand there for a moment—frozen in time and forever etched in Esther's memory—before she crumpled into a heap on the front steps. The soldier simply stepped over her and pushed Esther ahead.

"No!" Esther screamed, but Father was there pulling her away to join what seemed to be the entire neighborhood. They all looked shocked, stunned beyond comprehension. What could they do? Nothing but survive.

Father, Ad, and Daan became a wall of protection to her as they were herded down the streets of Amsterdam. Those men that followed the horrid news of the day knew where they were going: Camp Westerbork. The camp had originally been constructed for the many Jewish refuges that had fled Germany and Poland. The Netherlands would not turn them away, but instead made a place of shelter for them. Esther knew of the place. Several times over the past few years, she had brought baskets of food to the train station intended for the shelter. That was before they had been forbidden to do so.

Mother had been impatient then as well, Esther remembered, never able to tolerate injustices. More tears silently streamed down her cheeks. What would happen to her mother's body? She could hardly bear the thought. Esther would soon learn that many thoughts had to be pushed down deep, buried in the depths of her soul somewhere where she couldn't find them. It was a hard thing, but it was the way of survival.

They were marched to the train station—the same station that would have taken her in a totally opposite direction just four days later.

* * *

Bewilderment, fear, confusion—Esther could not ascertain which monster was ruling her. Perhaps all three were vying for complete control of her spirit. Ad and Daan sat in front of her and Father—heads down and motionless except for the constant swaying of the train. Her father, too, was still, like a defeated warrior returning from battle.

She had been confused at the station by the German soldiers' seemingly genuine kindness. The Jews were told that this move was for their protection during these unstable times. They would be cared for—watched after. And yes, they would be asked to work for the cause of the Third Reich, whatever that was. They were told that they were prisoners of war—no more, no less.

Upon arrival at Camp Westerbork, there was a frenzy of activity: index cards filled out, identification numbers given, and housing assigned. Everyone moved as in a daze toward their given shelter. To Esther's horror, she would be separated from what was left of her family. The men's barracks were separate from the women's.

"It will be alright, Esther," Father was saying, although his face showed no confidence. "Here, take this." With those words, Father pressed his Ketuvim* into her hand. "I was just getting ready to read our morning portion when the confusion happened."

Tears threatened his eyes as he realized it had only been six hours earlier. Now, his wife was gone, and he was being separated from his dear girl. "Read your story, Esther," he said, his eyes penetrating all fears in her own. "It will be a strength to you!" And with that, he was gone.

She stood for a moment watching him and her brothers walk away. Then she turned and for the first time, her eyes were opened to the reality of it all. She looked upon her new home. No more color, no more soft beds or warm blankets. No more of anything but the barest of necessities. Esther did her best to pick her way through the streets, nothing more than muddy ribbons tied around rows and rows of monstrous bunkers. More than once she felt the soldiers' eyes upon her and she found herself wishing she were ugly.

30

"Esther!"

At the sound of her name, she turned to see Gabriel's mother. Before she could respond, Mrs. Bachman held her in a wonderful, motherly embrace. There didn't seem to be any tears left. There were no words either, but she didn't need any, for Mrs. Bachman was speaking. "I'm so sorry about your mother," she said.

And with that, all strength seemed to leave her body. Had she not been supported by this dear lady, Esther would have been in a heap on the ground.

"I'm here for you, dear one. I know I could never take your mother's place, but I will do all that I can."

"I—I—" She had nothing to say. Empty of even sorrow, she simply allowed herself to be led away.

* A Jewish sacred book containing Esther through Song of Solomon.

Chapter Five

*"Behold I have refined thee, but not with silver,
I have chosen thee in the furnace of affliction."*

Isaiah 48:10

The next morning, Esther couldn't remember much. She opened her eyes expecting to see sunshine streaming through her doorway, colorfully skipping its way across the carpet and up to her bed. Instead, she saw row after row of iron gray triple bunks. She tried to comprehend, thinking perhaps she was not awake—that this was all a nightmare. Didn't someone once tell her that dreams were in black and white? Certainly the scene before her lacked any hint of hues.

As she mused, hushed voices wound their way to her from below—familiar voices. She peeked over the side of her bunk and saw all the ladies from her neighborhood. And then she remembered. Flinging herself back onto her cot, she lay motionless, trying to stop the swirling images of yesterday's fiasco. That's when she heard her name.

"Poor Esther. What an awful sight to witness—your own mother shot to death. If only she had held her tongue; but then, that was never her way."

Esther squeezed her eyes shut, trying to stop the tears. She thought that she had none left, but it seemed as though she had been granted a fresh supply for the day. *No! I will not give in to this!* The words coming from the group below gave her added resolve.

"We must all help her along. She has no one."

The words stung Esther deeply, taunting her. *No one! No one! Alone! You have no one!* As she rolled over to stifle a sob, she felt something cool and smooth touch her cheek. There, beside her pillow, was Father's sacred book. It seemed to draw her to itself.

Read your story! Those had been Papa's last words to her. *My story—the story of Esther.* At first she wished that it was the Torah, which contained all her heroes: Abraham, Joseph, Moses. But then she wouldn't have had the Psalms, Proverbs, Job, and of course, her story. With a strength that came from deep inside, she tenderly lifted the book and opened it to the account of another lonely girl. She was also taken from her home, her parents gone—she too was alone even though surrounded by people. How strangely similar were their situations. Esther lay there devouring every word, letting them sink down into her soul. A strange peace came over her. She remembered it—she had felt it at the synagogue on the Shabbat.

With her courage bolstered and her spirit refreshed, she descended to the floor below. By now, the ladies had scattered, to where she was not certain. Where should she go? There didn't seem to be a washroom anywhere in sight, and her body was reminding her of the lateness of the hour. As she made her way to the door, she passed a bunk where a teenage girl lay huddled into a ball; she looked strangely familiar.

"Silla?" she questioned. The form rolled over, revealing disheveled hair and red puffy eyes.

"Esther!" With a bound, Silla was off her bed and embracing her dearest friend on earth. She sobbed against Esther's shoulder, muffling her words. "What is happening, Esther? Why are we here?"

"Come with me, Silla. Walk with me to the washroom."

Like an obedient little child, Silla allowed Esther to lead her from the barracks to the latrine. When Esther finished in the washroom, she found Silla still sitting on the bench in front of the latrine, head down, hands folded on her lap. The life was gone from her. She reminded Esther of an unlit lamp—useless and completely ornamental. She sat down beside her, not knowing what to do next. What was expected of her? Where was she to go? What was she to do? Everyone seemed tense and agitated.

"Esther, why are we here?" Silla asked again, like a confused, frightened child. She waited for Esther's response—eyes pleading. It tore at Esther's heart, and she drew strength from her earlier time in God's Word.

"I don't know, Silla. Somehow we got caught in a web of injustice."

"But it's not fair! We obeyed their rules! We wore their stupid star!" The tears were again flowing freely. Esther knew she needed to be the strong one. How would a girl like Silla survive in a place like this? And what if ...

Esther wouldn't allow herself to think of what tomorrow might bring. Already, without realizing it, Esther was learning the basics of survival—think only about today, this moment. *I must get through this day, one hour, one minute at a time.*

Just then, Silla's mother came rushing up to them. "Silla, I was worried about you! I didn't know where you were." Her eyes were frantic.

"It's alright, Mother. I'm here with Esther." She gave Esther's hand a squeeze, and for the first time that day, she smiled. It was a bit wobbly, but it was a heroic effort on Silla's part. "What are we supposed to do, Mother?"

With a sigh, Mrs. Schenck replied, "Nothing for the moment." She looked nervously about the camp. People were mostly walking in groups, talking in hushed tones. The tension in the air was stifling.

"Why is everyone so tense?" Esther asked.

"Today is Tuesday," she replied, and went on to explain. "Evidently, every Tuesday a train leaves to who knows where jammed packed with our people."

"What do you mean, Mother?" Silla's voice raised with hysteria. "Who goes, and who stays?"

Esther wished Mrs. Schenck would have been a little more discreet with her daughter. Yet Silla needed to grow into the times in which she was living or she would not survive.

"I don't know how they decide. It sounds as though there is no rhyme or reason to what happens. All I know is what I have heard: Tuesdays are like this, and then everyone settles back down for another week, going about their business." She shook her head. "Come, let's walk back to our place and see what the others are doing."

With that, the three made their way across the grounds between the rows of barracks. As Silla linked her arm into her mother's, a pang of sorrow swept over Esther—how she wished for her own mother! But even as she thought the words, she rejected the idea of her dear mama living in such a place. No. As much as she missed her, she was glad she was not here.

And what about Gabriel? *In three days I would have been on my way to him!* She couldn't dwell on it or she'd go crazy. *Tonight, I'll think about him.* And so that became part of her daily routine. Her days started with her God; they ended with thoughts of the man she loved.

***

In America, Gabriel was facing torment of his own: the nightmare of not knowing whether his family and the woman he loved were safe. When two days passed without a letter from Esther, he tried not to be concerned. It could be the mail. Perhaps she was too busy preparing for her departure to write letters. But when a week went by, and then two, he became frantic. He had not heard from his mother either—that too was out of the norm. What could he do?

He shared his concerns with his uncle, but Gabriel could sense that his uncle was not sensitive to his plight. How could anyone here in America understand?

"Perhaps it's the mail," his uncle suggested. "This war has spread to the seas as well, Gabriel. The Nazis could be intercepting the mail ships. Some of our European connections have been interrupted, making our business transactions next to impossible."

As much as Gabriel was grateful for the opportunities his Uncle Jacob had made available to him at J.B. Investments, he was disappointed with his uncle's attitude about life. Work, work, work! Work came before everything—even his family. Of course, anyone could see the fruits of his labor. They drove the fanciest cars, their home was the biggest on their street, and Gabriel's cousin, Nelson, did not lack for anything—except character. Gabriel could already see the same demon of covetousness that controlled his uncle taking root of Nelson's soul.

With a heavy heart, Gabriel returned to his work, his mind whirling with unanswered questions. If he knew just how long it would be until he would ever hear from any of his people in the Netherlands, he too would have felt the pull toward insanity.

***

Slowly, one wretched week at Camp Westerbork slipped by. The Shabbat was kept, and it was the first time Esther had seen her father and brothers all week. What joy their reunion brought to her heart. They all seemed to be faring well enough. As the singing portion of the service began, there seemed to be no spirit left in her people;

35

however, as they continued to sing, their voices rose with a swell of hope gathered from God's promises. It encouraged Esther, and she left feeling her inner strength return.

After the services, Father took her aside to the back wall of their makeshift synagogue, where a box sat in the corner. He lifted it and handed it to her. "Here are some of your things, Esther." Recognizing the surprise in her eyes, he explained, "One of my Gentile associates from the glassworks was granted permission to go to our home and gather some of our things for us."

The thought of a stranger rummaging through her belongings did not sit well with Esther—just another adjustment to their new way of life.

"I wasn't sure what to tell him to get, so I hope you will find the things useful." He smiled at her and leaned closer to her ear. "I did tell him to get the letters."

By the glow in her eyes, he knew it had been the right thing to do. At first he hadn't been sure if it would only make things worse. But the few items of his wife's that he himself had requested had already been a great source of comfort to him, helping him feel her close to him again. He awkwardly held Esther in his strong arms; the show of affection in public was not an easy thing for him to do.

"Thank you, Father. They will be a great joy to me."

"If only ..."

"Don't say it, Papa. You did your best." She knew he felt responsible for their situation and was determined to persuade him otherwise. "I've been reading my story. It has been a great blessing to me." She paused for a moment, searching for the right words. "Somehow, I believe God has allowed this in my life for a purpose."

Father looked at her, amazement furrowing his brow. "What do you mean?"

"I'm not sure, Papa, but when I see the good that Queen Esther did for her people, even though she too was taken to a strange land and forced into an awful situation with the king, God turned it around for good—not only for Esther, but for all the Jews."

Her father held her again and said softly, "You are growing into a wise woman." Holding her by the shoulders as if giving her a command, he continued. "Esther, always—always look for God's good in any situation, no matter how difficult. When I think of your mother," he looked away from her eyes, his own eyes clouding with the

36

memory, "I can hardly believe what has happened, why it happened. But when I see this place, I am thankful she never had to be here."

"I've thought the same thing, Father. She wouldn't have been able to stand it. I see the women in our barracks and around the camp, just walking as if in a daze. The life is gone out of them. I wouldn't have been able to stand seeing Mother like that. The last few weeks at home were hard enough."

"She was a proud woman, and I loved her for it," her father replied. A tear gently slipped down his cheek, and Esther reached up to wipe it away.

"Are you okay, Father? I mean, do they treat you well?"

He straightened and blinked away the rest of the tears. "Yes. In fact, one of the officers came and actually apologized for Mother's death. He said that the soldier in charge was way out of line and lost his ranking because of his actions. I believe that is why Mr. Thomlin from the office was allowed to help us, and I'm hoping that it will keep us here, too." Hope tried to make its way from his heart to his eyes, but it was a difficult journey. How many times had they hoped, only to be disappointed?

Esther took his hand. "It might, Father, it just might."

The room was now cleared, and both knew they needed to part. She managed a smile for him, squeezing his hand as they left. Ad and Daan had been talking with others from their neighborhood outside the door, sensing that their father and sister needed time alone. Each gave her a quick hug and together, as a family, they walked the short distance to where their paths divided.

"Ad's volunteered to take over the kitchen and show the Germans how to make real food," Daan commented as they walked.

Esther looked at him incredulously, "Are you serious?" She first looked at Daan, then to Ad and back at Daan again. Ad's face, which always spoke the truth, betrayed his brother's attempt for levity.

"Yes," Ad replied, "and I've volunteered Daan's services as a dumb waiter."

Now even Father's face crinkled into a smile. "Oh, the food is not so bad, boys," Father interjected. "It just takes a little imagination."

The three men chuckled. Oh, how she missed them all! Even here, Daan's desire to lighten the atmosphere lifted the burdens of the heart. She was glad they had each other.

37

Alone with her box, Esther was too deep in thought to notice the hunger pangs rattling about in her stomach. She hurried to her barracks and quickly climbed up to her bunk—it was the only home she had left. There, she slowly opened the box. How thankful she was for the few articles of clothing that were included. She had borrowed a few items from some of the women, but she would be glad for her own things.

Underneath all the clothes, in one corner, were her letters. Neatly tied together with a ribbon along with her writing paper and stamps, they were just as she had left them. She was thankful that Mr. Thomlin had respected her privacy.

As she lifted the letters from the box and reverently laid them on her bed, she turned back to her digging. As she lifted the clothes from the other side of the box, she saw her dearest treasure other than the locket—its rosewood container. How did he know to take this? She thought of its beauty and realized that anyone could see its worth.

She held it close to her heart, rocking back and forth, remembering the night she received it: Mother's eyes full of emotion, Father's strong voice. How special the memory was. And the Lord had brought the box back to her!

Chapter Six

"For the hurt of the daughter of my people am I hurt;
I am black; astonishment hath taken hold on me."

Jeremiah 8:21

That Monday evening, all the people were summoned to gather on the boulevard—the main road that divided the camp in two. It was obvious that the people who had been there longer knew what this was all about. Eyes darted, panic edged every voice.

For a crowd this large, Esther would have expected much more noise—the near silence was unnerving. Several German officers were on the platform, talking and laughing among themselves, adding confusion to Esther's thoughts. Some laughed, some cried—it just depended upon one's origin of birth. The thought brought anger to Esther's usual quiet demeanor.

Before she had time to continue her thoughts, one officer stepped forward and rattled off a string of sentences containing instructions and details concerning tomorrow's departure. Esther had missed the previous Tuesday's ordeal. Had she wandered over to that part of the camp, she would have understood the anxiety on the faces around her.

When the regimental instructions were over, the main purpose of the meeting began. Names were recited in alphabetical order. As if shot by a sniper, those people to whom the names belonged each reacted in their own way, some wailing, others weeping and moaning, and still others just moving away in utter dejection. As the list continued, Esther realized that they were already past her family name. She was staying. Perhaps her father was right. *Oh Father, let it be true.*

The relief that washed over her was only momentary. She tuned back into what the officer was saying just in time to hear him call, "Schenck, Abraham, Drika, David, Silla." She didn't have to wonder where Silla was standing, for she heard her cry.

"No, no, no!" Her voice started as a cry of unbelief and rose to a tone of defiance. Images of her mother flashed through her mind—angry words and then the total blank stare as she fell to the ground. She rushed to where Silla was standing with her family. How could she bear this? *You must be strong for her, Esther! Be strong!*

"Oh, Silla!" She pulled the girl into her arms and held her while the list continued. Silla was shaking uncontrollably as her heart-rending sobs added to the cacophony around them.

"I can't do this, Esther. I can't take any more! Where are they taking us? I just want to go home!"

Mr. and Mrs. Schenck were there, trying to comfort their spoiled little girl. Perhaps they should have been more honest with her while they were still in the comfort of their own home; but then, who really knew what was going to happen? No one had any answers—not then, not now.

Mr. Schenck was speaking. "We will be alright, Silla. We are together as a family."

As he spoke the words, Esther thought of her own loved ones for the first time. Where were they? As she turned to look, she saw them coming toward her—her three pillars. Other neighbors were gathering as well. Words of comfort and encouragement were meagerly doled out in small fragments—no one had too great a reserve of them. Little could be said; little hope was left. All they could do was survive this day, and then the next, and then the next.

There wasn't much packing to do for those who were going—no one had very many possessions. Esther wandered over to Silla's bunk. How did one say goodbye for what might be forever? She had been able to say goodbye to Gabriel, but with that goodbye, there had been the hope of letters and a future. She hadn't been able to say goodbye to her own mother, and the thought nearly made her crawl back to her bunk and hide. But her friend needed something—some word or gesture of friendship and faith.

Silla had never taken her religion very seriously. Esther doubted if she had ever read any of the sacred writings for herself—though she hadn't either, until coming to this place. The treasures hidden within the Ketuvim gave her strength that she knew was not her own. *I need to share this with Silla,* she thought as she clutched the precious book.

40

As she approached her bunk, Silla was sitting there, toying with the strap on her satchel. No one else seemed to be nearby, for which Esther thanked God. The evening had been a draining one, and most of the ladies were coming and going to the latrine. It was not far, but there was no hurry. Life just seemed to keep going in slow motion.

"Hello, Silla." Esther sat down beside her, the springs squeaking out their rusty complaint.

"Hello, Esther." Even those two words were hollow and empty. Silla had been completely drained.

An awkward pause came between them as Esther sighed and took Silla's hand. She thought Silla would cry, but there were no more tears. "I've never really had to say goodbye to anyone, Silla, except Gabriel."

Silla's vacant eyes looked up at her, completely void of emotion. She hurried on. "When the soldiers came to our house, Papa was just getting ready to read from the Ketuvim. He still had it when we got here, and when we separated, he gave it to me. It has been a great comfort and strength to me."

Silla's brows furrowed, and she looked confused. "How? It's just an old book."

"No, Silla!" Esther protested fervently. "It is a letter from God! It gives me strength to face another day." She reverently opened the book and was about to read when she heard Silla groan.

"There is no God."

The words shocked Esther. "You don't mean that!"

"There is no God." Silla spoke the words louder, with disdain. Others looked their way, and then shifted their gazes elsewhere, uncomfortable by the spoken words that many had thought in their own minds. Silla looked at Esther with cold, hard eyes. "Don't tell me about God! How can a God let this happen? Where is He?"

With more conviction than she thought she had, Esther pointed to her heart and softly replied, "He's in here, Silla." Her own eyes—gentle but penetrating—tried to break though the hardened shell that Silla was building up around her. Was she too late to pierce the darkness that had taken over her dearest friend's soul? "You will never make it without God's strength. None of us have the kind of power we need to fight this evil—only God, Jehovah, can help us."

Silla shook her head as if to fight off the words. The disappointments and difficulties of simply existing combined with the

41

spiritual battle that was raging within her. It was more than she could absorb; her heart had already become too hard.

With a sigh and a look of utter rejection, Silla valiantly tried to put on a cloak of confidence. "I'm alright, Esther. If God is helping you get through this, then I am truly happy for you. Let's not waste our last evening together talking like this."

And with that, she jumped from her bed into her usual bright self with marginal success. "Come on, let's take a walk—it's stuffy in here."

Esther knew that the door to any serious exchange was closed—perhaps forever.

Outside, a dusky golden color was washing over their bleak surroundings. Somehow it brought peace to Esther's heart. The sun would keep rising and setting wherever they were. She put her arm around Silla, like they used to do as children, and gave her a squeeze. "We've been friends a long time, Silla," Esther commented, seeking a safe place of conversation. "Remember Mrs. Cohen, our fourth grade teacher?"

A mischievous smiled played on Esther's lips, and she was rewarded with her hoped for response: Silla smiled.

"She was special—that whole year was special—fourth grade!" Silla seemed deep in thought. "Remember the time we dumped Amiela Goldstein's desk all over the floor to clean it out for her? What a mess that girl was! How she ever stuffed all those papers into her desk, I'll never know!"

They continued to share stories as they walked across the compound. The sound of music seemed to draw them to a building they had never seen before. From inside, the lonely sound of a single violin floated through the air. Someone was playing one of the songs of Zion: *By the waters of Babylon, we lay down and wept for thee Zion. We remember, we remember, we remember thee Zion.*

Each girl, deep in thought, entered the back of the auditorium and took a seat, not wanting to cause the music to stop. Memories flooded their minds—bittersweet memories of singing together in school, at the synagogue, and in their homes. For one, the melody and the memories brought a warmth to her soul; to the other, it brought only torment and more tears. The walk back to the barracks was much quieter. Most of the people were already in bed for the night.

42

"I'll see you in the morning," Esther quietly whispered to Silla as she gave her one last hug before going to her bunk. There was no answer from Silla—just the same empty look that had been there earlier.

***

Sleep did not come easy to anyone that night—except perhaps First Lieutenant Albert Konrad Gemmeker. Although he was in charge of the operations, someone beneath him always carried out the dirty work. He saw only names, not faces or individuals. He would sleep well. This group had been fairly cooperative. What happened to them after they left this place was no concern of his. He need only involve himself with the task at hand—keeping peace and moving people.

To Esther, it seemed like the longest night of her life. She wrestled with nightmares the whole night through. What would happen to Silla and her family? Where did they take them? Somehow she knew it was not to a better place, no matter how much the Germans tried to convince them otherwise.

She slept later than she had planned to, and after a hurried morning routine, she returned to the barracks, planning to visit with Silla until she needed to leave. As she approached her building, she could sense swirling commotion. The detainees from her barracks were being sorted according to who was going and who was staying. She rushed forward to find Silla.

"You there," a soldier shouted at her. "What is your name?"

"Esther Raul," she answered. "I'm staying," she added, a bit too forceful for his liking.

"We decide who goes and who stays!" He shuffled through his paper, hoping to find her name there. If it were up to him, he'd send her too—mouthy little Jew. He shuffled through the papers again, stopping as if he had found her name. The effect he hoped to accomplish could be seen on her face—a look of terror. He felt satisfied but lingered a moment longer as if debating her fate. "Go on then, into your quarters," he shouted, moving on to his next victim.

Esther quickly moved in through the door, shaken by the exchange. It wasn't until she was half way across the room that she remembered Silla. She turned to go back through the door, but someone was pushing it shut and locking it. What did this mean?

43

Turning to an unfamiliar elderly lady, she frantically asked, "Why did he lock the door?"

"It helps to lessen the confusion. Besides, dear, you wouldn't want to be out there. Be thankful that you are safe for another week." And with that, she hobbled away.

"But I didn't get to say goodbye to Silla," Esther said, mostly to herself. No one else was listening. There was no more to say, nothing to do but wait for the door to open.

***

Two more weeks passed, and Esther was thankful that the Bachmans hadn't been taken anywhere. Mrs. Bachman was the constant source of encouragement and motherly love that Esther needed. The waiting was nearly unbearable. What were they all waiting for anyway? A deliverer? America? The Messiah? It seemed to Esther that all she ever did was wait—wait for Gabriel, wait for America, wait for anyone to put an end to this madness. Would her whole life be one of waiting?

She had written Gabriel a long letter explaining all that had happened. Her greatest hope was that she would receive a letter from him soon, before anything changed. As she wrote, she labored over what she should say. Should she tell him all and needlessly worry him, or should she put on an air of nonchalance to quiet his worries? In the end, she decided to tell him everything. Mrs. Bachman also enclosed a sheet that looked as lengthy as Esther's. On the Shabbat, she handed it to her father, knowing that he would have a better chance of getting it out of Westerbork than she would.

As she gathered with the others that Monday night, a sense of foreboding settled in about her. She noticed a group of Jews, mostly German, who had been there since before she had arrived. But as she looked around, most of the other faces she saw were people who had arrived after her. It made her pulse quicken, and she searched the grounds for her father. He was behind her, just coming into the courtyard, the men's barracks being much further away than the women's. Ad and Daan were there too, and she pushed her way to them.

It didn't take the officer in charge long to start the list. "Alfons, Amsel, Antje, Bachman ..." Esther's heart skipped a beat. The Bachman's were going.

The officer continued calling out names: "Baumann, Berkowitz, Blum, Bohmer, Goldhirsh, Greenberg, Pascal, Prinz, Rapp, Raul, David, Ad, Daan, Esther …"

Now she knew how the others had felt. Her brain seemed to work in slow motion as she turned to Papa. Her head was resting against his shoulder. He was hugging her and the wetness of his tears fell on her hair and cheek.

When she returned to the barracks, she noticed the little old woman who she had spoken to on the day of Silla's departure. She too was placing her few belongings into her bag. Esther felt she needed to talk to her. Walking over to that side of the room, Esther cleared her throat to get her attention. The woman turned and half smiled. "So, you are going too?" she asked.

"Yes, my father and two brothers and I were called today." Esther hesitated, "Do you have any family?"

"No, my husband was gone before all this started. My sons and their families live in England." Her look was wistful as she spoke. "They wanted me to come, but how could I leave my home and neighbors? I never thought it would come to this. All this moving about—I am too old. I will not survive." She sadly shook her head.

The woman's candid remarks brought a lump to Esther's throat. "Oh, don't say that! You will be fine. You are strong in body and in spirit." She hoped her words were an encouragement to this dear woman. She could have been Esther's grandmother—she seemed older than time itself.

The woman smiled again. Her face was all crinkles and wrinkles. "What is your name, dear?" she asked.

"Esther. Esther Ruth Raul."

"What a beautiful name." She studied Esther's face as if debating whether to share her thought. "Esther, you are young and full of life. And I can see the spirit of God in your eyes. I heard you as you talked to your young friend the other night. I was so glad to see a young woman with such a strong spirit! Don't lose that."

She took Esther's hand and patted it. "And don't you worry about me. I've lived my life. What happens to me happens. I am not worried. But you! Fight to live, dear Esther!" Her words became passionate. "Who knows if our God will not use you as He did Queen Esther? Perhaps you have been brought here for such a time as this!"

These words would come back to speak to Esther for many days to come, sometimes taunting her, at other times strengthening her resolve to live. Esther started to walk away but turned to the old woman and asked, "Excuse me, but what is your name?"

The woman smiled. "Miriam Pascal," she replied.

"Yours is a beautiful name too, and with so much meaning."

"Yes, my father was a rabbi from the Levitical line, as was my mother. My husband too was a rabbi," she said as her eyes began to mist. "He could be as bold as the Lion of Judah, and as gentle as his name: Pascal, the Passover lamb. And every day I miss him more."

Esther moved forward to give the woman a hug. It was received hungrily, like one starving for a touch of human kindness.

Part Two
Auschwitz

Chapter Seven

"Through the wrath of the LORD of hosts is the land darkened,
and the people shall be as the fuel of the fire."

Isaiah 9:19

August 28, 1944

Tuesday morning dawned without the sun in sight. Thick clouds were rolling across the skies, promising rain before the day would end. It seemed appropriate to Esther that the sky would cry on this day.

She had gathered her things and said goodbye to her bunk. It had become her haven of rest away from the world, and she was surprised at how much she hated to leave. She hadn't felt this way when leaving home, though she hadn't been given any warning on that day.

As she came down from her bunk, she saw Mrs. Bachman gathering up her belongings. "Here," she said to the older woman. "Let me carry that for you," and she picked up the dear woman's bags.

Mrs. Bachman gave a sigh and followed her to the door. They walked silently between the rows of beds. Many others were filing out as well, making Esther realize that their barracks would be nearly empty. For the first time, Esther thought about those who had been here before her. How many women had passed through this place, and how many more would continue to shuffle out the door? The idea of it made her shudder.

"Are you chilled, Esther?" Mrs. Bachman asked with concern in her voice.

"No, no—it was just a little shiver," Esther was quick to reply. She had no desire to frighten anyone with her morbid thoughts.

They came to Mrs. Paschel's bed, where she was busy placing the last of her toiletries in her bag. Turning back to Mrs. Bachman, Esther said, "I want you to meet someone," and she walked over to the older lady. "Mrs. Paschel," she called, then waited for the woman's response.

Mrs. Paschel looked up and smiled. "Why, Esther, how are you this morning?"

Esther was amazed by the woman's calm spirit. She was a true soldier of the faith. "I'm fine, and there's someone I'd like you to meet." Esther stepped back so the two women could face each other. "Mrs. Paschel, this is Mrs. Bachman. Mrs. Bachman, please meet Mrs. Paschel."

The two women exchanged pleasantries, and for some reason, the exchange warmed Esther's heart. How nice it was to hear a normal everyday greeting.

"If you are ready, we would be glad to walk with you," Mrs. Bachman offered. Her gracious manner reminded Esther of the woman's son. Strength of character ran through both generations of Bachmans and would continue to flow to the next, Esther was certain.

As the ladies approached the doorway, their movement was slowed by the volume of women exiting the building. No one was talking much; none were in a hurry. Thankfully, the rain was holding off. The thought of having to sit on a train for who knew how long in wet cloths did not appeal to Esther. However, the cloud cover did cool the day, even if it also added to the gloom.

At the crossway stood Father and her brothers, who were waiting for her along with Mr. Bachman and their two younger sons. How much they looked like Gabriel— especially Reis, who was only two years younger! Esther found herself staring at him until he looked her way. She smiled and quickly turned to her father.

"Good morning Father, Ad, Daan," she greeted then. Each in turn nodded their greeting. "Father, this is my friend, Mrs. Paschel." Father stepped forward, and they shook hands.

"Nice to meet you, Mrs. Paschel," Father spoke warmly.

"And a pleasure to meet the father of such a dear young lady," Mrs. Paschel replied. Esther's eyes dropped at the sound of such flattery. What must the Bachmans think? But just then, she heard Mrs. Bachman chime in.

"Yes, Mr. Raul, you have much to be proud of. Esther has been a strength and a help to us all." Then putting an arm around her, Mrs. Bachman continued. "She is the daughter I never had." Her words caught in her throat as she gave Esther a watery smile.

"Good words for a father to hear," Mr. Raul replied, smiling tenderly at his treasured daughter. "'*They that wait upon the* LORD

50

shall renew their strength; they shall mount up with wings as eagles.' "
A silent message passed from father to daughter as real as the passing of the sacred book just a few weeks earlier.

The group moved on to the boulevard, where the train had just pulled in. To Esther and everyone else's surprise and dread, the engine was not followed by passenger cars, but cattle cars. Soldiers and detainees alike were moving down the line opening the huge wooden doors, which creaked and moaned against their efforts. The gaping mouths of each car stood ready to swallow them all. Where would they be spewed forth, Esther wondered?

When all seemed to be assembled, several officials scattered throughout the group, pulling out index cards, checking the names of each person and assigning them to cars. All was done quickly and efficiently—weeks of practice had honed their skills. The Rauls and Bachmans along with Mrs. Paschel were all to board the same car and were some of the first to go in. After scrambling up the step, Father took Esther's hand, then Mrs. Bachman's, and then Mrs. Paschel's. All the men followed.

David Raul chose a corner that had a small air vent above their heads in the wall of the car. As if signaled from somewhere far above by someone who was witnessing the whole affair, a clap of thunder rolled angrily through the air. One after another, the thunder rolled, hurrying the soldiers' proceedings.

People continued to pack into the car. "Spread out a bit," Father fiercely whispered to their band. "Keep as much room as you can."

Children were crying, women wailing, men complaining, and then the door was shut. Thunder rolled on and on outside, and the rain began to fall, skipping the usual warning sprinkle. Sheets of a torrential downpour were pounding their way across the tops of the railroad cars, drowning out all the cries.

Human cargo—that was all they were. Any shred of dignity was slowly being stripped away, and this was only the first step. Hour after hour went by with no stops, no food, no water, hardly enough air to keep them all alive. Esther thanked God for the rain; it kept the temperature in the box car bearable, although it didn't seem to help the tempers of the people.

As she looked and listened, she realized for the first time that not all Jews were like her family and neighbors. Some cursed God, as

51

Silla probably would have done. Anger once directed at the German soldiers now rose against whoever was closest. Again, her three men were a wall of protection to her.

***

When she thought she could not stand it for one more moment, she felt a shift in the train's forward movement. She looked up at Papa and knew that he had felt it too.

How proud she was of her father. He stood there like a rock, his anchor on Jehovah held fast. He was so smart and astute. Because of his foresight, they had had enough room to move around a bit, even if it was only to squat down for a while, and the small vent above had been a lifesaver. The cool air sifting in through the bars had revived her. She couldn't even imagine what it must have been like further in the middle of the car. *Thank you, Father,* she prayed. *Thank you for Father, Ad and Daan, and thank you that even in this horrible situation, I can see your hand.*

Now everyone was aware of the train's decreasing speed. A sense of relief was mixed with foreboding. What would be next? They wouldn't have to wait long to find out.

As soon as the train slowed to a stop, the door was pulled open. The sunlight, though clouded, was blinding. Everyone shielded their eyes from the brightness. Orders were being given by voices sharp and angry: *"Schnell, raus, raus, schnell, schnell!"*

Out into the confusion they went. As her feet touched the platform, Esther noticed the rod-iron sign above the entrance way: *Arbeit Macht Frei.*† What did it all mean?

Above the turmoil, she noticed an officer watching her. He motioned to her, and she was taken from the crowd. One look back, one last cry of anguish, and she was taken from all that she held dear—except her locket.

† "Work Will Make You Free"

Chapter Eight

*"My times are in thy hand: deliver me from the hand of mine enemies,
and from them that persecute me."*

Psalm 31:15

Kurt Gerstein needed to pull himself together. His mind whirled with images of corpses and naked children walking innocently to their deaths. Could this really be happening? How could this be happening?

His own reputation now tainted as a flesh-loving predator, Kurt searched for young Jewish woman whose lives could be spared by a life none of them would choose. Today was Tuesday, and his schedule told him that a new shipment would soon be arriving from Westerbork. He stood near the platform that would shortly be filled with unsuspecting Jews who would be gassed, worked to death, or starved. At times, his own plans seemed so futile, but it was all he could do for now.

"Waiting for the next arrivals, Gerstein?" Officer Höcker jeered at him with a leering smile.

It sickened Kurt, but he played his part. "Yes, I hear the Dutch Jews are the prettiest."

"Who cares if they are pretty, just as long as they are young and ... fresh, if you know what I mean." With a jab in the ribs, Höcker was off to torment someone else. It sickened Kurt to hear a man talk in such a way, especially a married one, but there was no fear of God in this place.

From the distance, he could hear the train before he saw it come rolling down the tracks. Others were now gathering—they as well winked and jeered at him. *It's for the life of one more soul, Father,* he whispered under his breath. Coming to a slow grinding halt, the train now stood directly in front of him. He could already hear the whimpers of children and smell the stench of too many bodies cramped into a small confine for too long.

As the doors were opened, Kurt could see the usual distorted faces as they tried to adjust to the blinding sunlight and their new surroundings. The lying facades of the soldiers sickened him as they spoke condescending words of comfort to the people, assuring them that all would be well. His own mask of total nonchalance nearly slipped when he saw her—a young woman, perhaps sixteen to eighteen years old, and beautiful, in spite of her ragged appearance. She was being sheltered by three men, probably a father and two older brothers.

He stepped forward. "You there," he commanded. He could see the startled look on her face and the horror on her father's. If only he could tell the truth about what he was about to do. "The girl. Come! Stand here," he ordered, his features masked in false indifference.

Another wrenching goodbye. Another tear-stained face. Another life saved. Surely the old man and the two younger might make it, but he knew she would not. He wondered about the mother, almost glad she was not here. He casually chose nine more girls and led them ahead of the others.

***

If Esther had learned only one thing from her mother, it was to quietly obey no matter how difficult. She followed silently as the girls beside her questioned each other—asking questions that none of them could answer. They were taken to a building and ordered to drop their belongings by the door. The officer handed the woman in charge a slip of paper.

"Here are their numbers. Remember, they are mine. You know what to do and what to leave undone." He turned and was gone, never looking into the girls' faces.

"Humph," the woman muttered to her co-worker. "He's a strange one."

The other woman laughed a short, tight laugh. "I'll wager that there are many SS officers who would like his job." Her eyebrows rose as if to say, *you know what I mean?*

Another "humph" from the other, then they started their work. Directing their statements to the ten frightened teen girls, all strikingly good-looking in spite of their terror, one woman commanded, "Everything off and into the showers."

The girls stood there, stunned.

"You heard me! Now move! We have no time to waste." Then, redirecting her words to the other woman, she added, "This place will soon be swarming."

Esther led the way, quickly removing her shoes and hose. Her mind was racing. *How can I hide my locket*? Thankfully, her long hair was pulled back today. As she deftly untied it, she unfastened the locket as well and held the treasure loosely in her left hand while removing everything else.

The girls were led to a shower room, where they were instructed to wash quickly. Thankfully, the other girls made such a fuss that the guards' eyes were on them and not Esther. She finished quickly, toweled, and took the clothes that were given her. She wondered where they had come from, whose they had been. *Stop*, she ordered herself and hurriedly dressed. Strangely, there were no undergarments.

With her dress on and buttons fastened, she waited for the right opportunity to replace the locket. Some of the girls were still in the shower, but the water must have turned cold. Amid the girls' shrieks and cries, the guards harassed them to finish, giving Esther the moment she needed. By the time the woman guard was back to her desk, the locket was safely hidden once more.

"Come! Stand here," the next woman ordered, standing rather impatiently with shears in her hand, razors waiting on the table beside her. To Esther's horror, she realized that they planned to cut her hair, which would expose the locket's chain. What would they do to her if they discovered that she had hidden such an expensive possession from them? She slowly walked toward the barber.

"No, Elsie. These are Gerstein's girls, remember?" And with that and a curse beneath her breath, the woman motioned Esther to the next room.

There sat another German woman with some sort of apparatus on her table. A strange, medicinal odor filled the room.

"Sit down and place your right arm on the table," the woman instructed as she picked up what looked like a needle. She wiped something across Esther's arm and took another look at the paper that Esther had seen the officer give the first woman. Numbers? Esther's mind tried to comprehend. *I am no longer Esther Ruth Raul—I am only a number.* And with that, the woman tattooed *14777* on her arm.

55

Esther was ordered to stand by the door and wait for the other girls to finish, pain shooting up and down her arm from the tattoo. Finally, the last of the girls were finished, most of them whimpering from the pain and fear of what was happening. What next? *Who cares,* Esther thought morbidly.

As she leaned against the wall, to her horror, she felt her locket give way. She frantically clutched at it, but before she could grab it, it clattered to the floor at her feet. All eyes were upon her as the woman officer, who seemed to be in charge, looked at her with eyes of menacing steel. She coolly and slowly walked over to Esther, standing inches from her; the woman's hot breath blew from her nostrils into Esther's face as she coldly stared into her eyes—pools of terror. Without warning, the woman struck a hard blow across Esther's face, sending her reeling to the floor. She felt a shoe on her neck as the woman reached down to pick up the necklace.

"You little fool," the woman spat at her. "Take her out of here!"

"You forget whose she is, Frau Stedder," a voice as calm and cool as an Artic breeze spoke. Esther could not see him, but she knew it was the officer who had taken her from the platform.

"But Officer Gerstein, you know the rules! She tried to hide this from us," the woman whined, waving the locket in his direction.

Gerstein casually glanced at the locket and then back at the woman. "And are you more concerned with the rules or with keeping the trinket?"

Kurt knew much of the Jewish jewelry never made it to the official stockpile. Stedder would keep quiet, for she knew that he too would keep her secrets. She vehemently dropped the locket into his outstretched hand, spun on her heels, and returned to her desk for the tattoo order form. She curtly placed it in his hand and, without a word, continued her duties, dismissing him by her silence.

He turned to the girls, his eyes locking with Esther's for just a moment. "Follow me." Esther scrambled to her feet. As they all reached for their satchels, Gerstein simply stated, "Leave them."

As they left the building, each girl instinctively looked toward the train platform where the people were forming rows of five abreast. Some were passing through the gate and moving to the right, others to the left. They could only guess what it all meant.

56

Kurt turned to the girls and instructed them to form their own squadron of ten: five rows of two. Esther did not know any of the other girls, although she had seen them on occasion at Westerbork. They walked past rows and rows of barracks; Westerbork was small compared to this place. Esther could see two brick buildings farther ahead with giant smokestacks belching out an acrid smoke. They were probably responsible for the horrible smell that hung in the air.

It seemed as though they were marching straight for those towering stacks when the officer suddenly turned left. He stopped in front of the last barrack on the right. It looked different from the rest and was set apart from the others. Having only one floor and more windows, the building seemed to be much newer and was much smaller. There was a porch carved into each front corner.

The SS officer ushered them to the porch and mechanically turned to face them. He seemed as though he was wearing a mask. Esther had seen him slip her locket into his pocket, and she wondered if she would ever see it again.

"These are your living quarters. You have been chosen for special duties—some of which you would not choose for yourself." There seemed to be pity in his eyes. He quickly shifted his gaze away from their eyes and to the back wall.

"Two will be assigned to a room. During part of the day, you will help with the laundry of the officers and their families." He hesitated, as though struggling to relay the message. "And in the evening, you will entertain guests."

His short recitation ended, and he turned on his heels and opened the door. For some reason, Esther felt empathy for this man. He seemed different from the other soldiers that she had seen—he seemed to have a heart. But how could that be? She quickly dismissed the thought.

The building was nothing more than a long hallway with doors on either side, some of which were open and others shut. At each open door, he stopped, turned to two of the girls, and assigned them to the room. All were too numb to understand the reality of the situation. By the time he reached the other end of the hallway, Esther was the only one left. The last girl was placed with a young woman who was already in the room. Esther could not discern the look on her face. Was it pity, disdain, hatred? She wondered about her own fate.

The officer continued to walk to the last door on the left. Reaching into his pocket, he pulled out a key and unlocked the door. Clearing his throat, he hesitantly stated, "This is your room." Their eyes met shortly before he stepped back to let her in. The area was actually made up of three rooms—two separated by a wall, and a door to what she assumed was the toilet facility. There was no door between the rooms, only an entryway through which she saw a window.

She slowly entered the room, unsure what to do next. She was surprised when he followed her into the room, closing the door behind him. Panic coursed through her veins. He did not miss it.

"Please, be calm. I will not hurt you." His voice was gentle, yet strained. He looked like a man who carried a heavy load: Too many secrets seemed to be buried in his soul.

Esther stood waiting for him to speak, afraid to look at him and yet afraid to look away. As much as he wanted her to relax, too much had happened in too short a time for that. Her lower lip began to quiver in spite of her resolve not to cry. One lonely tear hung precariously from her long lashes before meandering down her cheek. She was surprised to see compassion in his eyes as he slowly reached down and tenderly wiped the tear away.

"I know you cannot understand all this. I will try to explain when I return. For now, please know that you are safe as long as you keep this door locked. Do not open the door, no matter what you hear." His gaze was urgent and penetrating. "Do you understand?"

She simply nodded. Her enormous dark eyes so reminded him of Elizabeth—beautiful, childlike, and terrified. He wanted to stay and reassure her, but he knew he would be expected at headquarters. Hesitatingly, he turned to go. "Remember, do not open the door, no matter what you hear. And don't turn on the lights. It's better if no one knows that you are here." And with that, he was gone.

She could hear him locking the door. She walked to the other room and looked furtively out the window. There weren't many people out on the walkway. She saw him hurrying down the road toward a building across a lawn, set back away from all the other buildings. She could see the brick building with the giant smokestack across the way. It looked ominous. At the moment, there was no smoke spewing forth. All seemed at rest. *What time is it anyway?* Esther wondered. She had no way of knowing. The sun had long since set behind the western wall. Had it been a beautiful sunset? Somehow, she couldn't imagine any beauty in this place.

She turned back to her room. It was more pleasant than she would have expected. In the back room was a bed complete with sheets and a cover. A small table stood between the bed and the outer wall, which held a small lamp and a book. Curious, she walked over and cautiously picked it up. It was a Bible.

Her first reaction was to throw it down. It was a forbidden book to her. She would read her Ketuvim. Then she remembered that her Ketuvim was gone—along with everything she held dear. *Gabriel's letters!* The thought of them in a stranger's hands made her heart ache.

The book in her hand brought her back to reality. Had she not heard that part of this book was like her own sacred writings? She hesitantly opened the front cover. The first page bore an inscription:

To Kurt,
With love,
Father and Mother

Strange! As she continued to turn the pages, she realized that it was indeed the same as the Torah. With hope in her heart, she continued fanning the pages. The familiar books were all there—First and Second Samuel, Kings, Chronicles, Ezra, Nehemiah—even Esther. Pulling the book to her chest, she fell to her knees and wept tears of joy. *Oh Jehovah, how great thou art!* She could speak no more; she simply allowed the tears to wash away all the horror of the day.

***

Esther didn't know how long she was there; exhaustion from the days' events and the lateness of the hour had caused her to fall asleep on her knees, her head resting upon the bed. She was still clutching the Bible when a rattle of keys startled her awake. Where was she? What was she doing on the floor, and why did her legs refuse to move?

As she gathered her wits about her, she looked up into the face of the SS officer. She gasped, ready to scream, when she remembered the face, the kind eyes, and the gentle touch. He was looking at her, staring at the Bible in her hand. *How foolish I must look!* She tried to stand, but her nap had caused her feet and legs to fall asleep as well. As she struggled to get up, he pulled a chair over to her.

"Here, sit down," he said as he held out his hand. Esther looked at it, hesitated, and then reached out. Once she was seated, he reached across her and turned on the lamp. He then moved to the window and closed the curtain. There was another chair on the other side of the window. Wearily, he lowered himself into it.

"I am sure you are wondering why you are here."

She only nodded.

"What is your name?"

She instinctively looked at the numbers on her arm.

"No, not that—your name."

"Esther Ruth Raul." It gave her great satisfaction to say it. Perhaps she was more than a number after all.

"What a beautiful name. Esther." He spoke it with thought. "You are named after a wonderful woman."

"*Sie kennen die Geschichte von Esther?*" she asked incredulously before she knew she was speaking.

He looked at her in surprise. "You speak German?"

She shyly nodded her head before explaining. "Our teachers thought it would be wise, considering the circumstances." For some reason, she did not want to offend this man.

"They were very wise." He hesitated before going on. When he did, his words were fierce, full of anger. "I am ashamed of my country and what it has done and is doing to your people."

He lowered his gaze to the floor and paused. "I need to explain who I am and why you girls were brought here. This is a horrible place. You are at Auschwitz." Seeing that she recognized the name, he continued. "I have seen firsthand what is happening. When I spoke against the Nazis, I ended up in a concentration camp, where I was asked to reconsider my loyalties. I determined then and there to re-enter the Nazi army and fight the evils from within."

He left his chair and was pacing the room, gesturing with his hands as he spoke. "I have tried to tell the outside world what is happening here, but no one will listen." He ran his fingers through his thick blond hair, a habit Esther would learn to recognize as an act of frustration.

He sat back down in the chair, looking full into her eyes. She held his gaze. "You would have died out there had I not brought you here," he stated.

What is this place that he is so hesitant to tell me? Esther wondered.

"They would have worked and starved you to death," the officer continued.

She could wait no longer. "What is this place?"

Her innocence broke his heart. "This is a brothel."

Again, he waited to see her reaction. She looked at him with question in her eyes. He cleared his throat, looking away. How could he tell her? He was sure the other girls already knew.

"Men will visit the girls in the evening ..."

He didn't need to say anymore. Her hands went to her mouth to stifle a cry. "No!"

The look of sheer horror on Esther's face cut him to the heart. He quickly went on. "But not you, Esther. You will be safe here." He saw the question in her eyes. "This is my room, and I will never hurt you in any way."

The wonder of it all was too much to comprehend. She looked around her. *Yes, this is a man's room.* And then she realized. "You are Kurt."

He looked at her incredulously, "How did you know my name?" She looked down at the book she still held in her hands. "It has your name in the front."

Again, amazement was written upon his face. "You looked at my Bible?"

Fear gripped her heart. "I'm sorry. I didn't mean to look at your private belongings." Trembling, she handed the Bible to him.

"No, it's not a problem with me. I am just surprised that a Jew would look at it."

At first, she felt compelled to defend her actions; but the kindness and concern emanating from his eyes stopped her rebuttal. She began to explain with quiet resignation in her voice. "When we were taken from our home, Father was reading the Ketuvim to us— me, my mother, and two older brothers. He took it with him and then gave it to me while we were in Westerbork. It was a great source of comfort and strength to me."

"The Ketuvim? I've never heard of it," he replied.

61

For the first time in a long time, a smile spread across her lips as she explained. "It contains part of your Old Testament: Esther to the Song of Song of Solomon. When I saw it here on the table, I realized my own sacred book was gone and wondered if what I had heard was true—that your Bible contained my story." She finished lamely. "I guess I got carried away and fell asleep."

She tried to read his thoughts as he sat staring at her. Was he surprised by her boldness to read a book that didn't belong to her and then smile at his ignorance? Again, she felt shame and confusion.

Kurt stared not in disdain but wonder. Had God led this beautiful woman to him? Indeed, her presence had already been a joy and comfort to him. He admired her faith and courage, and her extraordinary beauty held him spellbound.

"Again, I am sorry," Esther said, barely above a whisper. "I am afraid I have offended you."

Shook from his thoughts, Kurt was quick to reply. "No, on the contrary." His eyes searched her face as he sought his soul for the right words. "I believe that God has brought you here. You cannot know what a great blessing it has already been to talk to someone who shows such faith and character. You have lost everything, and yet you cling to God's Word. There is no bitterness in your voice, no anger, just strength."

With shoulders drooping and head held low, he simply said, "I envy your strength and faith in God."

Esther could not explain the peace that was in her heart. "I have thought all along that God had a reason for sending me here." Dare she share her inner thoughts with this stranger? The longing look in his eyes gave her resolve to continue. "Queen Esther was brought into a foreign land for a purpose. If God has done the same with my life, my only prayer is that He will give me the strength to do His bidding."

With amazement still plainly displayed upon his face, Kurt hesitatingly looked at his watch. Shocked by the lateness of the hour, his concerns turned toward her comfort.

"You must be very tired, and I'm sure you would like to wash up before you sleep. The washroom is through that door. Take your time."

He went to the bottom drawer of the chest and pulled out a night shirt for her. As he hesitantly handed it to her, he explained. "I've

62

been bringing young girls here for the past few months. I had always thought to have one stay here as you are, but it never seemed right. I can't explain it, but when I saw you, I somehow knew that you were the one to be here."

An awkward silence hung in the air before he continued. "You see, I am a Christian, a true believer in Jesus Christ. I grew up in a God-fearing home. We were faithful to church. I even thought at one time that God was calling me to be a pastor someday."

Again, the frustrated hand ran through his hair. "That was a long time ago. I've lost touch with God. I guess I blamed Him for all this. But you have stirred a spark that has long been dormant." His smile was a bit crooked, but it took twenty years off his face.

Esther gingerly took the clothes from him and left the room. She could not look into his eyes. Their conversation had somehow quelled her fears and anxieties, but it replaced them with other feelings that she could not name or understand.

After closing the door to the washroom, she stood there for a moment, leaning against it. Her cheeks were flushed. *O Father, what are you doing? Who is this man? Can I trust him?* She was much like her father, who always thought the best of everyone. This German soldier seemed so genuine, so sincere, and so lost in a world in which he did not wish to belong. *Help me, Father, and give me strength and wisdom.*

It felt so good to wash her face. She longed to linger but knew the man was waiting. Quickly, she stripped off the ugly dress that had been given to her and put on the clean nightclothes. She hesitated at the door. No man had ever seen her in only nightclothes before. *I must go out*, she told herself and quietly opened the door.

She could only see the bedroom; the angle of the doorway hid the couch in the living room. Kurt Gerstein was nowhere in sight. At first, she panicked. Had he left her alone again? As she listened, she could hear the regular breathing of someone fast asleep. Tiptoeing to the partition, she peeked around the corner.

He was lying on the couch. His immaculate uniform was a bit twisted. The tie had been loosened, but his shoes were still in place. His hair had been tousled and lay impishly across his forehead, giving him a boyish look. At that moment, a shiver ran across his face. Thinking he might be cold, Esther tenderly took the extra blanket from her bed and hesitantly placed it over him, breathing a prayer that he would not stir.

As he reached down to pull the covers around his face, he mumbled, "Thank you Elizabeth. You are so good to me. You..." and he was puffing again.

"Elizabeth?" she whispered. Her thoughts were a jumble as she slipped under her own covers. A masculine scent lingered around the coverlet, forcing her thoughts back to the man sleeping on the other side of the wall. *Who is Elizabeth?* she wondered. Was he married? If so, where was his wife?

It was obvious by the room's furnishings that they did not have a woman's attention. Although everything was neat and clean, but there were no frills. But perhaps that was the way of German women—especially ones who were at war with the world. Did she live somewhere else? Did he have children? But wouldn't he also have pictures?

Her hand instinctively went to the missing locket. It was gone. Vaguely, the memory of the day came back to her. She had had it when she left the train. *Pappa! Ad and Daan! Oh, where are they?* The locket—she had tried to hide it. Yes, and then it had fallen, and that woman had taken it. But then she remembered: Kurt Gerstein had taken it from the woman and put it in his pocket. Was it still there? She dared not look.

The thought that perhaps her beloved locket was still within her reach—indeed, nearly in the same room—gave her an overwhelming feeling of joy and peace. The faces of her family flashed across her mind. Then another face: her gentle Gabriel. Would she ever see him again? What was he doing right now? He must be frantic.

Although her usual evening ritual of reading his letters was now impossible, she rolled to her side and began praying for everyone she could remember, but most of all for Gabriel. That night, her prayer even included Kurt and Elizabeth Gerstein.

Chapter Nine

"He hath delivered my soul in peace from the battle that was against me:
for there were many with me."

Psalm 55:18

Kurt quickly and quietly arose from his sleep. As far as he could tell, he had not called out in the night. In fact, he couldn't remember anything about the evening, which was a first. How had the blanket gotten on him? Had Esther placed it there? He neatly folded it and placed it on the back of the couch, then headed for the doorway.

He hadn't planned to look over to where Esther lay, but he couldn't resist. In the dim light, he could only make out her dark hair. How thankful he was that she didn't have to lose it. He was also thankful that she seemed to be sleeping peacefully. A shadow crossed his face at the thought of the other girls in the building. Was he doing the right thing? He was sure most of them would hate him for what he had done, even if it did mean saving their lives.

Washing quickly, Kurt left the room, securely locking the door behind him. As he headed across the road, his mind was in a whirl. He would need to check into headquarters and start making the necessary arrangements. His plan was to go directly to his office and hopefully avoid any contact with the officers. They often leered and hovered like vultures when they knew new girls had been brought to the compound. How they could face their wives and children was beyond him. For some reason, male prisoners who were rewarded with this special "privilege" didn't bother him as much as the officers who took advantage of the situation. Unfortunately, prisoners were just nameless faces whose destiny he could not control—perhaps with the exception of one.

A list of numbers was already on his desk. He methodically matched these numbers with the numbers on his list. He had removed Esther's number and hoped against hope that no one would notice.

***

By the time Esther awoke, the sun was making a feeble attempt to break through the murky fog that had crept in at dawn. It seemed appropriate that nature was doing its best to hide this place. She sensed more than saw that Officer Gerstein was gone.

As much as she hated it, she slipped back into her ugly issued dress. What was she to do next? She felt like a prisoner. The thought made her feel foolish. She was a prisoner—albeit a safe one—and she didn't want to do anything that would jeopardize Officer Gerstein or herself. She would redeem the time in God's Word, drawing strength for whatever this day would bring forth.

After tidying herself and the rooms, she took the Bible and made herself comfortable on the couch. As she read Esther's story, she was again encouraged by the strength the biblical woman showed in her adverse situation. She hadn't known her destiny when she had been taken by the king's men.

So it came to pass, when the king's commandment and his decree was heard ... that Esther was brought also unto the king's house, to the custody of Hegai, keeper of the women. And the maiden pleased him, and she obtained kindness of him ...

Reading these words from Esther 2:8–9, Esther was again amazed at the similarities between her situation and Queen Esther's. At Westerbork, she had felt her beauty was a curse, knowing that it drew unwanted attention from the SS officers there. Had her beauty caught Kurt Gerstein's attention as well? She hoped that he would see more than an outer beauty in her.

After reading through her story, she ventured to the Psalms. Psalm 22:1 caught her attention. *My God, my God, why hast thou forsaken me? Why art thou so far from helping me, and from the words of my roaring?*

She was struck by the words. Forsaken of God? Who would feel that way? She had always felt that God was always with her—even in the difficult times. As she read on, it seemed that King David was writing about someone else.

I am poured out like water, and all my bones are out of joint: my heart is like wax; it is melted in the midst of my bowels ... they pierced my hands and my feet.

Was this figurative? Esther knew well the story of King David— he had been one of her father's favorite characters, and he read it to her often. She couldn't remember ever hearing of his hands and feet being pierced. What did it mean?

She was so absorbed in her reading that the rattling of keys in the lock startled her. She found herself holding her breath, hoping that it was Kurt Gerstein. He entered, quickly locking the door behind him. As he looked at her, his eyes fell again to the Bible. She awkwardly laid it beside her, absentmindedly smoothing the wrinkles from her dress. He walked to her and knelt before her, gazing directly into her eyes. They were brimming with emotions, but Esther couldn't discern which ones. Not anger. Not pity. Perhaps just sadness.

"Esther, I don't know what is going to happen to any of us, but while you are here, in this room, please know that it is your room. You may look at anything, read anything. I have no secrets—nothing too personal that I would not want you to see it."

He picked up the Bible, and placed it back into her hands. "But especially this Book." He hesitated, not wanting to startle her by his forwardness. "At Auschwitz, there is no time. We just continue blindly in our routines as if moving through a nightmare. We forget what real life is like."

Again, he halted, and the silence in the room was stifling. His closeness made the hairs on the back of Esther's neck rise; she could hear his labored breathing, as though his next words were costing him a great deal. "I used to read the Bible every night. Perhaps we could do that together." There was a subtle pleading in his voice.

Before Esther could respond, he continued on in a different tone. "When we are outside these doors, I must treat you as if you are no different than the other girls. During the day, you will eat with them and work with them, but at night you will be protected. If the other girls talk about ... their situation, it would be wise if you did not reveal yours."

He was visibly shaken. He absently massaged his forehead between his thumb and fingers, seeking to drive away the pounding headache that had started at the office. "When you are finished for the day, you may visit with the other girls or come here, but do not have any of the girls come to this room. Lock the door behind you. And I would suggest that once you are in here, stay in here."

He stood to his feet and walked to the door. He held the knob for a moment and then turned to face her. "Tonight will be very difficult for the girls. You may hear things. If I am not here, please do not open the door for any reason. Even if someone knocks and demands you to open, just ignore it. I cannot stress that enough."

He was so urgent. He turned back to the door and paused, taking a deep breath and exhaling it slowly. The drooping shoulders squared, transforming his entire appearance. He looked like the SS officer his uniform portrayed. Esther would find herself wondering at his dual image: the stern SS officer and the kind gentleman caught in a web spun by the Third Reich called the Final Solution.

He quickly strode down the hallway, knocking on each door as he went. Esther timidly went to the doorway. From each room emerged the two girls he had left there the night before. Esther's heart went out to them. Their faces were full of terror at the unknown. Eyes red and swollen, some had obviously cried through the night and well into the morning.

Esther was surprised at the change in Kurt Gerstein. He was all business—cold and unfeeling. There was no compassion or concern, and Esther had to wonder which image was the true Kurt Gerstein.

Standing at attention at the opposite end of the hall, he succinctly barked out the orders. "If you did not realize it by now, you are at Auschwitz. Your days will begin at 0800 hours with breakfast. It will be brought to this room and"—he paused, ruffling through his papers—"14789 and 14790 will make sure that each room receives their portions."

Each girl instinctively looked at the tattooed numbers on their arms to see who had been chosen for this task.

"Your rooms are to be immaculate. Cleaning supplies are in the closet halfway down the hall on my right." As he tipped his head toward the closet, the girls noticed one door still closed. "At 0830 hours you will be expected to be ready and waiting outside your doors, and will be taken to the laundry facility. You will be back in your rooms by 1800 hours. Your dinner will be here. You will then be expected to be available for the rest of the evenings in your rooms. Frau Wilheim will answer any further questions you may have."

He turned on his heels and saluted the woman standing next to him, who had slipped in the door behind him during his opening statements. She was a large woman. Her hair was pulled back in a taut bun, giving her already austere face a ridged, angular effect. There was a coldness in her eyes that seemed to reflect the hatred in her soul. Herr Gerstein was out the door in a flash.

Frau Wilheim surveyed the group. The girls' terrified looks seemed to bring her great pleasure and fuel her hatred. She spoke in short, clipped sentences that seemed to convey more of a message than her words. "I do not want to know your names. I do not want to hear your woes. You have been given a great privilege. You will serve the prisoners who have earned special privileges as well as some of the finest officers at our facility. I only need to know when you cannot serve due to your natural physical limitation. Do *not* lie to me about this, or there will be grave consequences."

She paused and surveyed the group to emphasize the importance of the last statement. "You were selected. You are privileged to be here. If you doubt my words, just look around you and remember: *Arbeit Macht Frei*—work will make you free! It is the motto by which we all live."

Under different circumstances, her sense of blind loyalty would have been seemed almost laughable. Then, as if on cue, an emaciated, head-shaven woman came through the door with a large tray stacked with loaves of bread, stooping beneath the heavy load. She wore a drab, striped sort of uniform. After depositing the tray into the first room, she quickly hobbled to the door, her eyes never lifting from her feet.

It was the girls' first glimpse of what lay outside the walls of their building. Esther was glad she had been at the other end of the hallway. Even at that distance, she saw too much. Frau Wilhelm turned and followed the woman out, giving her a cuff to the head for no apparent reason.

Numbly, the girls whose numbers had been announced earlier gathered the loaves and started handing them out. Each girl took the sustenance and headed back to her room.

Chapter Ten

"Thus I was; in the day the drought consumed me, and the frost by night; and my sleep departed from mine eyes."

Genesis 31:40

Life is often like a pearl necklace: ordinary days all strung together on a string, one no different than the next. One after the other, they fly by—each containing fragments of what we call normal. Even at Auschwitz, a daily routine was soon established for Esther and the other Gerstein girls.

Every morning, Esther rose early for her personal time with God. Although she and Kurt had also developed a routine each evening for Bible reading, she felt she needed some time alone. Starting each day consumed with pity for the other girls took its toll on her whole being; however, she knew her pain was nothing compared to the anguish she read on their faces. The eyes on their young faces mirrored the struggle of their bodies and souls. They would soon learn to console each other, knowing that each suffered the same demise— all except Esther.

Esther was glad to have work to do. The washing and ironing kept all of their minds off the evening's fiasco. Indeed, life could almost seem normal while they worked. Even while at home, Esther had always enjoyed laundry day. As her hands washed, hung, and folded, her mind went back to the carefree days that seemed a lifetime ago. Being the only girl, she had often toiled side by side with her mother, never realizing just how wonderful normal could be.

Oh, how much she had taken for granted: the sweet smell of lavender that Mother always put in with her clothes; the sense of security she felt in their backyard as she hung the cloths to dry, listening to all the local gossip as her mother visited with their neighbors; the variety of colors displayed in her dresses as they flapped in the breeze, waving hello to the trees. The thought of Mother often sent a tear into the soapy water.

She pictured all the trees in their backyard—trees that offered shade, scent, and beauty to their home. Father had planted so many varieties around their house. Here there was one lone tree that grew between what she had learned was the main headquarters, which housed Kurt's office, and the laundry facility where she worked. Unlike the poplars that stood like sentinels alongside the barracks, this lone tree seemed to stand apart from the rest. It became a symbol of her own life—alone and different from everybody else. It was a large maple, one of Esther's favorites, and it gave her comfort to see it growing there. By it, she would mark the changing seasons as the color in each leaf started to fade, eventually letting go of its branch and floating lifelessly to the ground in one last graceful dance.

She also welcomed the time at work to help her to forget what she saw nearly every day on her way back to her room. Early on, she had learned the meaning of the brick buildings with the giant smokestacks. She was horrified to see long lines of mostly women and children standing, waiting to be "deloused"—or so they were told. Esther had thought it strange that she never saw anyone come out of the building. She had finally come to realize that these buildings were responsible for the deaths of thousands of her people.

She remembered now Kurt Gerstein's anguish when she had first come as he tried to explain this place. The horrid smell that constantly hung in the air, so much so that you could taste it, was the smoke of her people being destroyed. How could such atrocities continue without anyone from the outside world realizing it? But Esther had observed that, except for a few scattered villages around the area, Auschwitz was very secluded.

Dear God, Esther prayed while she walked across the way, *You must look down with great sadness upon this place. How could Your creation have gone so wrong? Who could be so hateful against Your people?*

As she watched the little children—so frightened, clinging to their mothers—she wanted to run over and take them away to her own safe haven. She thought she'd go mad with the realization of their short destiny. But no matter how torn her heart would become, she knew there was nothing that she could do. Her admiration for Kurt Gerstein's small effort grew daily. As she observed the other girls' disdain for him, she wanted to cry out and defend his actions. *At least you are alive, no matter how many scars are placed upon your body and soul!*

Esther was not bitter against the girls. Indeed, she could not even imagine what they must be going through. Why had she been spared? Why was she not being forced to entertain men all hours of the night? She had heard their cries, especially during the first few weeks, but now there was little commotion on the hall—just the shuffling of feet and the barking orders from Frau Wilhelm. She ran a tight ship. There would be no strikes against her record for disorderly conduct.

Because of Esther's situation, she had extra time on her hands, and she decided to use the time to do the extra mending that was part of their work. All the girls were required to do so, but she often took the majority of the work. Thankfully, none of the others had questioned her about it.

She was also thankful for the time spent with Kurt. At first, the air was thick with awkwardness between them. She still remembered that first night. He usually came to the room around seven o'clock in the evening. She had returned to the room not much earlier, perhaps around six thirty. It had been a long, exhausting day. After all the waiting and sitting around at Westerbork, she was not accustomed to a full day's work. Her whole body ached—especially her feet. Standing on the cement floor all day in bare feet had taken its toll, and the sight of the couch was so inviting, she went no further.

Curling up in it at one end, she instantly fell asleep. Kurt had startled her as he entered the room. *He must think I'm impertinent to just take over his sleeping area.* But again, she was surprised by his desire to put her at ease.

"Please, make yourself comfortable. I know you must have put in a long day," he said with a smile that didn't quite reach his eyes.

He went through what Esther would come to realize was his normal routine: off with the uniform jacket, neatly hung in the closet; then the shoes, also placed in the closet, replaced by a pair of loafers; the tie was loosened and hung on a hook behind the door; lastly, the hat was hung over the tie. He started to empty his pockets: wallet, keys, some papers ... he hesitated. His hand had clasped something. He looked into Esther's eyes. Now his eyes were lit with excitement as he came over to sit beside Esther.

"Open your hand," he gently commanded.

She looked quizzical but obeyed. Her mind was still a bit clouded; she hadn't realized how deeply she had fallen into sleep.

Slowly, he drew out his hand. She could see nothing until he opened it into hers. There lay her locket.

She gasped. Words formed in her heart but seemed reticent to come to her lips. "My locket," she whispered.

Her fingers traced the intricate etchings, running over the surface of each smooth stone. How could it be? After all she had been through, how could it still be here with her? She looked up, unhindered tears sliding down her face.

Kurt was watching her. He had forgotten about the locket last night in all the confusion. He had been thankful that it had not fallen to the floor in his sleep. How could he forget? As he stood before SS Rudolf Höss, he had placed his hands into his pockets and touched the locket. It had taken all his willpower not to pull out the piece and examine it. It felt cool and feminine and reminded him of the beautiful young woman in his room.

"You are flushed, Gerstein. Are you ill?" Höss had asked.

"No sir, just a bit warm," he'd tried to answer calmly.

Now, as he sat and watched Esther's face, he was so very thankful that he had been able to retrieve the piece from Frau Stedder. "It is an heirloom, is it not?"

Esther didn't trust her voice, but she knew she must answer. Trying to clear the lump from her throat, she pulled her gaze from the locket to his face. "Yes, it was given to me by my parents on my sixteenth birthday." *Had that only been five months ago?* "It has been in my mother's family for five generations, always passed down to the oldest daughter on her sixteenth birthday."

She snapped it open. Tears now fell onto her trembling hands. "This is my mother and father and my two brothers, Daan and Ad," she managed to choke out between her sobs.

"I don't remember seeing your mother at the train," Kurt noted, the words slipping out of his mouth before he could stop them.

Esther tried to compose herself. "She was shot in the back on our front doorstep."

She saw the pity in his eyes and continued. "Mother was always a proud woman. Her ancestors had settled the Netherlands and were also responsible for settling New York City in America. One of her relatives was the first rabbi in the New World." It felt so good to talk

73

about Mother and her family. She hadn't been able to talk to anyone for so long, and Kurt was a good listener.

He instinctively reached over and squeezed her hand. "They are not only your mother's ancestors, Esther—they are yours." He spoke quietly but fiercely. He could see the effect his words were having on her.

Her eyes filled with wonder. "I never thought of it that way. I guess when Mother was alive, they were *her* heritage."

"Perhaps a sixteen-year-old does not think of ancestry," he said with a wry smile. Suddenly turning serious, he continued, "But you should."

She laughed a dejected laugh, "But why? Will I ever leave this place alive?"

Kurt hadn't let go of her hand. He gave it a reassuring squeeze. "I believe you will, Esther. I believe we both will."

***

They decided that it would be best if Kurt kept the locket during the day, and Esther could wear it at night if she wished. The times in which they were living were so volatile. Kurt never knew when he would be sent out on a mission of some sort. His dealings with the Zyklon B poison used in the gas chambers kept him connected with the outside world. When he left, he never quite knew if he would get back. If something should happen, the locket would have a better chance of surviving with Kurt than with Esther. As he carried it in his pocket, he felt a growing closeness to its owner. It became part of his ritual to place the locket in her hand after emptying his pockets each evening.

He had no right to feel anything, but each night, their time together became the highlight of his day—and Esther's as well. They had agreed to read the Bible together, starting at the very beginning: Genesis, the book of beginnings. How ironic it seemed to Esther, when it appeared that her world was coming to an end. They took turns reading passages, discussing each section as they went. Kurt was surprised at Esther's knowledge of the Scriptures.

"Did you think I wouldn't know the Scriptures because I am Jewish, or because I am a woman?" Esther asked one day, a quizzical smile on her lips.

Kurt was caught in her trap. How could he answer her? "Well, to be quite honest, both."

"We are in the twentieth century, Herr Gerstein, and I did attend Sabbath school as well as our own Jewish day schools. We heard and studied the Torah every day, but I believe I learned the most on my father's knee." A shadow passed across her face. They had been together for nearly five weeks now, yet she still had not gained the courage to ask that which was so heavy on her heart.

Kurt could sense her hesitation. "What is bothering you, Esther?"

It seemed like an odd question—one that almost made her laugh. *What was wrong? What was right?* And yet, even as she thought the words, she was rebuked. *Look at all that is right, Esther.* She felt shame at her ingratitude. Yet, could she ask him? The only thing she had to lose was the continual uncertainty that nearly drove her crazy with worry.

"Do you know where my father and brothers would be?" Even as she spoke the question, she could see the sorrow on his face.

"I don't know, Esther. All I can tell you is that when your family got off the train, all three men were taken to the right. That means that they were taken to the labor camp and not the gas chamber." He hesitated, and Esther sensed it.

"What are you not telling me?" She was surprised by the hysteria in her voice, but she couldn't help it. Six weeks of knowing nothing had put it there.

"How old is your father?" Kurt asked.

"He is, or will be, sixty-one this December," she replied.

Again the hesitation. Kurt was smiling. "He is a very young-looking man, strong and wise." He smiled wryly. "He must have lied about his age. The SS will only take men under the age of fifty. Even they know that the older men will not survive."

He could see the hopeful look in her eyes. "You never know, Esther. He is strong and wise, and I believe that that combination may see him through. We will pray every night for them."

"Is there any way you could find them?" Her lip trembled, her eyes watered. She sniffed.

He pulled a handkerchief from his back pocket and handed it to her. "I wish there was something that I could do, Esther. My situation

75

is already precarious. There is one rule in this place for SS officers and prisoners alike: Don't ask questions."

He didn't mean to sound so harsh. Perhaps it was not his words as much as it was the bare facts that sounded that way. Esther seemed resigned to the situation.

***

Esther had known for some time that Kurt would have liked to open the New Testament to her. She had to admit, during her morning devotions, she had gone beyond the point of temptation and had turned to the pages of the second half of the forbidden book. At first, she just flipped through, looking at the titles of each book. They seemed to be named after people or places. When she felt her curiosity being piqued too far, she panicked and quickly flipped back to the safety of the Old Testament; however, there seemed to be an irresistible urge she could not control to continue in her discovery.

With her future being so uncertain, she reasoned that she needed to know what was on those pages. And so, by last evening, Esther had already completed the first book—Matthew. The beginning genealogies fascinated her, but the story of Jesus' life seemed too incredible to be true. His birth was certainly abnormal. No wonder her people had rejected Him. Did His parents really talk to angels? Why would wise men from the east follow a star and bring such strange gifts? Then the sudden trip to Bethlehem—it all sounded like an easy way out for covering up a bad mistake.

That evening, they had read the seventh chapter of Isaiah. Kurt stopped after verse 14: "*Therefore the Lord himself shall give you a sign; Behold, a virgin shall conceive, and bear a son, and shall call his name Immanuel.*"

He turned his gaze upon her. "What do you think this verse is talking about? How could a virgin bear a child?" He knew he was being unfair—certainly she would know nothing about Christ's nativity.

As if she read his mind, she impulsively gave him the answer he would never expect. "Supposedly, your Jesus was born of a virgin."

The expected shock registered on his face. Esther ducked her head to hide her smile. "But how would you know about that, Esther?" he asked.

She looked up. His eyes searched deeply into her own. He seemed to be looking for the answer he hoped to hear. Her amusement turned to resentment. Esther had abruptly blurted out her secret, and now she felt exposed. Her emotions were a mix of shame and defiance—shame because she had let her family down by reading the forbidden book, and defiance because this German Gentile, who was part of the murderous plan to destroy her people, thought she would not, or could not, read it.

"Esther?" His voice came softly. "Have you read the New Testament?"

He seemed to be holding his breath, waiting for a reply. After what felt like an eternity to both, Esther's short, simple answer released a flood of emotions. "Yes."

Kurt let out a long breath, "Oh, Esther. You have no idea how much I've wanted to talk to you about this."

"Oh yes I do!" she shot at him. Her air of rejection chilled his blood. She raced on. "Yes! I have read some of your New Testament, and how anyone can believe these—these lies are beyond me!" The floodgate of pent-up anger had burst. "My people know the truth—they have always known the truth! They are God's chosen people, and look at what your religion has done to us!"

She knew that she was being unfair, but the whole conversation had unnerved her. She stared at her trembling hands. The room was still, yet charged with energy from her explosion. She knew Kurt was staring at her, but she would not look up.

Kurt's mind was whirling. He felt like she had slapped him, and indeed, her words had hit him like a fist to his midsection. He fervently prayed for the right words. Since Esther's arrival, he had confessed his bitterness and anger to God, and he had reestablished the sweet fellowship with his Lord that had once been the foundation of his existence. *Give me wisdom, Lord. Fill my mind with your thoughts and my mouth with your words.*

"Could I share some verses with you from the Old Testament?" he asked.

Keeping her head bowed, she simply nodded.

Beginning with Genesis 3:16, Kurt shared verse after verse that prophesied the Messiah. He wove his way through the sacred writings. In Genesis, Jacob foretold that Shiloh would come from the tribe of

Judah. Kurt seemed to favor Isaiah 49:6, which said that the Messiah would not only restore Israel but would give His light to the Gentiles.

Esther was amazed that Micah foretold that the Messiah would be born in Bethlehem. Had she not read that the priests had told King Herod and the wise men the same thing? Why hadn't she ever seen this before?

He read Isaiah 40:5—"*The voice of him that crieth in the wilderness, Prepare ye the way of the LORD, make straight in the desert a highway for our God*"—and explained how a man named John had done just that. He read her Zechariah 9:9 and told her that just as Zechariah had prophesied, indeed, Jesus had ridden into Jerusalem on a donkey, heralded by all the people only a week before his death.

He deftly turned the pages to Zechariah 11:12, "*So they weighed for my price thirty pieces of silver.*" He peered at her, almost a fierceness in his eyes. "Judas was paid this exact amount to betray his Lord. And Esther, there are so many verses about His death on the cross."

The rustling of the pages matched the flurry of her thoughts. Kurt continued, "Isaiah 50:6 says, '*I gave my back to the smiters, and my cheeks to them that plucked off the hair: I hid not my face from shame and spitting.*' They did this to Him. They took Him before Pilate, and Roman soldiers beat Him with whips. They pulled out His beard. The chief priests blindfolded Him and slapped Him in the face, mocking Him and asking who had hit Him." It seemed difficult for him to speak of such shameful actions. "And they spit in His face."

He paused as he slowly, reverently turned over just a few pages to Isaiah 53:7.

He was oppressed, and he was afflicted, yet he opened not his mouth: he is brought as a lamb to the slaughter, and as a sheep before her shearers is dumb, so he openeth not his mouth. ... And he made his grave with the wicked, and with the rich in his death.

He kept flipping through the Bible. "Some of the saddest verses are found in Psalm 22. I do not know if David had any idea that he was writing about his Messiah when he penned this psalm, but here, verse after verse matches perfectly with what Jesus suffered on the cross."

As Kurt slowly read the entire Psalm, Esther sat spellbound by his words—God's words—which miraculously foretold every detail of what she had read in Matthew surrounding Jesus' birth and death. The verses that spoke the loudest, though, were the ones she had read in

Psalm 22. She could not admit her intrigue to this man, but it was evident on her face. Her heart was torn in two—one half resisting the truths and holding fast to her traditions, the other half drawn to the truth and wanting to know more.

He was not sure how to interpret her quiet stare. He sensed that he had said enough. God was working in her heart, but he longed to know how she was reacting. Would she reject the truth or embrace it? He didn't want to push her too hard.

These past few months had been like a breath of fresh air on his clouded soul. This young Jewish woman had changed his life. Now he felt he had a reason to live, but it was more than that. Living in such close quarters with her was taking its toll on his heart.

Her usually sweet spirit, her thirst for the Word, and her kindness toward him had all given him a desire to know her more. He could hardly keep his mind on his gruesome tasks for thinking about Esther. Her name sang on his heart, and her image played across his mind continually. She was everything that he had ever hoped to find, and he was certain God had brought her here to him—possibly even *for* him.

"It's getting late," he finally managed to say. "Do you mind if I pray?"

Up until now, their readings seemed to stop abruptly each night without an ending. He hadn't had the nerve to pray with her before, but his heart had been made right. After his renewed dedication, it was all he could do *not* to pray. Tonight gave him the resolve for which he had been waiting.

Esther felt as though she was suffocating beneath a blanket of knowledge. Her mind was a jumble of mixed emotions. Her thoughts were in a whirl, but one thought pushed its way to the top. *Apologize!* It screamed at her over and over. As much as she tried to resist it, she knew the voice was right.

"Before you do, I must apologize for my outburst." The look in his eyes nearly stopped her from going on. They held such hurt and desire—no anger, no pity. "You have treated me with only kindness, and I have been completely unfair to you tonight. Can you forgive me?"

It was a simple question, but he hated to answer her. "You don't have to apologize, Esther. You have been through so much. We have talked about a lot of different ideas tonight. I think it would be best if we just commit all our thoughts and our time together in His Word back to the Lord."

She nodded her approval, and Kurt slipped to his knees to pray. His posture caught her by surprise. It seemed so humbling for him to be there kneeling beside her, yet it fit him. Esther wondered if she had ever met a more humble man. Humility was not a common attribute among her people. Perhaps it was because they were always fighting to justify their existence.

Just then, his words cut into her thoughts. His voice was so gentle and loving. He spoke to God in the same manner that he lived his life—at least his life with her. "Dear Heavenly Father, we come before Thee in prayer, first thanking Thee for thy Word. Lord, we know that our days are in Thy hands. Thou hast proven to us both that Thy plan is not our plan. Truly, Thy ways are so much higher than our ways. They are past finding out. We thank Thee for the times that Thou hast given us to read Thy Word together."

He hesitated. Esther wondered what thoughts were flying about in his head. "I thank Thee that we can trust Thee and Thy Word. Please help me to know what to say and what not to say to Esther. And please, Father, help her to know the truth and to understand it. In J—" Again, he faltered, then resumed. "In Your name we pray, amen."

Esther wondered why he stumbled. What was he going to say? She had never prayed with a Christian before. She couldn't contain her curiosity. "What were you going to say?" She could tell he didn't want to answer. "Please. How do Christians pray?"

He cleared his throat, reached for the Bible, and flipped to John 14:13, "'And whatsoever ye shall ask in my name, that will I do, that the Father may be glorified in the Son.' We believe that we should always end our prayers in Jesus' name."

Silence. He was still on his knees. As he gazed up at her, she felt flushed, unnerved. His face was just inches from her own. Something was passing between them, but Esther didn't know what it was, or perhaps she didn't want to admit what it was.

Kurt broke the spell by coming to his feet. *Control yourself, man*, he reprimanded himself. Walking to the closet, he busied himself there until he heard Esther leave the room, quietly closing the door of the bathroom behind her. He let out a slow sigh. If he had interpreted the look in her eyes correctly, life had just gotten a little more complicated.

Esther couldn't seem to catch her breath. She was trembling. *What is wrong with you? What are you thinking? First, you start reading about the Christian Messiah, and now your heart is falling for a Gentile! What would Gabriel think of you?*

Her face burned with shame and confusion. She must remember who she was—and who Kurt Gerstein was as well.

Chapter Eleven

"This is my beloved, and this is my friend, O daughters of Jerusalem."

Song of Solomon 5:16

As the weather turned cold, Esther tried to chill the atmosphere in their shared dwelling as well. She had tried to stay away from the words of Jesus, but they captivated her. Now, Kurt freely shared his faith with her as well as his insights into the Scriptures. She was amazed at how much he knew and how easily he could explain things to her. She tried to stay aloof, but it wasn't as easy as she had hoped.

In spite of Esther's efforts to remain superficial, she was intrigued by his life. Living in the Jewish quarter of her home city of Amsterdam did not give her much contact with the outside world. Everything and everyone she knew was Jewish. Coupled with the fact that he was raised in Germany, his life was so different than her own. His intrigue matched hers, and she enjoyed sharing stories of her childhood; it brought her great comfort to talk about her family.

One day, as she was telling him about her last days at her home, Gabriel's name came into the conversation. She had purposed not to tell Kurt anything about that part of her life, but it was too late. As soon as she said his name, she knew that he could sense the tension in her voice.

At first he said nothing, and she wondered if she saw hurt in his eyes. At last, he spoke, quietly yet with an air of resignation. "Was he your beau?"

She felt like a schoolgirl instead of a prisoner in a brothel. Why did she hesitate to tell him? Was she ashamed of her love for Gabriel? And what about Kurt's life? Before she could think, she answered, "Yes. And is Elizabeth your wife?"

As she saw the bewilderment on his face, she wished for once she would have thought before she spoke. "Elizabeth?" he asked. "I don't know who you mean."

One thing that Esther had learned in their short time together was that Kurt was not only gentle, kind, and humble, but he was also honest. She was determined to be the same with him. "You called out her name when you were sleeping, the first night I was here." She hesitated. "When I covered you with a blanket, you pulled the covers up and said, 'Thank you, Elizabeth.' I just assumed she was your wife."

Bewilderment changed to understanding, and then to amusement. "Elizabeth is my niece. I have never been married." He vehemently shook his head. "This is no place to have a family."

"But many of the officers do," Esther replied. She could see his expression darkening even further.

"Yes, and what must their children think?" He spat out the words, as though trying to rid himself of the horrible taste they left in his mouth. Esther could tell that she had touched a raw nerve.

He went on, repulsion lacing every word, "And how can any loving mother let her children be exposed to these atrocities? I will never understand the heart of my people. No, they are not my people!"

He stood to pace the floor, his hand raking through his hair. She could tell something other than Gabriel was on his mind. It amazed her how much she had come to understand this man before her.

"What's wrong, Kurt? What are you not telling me?"

He continued to pace frantically, like a caged animal. Her heart broke for him. She stood to her feet, stopping him mid-stride. Taking his hands in hers, she pulled him to the sofa. "Sit, please. What is it, Kurt? You can tell me. I am not a child."

She had never seen a grown man cry before, but now the tears were flowing across his contorted face. "There are so many coming in every day, Esther—more and more." He was frantic. "There is a tension in the air like never before."

His eyes were wild. "I have heard talk of exterminating all the prisoners. When will all this madness end?"

He burrowed his face in the couch and cried like a wounded animal. Sobs racked his body as he tried to stifle his cries. Esther sat motionless, too stunned, too filled with agony to respond in any way. She was frightened, and she was sad for her people and for Kurt. But above all, she was overwhelmed by the enormity of the empathy this SS officer held for her people. Hesitantly, she reached out to smooth his hair, trying to calm him.

Slowly, the sobs subsided. He reached for her hand and brought it to his lips. The tears were still flowing. She felt their wetness. He drew her to him and held her close. "I could not survive if it weren't for you, Esther." He whispered in her hair. "You are the only sanity that I have left."

Holding her close brought such comfort to his rankled soul. She could feel the tension ebbing away. For one short moment, time had stopped. Life had returned to normalcy. All was well.

She pulled away, but he wouldn't let go of her hands. She knew there was more to be said, and she sat still, not sure she wanted to hear. Kurt wiped away his tears and looked intently upon her. "Esther, I can't do this any longer. I can't keep living like this."

Confusion etched her features. What was he saying? Would he leave her? "But what do you mean? Where would you go?"

He saw her panic. "I'm not going anywhere—not without you."

"But where could I go? You know I can't leave."

"Esther," he spoke, but his voice was nearly inaudible, "I know I shouldn't ask you this. It is totally unfair of me. But our lives are so uncertain." He held her hands tightly. "Esther, do you ever think you could consider becoming my wife?"

How many thoughts raced through her mind, Esther could not tell. She could only think of the verse they had recently read, that a day with the Lord was as a thousand years, and a thousand years as a day. This moment seemed like time was truly standing still and yet racing out of control at the same time. Is this how it was with God? *What a strange thought at a time like this!*

She pulled her thoughts back to Kurt. Marry him? How could she? She was a Jew—and he was a Gentile. How could she betray Gabriel? But at the same time, she reasoned otherwise. What made her think she would ever leave this place alive? Hadn't she heard one of the older women say that the only way for a Jew to leave was out the chimneys?

He was watching her. Could he read her thoughts? Why was she so calm? She gazed into those deep blue eyes that she had come to respect. Did she love him? She could not tell, but if love meant sacrifice, she was willing to sacrifice all her dreams, all her future to give this man a few moments of happiness. He was here; he had saved her life.

84

Before she could say the words, he said them for her. "I love you, Esther."

"Yes, I know you do." A crooked smile sprung to her lips. Slowly, a peace and contentment she had not known for a long time emanated her soul.

They sat there in the stillness, comfortable and calm. Her answer came slowly, but with resolve. "Yes, I will marry you."

She could see as well as sense the love flowing from every part of his being. He gathered her into his arms and pressed a kiss upon her forehead. Like a flash, her mind went whirling back, back to another time—a lifetime ago, another man, another kiss, a goodbye. She squeezed her eyes shut to fight back the tears.

***

Kurt Gerstein's steps were a bit lighter than they had ever been before. He wasted no time making the arrangements, thankful that he had befriended the minister in the nearby town. Pastor Martin Houser had been a help to him, especially after he had made his heart right. He knew the pastor was opposed to all that was happening at Auschwitz, but he, like so many others, had gotten used to looking the other way.

When Kurt showed up on his doorstep, the reverend knew something had happened to the usually taut-faced officer. Kurt Gerstein carried the weight of a thousand burdens on his shoulders. Indeed, Kurt had shared his heart with him more than once, and the reverend was empathetic toward the young man. Pastor Houser quickly ushered him into his office, looking both ways to be sure no one had seen them.

"Herr Gerstein! *Guten tag!* How good it is to see you, and what a smile is on your face!"

The men shook hands and were seated in their usual spots: Kurt in the rocker beside the bookcase, and the reverend behind his rather cluttered desk.

"It is good to see you, Pastor Houser, as always." Kurt fairly glowed. As was his custom, he came directly to the point. "I need to ask a great favor of you." Kurt nervously fingered his hat.

"Yes? What is it my son?" Pastor Houser had an affectionate way of speaking to this young man. Indeed, he would have gladly owned him as his son.

Now that he was here, Kurt wasn't sure how to go about asking. "I have met someone, and I would like you to marry us … tomorrow."

Kurt could see the surprise on his dear friend's face. "But who is this most blessed woman, and where is she?"

Kurt's face clouded a bit. He had to word this all correctly. "She is a near child of God." The pastor waited for him to go on. "She is a prisoner at the camp."

The reverend's eyes widened. "A Jew," he said incredulously. "Kurt, how can you do such a thing?"

Kurt had never shared his secret operations with anyone outside the walls of Auschwitz, but he knew he had to make his case with the man before him—the only man who could accomplish his dream. As Kurt unfolded the whole account, he could see shock, then disgust, and finally sympathy written on Pastor Houser's face.

The reverend pushed back from his desk, deep in thought. Several times he shook his head. Kurt waited patiently, quietly, hopefully. Finally, the man spoke and shook his head. "I can see your dilemma, but Kurt, you ask a great deal of me."

"Please, Pastor Houser, she is the dearest thing on earth to me. I have sheltered her as much as I can. I want to keep on sheltering her and drawing her to our Savior. She is very near, but our time—who knows how much time we have?"

"But Kurt, is it necessary to marry her?" The minister looked doubtful.

"Father, we are living in the same rooms. As of now, we have been able to keep our relationship pure before God, but I don't know how much longer I can live like this, and I love her."

Pastor Houser could not miss the sincerity and passion in Kurt's voice. A cold wind shook the tree outside his window, causing the branches to scrape against the glass. The ancient grandfather clock quietly ticked the minutes away. Finally, the pastor answered, "I will go with you."

Relief flooded Kurt's face. He presented his plan to the reverend.

Kurt left to fetch the reverend the next day around five o'clock, when the gates were the busiest. The guards were used to seeing him coming and going from the compound—another privilege of his particular position. This day, he brought along another uniform for the reverend to wear.

As he and the reverend approached the gate, Kurt whispered a prayer of thanksgiving. There was some confusion in the car ahead of them and several cars behind him. He knew they would just wave him through, and they did. He parked farther away from the office than usual and was thankful no one was around.

As they left the car, he could sense the tension in Pastor Houser's movements. "Reverend," Kurt urgently whispered, "you must walk and act confidently. Please!" Kurt lengthened his stride and was thankful when the reverend matched it.

Kurt was never so glad to be in his own room as he was that day. The reverend sat nervously, eyeing the room. Kurt had told him everything, and the evening activities in this building made him very edgy. He couldn't wait to be on his way.

Just as Kurt came out of the bathroom, Esther opened the door. The look of surprise registered on her face as she saw an unfamiliar SS officer sitting in the room. At first, she backed away, out into the hall, but Kurt quickly came to her, pulling her in and shutting the door. "It's alright, Esther. This is Pastor Houser. He is just dressed this way to avoid suspicion."

Years later, Esther would often wonder if it was seeing a reverend and not a rabbi that had made her question her decision. What was she doing? She felt her identity being torn from her, just as she had when they had tattooed her number to her arm. Her short-lived dreams of a life with Gabriel were dissolving right before her face, but it was too late—her course seemed to be set by a power much higher than her own.

"Are you ready, Esther?" Kurt was asking her.

She had at least gone into the bathroom and freshened up. There was no special dress, no veil, no chuppah, ‡ just the man who had saved her life.

.

Looking at Esther, Kurt knew the struggle within must be tearing her apart. He longed to comfort her, reassure her. "Be strong, my dear Esther."

She looked up into his strong face. This simple statement, spoken with so much adoration, gave her the resolve she needed. She knew what she had to do.

The words of the man before them sounded so strange and unfamiliar. Every so often, a phrase caught her attention—something from the Bible, she was sure. He was asking her a question. What was she to say? But before she could ask, he supplied the reply, "If so, answer 'I do.' "

"I do."

She watched Kurt's face as he listened to the pastor repeat the same words. He turned toward her, holding her hands, and with such intensity it caught her breath, he uttered the same words, "I do."

"I now pronounce you man and wife. Let us pray. O God of our fathers, of Abraham, Isaac, and Jacob ..."

Neither Pastor House nor Kurt missed Esther's short gasp; Kurt would be sure to thank him for his thoughtfulness.

Before Esther had recovered from the joy of hearing the pastor's beginning lines, he had finished his prayer. He smiled at them and said, "You may kiss your bride."

Her pulse was racing. She knew her cheeks were flushed. Kurt turned to her, lifting her chin to his face. He paused for a moment, looking deep into her eyes, wet with unshed tears. Oh, how he loved her! Gently, he brought her lips to his. Once, twice—sweet and full of meaning. He held her in his arms, giving her strength. She held him too, glad for the power of his arms around her.

"I must take the reverend home, Esther. I won't be long," he whispered in her hair. Pulling away, he bent down to look into her eyes. "Will you be alright?"

She numbly shook her head, and they were gone. She stood there alone, wondering how she should be feeling. As in a daze, she looked around. There, on the end table, lay Kurt's Bible, their Bible. She went to it and found her story. She would be strong, like Queen Esther. She would read her story.

‡ A canopy under which a Jewish couple stands during the wedding ceremony.

Chapter Twelve

"For how can I endure to see the evil that shall come unto my people?
or how can I endure to see the destruction of my kindred?"

Esther 8:6

October 7, 1944

Saturday was not that much different than any other day, except that there were not as many officers on duty and the laundry was proportionally less. Because of this, coupled with the fact that Friday nights were especially busy and long for the girls, they were given an extra hour to sleep.

Kurt as well did not have to report to the office as early. In fact, Saturdays had been a bit awkward for them: Esther left, and Kurt stayed behind. For Kurt, it was a time he relished—his time alone with God. It was also the only time of the week that he was able to think and sort things out in his heart.

But now that they were married, all that changed. Everything was all so new to them both. He knew there was much on her heart that she as yet could not share with him. He did not fool himself into thinking that she loved him. Their marriage had been a desperate act to add honor as well as peace and stability to their insane lives. But he did know one thing: he loved her more than he could express.

Now, he always woke before Esther. He cherished these quiet moments in the morning. Truly God's Word was correct when it stated that *"Two are better than one."* He turned to face her, to watch her sleep—so peaceful, so child-like. How much longer would he be able to protect her? And what would happen to them if they were found out? The thought made his heart race. He instinctively reached over and drew her close. She snuggled next to him, slowly arousing from her sleep. At first, she seemed startled to see him there. He was usually dressed and leaning over her when she awoke. Why was he here?

She propped herself up on one elbow, searching his face. A hand instinctively felt his forehead. "Are you ill?"

89

He smiled, "How could I be ill when I'm married to the most beautiful woman in the world?" He kissed her nose. "It's Saturday, my love. We get a few extra moments, remember?"

Understanding registered on her face. Now she smiled and closed her eyes. "Ah yes, Saturday, and you loaf while I slave." His embrace tightened. How he wished they could spend the whole day together. Maybe someday they'd be able to.

Esther reluctantly rose and readied herself for the day. She was still in the bathroom when she heard an explosion that shook the quietness of the morning. She rushed out to see Kurt dressing quickly. "What is it?" she cried.

"I don't know." He was slipping on his shoes, looking up at her. "Stay here until I find out. If the other girls ask, tell them to stay in this building until they hear from me." He was about to race out the door when he turned, came back to her, and embraced her. "I love you." Then he was gone.

Esther hadn't missed the fact that every time he said those words, he never left time for her to respond. He seemed afraid of the message that the silence gave. She hadn't yet been able to tell him how she felt—she wasn't sure herself. But as he raced out the door, people shouting in the background, she realized that she would be lost without him. Did she love him?

She had been taught that love was a choice. Just as Isaac had grown to love the bride that his father's servant had chosen for him, she too might have had to choose to love her husband if her father had not been more forward thinking than some of the fathers in her community. She knew some of the wives on her street in Amsterdam had had to do so. With Gabriel, it had been different. It was not a choice to love him. Love had taken root in her heart and had continually grown even before he had shared his feelings for her. Then, as she had received his letters and read his love in every line, how could she not love him in return?

As always, thoughts of Gabriel brought such a deep regret and heaviness on her heart. *Oh, Gabriel, what would you think of me now? I am so sorry.* She walked back to the window, where she froze. The crematorium was in smoke. Soldiers were running everywhere. What did it all mean?

She tried to find Kurt. She watched as soldiers began to shoot any prisoner in sight. She had not known such terror since the day she watched her mother die at the hands of a murderous soldier. What if Kurt had been shot accidentally or hurt in all the commotion? Was it just because he was truly her savior that she felt a need for his presence?

She crossed the room and fell to her knees. *Oh, Father! What is happening? Is this the end? Dear Lord, am I, as a Jew, allowed to love this man?* She waited, as if listening for a response. She wished that she knew her Torah as well as Kurt seemed to know his Bible. Had Queen Esther loved King Ahasuerus? As she thought back over the story, she realized that the king certainly had shown his love to her. Had he not offered her half the kingdom? What had this Jewish queen done that had made him feel this way? Surely she must have shown him love.

Slowly she replayed the last few weeks over in her mind. She thought about how she felt every time he came through the door, when he held her hand, when he looked at her, spoke to her, shared his heart and faith with her. Those feeling were not just respect or appreciation. Her pulse was racing as she realized, for the first time, that she truly did love him. But could she truly love two men? Just thinking the thought made her feel disgraceful. There was so much she did not understand, but one fact seemed to dispel all doubts: She did love Kurt Gerstein. Her heart sang as she poured out her thanks to God for her husband.

Suddenly, all was quiet. She jumped to her feet and went to the window. The dead bodies were being thrown onto a wagon. It seemed as though the fire within the remains of the crematorium was being contained. She strained to see Kurt, but still without success. Would she have the opportunity to tell him of her new discovery? Her heart raced at the thought of losing him. She had herself in a near panic when she heard his voice in the hallway. He was calling the girls to come out of their rooms.

As she came out into the hallway, he was standing at attention at the other end of the hall. The cold, hard mask of reserve was on his face. As soon as the girls were assembled, he began, "There has been a planned revolt among the prisoners. If any of you knows anything about this, it would be to your best interest to tell me at once."

He hesitated, as though sorting out his own thoughts. Obviously this was not a planned speech. Esther found herself praying for him. "Rebellion causes difficulties for everyone. There will be repercussions because of this. However, for you, it will be a blessing in disguise." His tone softened ever so slightly. "There will be no evening visitors until I return. Make good use of your time. You will not be reporting for laundry duty today either."

At that moment, Frau Wilhelm entered with her charge. The whole compound could blow up, but Frau Wilhelm would be there, making sure *her* duties were fulfilled. She glowered at the girls. "Mind you, this is only temporary."

Esther received her rations and went to her room. Kurt must have circled the building and came in from the other side while the others weren't looking, for he was already in there when she opened the door. Such relief washed over her. She tossed the loaf aside and ran to him. He gathered her into his arms, a bit bewildered by her outburst. "Shh, there, there. What is all this about?"

He smoothed her hair, then dried her tears. As she looked up at him, she felt shy and hid her face on his chest. It was then that she noticed the smudges of dirt and grime and the smell of smoke on his jacket. She pulled back to look up into his face. She *must* tell him.

"Oh, you are here, alive! After you left, I was so afraid that something had happened to you. The men were screaming, and everyone was rushing around. Then I heard the gunshots. I was afraid that you might be dead, and I couldn't bear the thought of you being gone and never knowing."

She stopped abruptly.

"Knowing what, Esther?" He searched her face.

She could tell that he had no idea about what she was about to say. "I—I love you."

Her gaze was childlike. Her lashes blinked quickly, trying to hold back more tears. Kurt was staring at her in unbelief. She watched as the truth registered on his face. Intense joy sprang from deep within Kurt's being, slowly illuminating his face. He pulled her into a fierce hug, rocking back and forth, laughing and calling out her name, smothering her hair with kisses.

"You will never know how happy I am." His voice was thick with emotion. "I have never been so happy, Esther."

The day, the explosion, the entire outside world was lost for one brief moment—too brief. Kurt pulled her to the sofa, his expression again serious. "We need to talk."

Unwillingly, they came back to reality. "I need to tell you what has happened. Some of the prisoners have blown up Crematorium IV and killed several guards."

"But how could they? How could it be possible?"

"There is a group of prisoners called the *Sonderkommando* that remove the bodies from the gas chambers." His countenance grew somber as he tried to imagine such an awful task. "They somehow were able to smuggle gunpowder in from some nearby factories."

"But how could they get the gunpowder in here?"

"We do not know yet. That is why I spoke to the girls. I cannot imagine that any of them would be involved, but SS Höss said that the gunpowder was brought in by women."

Esther was incredulous. "What were all the gunshots?"
Kurt sighed. "They shot all the prisoners."

Esther leaned against his shoulder. "I am glad you are here and safe."

He was quiet—too quiet.

"What is wrong, Kurt?" She could see worry in his eyes and knew there was more. "What are you not telling me?"

He could see the same panic that he had seen too often before. "I must leave ... this afternoon. I am being sent to get more Zyklon B."

He raked his hair. Esther realized that he hadn't combed it or shaved. He looked a mess.

"I used to look forward to these trips to get away. I would stay away as long as I dared without becoming suspicious. But now ..." He squeezed her shoulder. "I will be back as soon as I can. As I said, the girls will not have nighttime visitors, so you all should be safe."

She could tell that he was as uncertain about that statement as she was. She must be strong for him. "Do you have any idea how long you will be gone?"

Again he sighed, his shoulders drooped. "It will take me at least seven days."

She touched his cheek with her hand. "Don't worry, we will be alright. I have come to realize that my safely and yours as well does not depend on us, but our Heavenly Father."

It was a simple statement filled with childlike faith, and Kurt loved her all the more for it. They spent the remainder of the morning together reading and praying since they would be apart for the evening. A sense of foreboding hovered around them, seeking to devour their sweet communion, but the words from their Heavenly Father were especially sweet that day.

Since the other night, Kurt had read only from the Old Testament, but with their pending separation, he felt an urgent need to try one more time to convince her that Jesus was the Christ, Israel's true Messiah. He read Psalm 2:7, "*The LORD hath said unto me, Thou art my Son; this day have I begotten thee.*" He then turned to John 1:14, which spoke of the Word being made flesh and dwelling among people. Kurt finished with Hebrews 1:5, "*For unto which of the angels said he at any time, Thou art my Son, this day have I begotten thee? And again, I will be to him a Father, and he shall be to me a Son?*"

Following the reading, Kurt said no more, but slid to his knees. Today, Esther followed his example. His prayer was full of praise and petitions. He was pleading with his God on her behalf. After he closed, he stayed there, head still resting on his folded hands. Esther didn't dare to move, wondering, yet knowing, what was coming.

Kurt finally turned to her and gently kissed her. He lingered close to her, his head resting against her own. She could feel his breath upon her face. "Esther, can you believe?"

It was all he said. She felt more than saw the agony in his soul. Oh, how she wanted to please him, but this? "I want to, Kurt, but I can't."

He too felt the struggle in her soul. God had led him to choose her, to help her, to protect her. But this was a decision he could not make for her. She had to believe. She had to accept by faith all that had been given to her. "You are not alone, Esther."

He flipped through the pages of John until he found what he was looking for. "Even Jesus' disciples had a hard time believing." Handing the Bible to her, he asked, "Would you read this passage?" and pointed where to start.

Hesitantly, she took the book. She looked at him, then at the words. She slowly began to read the story of Thomas, who refused to believe in Jesus' resurrection until he had seen Jesus' wounds for himself. Esther was struck by Jesus' words: "*Blessed are they that have not seen, and yet have believed.*" She closed the book and held it tightly before handing it back to Kurt.

He wanted to say so much, but knew he should say very little. "You will think in this, please?"

94

"Yes," she replied, smiling. "I will think on this, and on you!"

He pulled her close, and she rested her head upon his shoulder. "Oh, how I wish I did not have to leave you."

"Well, I suppose I could put on one of the SS officers uniforms." He pulled back, staring at her. Then she smiled, and they both laughed.

"Now wouldn't that be a sight," Kurt mused. "I'm sure you would be the best looking SS officer I have ever seen!" He stood, pulling her up from her knees. "Well, I must pack some things and be off."

She sat on the couch, watching him prepare to leave. "I wish there was something of yours that I could keep with me while you are gone."

"I have nothing to give"—he looked down at the book in his hand—"except this." He gazed intently at her, trying to memorize every feature. As much as he hated to part with his Bible, he wanted her to have it. He folded his hands around hers. "Keep reading it, Esther. I believe you will come to know your Messiah."

He pulled her close once more, the Bible still in her hands. One last hold, one kiss, one look that Esther would cherish forever, and he was gone.

Chapter Thirteen

"For my thoughts are not your thoughts, neither are your ways my ways, saith the Lord. For as the heavens are higher than the earth, so are my ways higher than your ways, and my thoughts than your thoughts."

Isaiah 55:8–9

November, 1944

"How could this have happened?" Schindler's voice was tired from fighting too many battles. Would there ever be an end to all this madness? He sighed and anxiously looked at the papers in his hand, shaking his head in unbelief. "This can't be possible."

"I'm sorry, sir, but these three hundred were somehow separated from the others in transport."

Amsel Sokolsky had been with Oskar Schindler since before the war. His Jewish features could not be hidden. Dark hair fell across his forehead just above his large brown eyes. He stood before Schindler, distress shadowing his every feature. The young man worshiped Schindler and hated to disappoint him.

Schindler let out a long sigh. "But you know that they will never come out of Auschwitz alive." Then, as though the statement empowered Oskar Schindler with new strength, he sprang into action. "See that the arrangements are made at once. I must get there before it is too late."

Amsel knew what arrangements needed to be made. He returned just moments later with plenty of cash, a car with a full tank of gas, and Simeon Stolarz, his faithful driver. He wondered just how many more lives one man could rescue.

Schindler was already waiting for him, bag in hand. An air of confidence made Oskar Schindler a striking figure that few could do battle with and win.

Walking briskly to the car, hand on the handle, he turned to face Amsel. He had not missed the torment on the young man's face. Placing a hand on his shoulder, he spoke gently to the man. "This is not your fault, Amsel. I am sorry if you took my actions to mean such a thing. I would be lost without your brilliant mind." He reached up and patted Amsel on the cheek. "These things happen—especially in time of war." He gently squeezed his arm and turned to go.

"Godspeed to you, sir!" Amsel shouted as the vehicle roared into motion.

Oskar Schindler waved his goodbye, knowing that this would need to be his greatest performance yet. He knew SS Höss—had met him on several informal occasions.

SS-Obersturmbannführer Rudolf Höss had not risen to the head of Auschwitz by half-hearted actions. He was adamant about the cause and did his duties with supreme accuracy. News had leaked out about the recent upheaval, which would only make matters much more difficult. But if anyone could match the dedication and wit that Rudolf Höss demonstrated, it was Oskar Schindler.

The visions of Jews from the Kraków Ghetto being rounded up and shipped off like cattle would never be erased from his mind. Scenes of cold-blooded murder of anyone—man, woman, or child—who dared to question the Nazis or moved too slowly was forever etched into his memory. Their memories drove him onward. These three hundred women were his girls, and he would do everything in his power to get them back.

***

Esther had just finally fallen asleep when the commotion started. The emotionally taxing day had driven Esther to retire early. Now it sounded like hundreds of people were outside her room. Keeping the lights off, she moved from her bed to the window. Outside, several hundred women were being ordered about. This wouldn't have been unusual except that it was the middle of the night. She watched as several guards gestured toward her building.

"Schnell!" cried the guards to the bewildered group, and they all were pushed through the doors and into the hallway.

Panic seized Esther as she heard keys rattling outside her door. She quickly hid under the bed, just as the door was opened. How many people were being shoved into her room, she could not tell. Just that quickly, the door was shut. Esther could hear muffled voices from her hiding place. Some were crying. She sighed as she realized that they were all women, but she was at a loss as to what to do next. Her quandary was solved as a woman came into the bedroom.

"It looks as though someone has been in here," one voice spoke.

Esther gasped as a foot connected with her own.

"Someone's under there!" another voice hissed. Slowly, the counterpane was lifted, and several faces searched the darkness.

"You can come out," came the kind reply. "We won't hurt you."

Esther inched her way out from beneath the bed. The women before her looked different than others at the camp. Then she realized: They still had hair.

One woman pushed ahead of the others. She voiced the questions that all were wondering. "Who are you, and why were you hiding under the bed?"

How could Esther explain her unusual situation to total strangers? Instead, she decided to ask her own questions. "Who are all of you?" She panned the room, glancing at all the faces. Her eyes seemed drawn to one particular face.

The girl who had spoken earlier seemed to be the leader. She answered with a smile, "I am Anita, and we are Schindler's girls."

Esther looked confused. "I never heard of Schindler. What do you mean?"

Anita looked around the room at all the familiar faces. "Come. Let's all go to one room." She laughed, "That is, if we will fit. They squeezed us in here like sardines!"

Esther knew immediately that under different circumstances, she and Anita would be good friends. The thought made her sad. As though reading her mind, Anita reached for her hand and pulled her to the other room. To Esther's astonishment, there were at least fifteen women all crowded together in the space that used to belong to her and her beloved Kurt.

Anita was speaking again, bringing sense and order to the group. "Come now, things could be worse. If we arrange ourselves properly, we can all sit for a minute and get acquainted with our host before we turn out the lights."

As if on cue, the girls all found a place to sit—some on the couch and chairs, but most on the floor in neat little rows. They were all facing Anita and Esther.

Anita began her explanation. "Oskar owns a factory in which he hires Jews—us!" Anita said with a smile. "We were supposed to be on our way to a new facility, but somehow, about three hundred of us ended up here." Although she was trying to make light of the mistake, Esther could see a bit of fear peeking out behind those confident gray eyes. "It will only be a matter of time before Herr Schindler finds us and takes us home."

One small girl slowly shook her head. Her eyes held defeat. "He won't make it in time—at least not for me."

"Oh, Leah, don't say that. Look what he has already done for us." Anita's voice was fierce. "How many times does he have to save you for you to believe in his miracles?"

The girl cowered until Anita went to her and smoothed her hair. Leah's staring eyes were filled with unshed tears. Her face was pale, her skin taut.

Anita turned to Esther as if to offer an explanation. "We haven't had much to eat since we left Kraków. We have tried to share our food, but Leah was frail before we started." Her face softened as she continued to stroke the girl's hair. "Now, tell us about yourself. Why is it that you are not shaved like the usual prisoners? And why do you have a room all to yourself?"

Anita's questions were so forthright that Esther felt compelled to explain. She started from the moment she stepped off the train. She could see the look of horror in the girls' eyes as she detailed the duties of the girls. She didn't miss their disdain for Kurt.

"But Herr Gerstein also sought a way to save lives," she argued fervently. "He did not have the means to purchase a factory like your Herr Schindler, but he too works against the system any way that he can."

Before Anita could think, she blurted out, "But how could you do such a thing?"

Esther smiled. Thoughts of her dear husband filled her mind. She hesitated. Should she tell them? Could she trust them? Searching each face, she spoke with resolve, "I don't. I am Kurt Gerstein's wife."
She went on to explain the events of the last few hours. She could see the doubt in their eyes, but it did not matter to her. She knew her heart—his heart—and it gave her a sweet peace that she could not explain.

Anita cleared her throat. "Well, I believe we have all had enough confusion for the night. Leah, why don't you sleep in the bed with Sarah and Esther?" And with that, she laid out a plan for everyone to sleep. As Esther shared her bed with two other girls, she wondered what the morning would bring.

***

Morning came before any of the girls were ready for it. It had been a long night. Esther stirred at dawn, expecting to see Kurt's face when she rolled over. She startled to see the face of a stranger, then remembered the events of the evening. The girl named Leah was lying next to her. She looked so still.

Esther turned away, reviewing the events of the past twenty-four hours in her mind. Indeed, she had a hard time believing it had only been that long. Just twenty-four hours ago, Kurt had been here beside her. Her heart ached with loneliness. What was happening? She quietly rolled over and began to pray. *Oh, Father, be with Kurt, wherever he is. I'm frightened, Father! What is happening?*

As she felt her pulse quickening with fear, God's Word came to her: *"Fear thou not; for I am with thee: be not dismayed; for I am thy God: I will strengthen thee; yea, I will help thee; yea, I will uphold thee with the right hand of my righteousness."*

Trust me, the words whispered in her heart. She continued in prayer until she felt someone stirring on the opposite side of the bed. Esther decided she would get to the bathroom before the rush. Her feet hit the chilly floor, waking her completely. Her heart went out to those who had slept there.

"Leah ... Leah."

Esther heard Sarah trying to wake the girl.

"Leah!" Sarah's voice was nearing hysteria.

Esther turned to look at the girl. She was violently shaking Leah. Esther's eyes widened in horror as Sarah slumped to the floor, weeping into the covers. Anita seemed to appear out of nowhere. She took in the scene before her, grief showing in her eyes. Esther could see her resolve to carry this added burden on her slim shoulders.

She walked slowly to Sarah's side of the bed and examined Leah before covering her face with the sheets. Then she turned to comfort Sarah. One by one the girls began to weep. All had tried to be

100

so strong through it all, but this was too much. The sound of weeping grew until there was a harsh knock at the door.

"What's going on in there?"

Esther was shocked to hear Frau Wilhelm's voice. She would not be pleased. Pushing her way through the crowd, Esther pulled open the door.

"Frau Wilhelm, one of the girls that was brought in here last night has died during the night. We just discovered her this morning."

Frau Wilhelm's face twitched with disgust. What would the officers think? Why did this Jew have to die in her building? They were always causing problems, these Jews. "Well! Don't just stand there. Haul her out here into the hallway."

Shock registered on all the girls faces.

"Don't just gape at me—move!"

Esther led the way back into the room. As best they could, she and Anita wrapped Leah in the sheet from the bed and carried her to the hall.

"Why waste the sheet, you silly fools?" Frau Wilhelm. "Humph! Don't ask for another!"

Esther was going to remind Frau Wilhelm whose room this was, but she thought better of it. No questions and certainly no confrontations were always best.

"Put it by the door—the soldiers will get it later," Frau Wilhelm directed before marching down the corridor.

As Esther watched her go, she felt sad for the woman. How could a person live with such a stony heart?

"Girls, come here into the hallway," Anita ordered.

Esther stared in wonder as all the girls from her room squeezed out of the room. Before she could say anything, Anita was speaking again. "We must pay our respects to our dear sister."

Each girl bowed her head as Anita prayed. "Dear Jehovah God, we thank you for the life of Leah. She was faithful and true, and we will miss her so." A sob caught in Anita's throat, and she paused for composure before continuing. "She is in Abraham's bosom now. We can do no more for her. Oh Father, please help Herr Schindler to get here in time!"

With the prayer's conclusion, all eyes turned to their leader. "Back to the room," she whispered fiercely.

As the morning passed, Esther wondered about their rations. As if on cue, she heard commotion in the hall. Heavy feet stopped near her door. They paused. Angry voices barked back and forth. There was a shuffling and grunting, and she realized they were taking Leah.

From the other end of the building, Esther recognized familiar sounds. "Wait here, while I go and get our food," she told the others. As she walked down the hallway, the same scenario was played out at each doorway: the usual girl coming for breakfast and what seemed to be hundreds of questioning eyes peering from the rooms. To Esther's horror, she was given her usual loaf of bread. Her eyes flew to Frau Wilhelm's face. Steely eyes dared her to question. Turning on her heels, Esther returned with her bread. She carefully divided among the girls, each getting a few bites. That would be all until the evening.

As they all settled down to await their destiny, Anita once again took charge. She could feel the hysteria mounting within the crowded room. "Now girls, it's not all that bad," she said, trying to convince them of what she did not quite believe herself. "As long as we stick together, we will be alright."

"We have no say as to what they do to us here, Anita," one girl voiced. There were several nods around the room.

Deciding to change the subject, Anita turned to Esther. "What is your usual schedule for the day?"

Esther could see Anita's plan, and her admiration continued to grow for this woman. "Usually, Kurt would go to his office. Then I would have a little time to read the Bible." The word was out before Esther knew it. Several gasps escaped around the room.

She went on, "I would read the Old Testament—it is very similar to our own sacred books. It has been my strength and high tower here." She reverently ended in a near whisper. She could see acceptance, perhaps even admiration, in some of the eyes staring at her.

"Where did you get a ..." Anita seemed hesitant to say the name of the forbidden book.

"The first night I came here, I was so distraught. I had been taken from my father and brothers. Papa had given me his Ketuvim, but of course they took it from me with all my other belongings. When I came into this room, I saw a book on the nightstand. I reacted much like many of you did when I saw it, but I was so thirsty for God's comfort that I opened it."

She paused. "I read my story—the book of Esther." She looked toward the table where she had laid it the night before. Looking at Anita, who was nearest to it, she asked, "Could you hand it to me?"

Anita hesitated. She knew all the girls looked up to her. What would they think if she touched it? She looked at Esther. Her own respect was growing for this young girl who had already faced many trials. She looked at the Bible and picked it up, quickly handing it to Esther.

Esther smiled. "Thank you."

Anita nodded.

"You asked about my daily routine. After I read and pray, all the girls in this building usually go to the laundry facility across the street and work there all day. Then we return here." She hesitated. "The other girls are visited by male guests during the night. God has spared me from this."

"But instead you marry a Gentile?"

Esther rightly read disgust in the older woman's voice. "I do not expect you to understand, and I do not know what you have faced with this Herr Schindler." Her ire was rising. "He sounds as though he has been a savior to you. Indeed, Herr Gerstein has also been my savior. If he had not chosen me, I cannot even begin to imagine ..." She stopped, barely whispering. "He saved my life."

"Ladies," Anita was speaking, "I do not think this is the time for judgment or condemnation. These are truly desperate times." Her stare turned to Esther and softened. "I think we need to hear from God. Would you read to us, Esther?"

At the sound of the intake of air, Anita glowered round the room, defying anyone to challenge her. Satisfied, she turned back to Esther with an encouraging smile.

Esther opened the Bible to where a ribbon held the place. It would have been her turn to read to Kurt. Tears threatened to fall when she saw the passage: Psalm 37. Clearing her throat, she began to read.

Fret not thyself because of evildoers ... For they shall soon be cut down like the grass, and wither as the green herb. Trust in the LORD, and do good; so shalt thou dwell in the land, and verily thou shalt be fed. Delight thyself also in the LORD; and he shall give thee the desires of thine heart. Commit thy way unto the LORD; trust also in him; and he shall bring it to pass. ... Rest in the LORD, and wait patiently for him.

103

Fret not thyself in any wise to do evil. For evildoers shall be cut off: but those that wait upon the LORD, they shall inherit the earth.

On and on she read, sensing the power of God in the room, giving encouragement and hope. She heard murmurs of agreement uttered around the room. Her voice grew confident as she read the final lines.

For yet a little while, and the wicked shall not be ... But the salvation of the righteous is of the LORD: he is their strength in the time of trouble. And the LORD shall help them, and deliver them: he shall deliver them from the wicked, and save them, because they trust in him.

Quietly, Esther closed the Bible. The silence was good, as each woman searched her own heart and communed with the Lord. As was her habit, Esther slipped to her knees and began to pray. It was not a long prayer, but it included a petition for them all, including her dear husband.

***

The sun slowly moved its way across the sky as the girls shared stories. Esther felt such a kinship with them. It had been so long since she had talked to anyone but Kurt. It felt good and right.

"Esther, I think you should go with us," Anita suddenly blurted out.

"What do you mean?" Esther could see that Anita's mind was whirling with thoughts.

"You have no idea when your husband will return, and as you said, times are very volatile—especially since the explosion. If we leave this place, I think you should come with us in the place of Leah."

Murmurs of approval echoed around the room. Esther's mind was whirling as well. "But what if Kurt returns and finds that I am gone?" The thought brought panic to her mind.

"And what if he doesn't?" Anita quietly suggested.

"He would never do that," Esther adamantly argued.

"Esther, we believe you," Anita said reassuringly, "but these are difficult and uncertain times. If we go and you stay, and he isn't able to return, then what will you do? Who will protect you then?"

Anita could see that her statements were hitting their mark. She could not tell why, but deep in her heart, she sensed that Esther would never get out of here with or without Kurt Gerstein. She felt they were her only hope. "Please, Esther, consider it?"

Esther had to admit that the thought of these women leaving her behind was frightening. Images of the soldiers shooting everyone in sight after the explosion coursed through her mind. *Oh, Kurt, why did you have to leave?* "I'm just afraid that if I leave, he will never find me."

"We are not that far away, Esther. After the war, or perhaps even before, he will come for you. Herr Schindler has connections throughout the entire Third Reich. He is a very powerful man. He has done the impossible over and over again. If anyone can reconnect you with your husband, it is Herr Schindler. And"—Anita paused for emphasis—"I believe your husband would want you to be safe. Better leave here and live than stay and ..."

She left the thought hanging, but she could see that what she had said was making sense to Esther.

"Yes, I think you are right. Kurt would want me be to be safe, and I am really a ghost here anyway."

The girls looked puzzled. Esther explained, "Kurt removed my name from any of the lists that he could get his hands on."

"Good! Then it's settled."

To Esther's surprise, Anita came forward and reached for her hand. Clasping it, Anita pulled her into an embrace. "Welcome to our little group, Leah!" She smiled but quickly became serious. "It would be best if we all started calling you Leah until we leave."

All heads nodded in agreement. There was a sense of expectancy. No longer was the thought *if* they would leave, but *when*.

***

That had been a three days ago. This afternoon the call came—they had been ordered to stand outside in the bitter cold. It had been a long time since Anita Agorazo had felt the cold that she was feeling now. As she stood with the others, her mind went back over the last few days. She had thought they were just moving to Brünnlitz, a small town farther away from the atrocious concentration camps. How in the world had they ended up at Auschwitz?

Just thinking the name made her shiver from within. Her hope that Herr Schindler would rescue them was growing thin as she stood

105

with the rest outside in the freezing weather. Now she wondered if she had made a mistake in bringing Esther into the whole matter.

They stood waiting—but for what, Anita wasn't sure she wanted to know. The afternoon sun sent out little warmth. *How long, Father? O, please let me see Herr Schindler's face just once more!* Anita pleaded with her God. She was so glad that Leah was not here. She would never have made it.

As she looked about the compound, she spotted a tight group of SS officers off to their left. They seemed to be disagreeing about something, and Anita couldn't help feeling it had to do with them. They would read some papers, then look up at the girls, and then continue to argue. Finally, two of them left the group and headed their way. She wasn't sure if she should be glad or not.

Gruffly, one of the men stopped in front of them and said, "This way." That was all.

Anita looked at Esther and raised her eyebrows as though to say, *Do you know where we are going?*

Esther discreetly shook her head. She hadn't been this way since she got here. It seemed odd to be out and about, walking away from all she had known for the past few months. She had sewn a pouch under her dress so that Kurt's Bible would not be seen. She knew it was dangerous, but it was all she had. She would sooner die than part with it. How thankful she was that Kurt had taken the locket with him! She was certain it never left his pocket.

As they marched down through the tall buildings, Esther remembered coming this way before. They were heading to the entrance. Perhaps they were going to be safe. When they stopped in front of the building where Esther had first met Kurt, she panicked. Would the women remember her?

Anita saw the fright in Esther's face, again questioning her with a look. Again, Esther quickly shook her head and looked down. She moved ever so slightly to hide behind the girls in front of her. Anita seemed to understand and moved to shield her.

Once inside the building, each stood before the woman with the shears. To Esther's relief, she did not recognize any of the women. One by one, they each had their hair cut short. It seemed odd to Esther—no tattoos or showers, just the hair cut short. As her dark bountiful locks fell to the floor, Esther thanked God. Now she looked just like one of Schindler's girls. Some of the other girls wept. Esther could tell that the strain was getting to them.

Once outside again, Esther fully expected to head down to the railway, but after more angry words between the guards, they were ordered to return to where they had been. "That was a waste of time," she heard the one soldier complain.

Instead of heading to their building, the girls continued to walk forward. Esther had not been this way before either. With each step, her heart pounded. Her eyes darted back and forth among the women. They did not know. This road only led to one thing.

On they walked until the giant smokestack was right in front of them. At the sight of it, murmurs and cries could be heard. "Silence! All of you," the guard shouted. He herded them to the side of the road and commanded them to stay there until further notice.

The sun had already dipped behind the horizon. Dusk was upon them. On they stood, waiting. As the night wore on, they huddled closer to one another, trying to stay warm. No stars could be seen, only a cover of thick clouds. Esther prayed. *How could they do this?* Her emotions seemed to spiral from anxiety to anger, and finally to despair and total defeat. She no longer cared if she lived or died.

The night wore on. All hope was gone, yet as the sky began to glow with the early morning sun, it brought a glimmer of encouragement. They had made it through the night. Certainly that meant something.

As the camp awoke, people began to mill about, each doing their sordid business. As Esther looked down the road, she saw the other girls from the brothel heading to the laundry. She wondered if she would be missed. *I waited patiently upon the Lord, and He heard my cry.* Though her head was light from lack of sleep and food and her heart was heavy with fear that she would be discovered, she silently communed with Jehovah. Speaking the words in her heart, she bounced between praying and reciting as many verses as she could remember. She was amazed at the inner strength she felt. *Oh, Father, why should I be surprised when you have promised to be my strength until I see you face to face?* As she saw the smokestack, she was overwhelmed with the thought of seeing God—today.

Anita would always remember that day—that voice. She had watched as several SS officers had passed by them, not even looking their way. Anita was glad. With the gas chambers and crematorium right in front of them, she hoped that they would stay invisible, but how? She thought about dying. What would it be like? At least it would not hurt. *You have to give the Nazis credit for that much.* She nearly laughed at the preposterous thought. Was she losing her mind?

As she mused over her sanity, she heard a familiar voice. Was it just in her mind? Could it be real? She turned to look behind her and there he stood—tall and proud and angry.

"What are you doing with these people? These are my people," she heard him say.

The officers did not know what to do; they had their orders.

"I have my orders too," he protested, angrily thrusting them a slip of paper. It must have had someone's name on it with power, for now they could not do enough for Herr Schindler.

"We are sorry, sir, we did not know. We were just following orders, sir." Such politeness from the SS officers—such joy in the face of death for the girls. The group of girls surged with energy. They were safe.

Herr Schindler was now walking toward them, inspecting them. Anita read relief mixed with worry on his face. Some of the girls swayed precariously from exhaustion and hunger. She saw his jaw tighten as he searched each face, his eyes resting on Esther.

She had never seen such a commanding presence. He stood there like a champion. She watched him in awe as he commanded the officers to do his bidding. How could he wield such authority? Oh, how she wished Kurt was here to see him. Her musing was broken when his stare stopped upon her face. Panic seized her. What would he do with her? Would she ruin the escape of all these women? Was that what he was thinking?

Anita took it all in, in a matter of seconds. Her mother had always told her that her quick wit and sharp tongue would someday get her into trouble, but today was not that day. Today, she needed to save a friend. "Look, Leah," she said, emphasizing the name and looking straight into Esther's eyes. She then turned her sharp gaze upon Herr Schindler. "I told you he would come."

Anita held her breath, hoping that Schindler got her message. Slowly, understanding dawned on his face for just a moment before he turned fierce. "Anita, be quiet unless you are being spoken to!"

"Yes, Herr Schindler. Sorry, Herr Schindler." Anita played her part well and bowed her head.

Part Three
Brünnlitz

Chapter Fourteen

"Thou shalt preserve me from trouble;
thou shalt compass me about with songs of deliverance."

Psalm 32:7

The setting sun was shining like a big, beautiful golden ball of warmth in the sky. Its heat soaked into Esther's body until she felt as though she was part of the shining orb. She lay watching the rays dancing off the water.

But where was Kurt? He should have been here with her. He was missing this beautiful sunset. As she watched the sun glide its way through the sky, she saw him. He was running. "Kurt! Kurt! I'm here," she cried to him, but he didn't seem to hear her.

She tried to cry louder, but the pounding waves on the shoreline drowned out her cries. Frantically, she tried to get up, but the sand was swallowing her. "Kurt! Kurt! I'm over here! Please," she wept, "please help me!"

The sobs caught in her throat, threatening to drown her. He was looking for her. She could see him, but he didn't know which way to go. She saw him drop to his knees, his face buried into his hands. He was weeping. The waves crashed around her, and the sun slipped behind the horizon. Darkness overcame her, and she felt as though every degree of warmth was being stripped from her body. She was sinking down into nothingness.

"Has she aroused yet?" Oskar asked as he watched her brow furrow.

"No, sir," the attendant replied. "She keeps calling for her husband, sir."

Schindler's brows arched with doubt, "Husband? So you think her story is true? Or is she fabricating it to cover the sordid details of that place?"

"I think she's telling the truth, sir."

Schindler shook his head. Whether her story was true or not, he knew she would have a difficult time living with either scenario among her people—and that was all depending upon whether she would live. Since the nightmarish trip from Auschwitz in the bitter cold, Esther had arrived unconscious but alive, which was more than he could say for many of the others.

Those who had survived were sick with fevers and frostbite. His brick building looked more like an infirmary than a munitions factory. Thankfully, enough of the others were well and working hard to keep up their ruse of making the faulty ammunition. God only knew how many more lives would be saved beyond these 1,200, because a bomb didn't explode or a grenade fell mutely to the ground. He had to smile at the thought.

Etka, the attendant, was watching him, waiting for further instruction. From her expression, he could tell that she was wondering what had made him smile.

Oskar cleared his throat, "Keep a close eye on her, and let me know when she arouses."

Etka noticed that he said "when," not "if." It was just like Herr Schindler—always looking on the positive side. He walked away, checking on other sick girls as he went, giving a smile or an encouraging word to each of them; and he was adored by all because of it.

Esther's eyelids felt like sandpaper and were as heavy as lead. She struggled to open them. At first, it seemed impossible, yet something inside told her to wake up. She feared she would be late for work. What would happen to her if she did not show up at the laundry room? The thought added more determination to her effort.

She thought about Kurt. Would he be in trouble if she was late? Fighting the urge to submerge once again, Esther opened her eyes ever so slightly. The room was dark and unfamiliar. Confusion clouded her already fuzzy brain, causing her to let her eyelids slip shut again. *No! I must wake up!*

Her eyes once again fluttered open. She looked next to her. Kurt was already gone. No, there was no room for Kurt. Why was she in a single bed? Panic seized her, and she fought to get up. Her head came crashing down again on the pillow as pain shot through her. What was going on? A groan escaped her lips.

The sound startled Etka, who sat dozing in a chair next to Esther's bed. Etka had grown fond of the young Jewish woman while at Auschwitz. Her faith in God attracted Etka, who had never been deeply religious. She leaned forward, reaching for Esther's hand. The action startled the girl—her eyes became wild.

"Esther, it's okay. You are safe here," Etka spoke soothingly while rubbing Esther's fingers.

"Who—who are you, and where am I?" Esther questioned. She frantically looked around the room. "Where is Kurt?"

Etka looked at the wall clock. It was five-thirty in the morning. Knowing that Herr Schindler was probably already in his office, she focused on Esther. "Esther, you must lie still; you've been very ill. I must get Herr Schindler." She hated to leave the girl but knew her orders. "I will be right back."

Esther fought to get up, but nausea swept over her with any movement. Her head was swimming, and she was only too glad to lie still. She closed her eyes, still trying to sort through everything, when she heard the door open. The woman was back with a very tall man. He looked vaguely familiar.

Oskar bent down close to her and pulled up the chair behind him. His eyes were gentle and kind. Where had Esther seen him before? As she continued to sort through her thoughts, she realized that he was speaking to her.

"Esther, do you hear me?" he asked.

She focused on his face and nodded slightly.

"Do you remember who I am?" he continued.

Esther frowned as she tried to remember. Slowly she shook her head. "But I feel as though I know you," she said.

He smiled. "Good. Good. Then your memory is still with you."

"But how do I know you?" she asked. Confusion etched her face as she licked her lips. Her mouth was dry, her voice scratchy from lack of use. Etka instinctively poured a glass of water for her and gently moved it to her lips. She sipped the cool liquid slowly and lay back again to study the face before her.

Schindler gently took her tiny hand into his large one. The movement startled Esther, but she lay still. "Do you remember being at Auschwitz?"

"Yes."

"Do you remember some women coming and staying with you?"

Esther thought for a moment. *Yes!* She did remember that. She nodded.

"Do you remember getting your hair cut and standing in the cold for a very long time?"

Esther shut her eyes. She frowned, and then nodded again.

"And do you remember me coming and taking you away?" Esther's eyes popped open. "I remember you coming to us as we stood in the cold." She stared across the room, bringing up the memory.

"Yes. You were there, and then they walked us to the railroad station. They put us into a cattle car—like the one that I had come in with my family, except it was so cold."

She shivered at the memory; a tear slipped down her cheek. "Everyone was freezing, and we rode on and on. We stopped and then went again." She strained at the spot on the opposite wall, not really seeing it—not seeing anything but the cold and darkness of that eternal ride. Her eyes closed, squeezing the rest of the tears down her cheeks. "I can't remember anything else."

Oskar patted her hand. "You have remembered correctly. I am Oskar Schindler. I own these buildings. It is a factory, for the most part. You will be safe here. No one will try to take you or harm you in any way. When you regain your strength, I would like you to work for me. But you do not need to worry about that now. You only need to get well."

He started to get up and leave, when her small, strained voice asked a question. "Where is Kurt?"

He looked at her, not wanting to overwhelm her but knowing he needed to know the truth. "Who is Kurt?" he gently asked.

Her eyes grew wide with fear. "He is my husband. Is he not here?"

Pity filled Oskar's voice when he spoke. "I did not know anyone in that place had husbands."

He could tell that she was embarrassed but was surprised to see an air of resolution cross her face. "I do have a husband." She

114

instinctively tried to raise herself, but dizziness forced her back down. "My book, do you have my book?"

Etka walked across the room to a small dresser. She opened the top drawer and pulled out the Bible, handing it to Herr Schindler. He eyed it suspiciously.

"Open the front flap," Esther instructed.

Oskar obeyed and read the inscription. He hesitated. "But this is a Bible, and you are Jewish."

A faint smile reached Esther's face. She looked at Oskar and sighed. "I know it might seem strange to you, sir, but Kurt Gerstein tried to save lives, not destroy them. His efforts were certainly minor compared to what the girls have said of you; but in his small way, he too was trying to save lives. I never had to do the things the other girls were forced to do. I stayed in Kurt's room, while the others …" She couldn't finish.

"You need to rest Esther," Oskar replied, seeing the strain all of this was having on her already weakened body.

"No, please. Let me finish."

He nodded.

Her voice was weak but fierce. "We never did anything wrong. We became friends. He was completely honorable in every way. Several weeks ago, we were secretly married. Kurt smuggled a minister into our room to perform the ceremony."

She looked into Oskar's face. She could see the questions and doubts there, and she smiled. "I know you are wondering how a Jewish prisoner could marry a German SS officer. Life is very uncertain, wouldn't you say, Herr Schindler?"

He lowered his gaze from her and nodded.

Thoughts of her dear Kurt overwhelmed her. Sobs rose up within her, shaking her weak body. "He saved my life, and I loved him for it."

Oskar drew close to wipe the tears away. "There, there, Esther." He gently stroked her hair, like a father, "You rest. We will talk later."

He continued to stroke her hair until he knew she was again asleep. "When she wakes again, we must get some nourishment into her," he said, turning to Etka. "No more talking; and try to keep her calm." His eyes were full of pity for the girl. Perhaps her story was true.

115

"Yes, sir," Etka answered while pulling her chair close to Esther's side.

***

The next time Esther awoke, she remembered where she was. She lay still for a moment, trying to put her thoughts in order. It seemed like ages since she had said goodbye to Kurt.

Oh Kurt, where are you? She closed her eyes and rolled over, not ready to talk to anyone just yet. She knew the woman was watching her, waiting for her to wake up, but she needed more time.

Kurt had said he might be gone for only a week, but she had no way of knowing how much time had passed since she had left Auschwitz. How long had she been unconscious? And now what? Oh, this wretched war that continued to devour everyone she loved.

She lay quietly for a few more minutes, tenderly savoring the few sweet memories she had shared with Kurt, like dainties from the confectioner's shop. *Oh Father, please protect him and keep Your guiding, protecting hand upon Papa, Daan, and Ad.* It was strange how separated she now felt from them, even though she had had no contact with them since the day they were parted. She felt her emotions spiraling downward and knew it was time to think on other things. She was here now—and she was determined to make the best of it.

Rolling over, she managed a weak smile and greeting. The woman seemed genuinely happy to see her. She was soon out of the chair and by Esther's side. "Good morning to you, Esther. My name is Etka. Shall we see if you can sit up a bit and take some nourishment?"

At the mention of food, Esther's body seemed to signal two different messages: part of her felt that she could eat a horse, but the other part felt nauseous. She simply nodded.

With Etka's help, she managed to raise herself to a sitting position. Esther had never felt so weak. Etka propped the pillows behind her, then brought her a small bowl of broth. She sipped it slowly, thinking she had never tasted anything so delicious and was surprised that the nausea seemed to abate as she continued to sip the hot broth. Her whole body responded to the nourishment.

"Thank you, Etka, for everything," Esther said with a smile.

The woman smiled shyly in return. "It is not any more than anyone else would have done. We thought we were going to lose you with the others." Etka's voice became hard with bitterness. "And after all that Herr Schindler did to rescue us!" A disgusted look crossed her face. "Filthy pigs," she spat.

Esther was surprised at the woman's outburst, and her face showed it.

"Oh, I'm sorry, miss," Etka offered repentantly.

Esther began again "Etka, don't let their evil sew bitterness into your heart."

Etka felt rebuked. She didn't understand this girl. How could she have such wisdom at her young age? She questioned Esther, "How do you keep such a peaceful spirit in the face of all you have been through?"

Esther sensed a warmth inside her soul. She felt such pity for her people—they seemed so lost, like frightened children. Had they all forgotten their Heavenly Father in the midst of this horrendous storm?

"Etka, do you read our sacred writings?" She searched the older woman's face for any sign of belief but found only emptiness. "Didn't your parents teach you the way of God?"

Etka looked away. She laughed a cold, hard laugh. "My parents were too busy making money." She looked into Esther's transparent gaze. Her eyes seemed to be open all the way to her beautiful soul. "We would tip our hats to God on the Sabbath, but nothing more."

"Where are they now?"

"Gone," Etka said flatly. "All my family—my entire village—is gone. I happened to be away at school when they came."

Esther could see the torment in Etka's eyes. Her face twisted, and her voice broke, "Even my little sisters were taken and ..." She could not finish.

With great effort, Esther reached out to her and held her hand. She gently squeezed it before saying, *"Like as a father pitieth his children, so the LORD pitieth them that fear him."* Suddenly, she felt the room pitch. She quickly laid her head back on the pillows. Alarm registered in Etka.

"Oh, Esther, please forgive me. Herr Schindler gave specific orders not to tire you, and here I am prattling on and on." She took the bowl from Esther's hands and moved her back into a resting position.

"Thank you, Etka. No harm done. We will talk again, but I am feeling a bit tired."

Esther was again asleep before Etka could reply. For once, she was glad *not* to see Herr Schindler.

***

Kurt gripped the wheel as he sped along the narrow road. Ten days! It had taken him ten days to get the needed Zyklon B canisters of gas. Even as he heard them bumping together in the back seat, he wished he could bury them like he had an earlier shipment.

The tide was different now. Everyone was being watched as tension mounted. Hitler had not been heard from or seen in public for some time, and speculations about his leadership rose even higher when Himmler gave a speech in the *Furher's* stead. When the Allies dropped into Normandy in June, there seemed to be no stopping them.

If it hadn't been for Esther, Kurt would have been heading in the opposite direction, turning himself over to the hands of the French. But he couldn't do it without Esther. His heart ached to see her and quell the fears for her safety.

As he pulled into the compound, the sun had already set for the day. He needed to deposit the Zyklon B in his office before he could head to his room. The building stood dark and foreboding, empty of all humanity except for the night guard who was used to Kurt's unusual comings and goings. He quickly unlocked his office, shoved the box into a corner, and headed to his room—to Esther.

Oh, how he had missed her. He could see her dark hair and beautiful face waiting for him just inside the door. A smile played across his lips as he crossed the road. Soon he would have her in his arms. He looked up at their room window but noticed it was dark. That was not strange—it was late—but then he noticed all the windows were dark. Usually their dim lights burned well into the evening. Strange. Perhaps things were still not back to normal.

He tried not to panic, but the closer he came to the building, the greater the foreboding enveloped him. He opened the hall door to complete silence. Quickly, he unlocked his door. The room was eerily still. He flicked on the lights. The sight seemed almost normal, yet there was an untidiness about the room that spoke of use and quick departure. He slowly walked to the next room, hoping against hope that he had overreacted. As he turned the corner, bile rose in his throat.

The bed had certainly been used—by how many, Kurt did not know. But now it stood empty. All life drained out of him as he knew his worst nightmare had become reality: Esther was gone, and God alone knew where she was or what she had had to face in just ten days. He crossed to the wall and pounded it with his fists. "No!" he shouted, sliding to the floor and weeping uncontrollably.

Exhaustion overtook Kurt, and before his thoughts could even find any semblance of order, the sun was crossing the floor where he lay, driving him into consciousness. One quick glance and it all came back to him. *Think! You need some answers and a plan of action. She may still be here—somewhere.* But even as he thought the words, something deep inside told him she was gone. He rose and looked out the window. To his incredible shock, the crematoriums were gone. What could this mean? He knew he would have no answers until he reported to headquarters. Quickly shaving and changing his cloths, Kurt headed out the door.

A light snow had fallen, seeming to blanket the compound into further silence. He noticed the usually full parking lot was half empty and quickened his pace. Upon entering the building, he headed directly to Himmler's office and gave the door a rapid knock.

"Yes, come in," came the voice of the preoccupied *Reichsfuhrer*-SS officer. Gerstein entered and waited.

"Ah, Gerstein, we've been wondering if you would make it back," came the unusual reply.

"What do you mean, sir?" Kurt asked, trying to keep his voice steady. Himmler's usual cool manner seemed a bit strained and tense.

"We sent you on a useless mission." His words were rapid and intense with urgency. "As you have probably seen, the crematoriums have been destroyed. Our mission here is nearly complete."

Kurt's mind raced. What did this all mean, and how could he ever find out about Esther's whereabouts? "I don't understand, sir."

"We have been given orders to shut down operations. As our chief supplier of Zyklon B, we obviously do not need your services here anymore. You are being reassigned." He ruffled through some papers. "Yes, here it is—you are to report to Mauthausen immediately and take the Zyklon B with you."

119

He knew he was being dismissed, but he had to chance one question. "If I may ask, sir, where are my girls?" He hated to refer to them that way, but he knew he had a better chance of getting an answer by doing so.

"Ah, your little harem," Himmler said with a sickening grin. "Yes, well that operation has also been terminated."

Kurt pressed on. "Excuse me, sir, but were they also moved to Mauthausen? Will they be part of my responsibility there?"

Himmler chuckled. "No, I'm sure they were nearly useless in their duties by now. You are free to suggest your little enterprise at Mauthausen, but I suggest you start with a fresh group."

Kurt gave a precise salute and turned on his heels, his mind whirling. Would he ever know the truth? Dejectedly, he headed back to his room. His stomach told him it was way past time for some sort of nourishment, but he knew he could never eat.

As he opened the hall door, he heard a sound coming from one of the rooms down the hallway. As he pushed open the half-closed door, he could see someone. There, bent over one of the dressers, was Frau Wilhelm. She held a hairbrush in her hand, which she quickly shoved into her satchel before speaking. Her expression was cold and calculating.

"Herr Gerstein, I see you've made it back."

Kurt had never liked the woman. Her heart was made of stone. It was obvious that she was benefiting from the girls' quick departure. He also knew she had no love for him. Just how much she knew about him and Esther was always a concern, but now he knew that she was the only one who could give him the answers he needed.

"Frau Wilhelm, I see you are using your time wisely." He let a conspiratorial smile cross his face.

She stood there trying to discern whether he was complimenting her or condemning her. No matter—she knew he was finished here. He was no longer any concern of hers. She had done her job well and was glad to be rid of it. She knew the girls despised her and never appreciated their special privileges. None of that mattered now. "I suppose you will be leaving soon?"

"Yes, I just need to gather my things." He hesitated. "Can you tell me what became of the girls after my departure?"

They were playing cat and mouse, and both knew it. Frau Wilhelm knew what he was fishing for. She wasn't blind. She saw the way he looked at the one beautiful Jew girl. She knew he had saved her for himself. Could it be that he had feelings for the girl? The thought disgusted her.

"Gone," was all she said. She could see he was struggling for control and enjoyed the power it gave her.

Through clenched teeth, Kurt managed to compose himself. "Gone, Frau Wilhelm? Can you give me any more details?"

Her smile was maddening. "Gone the way of all good Jews— through the chimney." She bellowed forth a sickening laugh at her little joke and turned back to the task at hand. She knew he would never know the truth. All had been sworn to silence concerning the uppity Schindler fellow. She knew the whole mix-up had caused nothing but grief for them all.

Kurt turned away quickly so that she wouldn't see his face. He composed himself until he was locked away in his own room. It was true. She was gone. He looked around the room for any signs of struggle or a note—anything to tell of his beloved. Going to the bedroom, he searched the nightstand for his Bible. It was gone. Strange. Why would she have taken his Bible if she was only …

He couldn't finish the thought. He dropped onto the bed, holding tightly to her pillow. A faint scent of her hair still clung to the case. Torrents of tears drenched it, and sobs racked his body. He tried to stifle them, knowing that Frau Wilhelm would like nothing more than to report his actions to anyone who might listen.

As he lay there, a plan started to unfold in his mind. He had no reason to live. He thought of trying to end it all right there, but something deep inside of him told him his mission was not over. Yes, he would leave this place. He would continue to tell of the atrocities he had witnessed until someone heard him. He would not give up. But first, he had to leave.

He quickly started to pick up the clothes that he had been wearing when something metallic fell to the floor—Esther's locket. Reverently, he bent low and picked it up. He held it to his cheek. Its coolness acted as a balm to his torn soul. He would give it to Elizabeth. He knew it would be safe with her no matter what happened to him.

Chapter Fifteen

"O Madmen: the sword shall pursue thee."

Jeremiah 48:2

May 11, 1945

Esther's body had recovered from the ordeal that led her to Brünnlitz, but her soul was wracked with agony over Kurt. What must he be thinking? It had been several weeks since she had left Auschwitz. The people here in this strange place were so loving and gentle to her, but all their efforts to quell her anxieties failed.

As at Auschwitz, she was glad for the daily tasks she had been asked to do. It was a different kind of work than anything she had ever done—factory work. What would Mama think? She was now no better than those who had worked for her father in the glass factory. Somehow, it seemed ridiculous that she would even think such thoughts. Under normal circumstances, she might have gone to the university and pursued a career, but normal was gone. Or she would have married Gabriel when he finished his studies, and ...

Somehow, thoughts of Gabriel always left a sickening feeling somewhere deep inside. He had been pushed even further back into the crevices of her memory; to dwell in that place brought more pain than she could endure.

Now she stood on the assembly line, doing the manual tasks that were before her without much thought of the past or future. She was glad to be gone from Auschwitz but still could not imagine anything beyond the confines of war. Such thoughts etched a sadness into her eyes. How had these people managed to find happiness here? She furtively looked around her. The other women laughed and joked with each other while they worked. It seemed impossible that she would ever laugh again.

Etka had taken Esther under her wing and taught her how to prepare the missile shells for the black powder that would be poured into them farther down the line. It was easy labor, and Etka had chattered like a chickadee while she worked. She seemed in awe of Esther and her story. Esther knew her sadness bothered Etka, but what could she do? At times she wondered if Kurt had been real, or had it all been a bizarre dream? As the weeks passed, she was sure that he thought she was dead.

Etka often watched Esther out of the corner of her eye and wished for a way to cheer the girl. These were such awkward times. What did one talk about? All subjects seemed to be closed. Could you ask about family? No. About the future, dreams, desires? Perhaps. She would try.

Clearing her throat, Etka said, "Herr Schindler seems to think that there is an end in sight." She paused, waiting for any response. Nothing. "What will you do when the war is over?"

For a moment, Esther seemed startled by the thought; then the usual air of futility returned. Esther shrugged but said nothing.

Etka continued as if she didn't notice. "Herr Schindler says that it will take quite a long time to sort everything out, since so many have been displaced. He thinks they will set up refugee camps in the place of the concentration camps to help us get back on our feet."

Get back on our feet? The thought seemed to ignite a small ray of hope within Esther. "What will you do?" she asked Etka.

Etka was thrilled by the response yet tried to act nonchalant. "Oh, I don't know. I'll probably return to my village first and see who is left. Then, perhaps I will go to Palestine."

"Palestine? Why Palestine?"

Etka had a faraway look as she spoke. She smiled shyly. "Perhaps it was something that you said. I don't know my God, but I do know that my heart is bitter against the Germans. I just feel that I need to leave Europe. Palestine seems safe somehow; and besides, many of the men and women here are talking about doing the same thing." She paused, "They are the only family I have now."

Her comments brought the faces of her own family to Esther's mind. Perhaps she still had family. What if she were able to return to Auschwitz and find her father and brothers—and Kurt? Hope was kindling a fire somewhere deep within, and its light flickered dimly in her eyes. Etka did not miss it.

"What about you, Esther?" Etka ventured again.

Hesitantly, she replied, "Perhaps I will return to Auschwitz and try to find my family." She looked at her, "Do you really think we have any future, Etka?"

"Certainly, Esther, especially for you!"

"Why me?" Esther asked, bewildered at the statement.

Etka looked surprised. "Because of your condition. Certainly that should give you an added reason to hope for the future."

Esther had no idea what the woman was talking about. As that realization dawned on Etka, she wondered, *Am I the one to tell her?*

She chose her words carefully. "Have you not noticed a change in your body?" She searched Esther's face for any understanding. It was not there. "Have you noticed the nausea in the morning?"

"Yes, but that's because I had been so sick, isn't it?"

Etka smiled. "No, it is more than that. This condition will be with you for several more months, if my calculations are correct."

Understanding finally registered. Esther's face transformed from a look of question, then to doubt, and then to wonder. For the first time since Etka had known the girl, sorrow was replaced by joy. Her large dark eyes sparkled, adding a beauty that took Etka's breath away.

"But how will I—when—where—"

Etka laughed. Motherhood always seems to brighten the darkest landscape. It gives hope a future, and Etka was caught up in the expectancy of it all. "Those are questions too big for me to answer. Now here's one for you: Do you wish for a girl or a boy?"

The thought made Esther's head swim. She was going to have a baby—Kurt's baby. Her features sobered, "I wish for a boy, just like his father." *Oh, Kurt, will I—will we ever see you again?*

***

Esther walked across the compound, alone in her thoughts. The air was turning warm; spring was in the air. It felt so good to walk freely without a coat or hat. The weather was not the only change in the air. Herr Schindler had just gathered them together last night and explained all that had happened. Were the Germans really on the run? He had told them that the rumors were true—Auschwitz had been liberated back in January, and now Dachau was also set free.

The rumors about Hitler committing suicide were also true; in fact, it was said that Britain was declaring victory. Could it be true?

Esther absently rubbed her tummy, which was just beginning to swell. With all the weight she had lost, most of the nutrition she had been able to consume went to her own needs. However, just yesterday she had felt movement for the first time. Etka was like an older sister to her, already claiming the child as her niece or nephew. She smiled to herself, so absorbed in her thoughts that she barely noticed the ragged soldier riding into the courtyard. At the horse's whinny, she looked up, startled.

He was neither German nor American. By the looks of his uniform, Esther realized that he was a Russian officer. She felt uneasy until he smiled. How weary he looked! She didn't need to wonder long about his errand.

"Excuse me, miss. Could you please direct me to whoever is in charge of this place?" His words were laced with a heavy accent, but they held no threat.

She managed a half smile and pointed to the low building to his left. "There, sir. You will find Herr Schindler in his office directly through that door."

He tipped his hat and turned in the direction of the stated building as Esther watched with intrigue. He dismounted stiffly and tied the horse to the porch post. His steps were labored. Where had he come from, and how long had he been on that poor horse? She noticed that the horse was lathered and looked as weary as its rider.

Barely minutes later, people exploded from the building shouting and calling to others. Herr Schindler led the way.

Etka was there at her side, pulling on her arm. "Esther, did you hear? It's over! The war is truly over!" At Esther's look of astonishment, she continued. "The Germans have surrendered! Oh, it's over, Esther! It's over!"

Both women fell to their knees, embracing each other, tears mingled with their laughter. *It's over! Oh, thank you, Father!* It was truly too good to be true. Esther felt too stunned to take it all in.

"What does this mean, Etka? What do we do now?"

"Herr Schindler wants us all to gather here as soon as we can. He has a document to read."

Etka turned and headed to the far building to tell the others while Esther rose and stood mutely watching all the movement around

125

her. It seemed as though the world was moving in slow motion. Such happy faces! She had not seen such happiness since ...

Kurt's face came into focus. He was smiling down at her. She had just told him that she loved him. She could see the smile spread over his face as the truth became a reality in his heart. *Oh, he was so happy! I'm glad I got to tell him, Father. Please, protect him, wherever he may be.*

When all were gathered, Herr Schindler began speaking. "This is the day we have all been waiting for—surviving for." Many heads nodded in agreement, tears flowing freely. "I will read you the document this Russian officer just handed to me." He held it up and read out loud.

Instrument of Surrender of All German Armed Forces

    1. The German Command agrees to the surrender of all armed forces to the C.-in-C. 21 Army Group. This to include all naval ships in these areas. These forces to lay down their arms and to surrender unconditionally.

    2. All hostilities on land, on sea, or in the air by German forces to cease at 0800 hrs. British Double Summer Time on Saturday 5 May 1945.

    3. The German command to carry out at once, and without argument or comment, all further orders that will be issued by the Allied Powers on any subject.

    4. Disobedience of orders, or failure to comply with them, will be regarded as a breach of these surrender terms and will be dealt with by the Allied Powers in accordance with the laws and usages of war.

    5. This instrument of surrender is independent of, without prejudice to, and will be superseded by any general instrument of surrender imposed by or on behalf of the Allied Powers and applicable to Germany and the German armed forces as a whole.

    6. This instrument of surrender is written in English and in German. The English version is the authentic text.

    7. The decision of the Allied Powers will be final if any doubt or dispute arises as to the meaning or interpretation of the surrender terms.

    HANS GEORG von FRIEDBERG

KINZEL G. WAGNER
B. L. MONTGOMERY, Field-Marshal
POLECK FRIEDEL
4 May 1945, 1830 hrs.

He looked up, allowing his eyes to travel over the small group of survivors who had become his family, tears gathering in the corners of his eyes. "It is truly over my friends."

A loud "Hurray!" rose, followed by much cheering and clapping.

He waited for a moment, then held his hands up for them to be quiet. "However, my little ones, there will still be much to do before we will see any signs of normalcy return to our lives. Thousands of people have been displaced. I cannot fathom the task that lies ahead of the Allies to regain order to our towns and villages. You are all welcome to say here as long as it takes for you to decide your future."

Future? Esther thought. It sounded as foreign to her as the Russian officer's accent. She was barely seventeen, pregnant, and, at the moment, very much alone. As the crowd started to disperse, she was surprised to see Herr Schindler walking directly toward her. She could not explain the fear that gripped her heart. His tall figure stood before her, and he was smiling down at her.

"I am sure you are very anxious to return to Auschwitz to find your husband and any family that may have survived. Didn't you tell me that you had a father and two brothers there?"

"Y—yes," she stammered. "I have not seen them since we were separated upon our arrival. But I have no way of knowing if they are alive. Kurt was unable to make any inquiries while we were there." She could sense more than see the doubt in his face. "Do you still doubt my story?" she asked.

"I do not know what to think, Esther," he answered with his usual frank honesty. "But I will see that you are taken there as soon as possible. Time may be very crucial, especially concerning your father. Do you have any thoughts as to when you would like to leave?"

"Sir, I don't want to sound ungrateful. I am truly indebted to you for my life. But I would be glad to return as soon as possible."

He smiled and laid his hand on her shoulder. "I would make the same decision if I were you. Very well then, we will plan your journey for tomorrow."

"I have no reason to ask this," Esther said, "but would it be possible for someone to stay with me until I find some answers?"

Schindler admired her realistic view. "I will take you and bring anyone you find back here if necessary."

Her eyes shone with admiration. "Thank you, sir. You have been more gracious than I can express. How could I ever repay you?"

"Live, Esther! Live," he said with such fervency that Esther had to blink back the tears. He gave her an ardent embrace before turning and heading back to his office. She watched him go, noticing once again the long, purpose-driven strides that Esther had come to love and admire.

Chapter Sixteen

"I will rise now, and go about the city in the streets,
and in the broad ways I will seek him whom my soul loveth:
I sought him, but I found him not."

Song of Solomon 3:2

There it was, in black and white: GERMANY SURRENDERS! IT'S ALL OVER! Rumors had been flying around New York for weeks that the end was near, but no one dared to believe it. Gabriel could hardly keep his mind on his studies, even though finals were looming just around the corner.

His mind was filled with thoughts of Esther. *Oh God, where is she? What has she had to endure? Is she still alive?* It seemed impossible that only last year he had asked her to write. He thought of the stack of letters kept in his top desk drawer. They had long since lost the sweet scent of her perfume, but they were a nightly reminder of the girl he'd left behind.

How many times had he loathed himself for leaving? *Perhaps if I had stayed*, he kept thinking. But what? There were never any answers, just a deepening dread of the truth.

And now it was over. The news brought mixed feelings of relief and anxiety. How did a college freshman with no money or means go about finding the girl he desperately loved? His only resource was his uncle, and Gabriel had little hope there.

He had forced himself to wait until Friday to ask his uncle for help. Now he stood outside the huge oaken doors that separated Uncle Jacob's office from the rest of the workforce. It was the end of the day and the end of the week, but Mr. Bachman was still hard at work. The secretary had told Gabriel to go right in, but he always felt that he was a bother to his uncle. Little did Gabriel know that Jacob Bachman admired his work ethic, probably more so because of what he saw lacking in his own son, Nelson.

The young man shook all thoughts from his head and knocked. An absentminded "Come in" could be heard, and he opened the door. It was several moments before Jacob Bachman pulled himself away from his books.

"Oh, Gabriel. Good to see you." He looked at his watch and sighed, shaking his head and looking weary. "Is it that late already? There are never enough hours in the day." He gazed at Gabriel for a moment before asking, "What's bothering you, son?"

Nothing irked Gabriel more than to be called his son. He knew his uncle meant it as a token of endearment, but when Gabriel thought back over the past turbulent months—not knowing the fate of his parents—coupled with the lack of interest on his uncle's part, he had to work hard at disguising his true feelings.

Unclenching his jaw, Gabriel said, "With the war over, I would dearly like to inquire about my family."

Jacob could hear the tension in his nephew's voice. *Curse you Daniel! Why didn't you come to America when I did!* His thoughts went back to their little room. How he had pleaded with his brother to come with him to America. What was there for them in Amsterdam? Nothing, compared to the unlimited possibilities in America. *If only you would have come, I wouldn't be wondering where you are right now.*

"Uncle Jacob?" Gabriel's voice pulled him back to reality.

"I'm sorry, Gabriel. I was just thinking about the last time I saw your father."

Gabriel's eyebrows arched. "When was that?"

"Years ago. We were just teenagers." He smiled wryly. "I begged him to come to America, but he would hear none of it."

Gabriel became curious. He had never heard his uncle talk this way. "Why not?"

Jacob smiled. "Your beautiful mother! I was leaving by the end of the week, and he was just in the middle of winning her hand. I couldn't change my passage, and he couldn't leave without her."

Gabriel sighed. "In some ways, I wish they would have. At least then I wouldn't be wondering if they are ..."

Jacob came from behind his desk, putting an arm around the young man. "I know, Gabriel. I can't even imagine what you must be going through. I'm sure some of your thoughts are on that beautiful young lady as well?"

Gabriel's smile was weak but sincere. "How can I find out about them, Uncle? I think I'll die if I don't get answers soon."

"Well, there will be answers, but I'm afraid that 'soon' is not part of the same sentence." He walked Gabriel to the door. "I will make enquiries concerning both the Bachman and Raul families. It may take months, Gabriel. You will need to be patient."

"I just wish I could be there!" His look was filled with defeat.

"I know, son, I know. Listen, I just have a little business to finish here. If you don't mind waiting, I'll take you home."

"Sure, Uncle Jacob, and thank you for all you said." He smiled faintly and left the office.

As he turned the corner to wait in the lounge area, he ran straight into the new office girl. She had been coming around the corner in a hurry, anxious to finish her day's work and head home for the weekend. The papers she had been carrying flew everywhere.

"Oh, I'm sorry," Gabriel said as he bent to gather them.

"No, it was my fault. I need to watch where I am going." She stooped to retrieve the papers with him. "You're Mr. Bachman's nephew, aren't you?" she asked, though she already knew the answer. She had secretly hoped for an opportunity to meet him.

He looked her way and smiled. "Yes, and you are the new office girl, but I don't know your name."

"Deborah, Deborah Sherman." She smiled coyly. "Does Mr. Bachman's nephew have a name?"

Gabriel smiled. "Yes, I'm sorry. I'm Gabriel Bachman." He straightened and held out his hand.

"It is a pleasure to meet you, Gabriel Bachman," she replied shaking his hand firmly and holding it just a second longer than Gabriel would have liked.

He was amazed by these American girls. They were certainly more aggressive than the girls in the Jewish quarter of Amsterdam. He had seen the looks in their eyes as they watched him like a cat tracking the movements of a mouse. Some had made forward advances toward him, but he had always been able to politely avoid them. Now, as he watched Deborah, he saw some of the same look in her eyes. It sparked something deep inside. *I will not be treated like some little school boy*, he thought and looked directly into her gaze.

"I've seen you at the university, haven't I?" he questioned confidently.

"Yes, we're in Business Law together," she responded, smiling.

"Really?" Gabriel asked, feeling like the little school boy as his mouth gaped open.

She laughed, a light airy laugh that somehow seemed to brighten the room and put him at ease. "Yes, but I have the advantage of sitting behind you. I'm sure in a class of two hundred students, you wouldn't have seen me."

Gabriel admired her sweet countenance and effort to rescue him from this clumsy conversation. Perhaps he had found his first friend here in America. "Are you ready for the exam?" he asked.

She rolled her eyes. "I don't think I will ever be ready. How about you?"

"I hope to make some headway this weekend." He was curious about this girl. Why would a young lady be taking Business Law? "What is your major?"

"Marketing and Management. How about you?"

"Accounting."

Deborah looked at her watch and then back at Gabriel. She didn't want to sound too forward, but she did want to get to know this young man a bit better. Hoping not to scare him off, she proceeded cautiously. "I was planning to head to the library after dinner to study. If you think it would help, we could study together."

She watched as he weighed the matter. Gabriel was thinking about his queen. Would it be disloyal in any way to study with Deborah? *You could use the help,* he thought to himself. "Are you sure you don't mind? You might find that I am a dunce," he said in mock seriousness.

She smiled. Gabriel couldn't help noticing how different she was from Esther. Her light brown hair, which was pulled back loosely from her face, hung almost to her shoulders and curled gently in soft waves. She was stylish in her manner and dress. Gabriel thought about Esther in her school uniform, dark brown hair, and beautiful innocent eyes. The two were as different as Amsterdam and New York.

"I'll take my chances," she replied. "I'll be there around seven-thirty."

Gabriel smiled. "Good. I'll see you then."

She smiled at him, and he wondered if he had done the right thing. He shook the thought away. *You just think that every female is falling in love with you,* he chided himself. He had to admit that the thought of studying with someone else was a welcome change. *Perhaps it will help me to keep my mind on my studies instead of Esther*, he thought.

* * *

"What are sole proprietorships?" Deborah asked with a glint in her eye. She and Gabriel had been studying for more than an hour. They were well matched in their intelligence and dedication to be good students.

Gabriel let out an exaggerated sigh. "You are wretched," he said with a pout.

She stifled a giggle. "You know he's going to have that on the exam."

"Yes, but that was at the beginning of the semester." He shook his head in frustration. "I'm going to fail."

Deborah looked at him with pity. "You will not, Mr. Bachman. I have never had any of my tutored classmates fail."

Gabriel looked up in surprise, "You've tutored other students?" he asked incredulously.

"Of course! Ann and Andy always came through with flying colors."

"Ann and Andy?"

She smiled. "Yes, my Raggedy Ann and Andy were my strongest supporters through my high school days. We studied nightly together before we were all tucked into bed."

He shook his head and smiled. "I think I need to stretch my legs and see if I can get some of the blood back up to my head."

He stood and pulled out her chair. They had been studying on the second floor of the library, where it was quietest. Descending the stairs, they headed for the front door.

The night air was cool and refreshing. Gabriel sighed deeply, looking up at the stars, wondering if Esther could see them as well.

"A penny for your thoughts," Deborah said softly as she held her hands behind her back. She had heard that Gabriel had left his family in Amsterdam to study here in America, and it intrigued her.

Gabriel pulled his thoughts back to earth. Should he burden this stranger with his worries? It certainly would feel good to tell someone, but he hesitated. "You don't want to know."

133

She lightly touched his arm and looked at him earnestly. "Yes, I do, Gabriel."

Seeing the genuine concern in her eyes, he explained, "My family and the girl I love were probably taken to Auschwitz."

The statement was so simple, yet the weight of it nearly crushed her. "Oh, Gabriel, I had no idea," she gasped. "I am so sorry."

"It's nearly driving me crazy. And now the war is over, and I still don't even know if they are dead or alive. I should have stayed."

"Do you really believe that?"

"No, I suppose not."

"Tell me about her," she demanded gently.

Gabriel looked at her in surprise.

"What is her name?" Her gaze was steady and sincere.

"Esther. Esther Ruth Raul."

"What a beautiful name. Tell me about her, Gabriel."

For the next few moments, Gabriel poured out his heart to his new friend. Deborah was not playing games with him. As they had studied, she felt a kinship with him that she had not known before. She felt more relaxed with him than anyone she knew, and when he mentioned that he loved another, she knew she would make herself be happy with only a friendship.

***

Exams were now a dim memory for Gabriel. Deborah had been right: None of her tutored students did fail; at least Gabriel was a living testimony to her record.

He had seen her often that summer as they both worked full time at J.B. Investments. The end of the war reopened many business connections in Europe, which meant busy days and long hours. Gabriel's growing friendship did much to ease his anxiety over Esther, as well as spice up the conversations around the water cooler. He tried not to let it bother him, but the looks he received from the women—young and old alike—nearly drove him crazy.

Over the past few weeks, Gabriel and Deborah had gotten into the habit of having lunch together, either catching a bite in the cafeteria or bagging it in the park just a few blocks down the avenue. It was a bright sunny day in mid-August, and the park seemed to beckon to them.

"Good day for a picnic, wouldn't you say?" Deborah suggested. Her happy spirit and bright face always perked up Gabriel, no matter how dark his mood.

"Sounds good to me." He grabbed his lunch from beside his desk.

"See you later," a girl name Angela gushed with a sickening sweet smile on her face. She looked at Deborah, then at Gabriel, then back to Deborah with a wink.

Gabriel could see that Deborah was flustered. He waited until they were out on the street before approaching her. "What was that all about?"

She tried to brush it off. "Oh, nothing."

But Gabriel knew her too well. He waited again until they were seated on the only available bench and had asked God's blessing on His provision. Gabriel finished his prayer with, "And Lord, I pray that you will help Deborah to trust me with her problems as much as I trust her with mine."

She looked up with a chagrined smile. "I get your message."

Deborah wasn't quite sure how much to say. The girls were constantly teasing her about her "boyfriend," and she didn't feel that she could say much for fear of betraying Gabriel's confidence. She knew, however, that she needed to say something. "Some of the girls tease me about you."

Gabriel stiffened, "What are they saying?"

Deborah took a sip of water before continuing. "You know, the usual silly girl stuff."

Gabriel rolled his eyes. "I thought that would end in high school."

Deborah smiled. "No, it only gets worse." She could see his surprise.

"But why?" he asked.

She looked at him, wondering if he was really that naïve. His strong, handsome face with those piercing dark eyes showed that the innocent questioning was genuine, and it made Deborah blush. She tried to sound like she was reading her reply from the encyclopedia. "Well, in high school, even though a boy and a girl might be serious about their feelings for each other, everyone knows that marriage is out of the question."

A quick intake of air filled Gabriel's lungs with much needed oxygen. "How could I have been such a fool? I am so sorry, Deborah. Have I misled you?"

If he only knew my heart, she thought. *But I must set my feelings aside. He desperately needs a friend.* She had told herself this continually over the summer as they began to spend more time together. "No, Gabriel, you have been totally honest with me." *But I haven't with you.*

Gabriel turned to look her full in the face. "Deborah, if it would be better for you if we didn't spend so much time together—I mean, I realize that you may be wishing to spend time with someone else, who could—"

"Who could love me?" The words were out before Deborah knew it. In fact, she hoped that she had only spoke them in her heart, but the look on Gabriel's face told her otherwise. "I'm sorry, Gabriel. I—"

"No, I understand. You couldn't be the friend I have needed if your heart was made of stone." He looked at her, searching her eyes and then looked down.

"Oh, I do want to be your friend, and I will continue to be, but I would be lying if I said that I didn't wish for more than friendship."

Gabriel began to gather up his lunch. "I don't want to hurt you," he said as he got up to leave.

She caught his arm. "Wait," she cried, looking pleadingly up at him. "You can't go. This is all wrong. Please, sit back down."

Gabriel struggled with his emotions. He wanted to run, but he knew she was right. Slowly, he sat back down—his appetite long gone—and waited for her to speak.

"We need to be friends, Gabriel, and there is no reason why we can't be. You were totally on the level with me about Esther, and I admired you for it. I have never met anyone that I have enjoyed being with as much as you, and if that can only be a temporary thing, I will not sacrifice it because of the local gossips."

She was passionate in her speech, not even realizing that she still clung to his arm, squeezing it fervently. "Ouch," Gabriel teased with a dead-pan expression.

She looked at him questioningly.

"I guess I had better be your friend," he joked, looking down at her clenched fingers. "I'm afraid you might beat me up if I'm not."

She suddenly realized what he was saying and let go of his arm as if it were a hot iron.

"I didn't know you were so strong. Are all American girls so strong?" he asked with mock innocence.

"Yes, so you had better behave yourself around me, mister!" She smiled a teary sort of smile.

They sat looking at each other for some time in a comfortable sort of quietness that friends share—each lost in their own thoughts. Gabriel had to admit, he admired Deborah. He knew she wanted more than admiration, but at the moment, it was all he could offer. He marveled again at how different the two women in his life were. What would it be like to have Esther here in America? The thought had never occurred to him. His plans were to finish school and head back to the Netherlands. But the longer he was here, the more he wondered if he could leave the fast-pace ways of New York City and be satisfied with provincial Amsterdam.

***

"Deborah, you are to report to Mr. Bachman's office," the secretary stated as soon as the twosome returned from lunch.

She cast a nervous glance at Gabriel, who hunched his shoulders but gave an encouraging smile. "I'll talk to you later," he said, heading in the opposite direction.

Deborah knocked softly on the huge office door. She had been in Mr. Bachman's office before, but somehow, this interview unnerved her. Perhaps it was because of the lunch conversation she had just had with this man's nephew. Had he been in on the gossip? A hundred thoughts raced through her mind when she heard the summons to enter.

"Come in, Miss Sherman. Have a seat."

I wonder if executives have such humongous desks for work purposes or to intimidate people? she mused as she sank into the comfortable leather chair directly in front of the desk. *Perhaps he's not happy with my work.* The thought surprised her, more because she had never thought that way before. Her valedictorian career at one of Brooklyn's most prestigious Jewish high schools, and her high placement at the university gave her an air of confidence she rarely doubted. Mr. Bachman's words cut into her thoughts.

137

"I'm sure you are wondering why I called you in this afternoon. Please let me put you at ease by saying we are all extremely satisfied with your work. In fact, may I go so far as to say that I hope you will consider J.B. Investments as a place of opportunity after graduation?"

Deborah tried to stifle the release of air from her lungs. "Thank you, sir. I must admit, I was wondering if I had done something wrong."

He smiled, but it was fleeting. "No, it's nothing like that. Actually, it is a personal matter. I was wondering if you would join our family for dinner tonight."

Deborah knew that Mr. Bachman was known for his frankness, but this was a bit unnerving. "I beg your pardon, sir?"

He leaned back in his chair, wondering how much he should say. He looked at the letter on his desk before continuing. "I have noticed your friendship with my nephew."

"Sir, I can explain—"

"There is nothing to explain, Miss Sherman. In fact, I am very pleased that you have helped Gabriel find his way through these difficult times. I am not a matchmaker, and you may rest assured that is not my intent in asking you to join us for dinner. But I believe Gabriel will need to have you there tonight."

Again he looked at the letter. He looked up to see if understanding had registered on her face. Her eyes were filled with pity and sadness.

"I'm so sorry, sir. You need not say any more. I will need to call home and make the necessary arrangements, but I will be there."

"If it would suit you, you could leave with us after work. I have already informed my wife—she was hoping that you would come."

"I will be glad to be of any help that I can, sir."

"I know this will be difficult for you, but would you please not let Gabriel know that anything is wrong? If it would help, I will tell him that my arrangements for dinner are strictly business."

Deborah looked relieved. "Thank you, sir. That would really help."

"No, I thank you. I don't know what to expect. This is going to be a very difficult thing." He shook his head sadly. "So many of our people have died. It is unthinkable. The estimates are in the millions!"

"I am sorry for your loss. My family has been here in America for so long that we have few ties in Europe. I have prayed that your family would be spared."

Mr. Bachman looked up in surprise. "You are a wonderful young lady, Miss Sherman. I wish you the best." He rose as she got up to leave, nodding her goodbye.

Chapter Seventeen

"My soul melteth for heaviness."

Psalm 119:28

Gabriel was completely clueless as to why Deborah would be coming to dinner, but he did wonder at his uncle's invitation and rather nonchalant explanation. He wondered if Uncle Jacob was playing the matchmaker, or perhaps he had designs to introduce Deborah to Nelson. He also wondered why the thought bothered him so.

Mr. Bachman talked more on the way home than he had ever before. Gabriel mainly sat and listened. As much time as he had spent in the presence of both occupants of the vehicle, he learned more from their conversation together than he had from either of them separately. The time passed quickly, and Gabriel was surprised when they pulled into the driveway of the immaculate mansion. He glanced back at Deborah and saw the awe in her eyes. *Maybe she'll be just as taken with Nelson*, he thought darkly.

The meal was delicious as always, although Gabriel sensed a strain in the atmosphere. Nelson seemed his usual overbearing self. He was certainly trying to impress Deborah with all his tales of adventures that only the son of a wealthy man could afford. He noticed that Deborah was polite but not caught in the obnoxious web of self-praise.

At the end of the meal, Gabriel was surprised that his aunt and uncle directed him and Deborah to the drawing room, but not Nelson. He seemed a bit peeved but covered the awkward situation none to successfully with an excuse that he needed to go for a drive in his new convertible anyway.

The drawing room was large and spacious, located directly across the entryway from the spacious dining room. It was a room to be seen, not inhabited. In fact, except for his first evening in the mansion, Gabriel could not remember ever being in there. The furnishings were elaborate, with plush burgundy carpets on the floor, heavy brocade draperies on the floor-to-ceiling windows, and gilt framed portraits on the walls. Gabriel's favorite part of the room was the massive brick fireplace, sentineled on either side by beautiful mahogany bookshelves. He had often wished that he could just enjoy this room and its mountain of books. He could have sat for hours in the dead of winter pouring a good read by a roaring fire.

Mr. Bachman directed the seating, placing himself across from Gabriel and Deborah on the overstuffed chair and his wife beside him in the matching chair. Deborah looked pale, and Aunt Judith seemed to be lost in thought—sad thoughts. A sudden sense of foreboding fell over Gabriel. They knew—they had heard from one of Uncle Jacob's European connections.

"You know something about my family," he said quietly.

Aunt Judith began to cry. Gabriel looked over at Deborah and saw the tears forming in her eyes as well. She reached over and took his hand.

"Gabriel, this is the hardest day of my life," his uncle was saying before he choked on his own words. He cleared his throat, trying to gain composure. "I'm sorry, Gabriel, but they are all gone."

"All?" He could say no more.

"Yes." Uncle Jacob pulled the letter from his vest pocket and handed it to the young man before him—the one who was more like a son to him than his own flesh and blood.

Gabriel silently read the letter.

Dear Mr. Bachman,

I am sorry to inform you that Mr. and Mrs. Bachman and their sons were taken to Auschwitz. We have checked with the authorities at that location and there are no records of their survival. The Raul family was also taken to the same institution. The records show that Mr. David Raul was the only one to survive but was in the infirmary before he was taken to Brünnlitz by a Herr Schneider after the war. At this point, we have no way of knowing his whereabouts. We send our deepest regrets ...

The rest of the words swam off the page. Gabriel quietly laid the letter beside him and buried his face in his hands. Sobs racked his body uncontrollably.

Deborah looked at Mr. Bachman. What should she do? He simply nodded sadly, and she slid closer to cradle Gabriel in her arms.

He leaned slightly against her, taking her hand into his. She felt the wetness of his tears, and her heart ached; her throat felt tight.

"I'm so sorry, Gabriel," she cried softly.

Gabriel suddenly rose and went to the fireplace, resting his head against the cool bricks. "Why, why?" he cried, pounding the bricks. "Oh Father, Mother, Reis, Shain! Oh, Esther," he cried. "My beautiful Esther. What have they done to you?"

Aunt Judith put aside her own grief and went to her nephew. She pulled him into her arms and cradled him like a baby. He shed more tears, but the comfort of a mother's shoulder brought him a temporary sense of peace and stillness. The sobs were quieter and less often now. He pulled himself away and looked into his aunt's face. "Thank you," he said.

She touched his cheek, and he leaned upon her hand, taking it into his own and turning it over. He gently placed a kiss there.

"You are a good boy, Gabriel," Aunt Judith said, weeping. "Your family would be so proud of you. I know I speak for my husband when I say this, but you are like a son to us. We want you to know that this is your home. Our own son—"

She stopped as a sob caught in her throat, not finishing the statement. "We are so proud of you. Your mother and father have instilled in you a godly character, and I know you will pass on their heritage to your own sons someday."

Jacob Bachman rose to his feet and came to his wife's side. It was the only time Gabriel would ever see this man cry, but cry he did as though all the pent-up emotions of a lifetime were breaking upon the scene. He held them both and wept, causing fresh tears to flow. Those tears, the embrace, the moment infused a bond between them that would never be broken. However, the moment passed, and the business man reappeared, pulling a handkerchief from his pocket and wiping his eyes.

"I think it would be good for you two young people to have some time alone," he simply stated, nodding to his wife and heading out the entryway. She gave Gabriel a weak smile and another strong hug before following her husband.

Gabriel watched them leave, feeling suddenly awkward to be alone with Deborah. He realized that it was the first time they had ever been alone together, and it unnerved him.

142

"Gabriel," Deborah called softly. "I can leave if you would rather be alone."

He turned to face her, looking into her earnest eyes. "No, that's the last thing I want." He came and sat beside her, sighing. "I feel so numb. Is it really true, Deborah?"

A lost puppy, Deborah thought. *He looks like a lost puppy—so alone and vulnerable. Father, help me to be what I need to be for him. Give me Your words of encouragement.* She tentatively took his hand, as though it was a child's.

"There are no words to express your loss. I can't even imagine it. This whole war has been such a nightmare. I've never been to Europe—it's a faraway place to me, but to you it is home."

"No, Deborah, it's not." His words surprised her."When I came to America, I planned to get an education and return to Amsterdam to find work. I just thought I would continue my life right where I left off. My children would grow up in my neighborhood, attend my synagogue and school." He paused, shaking his head. "But since I have been here, I have grown to love New York. It is so different here, but the differences are good."

He was speaking fervently as Deborah looked on in wonder. His gaze shifted from that far-off spot to her face. His eyes were passionate, seeking encouragement to go on—she gladly gave it to him, but his mood had shifted.

He looked down at their hands, turning hers over and looking at them as though they were something strange, yet wonderful. He continued but did not look up. "I have to confess something to you, Deborah."

She found herself holding her breath as he looked up at her again with those piercing brown eyes. "I have not been honest with you."

He let go of her hand and stood to face the window. She sat in silence, waiting for him to go on, afraid of what she was about to hear. "When the days turned into months, and I heard nothing from Esther, I wondered if this might happen. At first, the thought of it tore me apart inside. And then, to think of Mother and Father—what did they have to face? I don't want to even think of it, Deborah." He absently wiped the tears from his face, and crossed his arms in front of him, looking to the ceiling as if to find the words written there.

He looked back to her. "And then you were there. You were always there. I tried to keep my heart faithful to Esther, but," he sighed, "I feel like such a traitor."

Deborah came to stand in front of him. "Gabriel, you could never be a traitor. I saw the love you had for her when you told me about her. I heard it in your voice." He looked at her in amazement. "Gabriel, you will always love her, no one—not even I—can take that out of your heart."

Gabriel shook his head. "You never cease to amaze me, Deborah Sherman. You were willing to be my friend anyway."

She smiled. "Forever friends."

He reached for her and pulled her close. How right it felt. "You are a balm on my aching heart, dear one."

***

Dawn came whispering in across the room and kissed Esther's cheek. She snuggled down into her bed, dreams of Kurt bouncing their little boy on his knee playing in her sleepy mind. They were all together, happy and free. She hung amidst that mysterious land that lay between wakefulness and sleep, when someone nudged her.

"Esther, it is time," Etka was whispering, and Esther came fully awake, remembering that this could be the day.

She quickly sat up, rubbing the sleep from her eyes. "Thank you, Etka. You are so good to me."

Etka stood beside her, holding a satchel. "This is for your things."

Esther couldn't miss the sadness in her voice. She stopped what she was doing and came over to the woman. "Oh, Etka, I might be back before you know it."

The thought darkened Esther's countenance—she knew if she did come back quickly, it might not be good news for her and her loved ones.

"Esther, I wish the best for you and all your family, but I will miss you terribly. You are part of our family now, and wherever we both end up, we need to keep in touch."

Both girls knew how difficult that might become but each hoped for the best.

There was a knock at the door, and Herr Schindler entered furtively—so unlike his usual character. "Are you ready, Esther? We must leave immediately if we are to reach Auschwitz at a good time."

She offered him a smile. "I'm nearly finished." She quickly gathered the last of her belongings—all articles that had been given to her—and instinctively reached for her locket. Of course, it was gone, but she knew it was safe with Kurt. "I just need to run next door and I am ready."

"Here, let me take your bag, and I will meet you in the car." His long strides quickly led him away.

Esther walked over to Etka and pulled her into her arms. They held each other for a moment. "Thank you for everything, Etka. Most of all, thank you for being my friend."

Etka could say nothing as Esther quickly exited the room.

***

Simeon Stolarz was not only a faithful servant, completely dedicated in every way, but he was also a skilled driver and was able to deliver them to their destination in just under four hours. The trip should have only taken three, but checkpoints and makeshift roads where tanks and bombs had shattered any semblance of pavement added extra time.

As they pulled up to the gate, Esther's heart raced. What would she find? The dread of finding no one mixed with the hope of finding everyone, working her into an emotional wreck. Herr Schindler looked back over the seat. "While we are here, I must use a different name, Esther. You are free, but I am now a fugitive. I will tell them as little as possible about me. Please remember to call me Herr Schneider— Fredrick Schneider."

He saw the tension in every detail of her face and smiled a consoling smile. "And Esther, try to relax. I have noticed that you are a woman of great faith. You will need to draw upon it now."

Esther felt an unexplainable calm come over her. As the car pulled into the all too familiar parking lot, she took a deep breath and opened the car door. Her gaze immediately went to the one-story building across the street, the last window on the left. So many memories raced through her mind. Turning to follow Herr Schindler, she entered the building where Kurt's office had been, not sure what to expect.

As she walked down the corridor beside Herr Schindler, she looked into any open doorways, half hoping to see Kurt sitting at one of the desks. The secretary at the door led them to one of the offices near the back of the building and knocked briskly on the door. When an answer came, he opened the door and left them with the officer in charge. He was obviously Russian and very busy—papers littered every available space on the huge wooden desk. He looked up at the unusual pair. "Yes? How may I help you?"

"Thank you for seeing us, sir. I can see that your time is limited, so I will get right to the point and keep things simple. This woman was a prisoner here for a time and is looking for any family that may still be here. The names would be Raul: David, Ad, and Daan. How do we go about finding out if they are still alive?"

Esther stood amazed at the self-control and confidence Herr Schindler always commanded. The man looked impressed, as well as relieved. He turned to a filing cabinet next to his desk and pulled out a folder.

"We have made a listing of all prisoners that are still here." He riffled through a few sheets of paper. Esther could see the letter *R* typed neatly on the tab. "Let's see. Yes, here we have it. David Raul. He is here, in the infirmary." He looked up at Esther. A brief trace of pity could be seen in his eyes. "He has not been well, but he is alive."

"Is that all?" She couldn't take it all in. "What about Ad and Daan?"

"I'm sorry, miss. We have no way of knowing the movement or demise of any prisoner. We can only help you find those who are here. Would you like someone to escort you to the infirmary?" She detected impatience in his voice.

"Yes. That would be helpful," Schindler was saying, taking Esther by the elbow.

"Wait. Please, I have just one more question." She felt Schindler stiffen, but she had to know. "SS Officer Kurt Gerstein. Can you tell me anything about his whereabouts?"

The officer looked puzzled but turned back to the cabinet and pulled open another drawer. He leafed through the files. "Yes, here it is. It looks as though he is being held in the Cherche-Midi prison in Paris."

146

Esther's sharp intake of air caused the man to look up. How could she explain? *I will find him,* she thought. "Please, could you write the name of the prison down for me?"

He wanted to question, but he really had no reason to do so. If this beautiful young Jew wanted to know the whereabouts of a German officer, that was her business. He had enough to do. He quickly scribbled the name on a slip of paper and slid it across the desk.

"Thank you," she said softly as she picked up the paper and allowed Herr Schindler to lead the way.

Esther held the tiny piece of paper in her hand, shoving it deep into her pocket, allowing her thoughts to return to the task at hand. Papa! Her pace quickened. At least Papa was still alive.

They walked down the sidewalk, following the man assigned to lead them. Esther realized that they were heading to the long building just past the laundry room. As they passed the building, she stopped before the tall, stately maple tree that had given her strength and a sense of the passing seasons. Its leaves had been so brilliant last fall before they faded and fell to the ground. She bent down and picked up one of the brown leaves, rubbing its leathery skin. *You were up there watching everything that happened to me, just like our Creator.* She gently placed the leaf in her pocket as Herr Schindler turned and gave her a quizzical look.

"Are you alright, Esther?" he asked.

"Yes, I—I was just remembering."

He came back to her and gently put his hands on her shoulders. "I'm sorry that I didn't ask about your husband back there. I'm glad that you did; but we must keep to the task at hand, Esther. We are not truly safe until we are back in the car heading far away from this place." He let his eyes take in the complete compound, overwhelmed by the lingering sense of death that still hung in the air like an evil spirit. She nodded and fell into step beside him.

At the front desk of the building, their escort stopped and spoke to the man in charge. The only words Esther could understand were David Raul. After several brief instructions and a look back at them, they were led to another room filled with beds. The smell was overpowering and nearly made Esther swoon. Herr Schindler tightened his grip. They stopped by the last cot in the room. It was pushed up against the wall, and its occupant was turned away from them. *This can't be Papa.* The person in the bed was so small and thin.

Herr Schindler cleared his throat to gain the man's attention, but he never moved. He looked at Esther and motioned her forward. "Speak to him," he whispered.

Esther came closer to the bed. She leaned a bit forward and gently spoke one word: "Papa?"

There was an immediate movement, the head jerked up.

Esther gained courage, "Papa, is that you?"

With that, David Raul slowly rolled over. He had the usual look of a prisoner: gaunt features, sunken eyes, his hair and beard just nubs. His once strong arms were just skin and bones, but they reached for Esther. "Esther," he called, though his voice sounded like a rusty hinge.

Esther looked deeply into the eyes and knew they were her father's eyes. "Oh, Papa." She knelt down and fell into his arms, sobs choking her throat.

"My dear Esther. How can it be?" He patted her head and embraced her as much as his emaciated body would let him.

Esther pulled away, stroking his face. "It's me, Papa, and we are going to get you out of here."

For the first time, David noticed the tall man at her side. He noticeably stiffened in fear, his eyes wild. "Who is he, Esther?"

Esther turned to look up into Herr Schindler's kind eyes. "Oh, Father, don't be afraid. This is Herr Schi—Schneider. He has been a great help to me." Her voice softened with sincerity. "He saved my life, Papa."

Herr Schindler smiled. He wasn't sure what they were going to do. Was this man strong enough to be moved? He doubted it, and he knew they could not afford to stay here too long.

He cleared his throat. "Sir, do you think you have enough strength to leave with us?"

David's eyes twinkled. "I will make sure of it!"

With that, he slowly swung his feet over the bed and pushed himself up into a sitting position. Esther looked down at his legs. They didn't seem strong enough to support his weight. David scooted himself forward and tried to stand, but he couldn't. His eyes turned on Schindler, pleadingly. "Perhaps if I had some help?"

"Wait. I will go and bring the car as close to the building as I can and take care of all the arrangements." With that, he turned and was gone.

Esther looked at her once robust father. The sight of him broke her heart. She gently sat beside him, wanting to ask a thousand questions but afraid of tiring him. She took his feeble hand into hers and held it, looking into his face. "Oh, Papa! I am so glad you are alive!"

"I never thought I would get out of here. I just assumed you all were gone when no other Raul showed up." Silent sobs shook his body.

"Don't, Father. You must use all your strength to leave this place." She tightened her grasp. "We will walk out of here and never look back."

A faint smile flickered across his face. "Oh, Esther, it is so good to see you! And you look so well! How is it that you still have hair? And you look so nourished!"

A shadow crossed her face. How would her father react to her marriage and coming baby? She looked down, speaking softly. "It is a long story, Papa. We will talk later."

"But that man that took you away from us, did he hurt you?"

Esther realized that he was talking about Kurt. What a horrible image he must have of her beloved—the man who took her away. "Oh no, Father. He is part of the reason I was not put into forced labor; and Herr Schindler is the reason I was able to get away from here." She shook her head in amazement. "It is quite a story! Jehovah God was caring for me every step of the way."

Her look was one of awe, as though hardly able to comprehend it all herself, let alone tell him the details. It created a thousand more questions, but David knew that she was right. He must use all his strength to leave here.

***

Esther feared that the tiny flicker of life in her father would be snuffed out before they reached Brünnlitz. It had been a long, exhausting day for all of them, but the relief of escaping Auschwitz yet again gave them the strength to go on. The sun was already beginning to fade behind the western horizon, casting a rainbow of colors across the sky.

149

Esther had never seen anything so beautiful and wondered how long it had been since her life was full of color. She was tempted to wake her father—no one loved colors as much as he did—but she knew he needed the rest. The beautiful sky seemed like a promise from God, like Noah's rainbow of old. This may be all that was left to their family, but they would have each other and the promise of another generation.

Again, Esther pondered the idea of telling Father about Kurt. The thought made her mind race. He would never understand. Oh, what had she been thinking? As she thought back, she realized that her decisions had been made assuming that she would never leave Auschwitz alive. But here she was, zooming away, pregnant, and accompanied by her father. *Oh, Heavenly Father, I will need Your wisdom and strength for this. Please give me the right words to make Papa understand.*

Chapter Eighteen

"And he said unto her, Daughter, be of good comfort:
thy faith hath made thee whole; go in peace."

Luke 8:48

Three weeks had passed since Herr Schindler had taken her to Auschwitz. Everything had changed. Schindler left the moment they arrived back at Brünnlitz. He had spoken the truth: He was now a fugitive.

Although all the Jewish workers at the factory told the Allies of his heroic deeds, they seemed hesitant to believe them. All was now in the hands of the Russians or the Americans. Esther wondered if their fate would have been better if the Americans controlled their town.

There was adequate food now that relief began coming in from other countries. With proper nourishment, the difference in their bodies was amazing, but their souls were recovering more slowly. What future did they have? All their family and belongings were gone. Many were misplaced with no means of getting anywhere.

Everyone talked about leaving Europe and migrating to Palestine. Some dreamed of an Israeli nation, but most just wanted to get out and get on with life. But how? With no money, few friends, and a barrage of regulations, the Jews did not have many options. However, they did have what their forefathers had always had—pluck and courage.

A band of Jewish men and sympathizers called the *Beriha* had been forming since January to move the displaced Jews out of Europe and into Palestine. Many of the men in their area were involved with it, and Etka wanted to be one of the first to go. "Come with me Esther," she begged fervently. "I can't do this alone!"

Esther had been sitting beside her father all morning, reading to him. Since their arrival, his health was slowly returning. He was now resting peacefully back in the room while she stretched her tired legs.

She looked at Etka's face, full of life and anticipation. "How can I Etka? I will not leave my father, and he cannot make such a trip."

They both moved to a bench positioned beside the building, where the wind gently refreshed them and, unknowingly, carried their words straight to David Raul's ears.

"He is gaining more strength every day, Esther. Perhaps the time is right for the both of you."

"I will not ask this of him. He has been through too much already."

"Haven't we all, Esther?" Etka's eyes were pleading.

Esther sighed. "I think it's too soon."

"But if you wait much longer, you will not be able to make the trip."

David left his bed and sat by the window. What was Etka saying? He feared for his daughter.

"Have you told him yet?"

Esther shifted uneasily in her chair. She had purposely worn loose clothing in hopes that her father wouldn't notice, but she knew she couldn't hide her secret much longer. "No. It just never seems to be the right time," she confessed.

"What do you think he will say?"

"I have no idea."

Both girls sat quietly in thought. David's mind was racing. He nearly called to Esther but decided he needed time to compose himself as well as gather his thoughts. Could he make such a trip? He was well aware of the political climate in Poland. Some of the men even talked that there might be another—what was the word they used?—Holocaust. All he knew was that they had no future here.

Palestine. Abraham had been an old man when God called him there. The Promised Land: Just thinking the name made his heart swell with pride. Could there once again be an Israeli nation—a land for God's chosen people? He remembered reading about the words that a respected rabbi named Herzl had written in his diary: "In fifty years, a Jewish State will be created." He tried to remember when that had been. The 1800s? Yes, the late 1800s, 1898 to be exact. Could it be that Israel would become a nation in his lifetime? Certainly every Jewish man hoped it would be true.

And was Esther's health deteriorating that she would not be able to go? He had heard about some of the cruel medical testing that had been done on his people at Auschwitz. Truly, the reports sounded so bizarre that he had dismissed them as the type of gossip that would be in a place like that.

He shuddered as he thought back over the months he had spent there. How was it that he and Esther had been the only ones to survive? Why had God done this? Why couldn't it have been his barracks instead of Ad and Daan's that had gotten the typhoid epidemic? His heart sank as he thought back. *Oh, Anna! I miss you so. But how glad I am that you have been spared all this! Must I stand by yet again and watch another of my loved ones die?* He determined then and there that Esther had taken care of him long enough; it was now his turn to carry the load.

When Esther re-entered his room, she found her father dressed and sitting by the window. She quickly came to him, alarmed. "Father, what are you doing?"

He looked up at her and chuckled. "Well, Nurse Esther, I am getting some fresh air, if that is alright with you." Her questioning look made him smile. He feigned seriousness. "Or should I stay in bed all day?"

She didn't know quite how to answer him. "Are you feeling better, Papa?"

"Yes, tremendously better. After all, how good can an old man get?" He shifted in his chair. If he was honest, the extra exertion had just about done him in, but he was determined not to cause her another moment of worry. He wanted her to leave this place as soon as possible. He decided to take the plunge. "So, when do we leave for Palestine?"

He could see the surprised look on her face. Esther's mind was racing back to her conversation with Etka. *How much had he heard?* She decided it was time for some answers.

"You heard Etka and me talking?" she asked.

"Yes, Esther." His voice seemed weak, but he forged ahead. "I think you should listen to your friend. If there is a way for us to get to Palestine, I think we must try."

"But Father, you are too weak," Esther argued. She felt his eyes boring into her soul.

"And what about you, Esther? What is it that you have not told me?"

153

Moments passed as Esther weighed her choices. Should she tell him the truth? How many alternative stories had she thought up at night? Would it be better to spare him the truth? But what about Kurt? And if she went to Palestine, would she ever see him again? To get to France from Poland was one thing, but to get there from Palestine was another altogether. *I must tell him the truth.*

She took a deep breath and began recounting her story. She recounted the brothel she'd been taken to, Kurt's mission to undermine the Nazis from within, the way he'd saved her from the same fate as the other girls. As she described her and Kurt's growing intimacy, she looked pleadingly into her father's eyes, hoping for some sign of understanding. How could she expect him to understand?

"Well, I am glad that he was such a gentleman and that he did not hurt you. But what is wrong with you that you may not be able to make the journey? You look very healthy," he demanded impatiently.

"Please, I must tell you the whole story, Father. But if you interrupt, I will lose courage."

David nodded his agreement.

"Herr Gerstein and I did become great friends, Papa, more than friends. We were spending every night together and got to know each other completely in just a short amount of time." She knew it was hard for him to keep his silence and hurried on. "In October, we were married, and I'm carrying his child."

"Oh, Esther, how could you? He is a Gentile! A German SS officer! Your captor!" Emotions swirled about them, causing tension to build. Her father looked older than he had ever looked before, and Esther feared for his health.

"I shouldn't have told you!" she cried, tears clogging her throat. She stumbled to the bed and threw herself upon it. She cried for Kurt, for her father, for Gabriel, for her baby. She wished she were dead.

She didn't hear her father come to her side. She didn't see the tears in his eyes. His heart was breaking for his daughter. What would become of them? Surely she would become an outcast—not accepted in their world or the Gentile world. But she was his daughter. He needed to protect her, not reject her. His hand shook as he caressed her hair. Moments passed before the sobbing subsided. "There, there, Esther. We'll make it through this too."

154

Esther sniffed and lifted her head to look into her father's eyes. She saw no condemnation there, only love. "You don't hate me, Father?"

A look of surprise washed over his face. "Oh Esther, I could never hate you!"

She laid her head on his knee. He continued to pat her and comfort her. As much as he hated it, there were questions he had to ask. "Do you know where he is now?"

Esther reached into her pocket and pulled out the crumpled piece of paper. She carried it with her everywhere. "This is all they could tell me."

"Cherche-Midi prison in Paris," he read aloud. "This does not look good, my daughter."

"But why?"

"Esther, he may have saved your life, but he is still an SS officer for the Third Reich." He hadn't meant to sound so blunt. He immediately saw the effect of his blunder on her face. Her jaw quivered, and the tears came again.

He pulled her close and rocked her in his arms. "I'm sorry, Esther."

What could he say to comfort her? Truly, it did look bleak. If he was in prison, he would either be found guilty by the Allies and hung, or murdered while in prison as a traitor. And yet, David Raul couldn't help but feel relief.

* * *

Esther's dreams that night were filled with prison cells and angry faces. She ran from cell to cell, looking past the bars and into darkness. Only taunts and jeers came from all she met, but on she went, down an endless corridor. She stopped and turned around and around, completely surrounded by prisoners and guards alike. She wanted to quit; her throat ached with unshed tears.

As she pushed through the crowd, she looked into the last room, all the way at the end of the hall. There she saw him, hunched over in defeat, his head resting in his hands. "Kurt," she cried, but he couldn't hear her. "Kurt! Kurt!"

Still no response.

155

She tried to get to him, but everyone stood in her way. She was pushing and crying, a sense of hopelessness weighing down upon her.

Her own sobs startled her to wakefulness. It was still dark, and she realized the night was far from over. She rolled over, looking up into the darkness. What was she to do? She knew what Etka and her father wanted. But if she left Poland, would she ever see Kurt again? Was he even alive? She could hear Anita's words echoing in her brain: *Kurt would want you to be safe, and staying here is certain death.* Was that still true?

She had to admit, she didn't like the looks of the Russian soldiers who had taken over the camp. There was a tension in the air—perhaps not as evident as during the war, but she knew they all wished her people would just go away. *I've got to know, Father. What should I do?* She walked silently over to her dresser drawer and dug out Kurt's Bible. She hadn't had the nerve to read it since her father had arrived, but now she needed to hear from her God.

Making her way down the hall to an empty storage room, Esther quietly shut the door and turned on the light. She sat on the floor and opened the book to the front flap. Heartbroken, her fingers traced Kurt's name.

For just a moment she let her mind return to their nights together. His kind face and gentle touch seemed to comfort her. She looked down at the book in her hands. *Read it, Esther. I believe you will come to know your Messiah.* Kurt's words echoed so loudly in her ears that she was startled.

She leafed through the pages, reading bits and pieces from passages that they had read together. She didn't realize that she was crying until a tear dropped upon the page. She was working her way through several passages in Isaiah when one particular verse—Isaiah 66:13—caught her attention: *"As one whom his mother comforteth, so will I comfort you; and ye shall be comforted in Jerusalem."* How long had it been since she had felt the comfort of her mother? The thought brought an ache to her tired heart.

She turned back to the verse and read it again. *"As one whom his mother comforteth, so will I comfort you; and ye shall be comforted in Jerusalem."* God would be like a mother to her? The thought brought such a peace and contentment in her heart. Then, two words stuck out from the page: *"in Jerusalem."*

She gasped. *Oh, Father! Is this your plan?* As though from heaven above, the thought came to her: *I can find out as much about Kurt from Jerusalem as I can from here.* Heart swelling and tears flowing, Esther bowed her head and praised her God for His leading in her life. She prayed for Kurt, knowing that he too was in God's hands. *Funny,* Esther thought, *he is a Gentile and I am a Jew, and yet I believe with all my heart that we pray to the same God.* The thought surprised her.

Gentiles had been such a foreign group in Esther's mind for the better part of her life; she never really thought about what they believed. *Read it, Esther. I believe you will come to know your Messiah.* She looked around, half expecting to see her father standing there, then slowly turned to the New Testament. She came to the book of Luke, remembering how the birth of Jesus had puzzled her so. She read it again, continuing on through the following chapters, again amazed by the genealogy of this Jesus. She read of His temptation, His healings, and His boldness in the synagogue. Who was this man? How could He do these great miracles? Her mind quickly reminded her that many other prophets did miracles.

As she continued, her eyes were once again drawn to the word "comfort." *And he said unto her, Daughter, be of good comfort: thy faith hath made thee whole; go in peace.* She shook her head in amazement. It seemed as though God's Spirit was again speaking directly to her. How could this be?

She rested her head on the wall behind her, closing her eyes and allowing the words to wash over her. Had she ever felt so loved, so comforted? A sudden drowsiness came over her. She stumbled to her feet and made her way to her room. She quietly put the precious book back in its hiding place and fell into bed, exhausted yet at peace with her circumstances and her decision.

Part Four
Israel

Chapter Nineteen

"I make a decree, that all they of the people of Israel ...
which are minded of their own freewill to go up to Jerusalem, go with thee."

Ezra 7:13

Esther's feet ached, her head ached, but most of all, her heart ached—for her father. They had been traveling for five days. The people in charge were caring and kind, but they were as desperate as she was. At the start of their journey, all were excited and full of hope and anticipation. The traveling had not been too difficult.

The Joint Distribution Committee from America had been very helpful, providing clothing, food, and shelter when possible. While most people headed back to their hometown, Esther and her father journeyed in the opposite direction, knowing that they had no other family and no other choice. As they made their way through Hungary and now Austria, they were so thankful to the *Beriha*. They seemed to be everywhere, all holding to the same goal: leave Eastern Europe.

Now she and her father found shelter in the city's beautiful synagogue. Esther had only been to the larger synagogue in downtown Amsterdam once. It had seemed gigantic compared to their own place of worship. She remembered that it had lacked the warmth of familiarity of her own synagogue, and the memory made her long for home; she wondered if it was even still standing.

For now, Esther was more than thankful for this cavernous building. They would need to rest before embarking on the most difficult part of the journey, and her thoughts were fraught with worry. How could Papa make it on foot across the Alps into Italy?

As she sat toying with her coffee cup, David Raul eyed her, seeing the lines of anxiety crease her brow. He too had had the same doubts and had thought about staying behind, but even as the idea came to his mind, he knew Esther would never leave without him. He could not explain it, but somehow he felt younger than he had in years. Perhaps it was the natural paternal instinct to protect a child that had given him strength. Esther seemed so strong, yet so vulnerable. She had been through so much, and yet he could see that the trials had made her faith stronger than ever, perhaps a little different somehow. He was not able to put his finger on the difference, but it was there.

He reached across the makeshift table in the quiet corner of the room and touched her hand. "Daughter," he spoke. She looked up, startled from her revere. David smiled, "You are just like your mother—you worry too much."

The half-smile did little to relieve the worry lines. She sighed. "Oh, Papa, how will we ever make it?"

"You are going to make it just fine, and so will I."

He spoke with such conviction that Esther wondered at him. "How can you be so sure?"

"I don't know, Esther. I just feel as though I've been given a promise from God that I will see the land of our fathers."

She squeezed his hand, hope springing to her face. "God is our strength, a very present help in trouble. We will not fear."

***

Before dawn had danced its way across the city, the Jewish refugees were being packed into any type of vehicle that could carry them. The *Beriha* were everywhere, helping people to get settled. They were so kind to Esther and her father—perhaps because they were surprised to find a man of his age. Possibly that was the reason they were given the front seat in the huge army transport truck.

David hoisted himself up into the cab with the driver's aid, then pulled Esther in beside him. The cool wind blowing down from the mountains could not chill the atmosphere charged with excitement. This was the last trek, and everyone was anxious to be moving again.

Their caravan left the city just as the sun peeked over the distant hills. They were heading south and would go as far as the roads would take them. As the way narrowed and the little towns grew farther apart, the fears returned to haunt Esther. Her gaze was fixed

161

straight ahead, her body rigid while her father chatted amicably with their driver.

"How will we know the way?" David was questioning.

"You will have guides," the man answered as he navigated a curve in the road.

"But who are they? Can we trust them?"

The man smiled. "You sound like a man who has been badly treated and locked away for too long." He saw the hurt in David Raul's eyes. "Sir, I mean no disrespect or rebuke. My heart aches for you. These guides are men you can trust. They are Palestinian Jews who are anxious for your arrival."

David looked amazed. "Palestinian Jews? Why would they care about us?"

"They desire to build the kingdom—the nation of Israel. The more Jews that come to Palestine, the better."

David turned to Esther. "Did you hear that, daughter? We will be welcome! Praise Jehovah!"

Esther stared in wonder at the childlike excitement that gleamed from her father's eyes. For the first time, she dared to hope that they would cross the finish line into Palestine.

As they traveled on, the road continued to narrow slightly. There hadn't been a town or village for several miles, but as they turned yet another corner, Esther could see a group of men in a tight knot farther up the road. Their truck, which had led the caravan, now pulled off to the side, just past the men.

Warm greetings met them as they gathered. The morning was gone, and Esther's stomach growled its complaint. As though in answer to it, dark bread and coffee were being served by their guides. With their small meal complete, a man not much taller than Esther came forward. His curly black hair twisted its way out from beneath the knit cap he was wearing. His face was serious, but Esther felt that it was a face that could break into laughter very easily.

His eyes danced with excitement. "Welcome, my people. My name is Isaac Hirsch, and I and my men will be leading you across the mountains. It is not an easy journey, but we will succeed!"

His gazed scanned the crowd of anxious followers and came to rest on Esther. He took in her beautiful features but did not miss the swollen midsection. His eyes flashed back to her own. She could read anger, then pity in them before he looked away.

"Please do your best to keep up with us, but as we progress, we will naturally divide into three different groups: those who are faster, then a middle group, and finally those who are slower. You will set your own pace. Do *not* overexert yourselves. We will stay with you until we reach the other side."

He continued on with further instructions, but Esther's mind was elsewhere, his look still flaming before her. *I do not want your pity, sir,* she could hear herself exclaiming to him. Gear was quickly packed away, and as a whole, the group headed toward the mountain, thinning out to a long strand. She would do her best not to be in Isaac Hirsch's group. But much to her chagrin, she and her father were soon lagging behind the rest, and that man was heading their group.

As she furtively watched him from the corner of her eye, she could see that he was filled with great compassion. He made his way among the group, asking names and making small talk with each individual, encouraging everyone he met. She knew her turn would come and soon realized that he had saved her and her father for last. As he approached, she stiffened.

"And how are you folks doing?" he asked.

"Fine, just fine," her father responded with a smile before Esther could even look up.

"And what are your names?"

Again, her father responded. "I am David Raul, and this is my daughter, Esther."

"It is good to meet you, Mr. Raul, and you too, Miss Raul."

"Esther Gerstein," she corrected. She felt more than saw the surprise on her father's face. It was the first time that she had used her married name, and she knew it bothered him.

"Gerstein," Isaac pondered. "That sounds—"

"German? Yes, you are correct. My husband is, or was, a German officer."

"Where is he now?" he asked. Esther could see the look of surprise in his eyes.

"He is in prison in France."

Esther felt all eyes upon her. She looked around to see a mixture of pity, surprise, and disgust register on the people's faces. She didn't care. She was Esther Gerstein, and she was glad.

"I'm sorry, madam," Isaac responded. He too was staring at her, but as Esther shot a defiant glance at him, she saw neither pity

163

nor hated, but rather compassion. Tears stung her eyes. "I wish for you the best. Can you tell me when your baby is due?"

The question shocked her. Why did he need to know? Isaac read the response correctly and continued, "For planning purposes, I really need to know."

Esther stammered, "I—I'm not exactly certain, but I believe he will come in July."

Relief washed over Isaac's face. "Good. That should give us enough time to get you and your father settled."

He hesitated before continuing in a hushed tone. "I do not wish to pry or meddle into your affairs, but you may wish to keep your husband's nationality quiet for a while. I do not say this lightly, Esther. You are among people who have known great hardships at the hands of the Germans. For your sake, and for your baby's sake, you may wish to—"

He didn't have the opportunity to say any more. Esther was ready to walk away from him, from all of them. "Thank you for your concern, Mr. Hirsch," she cut in. She left them as she pushed herself ahead, her mind racing, and her face hot with embarrassment and exertion.

What had she been thinking? Could she blame any of them? The reality of her situation lay heavy on her heart. She didn't want to be disloyal to Kurt, but she did have to survive. Her mind raced ahead. Would the hospital or midwives even help her deliver her baby if they knew that his father was German *and* that she loved him? She had seen the faces of the other travelers. Isaac's words echoed in her mind. *"For your sake and for the baby's …"*

She would do whatever it took to protect Kurt's son. She would lie if necessary, but when he knew where she was, he would come for her and take care of them both. Then people could gossip as much as they wanted. She would be Mrs. Kurt Gerstein, and Kurt would be proud of her.

At that moment, a memory came to her like a flash of lightening. She saw herself sitting in her own bedroom at her writing desk writing her name—practicing it over and over: Mrs. Gabriel Bachman. She shook the memory from her mind and walked even faster.

***

At the first sight of snow, Esther had felt like a child. Such excitement! She could only remember a handful of times that they had seen snow in Amsterdam. But now, as she trudged through it for the second day, she was ready for warmer weather. They had followed the path that the Palestinian Jews had obviously taken earlier.

Esther thought she could have found her way without the guides, but on the fifth day, the falling snow completely obliterated their trail. The guides assured them that they were making good time and were near the peak. The mountains were suffocating to Esther— their walls towered over her on every side. How she longed for the flat land of Amsterdam.

She was surprised that her thoughts continued to revert back to her homeland. Perhaps it was having Papa with her that made her mind skip over the past year and dwell on the land of her nativity. He never talked about home, but she knew it was on his mind as well. Crossing the mountains seemed to cut the last thread that connected them to the past.

***

Ten days. It had taken them ten days, but now they sat around a fire with the Alps behind them and the warm weather of Italy before them. It had been a quiet ten days for Esther. After her announcement of her marriage to a German SS officer, everyone gave her a wide berth— everyone except Isaac Hirsch.

She tried to avoid him, but the more she tried, the more often she seemed to run into him. He had taken a liking to Father—could she blame him? As she looked across the fire at him, she realized what a treasure he was. His strength seemed to grow as he walked on. The cold never seemed to bother him, and he was always giving a word of encouragement to the others in their group, in spite of their covert glances at Esther.   Now the three of them sat enjoying the warmth of the fire and a last meal before they reached civilization. Esther's heart was filled with gratitude to God and to their guide, Isaac Hirsch. She waited for a break in the conversation to tell him so, knowing she also owed him an apology.

165

She cleared her throat, reminding herself of Etka, who had sprinted to the first group before the first day had ended. "I'll see you in Palestine, Esther!" she had bubbled as she ran ahead.

Isaac and her father both looked up at her. She suddenly felt shy but forced the words out her throat. "I just wanted to say thank you, Isaac, for all your help."

Isaac smiled, and it unnerved her. The warmth in his eyes seemed so undeserving. "I am glad that I have had this opportunity. You have been a delightful group."

"Have you led others?" Somehow the thought had never occurred to Esther.

"Yes, but only one."

"Will you lead more, Isaac?" her father asked.

"Yes—at least that is my plan. But first I must stay in Palestine and work."

"Do you have family?" Esther asked.

A shadow crossed Isaac's face. "I had a family, but my father, mother, and two sisters died when a bomb exploded in the marketplace where they worked our fruit stand."

Esther could see the hurt in his eyes. Why had she been so pigheaded with this man? She felt ashamed of her selfishness. "Isaac, I am so sorry." His eyes flitted up to hers and then quickly returned to the fire. She went on, "And I am very sorry for how I have treated you. Isaac, can you forgive me?"

He kept his gaze upon the fire. How could he look at her? He feared that she would see the way his heart jumped to his throat every time she spoke his name. "There is nothing to forgive," he said quietly, trying to keep his voice calm as he absently stirred the fire.

Esther misread his actions—the low voice, the inability to look at her. *He can only think of me as a traitor,* she thought. She was surprised at how much it bothered her. *Get used to it, Esther,* she told herself.

Deep within her soul, the tentacles of bitterness wrapped around her heart and squeezed, transforming the beautiful young woman into a stone. *If I do not feel, then I will not hurt,* became her motto.

166

Chapter Twenty

"I bring near my righteousness; it shall not be far off,
and my salvation shall not tarry:
and I will place salvation in Zion for Israel my glory."

Isaiah 46:13

Like a matching bookend to the other side of the Alps, the snows receded, and their path slowly turned into a road, widening as they descended. One of their guides had pushed ahead to make arrangements for their group. As they gathered on a grassy knoll overlooking a small village farther down the road, Esther noticed for the first time that several vehicles were waiting for them.

The next few days became a blur as Esther and her father traveled with their group across Italy and the Mediterranean Sea. It seemed as though the *Beriha* had thought of everything; there was always a mode of transportation ready to make the next leg of the journey. Of course, they were the last of the three groups, and it sounded as though there had been other groups as well who were already settled in Jerusalem. Esther was thankful and ready to be done traveling.

The weather had been beautiful, and the ride across the sea uneventful. Now, on this final day of their journey, Esther stood by the railing watching the ship cut swiftly through the water. She had never sailed before and found that she loved watching the water ripple away from the stern in rhythmic fashion. Her eyes slid shut; the sun was high in the sky and warmed her skin as fast as the breeze cooled it. The salty sea air seemed to blow the cobwebs from her mind and the cares from her heart. Right now, she was just a passenger on a ship.

She was so absorbed in her thoughts that she hadn't seen or heard Isaac slip quietly beside her. He watched her, wondering—not for the first time—what he had done that had caused the wall to go up between them. As the wind tossed Esther's hair around her face, Isaac studied her profile. Her beauty was beyond that of any woman he had ever seen. He longed to touch her hair, feel the warmth of her tiny hand in his—protect her. *How do I get close to you, Esther?*

She turned and looked surprised to see him there. For a fleeting moment, Isaac thought he saw a longing for friendship in her eyes, but then the curtain fell, and the wall came up.

Isaac's heart was in his eyes. He tried to control his feelings and hold his voice steady as he spoke. "Your journey is almost ended."

She simply nodded and looked out over the sea. He had to try again.

"Esther," his voice pleaded.

She turned to face him, seemingly startled to hear such emotion in his voice, thinking that perhaps she imagined it. She looked into his eyes and saw it there as well, but she didn't know how to react. The look of confusion in her eyes nearly broke Isaac's heart.

"Esther, what have I done to cause you such confusion and hurt?"

"I don't know what you mean," she replied honestly.

"I just feel like we are enemies, and I don't know why." He came slightly closer. "I just want us to be friends."

Her face was a mask of stone, yet somewhere in her eyes was a vulnerable look that made Isaac press on. "I do not know what your circumstances were during the war. Your father has only told me about your growing up years in Amsterdam and that you were at Auschwitz. I do not want you to feel that you need to tell me anything, but can we not at least be civil to one another?"

Esther lowered her head, her cheeks hot with emotion. Why must he bother her? Why didn't he just leave her alone? She sighed deeply to still her pulse before answering.

"I just want to be left alone." Her voice was barely above a whisper.

"I can't, Esther. It goes against everything in my nature not to help someone in need."

"I don't need anything or anyone," she answered hotly.

Isaac was tempted to lose his temper—something that had been a frequent part of his nature in the past. When his family had been murdered, the anger and hatred that welled up inside him nearly ate him alive. The *Beriha* had been his salvation. It had given him a useful outlet for his anger and had taught him to see the needs of others.

168

Before him stood the most beautiful woman he had ever met. Yes, she had married a German officer who was at this moment in a prison cell. He doubted that she would ever see him again, but he chose not to voice his opinion. He could see the bitterness taking over like a cancer to the soul. He had experienced it and knew he could not turn away.

"I believe you are mistaken," was all he said.

She looked up at him, anger flashing in those dark brown eyes. "How dare you!" She reached up to slap him across the face, but his hand shot up as well, holding her wrist in an iron fist.

His look stopped her from saying more. Isaac Hirsch, who had always been so gentle and kind to her, now bore holes into her with such a fierce look that Esther stepped back. He looked ready to explode and would have if she hadn't looked so frightened.

His chest was heaving with pent-up anger, but he made himself be calm. His look softened only slightly when he said, "You are not the only one to have suffered loss, and you are a little fool if you do not accept the help that others want to give."

Their eyes locked for a moment before he let go of her and abruptly turned to walk away. She nearly called him back, but the ache in her heart held her in place. *If I do not feel, then I will not hurt.*

Confused, hurt, frustrated, and angry, Esther turned back to the water, hot tears sliding down her cheeks unchecked. The sea continued to lap the sides of the ship as it plied forward. "I will be so glad when this trip is ended," Esther spoke to herself.

She pushed herself away from the railing and slowly made her way below, walking with weary feet. She suddenly felt more tired than she had the whole trip.

***

"Esther! Esther!" The call came from a woman waving at them with all her might from the entrance of the waiting room. As Esther came closer, she realized that it was Etka. How welcome the sight of a familiar face was to her!

"Etka!" Esther ran to her and fell into her embrace.

"You made it! I have come every day to look for you slowpokes."

"When did you get here?"

169

"We arrived five days ago, and I have so much to tell you."

Etka had always been such an encouragement to Esther, and now she was doing it again. They were tired, dirty, and hungry, but they were in Jerusalem at last. The sight of it warmed Esther's cold heart. *My baby will be born in Jerusalem!* Truly, the only thing that kept her going was the thought of her baby.

Suddenly, she remembered the words of the man in charge of displaced persons. "Do you have any relatives here?"

"No."

"Any friends, acquaintances?"

"No."

"Wait in the other room until we can make some arrangements," he had said. That had been several hours ago. With each passing moment, Mr. Raul and Esther's hopes sank deeper. She thought back to the warm embrace Isaac had given her father and the curt nod he threw her way. Mixed emotions swirled in her throbbing head. It was at that moment that Etka had appeared.

"Oh, Etka, what are we going to do? We have no relatives here in Jerusalem, and we were told hours ago to sit here and wait." Her pleading eyes nearly broke Etka's heart.

"Wait here, I will take care of everything," she said confidently and disappeared into the other room.

Esther could hear her speaking in persuasive tones to the man in charge. She was tempted to peek around the corner and watch but didn't want to interfere, possibly jeopardizing any chance they might have of leaving this place. Etka sounded like a different person: confident and assertive, yet kind and cool. *What had given her this air?* Esther wondered as Etka stepped back into the room, face beaming.

"Come along," she said with a gleam in her eye.

Esther just stared, first at her and then at her father. He smiled, shrugged his shoulders, and stood to follow them. Anywhere was better than here.

As they left the building, Esther linked elbows with Etka.

"Where are we going, my secretive friend?"

Etka smiled. "To my place. Wait until you see! There's enough room for you and your father, and the people in the building have been so kind."

"But how were you able to find something so quickly? Did you know someone here in Jerusalem?"

Etka smiled the biggest smile Esther had ever seen. She thought that Etka never looked lovelier. She leaned closer. "Oh, Esther, I've met the most wonderful man!"

Esther looked shocked. "Already?"

"He was our guide." Her face was filled with love as her words began to flow. "He is so wonderful. His name is Jacob Hirsch, and he's led several groups across the mountains."

Esther stopped short in her tracks. "What is his name?"

Etka looked at her questioningly, "Jacob. Jacob Hirsch. Why?"

Esther looked pale. "Does he have any family?"

They continued to walk at a slower pace. "Yes, but he only has one brother left. The rest of his family was killed by a bomb."

Esther sighed and rolled her eyes. "And his brother's name?"

"Isaac." Etka searched Esther's face. "Do you know him? He was a guide too."

Esther smiled faintly, but her father answered, looking sharply at Esther. "Yes, he was our guide: a fine young man."

Etka's face screwed into a frown as she searched her memory. "I don't remember him, but then, I was in such a hurry. I nearly raced Jacob up the mountain," she said with a giggle that sounded more like a schoolgirl than a young woman. Etka looked across the street and pointed to an apartment building made of white block stucco, several stories high.

Esther was amazed at its height and beauty. Palm trees stood as sentinels in front, and she could see a British flag flying beside another flag with the Star of David in its center. As she looked at the star for the first time since she had worn it on her arm as a sign of scorn, Esther stopped and gasped.

"What is it?" Etka asked. She stared into the girl's face and followed her gaze to the flag. "Isn't it beautiful?" Her eyes were shining with pride and joy.

"It was such a disdainful thing for so long, I hardly know how I feel," Esther responded quietly.

"With pride, daughter." Esther turned to see tears flowing down her father's cheeks. "With pride!"

"Oh, Papa," she cried as they fell into each other's arms. Weeks of suppressed emotions flowed from them both. Her father shook with uncontrollable sobs that nearly broke her heart. *Oh, Father, forgive my hard heart,* she cried within her soul. *I have been such a fool!* It seemed as though a mountain of burdens fell from her shoulders. *I will ask for Isaac's forgiveness too, Lord.* Such a peace flooded her soul as she stood there on the streets of Jerusalem, embracing her only living relative in the shadow of their star.

"Etka!" came the cry from across the street as a tall man waved to them.

Esther pulled away from her father, looking into his eyes. He reached down and wiped her tears away. He could see in them the peace and sweetness of the daughter he had left behind on the tracks of Auschwitz. "We will talk later," he said as he turned to the approaching stranger.

Esther knew before he spoke that this was Isaac's brother. He was a carbon copy of Isaac, just older and taller. The dark curly hair and dancing eyes must have been a family trait, for Jacob sported them as well. Yet Esther knew in a moment that it was Etka that made his eyes shine. The love between them was a beautiful sight to behold after so much hatred and strife.

"Esther, Mr. Raul, I would like you to meet my friend, Jacob Hirsch," Etka said, nearly bursting with love and pride.

Esther smiled her greeting as her father warmly embraced the young man.

"Shalom, and welcome to Jerusalem," Jacob offered. "We are so glad that you are here."

"Jacob, they have no family or friends, so I told them that they could stay with me." The statement was so simple, as though Etka had been bringing fugitives into her home for years. Esther wondered again at this new Etka.

Her act of kindness brought a look of tender admiration to the man's face. "You are a good woman, Etka, always ready to help."

Etka blushed under his open adoration. "Oh, anyone would have done the same."

He snorted and shook his head. "No, you are sadly mistaken. Many only think of themselves in our land. But enough talk." He turned to Mr. Raul and Esther. "I'm sure you are very weary from your journey."

His words seemed to remind Esther just how tired she was. They quickly crossed the street and headed to the apartment building. Up close, it looked even taller, and Esther wondered if she would have the strength to climb the stairs.

The building sat back off the road and had a set of double doors centered in the front, giving it a symmetrical balance. As they passed through the doors, they found themselves standing in a large foyer decorated with potted plants. Comfortable chairs were tastefully grouped on area rugs. The prominent colors of green and ivory made the room feel like a tropical paradise.

They moved through the area to a hallway on their left. Etka and Jacob chatted as they moved down the hall to the third door on the right. Etka produced a key and stood back to let her guests enter first. The apartment was nicely furnished but economical in appearance compared to the lavish foyer. Esther was surprised at how cool the rooms felt.

Although it was small, the apartment had two bedrooms, one smaller than the other. Esther couldn't help but wonder where they would put a newborn baby. Perhaps by then she would have an apartment for her and her father.

The kitchen was sparsely furnished but looked like heaven to Esther. *When was the last time I stood in a private kitchen or cooked a meal?* She saw her mother bringing scones to the table, the glass shattering, the stone, the soldiers, the shots … She shuddered.

"Esther, are you cold?"

"No, I'm fine, just a little tired."

"Of course you are! How stupid of me. Here." Etka took her arm and steered her to the larger bedroom. "We will share this room, and your father can have the other one. Why don't you rest a while?"

"Yes," chimed in Jacob. "And please plan to join my brother and me for dinner. I have made a feast to celebrate his return."

Her father looked furtively at Esther, seeking her approval. She smiled weakly and nodded.

"You are too generous, Jacob. We would be glad to join you. Before you go," David stopped him, looking at Jacob beseechingly, "do you know of any work for an old man?"

Jacob smiled and touched the older man's arm. "We will talk later, my dear friend. You should rest as well." He looked over at Etka. "Perhaps I could get some help on the dinner's finishing touches?"

Etka looked at him coyly. "I don't know; I am terribly busy."

"Well," Jacob retorted with a sigh, "I guess I'll just have to ask Keturah." His eyes danced as he saw the flash of jealousy in Etka's eyes.

173

"You are a bad one, Jacob Hirsch!" Etka slipped her arm into his and escorted him out the door. "Rest you two," she flung over her shoulder with a smile.

***

A bed had never felt so comforting to Esther. How long had it been since she had slept in a room all alone? Again, her mind wondered back across what seemed a thousand years to her room in their home in Amsterdam. As she closed her eyes, her thoughts whirled across scenes from her past. Was she only seventeen? She felt old and stretched out like a worn garment, but she murmured her thanks to God for bringing her to this place. She thanked Him for the bed, a room, an apartment, Etka, her father—and even Jacob and Isaac Hirsch.

When she woke, Esther wondered where she was. In the sometimes bewildering land of semi-consciousness, she could feel a breeze blowing in from the open window to her left. The bed and window happened to be in the same proximity as they had been in her childhood bedroom. For a moment, she thought that she was back at home. She heard her father and brother talking and wondered if she would be late for school.

As she opened her disoriented eyes, she looked around the unfamiliar surroundings as her mind retraced her steps. She could hear low voices in the living room and then she remembered. Her stomach growled, reminding her of the promised meal, and the baby leaped within her as if to remind her of his presence. "Don't worry, little one. I have not forgotten you."

She slipped from the bed and straightened the covers. As she approached the door, she recognized Isaac's voice. Her heart raced. *Already, Father? Must I apologize already?* She smiled as the baby seemed to answer with a kick, and she quietly opened the door.

Conversation stopped as both sets of eyes turned her way. Her father was the first to speak. "Esther, you look much better. Did you sleep well?"

She glanced out the window, noting that the sun was already deep in the west. "By the looks of the sun, yes I did." She smiled. Isaac's eyes were apprehensive but not cold—perhaps indifferent. She quickly looked away. "And you, Papa. Did you sleep?"

174

"Like a baby," he said before he thought. All eyes seemed to travel to her swollen abdomen. Her face flushed. This time, Isaac came to the rescue.

"I believe Jacob and Etka have cooked up quite a meal, and I don't know about you, but I'm starved." He smiled and moved to get up.

Esther took a deep breath and rushed on, fearing that she would renege on her promise to God if she didn't act quickly. "Father, would you mind giving Isaac and me a moment alone?"

David pushed himself from the chair and smiled. "I believe I can find my way, but don't be long. You don't want to keep a hungry man waiting!" He winked at Isaac and turned toward the door, closing it softly behind him.

Esther felt glued to the spot. *Help me, Father,* she cried in her heart. She looked up to see Isaac looking at her with those kind eyes she remembered from the trip. At the same moment, both spoke the other's name. Isaac smiled. "You first," he said.

"Thank you," she spoke softly. "Do you mind if I sit down?"

"No, not at all." He rose and motioned to the chair next to him, waiting for her to be seated before sitting himself.

Esther sat, hands folded in her lap, looking at the carpet, wondering how to start. "I feel I need to apologize again for my rude behavior on the ship." She waited. No response. "When I first saw the flag with the Star of David, I just stared at it. The last time I had seen it, it was on our armbands."

Esther could see Isaac flinch and look away.

"I just froze, but Papa"—the tears sprung to her eyes at the memory—"Papa sobbed. It broke my heart to hear him cry so. I had let all the bitterness freeze my heart into a stone. I was determined to shut everyone out." She looked up at him. "Especially you."

"But why me?" Isaac asked innocently.

She sighed. "I saw the look of pity and anger in your eyes when you saw that I was with child. It angered me so, because it is not what you think."

"I've told you before that you do not need to explain, Esther."

"No, I do need to tell you. If we were living on the opposite end of town, perhaps I wouldn't. But by the looks of Etka and Jacob, we are practically related."

Isaac smiled. "These are strange times in which we are living."

175

Kurt's smiling face flashed across Esther's mind. Had he not spoken the same words to her? Isaac saw the look but remained silent. "Someone else said that to me once." She looked straight into his eyes. "My husband. When I arrived at Auschwitz with my father and brothers, I was taken by a man along with several other girls. We were taken to"—*oh is there any other name for it, Lord?*—"a brothel."

Isaac fought well to keep his face emotionless.

"The man who had taken us kept me in his room. He was a gentleman in every way and never touched me, nor did he let anyone else touch me. In fact, he erased my name from his list.

"He was so kind. We were never together in any untoward way—he slept on the couch and I in the bedroom. But living so closely and spending so much time together, we became very close. I knew that I was a temptation to him, but as I said, he was a complete gentleman.

"He asked me to marry him. He said just what you said: 'These are strange times in which we are living.' " She looked at Isaac and then out the window. She knew she must hurry. "I knew he loved me, and I also knew that he had saved my life. So, when he asked me to marry him, I said yes. We were married in October, and in November, he was called away." Her voice was barely a whisper. "I never saw him again."

"I'm so sorry, Esther," Isaac said with deep compassion.

She looked at him. "Please understand, Isaac. I loved him, and I am not sorry that I married him. I don't expect you to understand how I could do such a thing, but he was not like the others. He hated this war and all it was doing. I saw him weep for our people, Isaac. He tried to save only a handful of lives, but he did all that he could, and I loved him for it."

Isaac sat staring at her, trying to comprehend all that she had said. The hatred that he felt for the Palestinians who had murdered his family had been doubled against Hitler and his crowd. Now, here before him sat a young Jewish girl lauding one of Hitler's men. He wanted desperately to believe her and made a conscience choice to do so. "I will help you find your husband," he said calmly, though his eyes were intense.

Esther just stared at him. "But how?"

He got up and walked to the window, staring at the flag with the star. "The *Beriha* has many connections across Europe, including

176

France. We will make inquiries. But Esther, I can't promise that what we find will be good news. It sounds as though Herr Gerstein would have many enemies on both sides of the prison walls."

Esther looked confused. "But he was against the war," she said, defending her beloved.

"I understand that, but not everyone will. War is an ugly business. You have seen that firsthand. If Herr Gerstein's actions and loyalties are found out by those who are in prison with him ..." He left the sentence hang. "These are ruthless people, Esther, with no sense of right and wrong. Their world and empire has just crumbled. Vengeance is all they now know."

"Thank you, Isaac Hirsch," she said, looking at him earnestly.

"For what?"

"For not rejecting me. For believing me."

Isaac thrust his hands in his pockets. "I just have one question, Esther. Will your baby be Jewish?"

A single tear slipped down her cheek. "I don't know, Isaac."

There was a heaviness in the room. Isaac knew it was time to move on. He walked toward her and reached out his hand, smiling. "Well, Jehovah will lead you. Right now, I believe we need to follow that glorious aroma that has slipped down the hall and under the door."

Esther took the offered hand and laboriously pulled herself from the seat. All the stiffness from the last few days and the weight of her baby made her nearly topple over.

Isaac reached out to steady her. He held her arms and looked into her eyes. Esther knew what she saw and quickly pulled away, heading to the door.

Chapter Twenty-One

"And unto this people thou shalt say, Thus saith the LORD;
Behold, I set before you the way of life, and the way of death."

Jeremiah 21:8

July 25, 1945

There is no reason to live. You have failed everyone. The voices echoed these words over and over in Kurt's mind. He tried to ignore them, but the reality of their words plunged him into despair. *Oh, dear God, have mercy on my soul,* he cried, burying his face into the cot.

The past few weeks in Cherche-Midi prison had been a nightmare. After leaving Auschwitz, his heart felt dead with the thoughts that Esther had been killed like the rest. The horrible images of naked bodies being pushed into the gas chambers rose before him. There was his Esther, his dear Esther, whom he had thought that he could protect. He had failed her and all the others he had tried to save. How many people had he told of the atrocities? They all looked at him as if he was mad. Maybe he was. Had he only imagined it all?

On the way to his next assignment, he heard the rumblings that the Third Reich was falling. As he drove, he knew what he had to do, but first he would stop at his sister's house and say one last goodbye. He remembered dear sweet Elizabeth and her tears as he said farewell.

"When will we see you again?" she asked with a serious pout.

"I don't know, pumpkin," he said as he brushed his hand across her cheek. How thankful he was that she had been spared the horrors of the war, once again admiring his sister and her husband for their success in shielding her.

He bent down to face her and took her small hands. "I want to give you something to remember me by while I'm gone."

Her face brightened in anticipation. "What is it, Uncle Kurt?"

"Before I give it to you, you have to promise that you will take good care of it."

Her little face held such a solemn look that he smiled in spite of his breaking heart. "I promise," she said with all the dedication of a child's heart.

He reached into his pocket and pulled out the little box he had found. He held it tenderly, straining to hold back the tears. Slowly, he opened it and took out Esther's locket. The sight of it nearly pushed him over the edge, but his resolve was strong not to alarm Elizabeth.

He held out the locket for her to see. "Oh," she whispered, cautiously reaching for the necklace. He reluctantly let go and allowed it to drop into her hands. She held it with such reverence that Kurt's heart relaxed a bit, knowing that he was doing the right thing.

"Where did you get it, Uncle?" she asked while tracing her little finger over the twelve smooth stones.

"It belonged to a very dear friend of mine," he said softly.

"Who was she?"

"Her name was Esther."

"That's a pretty name." She opened the locket and saw the pictures. "Is this Esther?" she asked, pointing to the picture.

"No, that is her mother and father."

"Where do they live?"

Kurt looked at her with sad eyes. "I don't know, Elizabeth."

"Will Esther mind if I have her locket?" Elizabeth asked, looking into Kurt's eyes with apprehension.

It was almost his undoing. He took a deep breath and looked over her head, then back into her earnest face. "No, I think she would be glad that you have it." He drew her close and just held her for a long time.

From there, he drove into France, leaving his uniform and identity in the trunk. He found the French authorities in the town of Reutlingen and turned himself in, telling them everything he knew. At first they seemed pleased, but with Germany's surrender, they seemed to doubt him, and he became the suspect instead of the witness.

In July, after living in a hotel with little restraints, he was moved to the Cherche-Midi prison in Paris. Now he lay in his cell in silence. The whole world had been turned upside down—his hopes had been dashed to pieces and thrown to the wind, and his only relief was prayer. Although he had failed, he knew that God had not. He rolled against the wall and prayed yet again. *Father, forgive me for failing you. Forgive me for failing Your people. Forgive me for failing Esther. Please help me.*

"*Jude-Geliebter*," hissed from the cell across the aisle. Kurt looked over and saw hatred in the German's eyes. He did not know the man, but had heard this jibe before. The man started tapping the wall in rhythm, and he chanted the phrase over and over: "*Jude-Geliebter, Jude-Geliebter, Jude-Geliebter.*"

Other men in other cells picked up the chant as well. The phrase now reverberated up and down the hallways: "Jew-lover, Jew-lover, Jew-lover."

Kurt stared at the wall. The French authorities had promised him that his written statement would be kept secret; they had promised so much, but now he wasn't sure if they could even promise him tomorrow.

***

The weather had turned unbearably hot by July, and as Esther's time drew near, the heat bothered her more and more. She stood at the sink washing dishes, trying to keep cool, and wondering how her father was able to work in such heat. But then, he loved what he was doing.

When Isaac found out that David Raul had owned and operated his own glass business, his face lit with joy as he clasped his hands together, crying, "*Jehovah-jireh!*" A relative of his had such a business and was sorely lacking in the managerial end of things. Both men praised God for His infinite mercy and guidance.

Esther saw new life in her father and rejoiced as well. She had planned to join him in the factory, but neither man would hear of it. Secretly, she was glad. She felt as big as a house and knew that her time was near.

She hadn't told anyone about the pains that had started sporadically in the night. She knew that it could still be hours before her baby would enter the world; however, Esther was glad that Leah, the midwife, lived on the fourth floor and was home today. As another pain shot through her, she thought that it might be wise to visit the old woman.

No sooner had she climbed the last flight of stairs when a sharp pain made her double over and water began to dribble down her leg.

Don't panic, Esther. Women have babies every day and in all kinds of situations. She hurried to the woman's door and knocked furiously.

As soon as Leah saw Esther, she knew. "Come in, child, quickly." Leah drew her in and gently led her to a bedroom.

Esther had never felt such pain in all her short life. Leah continued to assure her that she was doing fine and that the baby was doing fine as well. Her words did little to comfort Esther—she thought she would die.

She lay back panting after the last contraction had passed, her forehead damp with perspiration, as Leah kept busy by her side. Suddenly she heard a flurry of movement in the other room. With a rapid knock, Etka came flying into the bedroom.

"Esther, your baby is coming!"

Esther offered a faint smile at the ridiculous statement. "I believe you are right, Etka," she said weakly.

At that moment another contraction was upon her, harder than any thus far. They came constantly and with such force that she felt she would break in two. "I can't do this, Etka!" Esther panted between the pains.

"Yes you can. Just keep thinking about that little boy that's going to be in your arms in just a few moments," Etka spoke.

"He's almost here!" Leah exclaimed. "One more push and he's here."

At that moment another contraction ripped through her, and Esther pushed with all her might.

"He's here!" Etka cried, looking on as Leah did her magic. Soon a husky cry filled the air, and Esther thought she had never heard anything so beautiful.

"It's a boy," Leah proclaimed triumphantly. She wrapped him securely and laid him in Esther's arms for a moment.

The new little mother looked down into the tiny face and saw the eyes of Kurt Gerstein looking up at her. "Oh, Kurt," she cried, holding the infant close to her.

"He will be proud of his son and his wife," Etka said, coming to kneel beside Esther.

"Thank you, Etka, and thank you, Leah. How can I ever repay you for all you have done?"

"By naming the next one Leah," the woman said. Laughter and joy filled the room and the heart of each woman.

181

Esther laid her head back and closed her eyes. "Thank you, Father. Thank you."

When David Raul entered the apartment calling for Esther, he felt great alarm at her absence. Where could she be? He looked around for any clues to her whereabouts and noticed little signs of a departure that had not been planned. At other times, Esther would leave a note explaining her whereabouts. Not only was there no note, but the radio was on and the dishes in the sink were only half washed. Etka was nowhere to be found either. He raced from the room to Isaac and Jacob's apartment.

"Have you seen Esther or Etka?" he panted, winded from the flurry of sudden activity.

Isaac looked at Jacob. Both men shook their heads. "Do you think it's her time?" Isaac asked.

"It certainly could be, but where would she go if that were so?"

"Leah, on the fourth floor," Jacob offered. Without any more conversation, all three were heading for the stairway, bounding to the fourth floor two steps at a time. The frantic pounding of three men on her door brought a not-to-happy Leah to her weary feet.

"Shhh," she hissed in their faces as all three began to speak at once. "If you will be quiet, I will show you the fruit of our afternoon's labor," she exclaimed in a vicious whisper.

Three contrite but excited men entered her apartment. Motioning them to sit in the living room with a jerk of her head, the midwife left them to check on her charge. She quietly entered the bedroom, where Esther had been sleeping for the past few hours. The precious bundle was tucked securely by her side, a look of contentment on both faces. How she had slept through all the ruckus, Leah was not sure. She was about to turn and exit when Esther stirred. Her eyes first went to her baby, and a look of mingled joy and sorrow crossed Esther's face. She bent over and kissed the baby's downy head.

"He's a beauty," Leah said softly.

Esther looked up, noticing the woman for the first time. "He certainly is."

"Are you up for some company?" Leah asked with a doubtful frown. In her opinion, men were such a nuisance.

Esther looked at her in surprise.

182

"There are three anxious men in my living room. You would think that you were on your deathbed. I don't understand menfolk. Don't they know that childbirth is as normal as the rising sun?"

Esther smiled at the woman's disdain. "I don't believe it's a subject that they will ever feel comfortable with. I don't mind seeing them, but I must look a mess," Esther answered, her hand automatically going to her hair.

Leah smiled. "Believe me; they will think that you and that baby of yours are the most beautiful sight they have ever beheld!"

The Hirsch brothers followed David Raul into the bedroom like two whipped puppies, looking a bit uncertain and hesitating at the doorway. David went forward, his eyes first on his daughter, taking in the smile on a face that had gained a maturity, which motherhood alone can bring. Her smile did much to quell his anxious feelings.

He held her hand as he gazed down at his grandson. He sat gingerly on the bed, gently picking up the tiny hand and caressing each perfectly formed finger. Wonder filled his eyes. "Oh, Esther, he is beautiful."

At his words, the little face scrunched into a frown and then a smile. His lips pursed and puckered, and his eyes blinked open. They seemed to stare right into the face of his grandfather, and David stared back in wonder. "He knows I'm his Papa," David said in grandfatherly confidence.

Esther smiled and squeezed his hand. "Don't you want to know his name?" she asked. His look gave her the answer. "David Kurtis Gerstein."

David bent and kissed her forehead and then pulled back to look into her face. "Thank you, Esther." He looked again at the little bundle beside her and bent to kiss his head as well. He stood and motioned to the two men who had become sons to him. "Come, look at my beautiful grandson," he said proudly.

Both men came forward shyly. Neither had spent much time around babies. Jacob smiled and said congratulations, feeling a bit awkward. He had not accepted the situation as well as Etka would have liked, even though they often talked about it late into the night. He stepped back to give Isaac a look.

Isaac came forward cautiously, his eyes first on Esther and then on the child. So many emotions swirled in his mind, but he controlled his reactions. To Esther's surprise, he knelt beside the bed, placing his hand upon the baby's head. "May I offer a prayer?" he asked.

All nodded in agreement.

He bowed his head and prayed, "Oh great God and Father of Abraham, Isaac, and Jacob. Our hearts are filled with praise for Thy goodness to us this day. We thank Thee for the life of this child. We thank Thee for his safe delivery and for the keeping of his mother. Oh Father, we pray that Thy hand will be upon this son, David. Make him a great warrior for Thy kingdom's sake. May his heart pant after Thee, O Lord. May he rise up to call Thee blessed. May he stand among princes and proclaim Thy word, O Lord."

There was a hesitation. Isaac struggled with his thoughts but continued. "Please, be with his father. Bring him safely to his son, as you brought Jacob to his son, Joseph. Amen."

Amens were heard around the room. Isaac looked up into Esther's watery eyes. "Thank you," she whispered.

Little David chose this moment to make his presence heard with a lusty cry. The moment was lost, but the bridge that had been built between the two friends could not be destroyed. To Esther's surprise, Isaac slipped his hands under the baby and lifted him to his face. "There, there, Little David," he crooned as the other men laughed. "Uncle Isaac has you. You don't need to cry."

For a moment, the tiny voice was silent, eyes looking in wonder at the face so near to his, but just as quickly the wails began again.

"I don't think you have what he needs, brother," Jacob interjected with a wry smile.

"Out with you all," Leah said, trying to sound more annoyed than she felt. She had been touched by Isaac's actions and was not blind to the love she saw in his eyes for Esther. *It would be the best thing for all if the father died the death he deserves,* she had thought while he prayed. She admired his compassion, but she had never been known for much of her own—at least not for anyone of the opposite gender.

***

Esther stayed with Leah for the next few days. Leah felt pity for the girl who had no mother to teach her the ways of motherhood. When the day finally came for Esther to head back down to the first-floor apartment, she worried about where they would keep Little David, as he was now called. Etka had come every day to visit. She held an air of secrecy about her, but when Esther questioned her, she just smiled and said nothing—which was rare for Etka.

"All packed!" came the cheery voice of her friend.

"Yes, thanks to Leah," Esther said. "I don't know how to thank you, Leah," she repeated for the hundredth time.

"I told you how," Leah said with a grin. She came to Esther and pulled her into her arms. "It has been my pleasure to have you here. The place will seem quiet once you leave."

"I'm sure it will without all the visits from one doting grandfather and two doting uncles," Esther replied.

"Yes, I can't believe I'm saying this, but I will miss them too."

"Please come and visit us often," Esther urged.

The old woman smiled, "I will, you can be sure."

Esther smiled, wondering if her father had more to do with the statement than her son. She hadn't missed the sparkle in her father's eyes as he teased with Leah. They had developed quite a friendship, although the average onlooker would have said they acted more like enemies than friends.

After the goodbyes, Etka led Esther down the stairs, toting baggage and baby. She could hardly contain her excitement as they met the men in their hallway. Eyes glittered with secrecy, and Esther couldn't help wondering what they were up to.

As they entered the apartment, Esther immediately noticed new furniture in the living room. She thought for a moment that they were in the wrong apartment and looked questioningly at her father.

"Come Esther," was all Etka said as she led Esther into her bedroom.

The double bed was gone; in its place stood a single bed and a crib. A changing table was nestled against the other wall beside a beautiful rocking chair covered with blue cushions. A tiny dresser stood between the bed and the crib, serving as a nightstand as well.

She turned to Etka. "I don't understand."

Etka came forward, gushing, "I could hardly keep from telling you. Jacob and I are married. I have moved in with him and Isaac so that you, Little David, and your father could have the room you need."

185

Esther looked into all their faces and knew that it was true. "I don't know what to say! But how can we pay for all this?"

Her father looked at her with mock insult. "You forget that I am a working man, my daughter!"

She looked into the eyes of each face. They loved her and her son. How could she have ever hoped for such a thing to happen? They had cared for her and met her every need. Tears filled her eyes. "I don't know what to say," she repeated.

"Say you'll have us for dinner," Etka chimed in. "I'm weary of feeding these three."

Laughter filled the rooms and echoed down the hallway. It was not the life that Esther would have chosen, but as she stared down at the infant in her arms, a product of love, and looked into the faces of her dear friend and father, her heart swelled with joy. *Thank you, Father*, she thought in her heart. *My cup runs over with Your blessings.*

***

Esther's days were filled with happy hours caring for Little David. She was amazed at the way a baby melted the hearts of people who had once looked upon her with disdain. They greeted her in the hallway and on the streets. She was a daughter of Zion, and her son was a child of Jehovah—no matter who his father was.

Daily, she prayed for Kurt. As the weeks flew by, her heart ached to see him again, but she found herself finding comfort in God's Word. She kept up with the aftermath of the war by reading any newspaper that she could get her hands on. Isaac had kept his promise and was making inquiries about Kurt, and Esther knew it was costing him his reputation in the eyes of the *Beriha,* who didn't understand a Jewish man's interest in the welfare of a German officer. What Esther didn't realize was that he had told them that he sought revenge for the ruined life of a precious Jewish girl at the hand of this German. He did not feel this way, but he knew that answers would come much quicker if this were the case.

Isaac had been away on another quest for most of the month of August. He knew their window of escape was closing; in fact, he doubted if they would be able to bring any more refugees across the mountains. Britain was feeling the heat from the Palestinians, who saw the number of Jews rising daily in what they claimed was their territory. Oh, how he hated politics.

As he entered the *Beriha*'s makeshift headquarters, the secretary, Sharon Shapiro, was seated behind the main desk and waiting for him. She was a young woman with a heart for her country. Isaac had long admired her zeal and courage, and he knew she would have been happy to start a relationship with him, but something held him back.

He had decided to take the plunge right after he got back from the last trip—the trip where he had met Esther. She had made him so angry that he had determined to ask Sharon out as soon as he had a good meal and a good night's sleep. And then there was Esther, right in his building. The rest was history.

He was anxiously awaiting news from France as well, but for totally opposite reasons. The thought disturbed him, but he pushed it away. He was leaving it all in the hands of his Heavenly Father.

"Isaac, I have news for you from France," Sharon said with a light in her eyes. She leafed through several papers on her desk until she found what she was looking for. She reread the note and handed it to Isaac, smiling. "I think you will be pleased."

He took the note and scanned it briefly before putting it into his pocket. He gave her a weak smile and a thank you as he exited the building. Once on the streets, he pulled the note out and read it again:

TO WHOM IT MAY CONCERN: KURT GERSTEIN, SS OFFICER FOR THE THIRD REICH, WAS FOUND DEAD IN HIS CELL, JULY 25, 1945.

So, it is as I thought it would be, Father, he spoke in his heart. *It is the answer I had hoped for, but why do I feel such sadness? Oh, God, help me to find the words to tell her.* He slowed his pace, trying out the words he would say in his mind. None of them sounded right. Before he knew it, he was standing at her door, staring at the doorknob.

As he reached up to knock, the door swung open, and Esther nearly ran into him. She held a basket of clothes on her hip. Her hair was covered with a scarf, and she had a smudge of baby powder on her nose that she obviously did not know was there. He thought she'd never looked more beautiful.

"Oh, Isaac, you're back," she said as she tucked a stray hair under the scarf.

"Yes, but I see that I've caught you at a bad time."

"Oh, no. I just thought I'd get a load of wash in the washer while little David sleeps. Why don't you have a seat, and I'll be right back," she said. She was gone before he could argue.

He stepped into the apartment and thought, not for the first time, what it would be like to call it home. Esther had added little touches of her own that filled each corner with her presence. Candles graced the table along with a bowl of fruit. On one end table was a picture frame that housed an armband with the Star of David. Esther had found it one day in the market place, probably discarded by a new arrival. She had picked it up and brought it home. She fitted it to a frame, saying that she wanted it as a reminder of who she was and what she had witnessed.

He walked to the bedroom and peeked into the crib, amazed at how much Little David had grown. He reached down and gently caressed the soft cheek with work-roughened hands. He couldn't ignore the tufts of light blond hair—so uncommon among the Jewish children. When he heard Esther enter the room, he withdrew his hand and placed it on the crib railing. She came to stand beside him.

"Has he changed much?" she asked.

"He's growing like a weed."

She reached down to hold Little David's hand for a moment before motioning for Isaac to follow her to the living room. She gently shut the door and went to the refrigerator to pour them both a tall glass of lemonade. After she handed one to him, she sat down and asked about his trip.

"All went well, but I'm afraid that it might be our last trip across the mountains."

"Really? But why?"

He was always grateful for her concern for his people, their people.

"Britain is getting a lot of pressure from the Palestinians and others around the world to keep our people out of Palestine. They fear we will accomplish what we have set out to do," he said fiercely.

Esther sighed. "Why must it be so hard for our people, Isaac?"

There it was, his name coming across her lips. *If she knew how it affected me, she would never utter it again,* he thought.

"I don't know." He sat looking down at his glass, wondering how he could tell her. He decided that there was no easy way.

188

"A letter was waiting for me at the office when I returned," he said, looking up at her. He didn't need to wonder if she knew what he was saying.

She stiffened and looked into his face. "What did it say?"

He pulled it from his pocket. "Would you like me to read it?"

She nodded, closing her eyes. He cleared his throat and read the message. Isaac wasn't sure what he expected her to do—perhaps fall into his arms weeping so he could comfort her? Whatever the scenario, he was not prepared for what happened next. Her eyes flew open wildly and she snatched the paper from his hands. She rose to her feet, reading and rereading the missive, pacing the floor, then hiding her face in the corner across the room like a child.

His heart broke as he went to her, gently turning her around and held her in his arms. He stroked the hair he had so longed to touch. His actions seemed to bring on another torrent of tears, but he stayed himself, willing to have strength for them both.

Later, he wouldn't remember what it was that he had spoken to her—just words of comfort and consolation. His mind whirled back to his own time of grief. Could he remember anything that anyone had said to him? He tried, but nothing came to mind. He knew it wasn't the words as much as the presence of those who came to share his pain as he would share Esther's pain.

As the weeping subsided, Isaac gently pushed her away from him and reached into his pocket for his handkerchief. He handed it to Esther, who graciously accepted it and dabbed at her eyes. She whispered a quiet thank you as she placed it in his hand. He pulled her chin up and gingerly wiped the baby powder from her nose, explaining, "You must have changed a diaper recently," and half smiled.

Her sad eyes looked up, but she only nodded.

"Come and sit down, Esther," Isaac urged, supporting her the short distance.

She sat down, staring at the tiny piece of paper that held such a gigantic message. She finally looked up at him. "Did you see the date?"

He took the note from her and read aloud, "July 25, 1945." He thought for a moment. Esther watched as understanding dawned on his face. "Oh, Esther, I am so sorry."

The tears again began to flow. "His died on his own son's birthday."

189

Chapter Twenty-Two

"But he knoweth the way that I take: when he hath tried me,
I shall come forth as gold."

Job 23:10

1948

Little David tottered to his mother across the grass, his blond hair glistening in the sunshine and his bright blue eyes sparkling with merriment. He loved the park almost as much as Esther did. She took him up in her arms and covered his face with kisses. He was a constant source of joy to Esther in spite of the disdainful glances that came her way because of him.

At two years of age, Little David's German heritage was all too obvious among his dark haired, olive skinned playmates. She was thankful that his innocence was untainted by the actions of others, but she also wondered when he too would feel the barbs and nettles of racism.

Time had passed quickly for Esther, and the days had helped to heal the deep wounds of her losses. At first, she felt that she had no reason to live. Her hopes and future had been tied to her bright star in the northern sky—Kurt Gerstein. Now he was gone, and all hope shattered and fell to her feet like so many shards of broken glass. Somehow, she felt that if she could have only seen him again, shown him their son, kissed him goodbye, felt his strong embrace once again, all would be well.

How she had depended upon the strength she saw in his eyes and heard in his voice, especially as he read the Bible and spoke of his God. It was all gone in an instant, and she didn't even know where he had been laid to rest. At times, the truth of the whole situation nearly pushed her over the edge. How had he died? What had been his last thoughts? Why had he been in France? There were so many questions, so few answers, and even less hope in ever finding out the truth.

Isaac Hirsch had become a source of strength to her. He was a faithful companion, though Esther knew he wanted more than that.

She didn't know what held her back. No, that wasn't true. She did know, and the thoughts made her desperate. Someone stood in their way—Gabriel Bachman.

When the reality finally sank deep enough within her that Kurt was truly gone, the weight of the matter seemed to release a flood of memories that had been pushed down and buried deep within her. His face, his letters, his love refused to be pushed aside any longer.

At first she fought any notions about Gabriel, feeling completely disloyal to Kurt. Wasn't Kurt the one who had saved her life? Hadn't he been there for her, protecting her from so many horrors and destruction? Was it not Kurt's face that she saw every time she looked into the precious face of her son? A battle raged within her until she thought she'd lose her mind. Thankfully, God had His servant there for her just when she needed it.

Etka stood and watched Esther from the doorway as she broke the bread into tiny pieces and fed them to Little David. Her heart ached for her friend, and she had longed for an opportunity to help relieve the pain. Today seemed to be that day. She quietly slipped into the chair next to Little David just as he reached for her, knocking over his glass of milk and spilling it over the highchair and onto her skirt.

Esther snapped, shouting at Little David, then dissolving into a torrent of tears over her outburst.

"I'll clean it up; there's no harm done," Etka reassured Esther as she wrung a dishcloth out at the sink. She wiped the spills from her skirt and continued to clean up Little David as Esther sat mutely, a look of utter defeat written across her face.

"I'm sorry, Etka, I don't know what's wrong with me," Esther said with a sigh.

Etka looked up into the face of her dearest friend on earth. "I think I do."

Esther stared at her, a look of questioning written all over her face. "What do you mean?"

Etka looked at her, weighing her thoughts, calculating the correct approach. "I see a war going on."

Esther furrowed her brow, "Well, yes, I see that too on every street it seems."

"No, not that. I see a war going on within you, a battle of two—no, three—men."

191

It was as though Esther's defenses had all been torn down. "How did you know?"

Etka smiled. "Because I know you, and I know what you've been through, and I am a woman. I did not know your husband or the young man that you pine for, and I'm obviously partial to the one that lives with me. But you need to settle this in your heart, Esther, before it tears you apart."

"But what should I do?"

"Well, to start with, you need to put your memories of Kurt Gerstein to rest." Etka saw Esther bristle. "I am not suggesting that you forget him, but all of us have suffered great losses. I have lost my whole family. At least you still have your father."

Etka knew it wasn't quite fair of her to play this card, but she knew it would help soften Esther's heart, and she was right. Esther visibly relaxed, albeit somewhat defeated.

Etka continued more tenderly, "God has given you a beautiful, living reminder of your time with your husband. Cherish him and his father's memories, but you must move on and live. You know that is what Kurt would have wanted."

Esther knew she was right but still said nothing.

Etka continued. "And I see someone else filling your thoughts. What was his name?"

Esther looked up with sad eyes. "Gabriel." Just speaking his name brought torment to her spirit.

"Where is he?" Etka asked compassionately. She feared he was dead or in parts unknown as well and wondered how she would have handled such a loss.

"America," came the unexpected answer.

Etka looked at her incredulously. "America? You know where he is?"

"Was. I know where he was before our capture. Right before we were taken, he left to live with his uncle and study at the university in New York. He asked me to write, and we did faithfully until my family was taken to Westerbork." The memories were so bittersweet.

Etka looked questioningly, and Esther continued. "It was a camp—not like Auschwitz. It was like a holding tank for our people before we were shipped elsewhere." Esther sat in silence, remembering Silla, Mrs. Bachman, Mrs. Paschel, Daan, Ad.

Etka hesitated before saying any more. Esther had been discussed often in her home with Jacob and Isaac. She knew well the special place that Isaac held for her in his heart. She had encouraged him to be patient, believing that if given enough time, Esther would end her grieving and seek Isaac's affections.

It had been two years since they had arrived in Palestine. The Jewish quarter in Jerusalem had swollen in number by the thousands. It was an exciting time to be living here, watching all the pieces coming together as she watched her people—her own husband and brother-in-law—work constantly at building their new nation. The meetings, rallies, and training had taken up a large portion of their lives; they had literally put their own interests on hold to work at creating a new Israel, knowing it would be worth it all. Even as Etka carried their first child, she looked forward to the birth of their nation as much as the birth of their child.

She knew that Isaac's fanatical dedication was, in part, to shield his heart from Esther. Etka felt that Esther had been coming around, but lately, she had withdrawn into her shell, avoiding them all as much as possible. She had wondered what was wrong with Esther. Then, she had come upon a new revelation by accident.

Just last week, as she stood outside Esther's door, poised to knock, she had heard Esther crying. The sound was so pitiful that Etka had decided to leave Esther alone; but as she turned to go, she heard Esther cry out another name: Gabriel. It hadn't taken Etka too much time to put the pieces together.

Esther was young and beautiful. She was the most dedicated, loyal woman that Etka had ever met. If there had been a young man before the war, Etka could imagine the double grief that Esther must have felt having married a German and now holding his son. She thought of her own brothers and wondered what their reactions would have been.

As all this flashed through her mind, and she knew what she had to say. "Do you have an address?"

The question seemed to startle Esther. "Why, yes. I wrote it so many times, I will probably always remember it."

"Then you must write to him," Etka said with more resolve than she felt.

All of the doubts that Esther had collected in her mind over the past few weeks were written plainly on her face. "I can't."

"Yes, you can, and you must," Etka shot back fervently.

"No, Etka! I won't! What would he think of me? I would be such a shame to him. Don't you see the looks I get every time I leave this room? He would hate me." Her voice broke. "I would rather him think that I was dead."

"How can you say that? He loved you! Was he that shallow of a man that you would think this way?"

The question brought Esther's head up with a jerk. "Of course not. He was one of the most decent, good, and wonderful men I have ever known." Tears flowed from her eyes unheeded.

Etka reached across the table and took Esther's hand. "Then I know you must write. For Isaac's sake you must."

There, it was out. Etka saw the look of surprise and question in the young mother's eyes. "Esther, you must have noticed by now. Can't you see that he loves you?"

Esther's face was defiant. "I never gave him any encouragement. Of all people, you must know that."

"Yes, you are right, but he still has feelings for you. He has put his life on hold for you."

"But I didn't ask him to," she replied softly.

"Either way, you owe it to yourself and to Gabriel to write. You will never have peace until you do."

***

Esther took Etka's advice. It was the hardest letter she had ever written. As she reread the missive, her face blushed with shame. It all looked so unbelievable on paper. Why should he believe her? Again, she shared her doubts and the letter with Etka.

"It is good, Esther. You would want to know if the roles were reversed, wouldn't you?"

Esther smiled wearily. "Yes, but I am not a man." She left the sentence hang in the air like a cloud of foreboding.

***

Judith Bachman sat in the drawing room absently fingering the cup of tea the maid had brought her over an hour ago. She mechanically took a sip from time to time, not noticing that it had grown cold—a fact that she usually detested. She looked nervously from the giant grandfather clock, which she would have sworn was not working properly, to the letter that sat beside her on the end table.

It normally didn't bother her when Jacob was late from work, but today she desperately needed him. What could the letter mean? It was like an evil little demon sitting there—taunting her. She had almost opened it, but she couldn't—not without Jacob. He would know what to do. He always knew what to do.

As her thoughts drifted back over their life together, she realized how few decisions she had made on her own. She was so unlike her sister, Madrid. Madrid was two year older and had the world by the tail. It always amazed her that she was the one who had married Jacob.

When he had started attending their synagogue, Madrid was the one who caught his eye—her vivacious ways and vibrant eyes always caught the boys' attention. Since Jacob was a newcomer to America, Madrid had taken it upon herself to be his personal tour guide. Mother had said it was scandalous the way Madrid acted, but Judith had always admired her sister's ways, wishing that she had more of her spunk.

In the end, Madrid had tired of Jacob and his work-driven ways. He was soon climbing the ladder in their father's business and had little time for Madrid or anything else. Judith had waited patiently, just as she was now. He finally noticed her, and in the proper time, had decided that he needed a wife. Judith was there—she was always there for him. She smiled in spite of the anxiety that kept her in its grip.

Again, she picked up the letter. There was no name, just an address from Israel. Who did they know in Israel? But then it wasn't for them; it was addressed to Gabriel, and it was obviously a woman's handwriting. Not just any woman—Esther Raul's. After all the letters that had come from Amsterdam, Judith would have recognized it anywhere. But how could it be? She stood to pace the floor, making her fifth round when she heard the front door open. She quickly turned to greet her husband, leaving the dreaded letter in its place.

She literally threw herself into his arms. "What's this?" Jacob asked as he quickly laid his briefcase aside to fully embrace his wife. He pulled her back and gave her a quick kiss, noticing for the first time the worry lines on her face. Panic seized him. "What's wrong? Is Nelson in trouble?"

"Oh, Jacob, I wish it were that easy," she cried, resting her head against his strong broad chest.

Again he pulled her away. "What is it, Judith?" he demanded. She took his hand and led him into the drawing room, picked up the letter, and placed it into his strong hands. With the letter, all anxiety seemed to transfer from her heart to his. *He will know what to do,* she thought as she looked into his eyes. He looked at her questioningly. "Who does Gabriel know in Israel?"

"Don't you recognize the handwriting?" she asked incredulously. But of course, he wouldn't. Jacob Bachman had more important matters to attend to than receiving the daily mail addressed to his nephew.

He looked up again, impatiently, turned over the letter, and opened it.

"Jacob!" Judith was surprised at his quick decision. "Shouldn't we just give it to Gabriel?"

But Jacob was not listening. He was quickly devouring the contents of the letter. His face went from shock to disgust. He literally threw the letter at her and walked to the window, leaning against the sill, arms crossed akimbo.

As Judith read the letter, little gasps left her lips. When she finished, she carefully put it back in the envelope and moved toward her husband. "What are we going to do?"

He quickly turned to face her, snatching the letter from her hands. "We are going to do nothing." His eyes were full of fire. He frantically looked around the room as though looking for a hiding place. He then moved to the fireplace, removed a match from the mantel, and struck it.

Judith gasped. "Jacob!" Before she could find the nerve to move, he had lit the corner of the letter and placed it on the grate, watching the flames lick up the paper. Within moments its ashes had joined those below the grate.

He let out a long sigh and shook his head, turning to Judith and pulling her to the sofa. As they sat down, he began, "Judith, what good would it do Gabriel and Deborah if they received this letter? They've been married for over a year now and are expecting their first child." He looked into her eyes, seeing the anguish there, and again shook his

196

head, as though trying to remove the contents of the letter from his mind. "As bad as I feel for this poor girl, it would only cause Gabriel such heartache. Hasn't he suffered enough?" He looked at her pleadingly, as though he needed her reassurance.

She had never seen him like this before. When had he ever asked for her approval? She squeezed his hand and smiled. "You are right. I feel so badly for this girl, but it would be better for her if she continued to find a new life for herself and her child there in Israel."

Jacob looked intently into her eyes. "We must never mention this to anyone, Judith. Do you understand? We must act as though we never received that letter."

He was squeezing her hands so hard that it hurt. "Yes, Jacob. It will be our secret."

Somehow the thought of them sharing something that no one else had a part in gave her a strange sense of security.

***

The war within Esther Gerstein was over, or perhaps merely the present battle had ended: She did not know. It had been six months, and there had been no answer from Gabriel. As the days slipped by, Esther fought the many sordid thoughts that haunted her. Had he despised her as she thought he would? Did he ever receive the letter? So many questions went unanswered, but she was determined to live for Little David's sake as well as her father's.

One thing she did know: The war that raged all around her kept her in a constant state of anxiety for the safety of her son. As patriotic fervor rose across the land promised to Abraham, Isaac, and Jacob, tensions also mounted with those who had claimed the same land as their own—not by a covenant with God, but through time and hard work. As the saying goes, "possession is nine-tenths of the law." Their ancestors had claimed the land, worked the land, and had fought for the land—and they were gladly fighting again.

How many had already died by the beginning of 1948? Hundreds? Thousands? She did not know, nor did she care, for she was too busy fighting her own battles.

The combination of the truth of Etka's words concerning Isaac and the truth that spoke loudly from the lack of any reply from America galvanized Esther's heart into action. She could not stay in

Israel and torment Isaac any longer. Yes, she saw the love in his eyes and actions, but she also saw the danger that she would bring down upon him and his career in the forthcoming Israeli state. Oh, how he loved Little David! It nearly broke her resolve, but she could not stand in his way. She would not.

Everything seemed to come to a head on May fourteenth, the day before the expiration of the British Mandate. Like the travail of suffering at the birth of a child, Israel came forth with a shout of victory. Oh, how many enemies the little struggling nation had to face! The Arab world had united against them, promising a complete massacre—but their threats died with them.

She would never forget the night of celebration. What joy! What a victory! Esther rejoiced with her people, but her heart was torn between her devotion to them and her thirst for peace. She knew what had started—if not completed—the tearing within her heart: her daily time with God in the forbidden book.

As much as she hated to admit it, her heart yearned for the words written there. Yes, she relished the holy times on Shabbat, worshiping Jehovah here in her native land with her people. But a seed had been planted by Kurt during their devotional times together that she could not ignore.

She fought it bravely and had even gone so far as to consider burning the book, carrying it out to the trash pile, hiding it in her pocket, with every intension of hiding it in the rubbish; but as she stood there, alone in the bright colors of the evening's sunset, her hand clasping her treasure fiercely, her heart would not let go of the only tie she had with her late husband. This was the only heirloom Little David would have from his Christian father, and if he chose to destroy it, that would be his decision, not hers.

Since then, every morning except the Sabbath began with her Bible reading. Her father would leave for work, and little David usually gave her an hour before he would start his day. She would settle down beside the window and drink in the morning sunshine as she fed upon the Word.

It was just an ordinary day. Esther's mind had methodically ticked off her duties for the morning as she reached for the living room curtains to pull them back, anticipating the warmth of the eastern sun. The sight that met her eyes brought shock and horror to her heart.

There, like a giant spider, was a swastika spray painted upon the window in black. She cried out and quickly drew shut the curtains as though this would erase the horrible emblem of hatred. Who would do such a thing? Did she have to think hard for the answer? No. Sadly, her mind was filled with countless faces, some she knew and some she did not. She collapsed to the floor in a puddle of sorrow, shaking uncontrollably. How long she sat there, she did not know. Time slowly slipped away as she formed a plan in her mind. She would need Etka's help.

She quickly peeked in to see Little David still fast asleep and then called Etka, trying desperately to keep her voice calm and failing miserably. Etka was there in less than a minute.

"What is wrong?" her friend enquired as soon as she came through the door. She held one-year-old Abraham on her hip, a bib still tied around his neck. Esther's call had obviously interrupted his breakfast.

Esther slowly walked to the window, half hoping that the horrible sign would not be there. But as she slowly pulled back the curtain, the swastika cast its evil shadow across her face. She heard the sharp intake of air as she stared at the window.

"Oh, Esther," Etka began. "How could anyone be so cruel?" She set Abraham on the floor and went to her friend. New sobs shook her shoulders as Etka held her closely. "I'm so sorry, Esther," she said as they rocked back and forth in the shadow of the spider.

Esther broke away and closed the curtain. She sat on the sofa, staring at the floor. "I'm leaving, Etka." Her voice was barely above a whisper.

Etka came to sit beside her. "But how? Where will you go?" "America. It is the only place I can go." She lowered her face into her hands as the tears spilled down her cheeks.

Etka placed a comforting arm around her. "I hate to see you go, but I don't want to see you or Little David get hurt." She paused. "Stupid people! Don't they see that they are just as bad as those who murdered their own people?" The words spat forth like venom.

Somehow, Etka's outrage calmed Esther. "No, they do not see. But you must not be angry with them. They are just reacting in fear of that which is different. Don't blame them. They have suffered too much."

"But haven't you suffered just as much, if not more?" Etka asked incredulously.

Esther smiled. "We have all suffered. We are all just trying to protect our children from the same suffering. That is why I must go."

***

Gabriel continued to pace the floor, looking out the window at the night skyline and then back to the clock, which now read 2:47 a.m. When was this nightmare going to be over? He thought back to the day when Deborah had told him that she was going to have a baby. It had been the happiest day of his life—he was to be a father! The memories flooded his mind: shopping, painting the spare bedroom, the baby shower that her family had hosted, and the myriad of gifts that they had received. He remembered Deborah's face, radiant when he would come behind her and wrap his arms around her swollen abdomen. And now this. *Why God, why?*

She had awakened around midnight in terrific pain; he could still hear her crying out. "Gabriel, something's wrong," she had whimpered clutching her stomach and rocking back and forth.

He had been in a dead sleep, but the scene before him startled him to complete alertness. He reached over to her, not sure what to do. As he pulled back the covers, his heart raced—the bed was saturated with Deborah's blood. By the time the ambulance had come, she was unconscious. Her last words to him had been, "Take care of our baby."

They echoed now in his mind, tearing at his already broken heart. He had stroked her hair as she slipped away, her face a sickening white. Now, almost two hours had passed without a word. The waiting and not knowing nearly drove him crazy. He tried to pray, but the words seemed empty and hollow.

The doctor found him seated on the faux leather chair, head in his hands—the picture of despair. How many times had he come to this room with the joyous news of a successful delivery? The Bible verse always came to mind at the delivery of a healthy infant: *"A woman when she is in travail hath sorrow, because her hour is come: but as soon as she is delivered of the child, she remembereth no more the anguish, for joy that a man is born into the world."* But these visits—they were the dread of his occupation. At times like these, he wished he would have followed the steps of his father and stayed on the farm.

He quietly walked over to the chair beside Gabriel and eased himself into it. Gabriel started, looking up with bloodshot eyes, pools of anguish.

Before the doctor spoke, Gabriel knew it was not good news, but what? "My wife—how is Deborah?"

Dr. Simes had always followed the adage of bad news first. "Mr. Bachman, I'm terribly sorry. We did all that we could, but she had lost so much blood before she ever arrived, there wasn't much we could do."

He paused a moment, putting his arm around the young man, trying to give any strength he had left. He had been up for twenty-one hours, and his aging body seemed to remind him that he wasn't getting any younger. He waited for the sobs, but they never came, just empty numbness. "It seems as though there was a tear in the uterus lining. It's strange that she did not have any minor bleeding before, but happening in the night like this—the tear could have started, and the movement of your baby could have made the rent worse."

He squeezed the strong shoulders that drooped before him. "You need to be strong, Gabriel." He didn't often use first names, but this young father was so close in age and stature to his own son. How would he feel if he had to give this news to his son? "You have a precious little girl in there that needs you."

Gabriel lifted his eyes to the compassionate gray eyes of the doctor, searching for understanding. "You mean the baby lived?" he asked incredulously.

Dr. Simes half smiled. "Yes. She's small, but you are the father of a beautiful baby girl."

The information swirled in Gabriel's head. How could this be? Deborah was gone. How could he raise their daughter alone? What was he to do?

Dr. Simes seemed to read his thoughts. "Would you like to see your wife and child?"

Gabriel blinked. His mind simply refused to function. He nodded as the tears began to flow. He buried his face in his hands and let all the anguish flow with the tears. The doctor simply held the man, acting on thirty-three years of experience. When the torrent seemed to ebb, he helped Gabriel to his feet and led him from the room.

He would later thank his staff for their thoughtfulness. Like a well-trained army, they were his support, doing all the unthought-of acts that made the room as comfortable as it could be under the circumstances. They were out of sight but not out of earshot, ready to assist if needed; but they knew their doctor, revered him, knowing that he would do what was best.

He led Gabriel to the table where his wife lay motionless, a pink blanket tucked under her arms. Except for the loss of color, she looked as though she were sleeping. Gabriel went to her. She looked so peaceful.

"Oh, Deb," he whispered. He picked up the cold hand and held it to his own hot cheek, kissing it before he laid it down once again, bending down to hold her one last time. His sobs wracked his body. "This can't be happening!" he cried as he tried to pull her close.

Dr. Simes always seemed to know just how much time was right before he interrupted. He came behind Gabriel, speaking softly. "Gabriel, we will need to make some arrangements, but there is someone else you need to meet."

He squeezed Gabriel's shoulders, gently pulling him away. Gabriel responded like an obedient child, as Dr. Simes knew he would. He led him through several doors. As they approached the nursery, Gabriel could hear the cries of a dozen babies; the sound seemed to alert every sense in his body. The doctor nodded to one of the nurses, who went to one bassinet and lifted out a tiny bundle of pink. She smiled down into the face of the little mite, talking to her as she came to the door.

She cradled the infant in her arms as Dr. Simes opened the door. "Gabriel, I'd like you to meet your daughter."

Gabriel just stared in wonder. The little baby was awake, eyes wide, searching with wonder, not really focusing on anything. Her little hands reached up and out, as if she was searching for him, needing his touch. He took the tiny little hand in his. She was so small and helpless. A paternal instinct of protection that Gabriel didn't even realize he had seemed to take over. "May I hold her?"

The nurse smiled and tucked her chin. "Of course, Mr. Bachman."

She tenderly placed the tiny baby into his arms. He felt awkward, but his mind and reactions seemed to spin back to his home in Amsterdam when he first held his brother, Shain. He wasn't very old himself, but he felt the same feeling of protection, only this time it was much stronger. He kissed the downy head and handed her back to the nurse.

"What do I do now?" he asked the doctor.

They both turned and exited through yet another door out into the hallway. "I think the best thing for you to do is to get some rest. Is there anyone you need to contact?"

Gabriel's mind raced to Deborah's family. Oh, how could he tell them? "Yes," he stated simply. He looked up into the doctor's face, "Thank you, sir, for all your help."

"Please, be sure to call me after you have slept. Just call the hospital, and they will know how to reach me."

They shook hands, and Gabriel turned quickly away lest the tears start again.

Part Five
New York

Chapter Twenty-Three

"And they shall comfort you, when ye see their ways and their doings:
and ye shall know that I have not done without cause all that I have done in it,
saith the Lord GOD."

Ezekiel 14:23

May, 1949

Esther leaned against the railing, enjoying the feel of the sea breeze whipping through her hair. Mid-afternoon seemed to be a quiet time aboard the ship, and it had become her favorite part of the day. She slowly inhaled the fresh sea air, looking across the wide expanse of water. The cloudless azure sky reached down to touch the edge of the ocean, making it look bigger than it had ever looked before. It was a fairly calm sea, but Esther had learned from her short time on the water that even on a calm day, the ocean surface gently rolled and lapped the sides of the ship.

Little David was by her side in his carriage, taking his afternoon nap. She looked into his peaceful face. His cheeks glowed with the blush of sleep, and his lips were puckered against his fist. How she adored him—would do anything for him.

She had opted for a passage by sea rather than air, mainly because it was less expensive. However, she also knew that she needed the time alone to gather her thoughts and seek God's direction. It had been so difficult to leave her father. After the swastika incident, he had understood her desire to leave. But the thought of being separated from the only family he had left—especially his new grandson—made it nearly impossible to say goodbye.

If it had not been for his own little surprise, Esther wondered if she would still be in Israel. She smiled, remembering his face—like that of a schoolboy—telling his grown daughter about his decision to ask Leah to marry him. It was as if he was seeking her approval. It hadn't been a surprise to Esther. Leah often took meals with them, and her eyes watered a bit as the image of the older couple strolling through the nearby park after dinner came to mind.

She had reveled in watching her father blossom. Thinking back on their last night together, she knew Papa had sensed her need to talk and asked Leah to stay with Little David while he took his daughter for one last walk. They had enjoyed the cool evening, strolling in no particular direction—just enjoying the night sounds and each other's company. She remembered his hesitation as he questioned her again about her time at Auschwitz.

"I was wondering, Esther." He paused before going on, not wanting to pry too deeply into her private affairs. Esther braced herself, wondering what he was about to say, her heart still stinging from the swastika incident. "Do you know what ever happened to your locket?"

She let out an audible sigh of relief. Beginning with the shower-room incident, Esther described how she had tried to hide the locket and was then discovered. Her face clouded, recalling Kurt's intervention.

"That's when Kurt stepped in and truly saved my life. God only knows what that woman would have done to me."

Her father put his arm around her in a rare sign of public affection. He waited patiently for her to continue.

"Kurt had put it in his pocket, and I had forgotten about it until the next day when he gave it to me."

David interrupted excitedly, "Then you still have it?"

She looked into his expectant eyes. "I'm sorry, but no, Papa. When the prisoners blew up the one crematorium and Kurt had to leave, we thought it would be better if he took the locket with him." She fought tears as she remembered their last time together. "It was so hard for him to leave me, but what could he do?"

She laughed a caustic laugh. "We thought I would be the one to die. Who would have thought that I would live and he ..."

She could not say the words. She paused, thinking back, wondering for the umpteenth time what had happened to her husband. How had he died? She hadn't really thought about the locket but hoped that it had brought some comfort to him.

They continued on, unexpectedly finding themselves in the nearby park. Both headed for their usual bench, which afforded them the seclusion they needed. She could sense that her father had more on his mind, and she didn't have to wait long to hear his thoughts.

He had folded his hands on his lap and sat staring down at them as he rubbed his fingers. "There is something that I must tell you, daughter."

Esther looked up at him. She could see the struggle it was for him to speak. "What is it?" She reached for his hand.

Squeezing her hand seemed to give him the strength he needed to continue. "The other day, I had some extra time on my hands. I had wandered through some of the ancient sites—at least the ones we are allowed to visit. I came upon the empty tomb of Jesus."

Esther gasped. She knew that it was not a place for any orthodox Jew. "But why, Papa?"

The look of confusion in his eyes broke her heart. "I don't really know. Anyway, there was a group of people there. I suppose they were Christians. One man in particular seemed very shaken by the sight. I was there when he came out of the tomb." He shook his head in astonishment and looked up at Esther. "He was crying. When he joined the group they started praying. Esther, I have never heard a Christian pray before. They were so sincere. They called out to God the Father and thanked Him for sending them Jesus, the Messiah."

"Oh, Papa." Esther didn't know quite what to say. She wanted to share her heart with him, but how? It seemed as though he was looking to her for answers. "Papa, I must tell you something too. I only have one possession of my husband's—his Bible."

A wry smile came to David's lips. "Yes, I know." He saw the shock in her eyes and quickly explained, "One day when you were out with Etka and I was caring for little David, he had made a mess of his outfit. I wasn't sure where to look for clean clothes, so I just started looking in the dresser drawers. I saw the Bible hidden under some clothes. At first I was furious and was ready to throw it out. But then I saw the inscription on the front cover." He paused. "As much as I wish that Isaac was Little David's father, it is not true, and I cannot blame you for what happened."

Esther felt such relief wash over her. "Oh, Papa! You cannot know what this means to me—you knowing and understanding. When I first heard Kurt pray, I too was astonished. He was so sincere, and he too was talking to Jehovah."

Her Papa's words came slowly. "Esther, are you a Christian?"

She looked shocked. "No Papa!" But then her voice softened. "Kurt prayed for me that I would know the truth, but I don't know what to believe. I feel like such a traitor to our people to even question our beliefs. But I must tell you, Papa, I would rather be disloyal to my people than to my God."

They both sat in silence, weighing each other's confessions, thankful for their mutual concerns but confused as to what it all meant. Then they had prayed together. The sweet memory of her father's heart-felt prayer would be forever etched in her mind.

Oh, how she would miss them all! A tear slid down her cheek— not for the first time. She let her mind wander over all the memories the past few years had given her, ending with thoughts of Isaac. He had made all the arrangements for her. He had even made plans for her to stay with some of his distant relatives in New York City. When she saw the address, she gave a quick intake of breath.

"What is wrong?" Isaac asked, searching her face.

Esther had been quick to cover her reactions with a falsehood. "I guess it makes it all seem so real: the American address."

She quickly shoved the paper in her pocket. One word had jumped off the page at her: Brooklyn. She didn't know what it meant, but she knew that Gabriel's address had had the same word in it. It may mean nothing—she knew that New York City was big. It could be a section of the city, and it could possibly be bigger than all of Israel.

Isaac had also driven her to the dock, helping with every detail. As they had stood waiting for clearance to board the ship, he had taken her hands and held them tightly. "Please, don't forget us," he had said, his dark clear eyes filled with anguish. It nearly broke her already torn heart. Was she making a mistake? Oh, why did life have to be so hard? She had tried to explain all the reasons she could not stay. He had been so broken—so much so that he begged to come to America with her.

"No, Isaac. You cannot leave all that you have worked for. It wouldn't be right."

"But I—" He had hesitated, weighing whether the words should be spoken. "I love you, Esther. Don't you know that?"

"Isaac, you are breaking my heart." She looked away, a sob catching in her throat. Gently, she reached up and pulled his head to her lips, kissing his forehead. He had moved with actions fueled by years of pent-up emotion—pulling her close, kissing her lips and cheeks and hair before wrapping her in his arms.

"How can I let you go?" he sobbed huskily.

She had just let him hold her, resting in his strong embrace before moving apart. "Perhaps I am chasing shadows, but I know that the Lord wants me to leave. If I do not find whatever it is I am looking for, I will return to you. Perhaps by then—" She hesitated, looking at little David, who had been busy taking in all the sights with wide eyes from his carriage. "Perhaps by then, people would be willing to accept us both."

She had been glad that the others had said their goodbyes at the apartment. Esther was sure that everyone was hoping that the time alone with Isaac would convince her to return with him. *If they only knew how close I came to doing just that.* One look at her sweet Little David and she knew this move was mainly about him; however, even as she spoke the words in her heart, she wondered if it was the truth.

What was she looking for? *Do you think that Gabriel will be waiting there for you, Esther?* She knew that he was a big part of her reason for heading to America, but it had been Isaac who had made the arrangements for her to dock in New York City, and he knew nothing about Gabriel. She had decided to let the Lord lead every step of the way. If He wanted her to see Gabriel, He would have to orchestrate it, not her. She smiled ruefully to herself, wondering how strong her resolve would be once the ship docked.

Esther returned to the room she shared with five other women. It was sufficient and clean but offered little in the way of comfort. Thinking back on the many modes of transportation that she had taken, it was more than adequate. Each of the girls had her own bunk as well as one of the lockers stacked behind the door. A sink stood in one corner below a small mirror next to a porthole, and a shower room was just down the hall.

At first, the girls had all stayed to themselves, but the long passage had forced them to become acquainted with each other. Esther had made it a habit to read her Bible often, so she shouldn't have been surprised when one of the other girls had asked her if she was a Christian.

"No!" Esther replied quickly, taken aback by the question.

"Oh!" The girl named Gladys had been equally as surprised. She was a rather tall girl with the curliest light brown hair Esther had ever seen. It was cropped rather short and circled her face like a halo. Lively green eyes peered questioningly behind a pair of wire-rimmed glasses. "I guess I just assumed you were when I saw you reading the Bible."

"Oh, I—" Esther hesitated. Did she really want to tell this stranger her whole story? There was something about this tall, slim young woman that put a longing into Esther's heart. Her casual stance—arms relaxed, head tilted slightly to one side—made Esther want to share the heavy burden that pressed down on her heart. She answered, "A friend gave this to me, and I'm just curious."

"Oh," Gladys said, seeming to want to say more.

"Are you a Christian?" Esther asked before she thought.

Gladys smiled as though a door had just been opened to her. "Yes, I am. But I haven't always been."

Esther looked at her questioningly.

Gladys continued, "I was not raised in a Christian home. My family never went to church."

"Were you Jewish?"

"Oh no, we weren't anything." Gladys saw the startled look on Esther's face. She went on hesitantly. "Are you Jewish?"

Esther looked chagrined. "How did you know?"

Gladys chuckled. "Well, for one thing, I noticed that you only read the Old Testament. And for someone to be startled that a person would have no religion and then ask if I am Jewish, along with your accent ..." Gladys shrugged. "I guess I just put it all together."

That had been the beginning of a wonderful friendship that Esther knew would last a lifetime. Gladys Porter was an American who had been visiting the Holy Lands in conjunction with a course that had been offered at the university she attended. She lived in New York City with her parents, two younger brothers, and a cat named Pasha whom she missed dearly.

It was all so foreign to Esther, but Gladys was glad to tell Esther all about this new land they were fast approaching. She was so easy to talk to, and Esther found herself relating her whole story to her new friend. Somehow, it didn't seem as degrading as it had in her letter to Gabriel. Gladys was warm and sincere in her sympathy. She supported Esther with her heart, never judging her, only loving her. Esther would

211

always remember the day that she showed Gladys the address that Isaac had given her. Gladys squealed with delight.

"Oh, I live in Brooklyn! And this address isn't that far from my home. I can't believe it!"

"Don't you believe that God can do anything?" Esther had said coyly.

Gladys had been sharing her faith with Esther, praying for the right opportunity to question her about her personal beliefs. She looked up from the address in surprise and then broke into her infectious laugh that Esther had quickly grown to love.

"Oh, you continue to surprise me, don't you?" Then her face grew thoughtful.

"Yes?" Esther could see the musings in her friend's eyes.

"I don't want to offend you, but how can you have so much faith in God the Father and yet reject His Son?"

Esther considered her answer before she spoke. "I don't reject His Son. I just do not believe that He has come yet."

Gladys considered the statement before answering. "I never thought of it that way before." A comfortable silence passed between them before Gladys went on. "But what do you do with all the prophecies that Jesus fulfilled in His coming?"

"I don't believe that I've read those."

Gladys looked at her questioningly. "Have you read any of Isaiah?"

"Oh, yes. That's one of my favorite books."

Gladys was now animated as she spoke. "Have you read chapter fifty-three? That whole chapter is about the sufferings of Christ on the cross."

Esther was quiet. Her mind whirled back to the times she had spent with Kurt. Had he not said the same things? The thoughts clouded Esther's countenance.

Gladys quickly replied, "I'm sorry. I have offended you."

Esther looked up quickly. "No, not at all," she replied. "You just remind me of my husband. Kurt would also get excited when he would talk to me about his Messiah."

Gladys tenderly laid her hand on Esther's arm. "He loved you very much. What a great gift you must have been to him. And God has given you such a precious reminder of your husband in your son."

Esther's vision blurred as the tears filled her eyes. "You would think that I had cried enough tears by now." She covered Gladys' hand with her own. "I miss him so much. My heart feels so empty at times."

"I know of Someone who can fill it," Gladys said gently. "In fact, He's the only one who is big enough to fill it."

Esther wondered at her new friend's words. If she was honest, she would have admitted to her dear friend that the empty place within her heart did seem bigger than the vacant place that Kurt, or Gabriel, or Isaac, or even her family had made. She would wonder at the thought for the rest of their journey; and if Gladys would have looked closer, she would have noticed that when Esther read her Bible, there were more pages resting on the left side of the book than on the right.

Chapter Twenty-Four

"I call to remembrance my song in the night: I commune with mine own heart: and my spirit made diligent search."

Psalm 77:6

On the final day of their voyage, Esther made certain that she woke early. She knew that they were scheduled to sail past the Statue of Liberty, and she didn't want to miss it. Little David had been such a joy to all the girls, and they had gladly watched out for him if Esther happened to leave the room. She did so now, tiptoeing to the door and heading for the stairway just down the narrow hall. It had become a favorite spot for her to read, especially during these early morning hours.

Most of the ship was still slumbering to the rhythmic motion of the sea. *I could sail on forever*, Esther thought as she settled onto the metal step. *Maybe I'll become a sailor.* She laughed outright at the thought, then quickly looked about to see if anyone had heard her. *What nonsense!*

She looked down at the Bible resting in her lap. By now, she had made her way through the first three books of the New Testament and wondered at their familiarity. They all seemed to say the same thing. It puzzled her until the day that Gladys mentioned that the first four books were called the Gospels. *What a strange word*, Esther thought.

She had so many questions but didn't have the nerve to ask for answers. Somehow, this adventure seemed to belong to her and Kurt. At times she felt as though he were sitting beside her, leading her across each page.

She was so fascinated by the story of Nicodemus and the woman at the well. This Jesus seemed to always have just the right answers for whomever He was talking to. She was riveted to every word as Jesus conversed with her people, when one verse seemed to jump right off the page: *"And ye shall know the truth, and the truth shall make you free."*

214

She looked up past the metallic white ceiling above her. *Oh, Father. I need the truth. Please help me to know the truth about your Son.* She returned to the words of Jesus, devouring them like a starved animal. As the Jews argued with Jesus, she tried to see their side. *"They answered him, We be Abraham's seed, and were never in bondage to any man: how sayest thou, Ye shall be made free?"* Well, that was certainly not true! How many times had her people been taken into captivity because of their unfaithfulness to God?

"Jesus answered them, Verily, verily, I say unto you, Whosoever committeth sin is the servant of sin. ... If the Son therefore shall make you free, ye shall be free indeed. I know that ye are Abraham's seed; but ye seek to kill me, because my word hath no place in you."

The thought overwhelmed Esther. *"My word hath no place in you."* *Oh Father! I want Your Word to have a place in my heart. Is this Your Word?*

She continued to read as the Jews debated with Jesus, trying to hold on to her heritage and yet finding peace with each word of the supposed Messiah. As she read on, she gasped: *"Ye are of your father the devil, and the lusts of your father ye will do."* She slammed the Book shut. *How dare He!* Her thoughts whirled within her mind. *My people are not Satan's people!* The thought made her face burn. *He must be an impostor—a liar!* And with those thoughts, the Evil One snatched away several of the seeds that had been planted in her heart.

She vowed that she would never look past Malachi again. *Of all the wicked things to say!* And yet as she climbed the stairs and angrily pushed open the door to the deck, the wind hitting her face, her steps were heavy. She walked across the deck to the railing and waited for the sun to make its appearance.

The sky was bursting forth with color—splashes of reds, orange, and pinks raced across the sky. She loved to stare at the eastern horizon, waiting for the sun's arrival. Each time, she was not disappointed as the brilliant orb popped up, starting as just a tiny slice of brilliancy. With each passing second, it seemed to majestically take over the whole of creation, as if to cry, "Here I am—ruler of all land, sea and sky!"

For the moment, she had forgotten her struggle with the Word of God, but as she stood there, enveloped in the rays of the dawning day, one seed remained out of the grasp of the Enemy: *"Because my word hath no place in you."* The phrase would continue to haunt her even as the ship slid past Lady Liberty.

Everywhere she looked, the words that she had read seemed to appear from nowhere and taunt her. Later that day, as Gladys quoted the words immortalized by the statue, "Give me your tired, your poor, your huddled masses yearning to breathe free," Esther's mind flew to the words of Jesus: *"And ye shall know the truth, and the truth shall make you free."* Would she ever be free? The heaviness in her heart made her doubt that it could ever be possible for her.

Questions continued to swirl in her mind like the little eddies that teased the ship's hull. She tried to keep her voice light and her steps quick, but Gladys saw the struggle and knew God was answering her prayers. *Time, Gladys,* the Lord seemed to whisper to her as she fervently prayed. *Give her time—be her friend, let my Spirit do the rest.*

✶✶✶

The girls had huddled in their room, exchanging hugs, addresses, and teary farewells before each gathered her belongings and joined the procession to the main deck. It surprised Esther to see how many people had been on the ship. She stood spellbound on the deck as the New York City skyline continued to tower into the sky. She had never seen anything like it. As their ship slowly churned the waters of the harbor, Esther's stomach churned as well, draining the color from her cheeks.

"Don't worry, Esther," Gladys spoke softly as she put an arm around her. "I know it is big, but it's my home." She smiled as Esther's eyes traveled up the front of one building that she would soon learn was the Empire State Building.

"I've never seen such tall buildings," she whispered in awe. "They make me feel so small."

"Yes, that one is especially tall—102 stories, to be exact, and you can ride to the observation deck at the top in an elevator and see for miles—or you can take the 1,860 steps, if you'd like."

Esther drew her gaze from the building to her friend with a quizzical look. Gladys looked chagrined.

"Sorry, the Empire State Building is somewhat of a hobby of mine. I've learned all I can about it." She looked dreamily at the giant skyscraper before them and sighed longingly, "I hope to work there some day."

The girls' reverie was soon broken by a surge of movement as the ship slid into port. Sailors were everywhere securing the boat, fastening lines to the huge posts, and lining up the gangplanks to the dock. It was just as fascinating to Esther as it was to Little David. Her mind couldn't help but go back to her voyage with Papa to Israel, making her heart lurch and her throat tighten. Oh, how long ago that seemed! A lifetime ago! She squeezed her son and focused on his myriad of questions and comments.

Esther didn't have to wonder which members of the massive group of people were Gladys' family—amid the crowd stood a tall couple with two tall boys. One boy sported the same curly hair that Gladys had obviously inherited from her father. They were waving and shouting as though Gladys was the only person disembarking from the ship. At first, Esther feared that she would be left to fend for herself, forgotten now that the trip had ended. But before Gladys' family had given her the attention she deserved, she turned her searching eyes toward Esther and David and pulled them toward her family.

"Dad, Mom, I want you to meet a dear, dear, dear friend who I found on the ship. This is Esther Gerstein and her son, David." She quickly turned to Esther with an endearing smile. "Esther, these are my parents, John and Linda Porter, and my brothers, Samuel and Johnny."

Esther smiled shyly and shook the hands that were offered to her. There was something in their faces that instantly put her at ease. She liked their friendly manner, feeling like she had known them for a long time.

Mrs. Porter smiled sweetly, first at Esther and then David. She reached out to tousle the toddler's hair. "Welcome to America, David," she said in a grandmotherly way.

David nudged his face under Esther's arm, peaking out and smiling in a shy sort of way. The effect was both comical and endearing.

"What a beautiful little boy you have been blessed with, Esther," Mrs. Porter said, her eyes shining with delight.

"Thank you," Esther responded. The pride could not be hidden from her voice.

Mr. Porter was the next to speak. "Is there anyone meeting you, Esther?"

217

Esther faltered for a moment, "I don't know. I have the name and address of someone, but I'm not sure what arrangements were made." She felt foolish and small, but Mr. Porter came to her rescue by asking to see the information.

Esther rummaged in her bag while David played peek-a-boo with Gladys. She produced the precious piece of paper and handed it to Gladys' father. It saddened her to see Isaac's manly script. Mr. Porter studied the paper and looked up at Esther as though trying to find an answer. "This address—"

"Is very near our neighborhood," Gladys interrupted. "Isn't that amazing?"

She looked at him with a look that only they would understand. As though reading his mind, she knew that he had realized that the name and address were Jewish, that Esther looked Jewish but had a German surname, and that her son, David, looked more German that Jewish. Gladys teasingly called her father Sherlock Holmes for his amazing deductive reasoning—another trait that she had inherited from him, making her a worthy opponent to the former chess champion.

John Porter took his cue. "Do you think they are here?" he asked while looking around.

As if on cue, a stern looking orthodox Jewish man and woman were approaching them from the left. The Porters had often seen the payots—long uncut locks of hair on the orthodox Jews—as well as their dark suits and top hats. They made imposing figures—ones that should have put Esther at ease but were causing the opposite effect. The man stepped forward, looking first at the Porters with an expression nothing short of unfriendly, then at Esther. "Esther Gerstein," he said, fairly spitting out the last name as though it were poison.

Esther stammered, "Yes, sir, I am Esther." She felt ashamed that she did not state her last name but seemed tongue-tied and stiff in this man's presence.

He gave her a quick nod and said, "We are Isaac's family. You are to come with us." He gave a curt look toward the Gentiles and then turned to go.

Esther looked at Gladys with the eyes of embarrassment. What could she say? What *should* she say? "Thank you for all you have done for me, Gladys," she stated simply and turned to go.

218

Gladys watched for a moment before snapping into action. "Wait!"

Esther stopped and turned. The Hirsches stopped as well, looking first at Esther with a look of impatience, then to Gladys with disdain.

Ignoring them, she went to Esther and took her hands. "Do you want to go with them?" she whispered fervently, "because you are more than welcome to come with my family. We have plenty of room, and you can stay as long as you like." Her eyes were pleading.

Esther felt torn. "I—I think I should go with them, Gladys." She pulled her friend close and whispered in her ear, "but please come to see me," she said desperately as she pressed the slip of paper containing the address into Gladys' hand.

As they separated, Gladys gave her a knowing smile and nodded. "I will, and soon."

As she turned to follow, David began to cry and reached for Gladys. She hugged him, murmuring words of comfort before letting them both go. Esther resumed following her people, leaving her new friends behind but knowing that something was not right.

She mused as she walked several paces behind the austere couple. *The Porters welcomed me with open arms, while my people continue to reject me, even here in America.* The thought made her sad. *Will I ever belong anywhere, Father?*

In silence, they made their way through the maze of people to a parked car. Mr. Hirsch opened the trunk and placed her belongings there, then opened the front door for his wife and the back door for Esther and David. Emotions swirled about in Esther's mind. She felt anxious about staying with these people, lonely for her dear friend Gladys, and above all, tired. If she could only be settled!

As Mr. Hirsch maneuvered into the busy streets, Mrs. Hirsch cleared her throat and turned slightly toward the back seat. "Did you have a good trip?" she asked, her eyes never quite meeting Esther's.

"Yes, we had smooth waters for most of the time." Esther could see that Mrs. Hirsch was making an attempt to be cordial.

"And how is our Isaac?"

Esther thought for a moment. *Brokenhearted that I left him,* she was tempted to say. "He is doing well. He was a wonderful help to me and my father." The words brought sadness that even Mr. Hirsch could hear in her voice.

"Isaac is a good man," Mr. Hirsch stated in a voice that said much more than the simple sentence implied. She wondered how much Isaac had told them about her. Her face reddened with anger at the thought of her private affairs being spelled out to these strangers in a letter. Who knows how many people had read about her—had formed their own opinions against her? The image of a swastika loomed in her mind. It seemed to mock her and laugh at her; however, Mrs. Hirsch had said something, interrupting Esther's thoughts.

"I'm sorry, what did you say?" she asked, trying to pay better attention.

"I said how is your father? I'm sure it was hard to see you go."

Esther's voice was just above a whisper, "Yes, it was hard to leave him there." She thought of him and Leah, glad they had each other. He would be safe there, and Leah would help him to build a new home.

She had hardly noticed which direction they had gone or how long they had been driving, but a glance out the window revealed different buildings. As they drove, the skyscrapers gave way to neighborhoods. She could tell that they had passed out of a Gentile community and into the Jewish quarter just by watching the people and their dress.

They had taken so many turns; Esther knew she would be lost. The rows and rows of buildings all linked together fascinated her. Some sections would bubble out and were made of different color block, but they all looked so much alike that she wondered how anyone could tell them apart.

Before she knew it, Mr. Hirsch was parking the car in front of one such building. As she looked more closely, she could see subtle differences in each townhouse. As he exited the car, she watched as Mr. Hirsch quickly walked up to the reddish colored section on the end of the row of townhouses. It was adorned with window boxes bursting forth with color. Tulips and daffodils nodded their heads her way. "Oh," Esther gasped at the sight.

Mrs. Hirsch looked at her with a startled look. "What is wrong, dear?"

Esther's eyes misted. "The flowers! They are so beautiful!" She hesitated to share her thoughts but felt she would burst if she held it all inside. "The colors—I've not seen such beauty since I left my home in Amsterdam," she finished haltingly.

220

Mrs. Hirsch's countenance softened. "You've been through so much for someone your age. I can't imagine the horrors of what you have seen and experienced."

She reached back over the seat and gently brushed the wayward strand of hair from David's forehead. He ducked shyly but did not turn away. Their eyes locked, and Esther could sense a kinship developing. She smiled for the first time, and it felt good.

The streets were busy with Jewish people everywhere, each coming and going about their business. She saw children clustered together, playing childhood games. It brought back so many memories of her own childhood. Down the street, standing in front of a doorway, stood a group of men, mostly older, their beards and payots bobbing as they held an intense discussion.

As Esther stepped onto the street with David's little hand in hers, it seemed as though every eye was upon her. As if in slow motion, she turned in every direction, looking into the eyes of strangers who already seemed to hate her. She gazed pleadingly into Mrs. Hirsch's face and allowed the woman to lead her into the townhouse. The older woman looked embarrassed and ready to get her off the street. At that point, Esther knew she would not stay here any longer than was necessary. Her face burned with indignation. Once inside, Mrs. Hirsch turned to face her.

"I'm sorry, Esther. People ask and talk and make everything their business." She seemed frustrated. "We were more than happy to help Isaac's friend; we just didn't realize all the circumstances." She looked hesitantly in the direction that her husband had fled. "Solomon nearly refused Isaac's request."

As much as Esther hated the situation, she felt sorry for this woman. "Please, don't worry. I will make other arrangements. I just appreciate your honesty." Her gaze trailed to the floor. "This is why I left Israel. I thought it would be better here."

Miriam Hirsch was not a strong woman. She did not like conflict and usually succumbed to her husband's demands. Having no children of their own, she felt the shame of her barrenness and ached for Solomon. After all, no heir was the worst thing that could happen to a Jewish man. Although they never knew the reason for the situation, Miriam blamed herself for her barren condition.

"I'm so sorry," Miriam said. "I will do what I can to help you." She turned toward the inner doorway that led into the townhouse and opened the door. Esther mutely followed. She was amazed at the spaciousness of the building. Directly before them was an open stairway. The woodwork was a rich, dark walnut that had been polished to perfection; a thick carpet runner with patterns of dark reds, black, and gold covered the center of each step, accenting the dark wooden spindles. The staircase curved near the top as the banister ran below a beautiful multi-paned window. The glass glistened as the late morning sun streamed through between heavy brocade draperies.

"Your home is beautiful, Mrs. Hirsch," Esther exclaimed.

"Please, call me Miriam," the older woman replied. "The God of the universe has blessed us—at least materially."

Esther could sense Miriam's sadness. As they climbed the staircase and walked past several bedrooms, all beautifully furnished, Miriam explained, "We have never had any children of our own. We had often hoped that Isaac could come to America. We could offer him so much! And then when his parents were so brutally murdered—" She stopped in the upstairs hallway and turned to face Esther. "What kind of people would do such a thing?" Her eyes were filled with hurt, causing Esther to reach for her hand.

"Wicked people," Esther said sadly. "They seem to be everywhere, hating and killing. Israel is no exception. But Isaac's heart is with many others there. He is working so hard to make a homeland for our people."

Miriam snorted. "And what do we need with a homeland? My homeland is here, not in some dusty piece of desert."

Her response surprised Esther. After seeing the fervor in everyone's eyes living in the Promised Land and sensing the excitement among her European counterparts in finally getting there safely, she just assumed all her people felt the same way.

"Here we are," Miriam continued almost in the same breath. "This will be your room." She motioned to the last door on her left and entered. The room was decorated in various shades of blue. Two large windows were heavily draped in a soft pastel blue pattern. Shears covered the windows. A beautiful four post bed sat between them, and matching tables and lamps were centered in front of each window. Another window graced the front wall and sported a window seat. Esther knew that would be a favorite spot, if she were to stay.

Miriam led the way across the thick white carpet to another door next to the window seat. "Here is your bathroom, and this door leads to David's room." She walked across the black and white tiled flooring to open yet another door. Esther's eyes grew wide as she stepped into the most beautiful nursery she had ever seen.

She had always known that her home in Amsterdam was in one of the wealthier communities. She had felt only pride in her childhood home—truly one of the finest on her street—but it could not compare to the wealth and opulence before her. It seemed as though every color of the rainbow was splashed about the room: in the nursery rhymes depicted on the walls and the abundance of toys in every shape and size that were scattered around the room.

Stuffed animals sat invitingly on the bed, in the chairs, and tucked into every corner. She heard a slow intake of air from David and looked down to see the wonder in his own eyes. "Oh, Mommy," he breathed before walking over to a little monkey sitting on a child-size rocker. The monkey's little beady eyes and inviting smile attracted David's attention above all the rest. He gingerly picked up the little friend and held him to his cheek, rocking back and forth. Miriam's eyes were shining as she walked over to David and knelt beside him.

"Well now, I see that our new little friend has caught your eye."

David instinctively held out the little monkey to the woman he was not certain he could trust. His actions seemed to melt Miriam's heart and any reserve she might have still harbored. "Oh, no David. You may hold the monkey," she explained as she gently placed him back in David's hold. He hesitated for only a minute before he squeezed him fiercely.

Miriam laughed. "But I'll warn you, he's a bad little monkey! He's always getting into scrapes."

She rose and went to the bookshelf that had escaped Esther's notice. It was loaded with children's books. She pulled one off the shelf and went to the rocker, which sat between the window and the shelves. Sitting down, she held the book up for David to see. On the front cover was a picture of the little monkey and his name: Curious George. David looked up at his mother as if asking for permission. She nodded, and he was on his way to Miriam's lap and the adventures of Curious George.

Esther smiled lovingly at the two, wondering just what she was to do. As they continued to devour the story, she turned back to her room. As she wandered about she wondered, *Am I to stay here, Lord?* Already she could see the bond that was forming between her son and Miriam. She knew he would be a balm to the woman's empty soul, and she could be the grandmother that David never had. *Lead us, Father, as you already have in so many wonderful ways.*

With the prayer barely off her lips, David came bursting through the room and into her arms. "Grandma Hirsch said I could keep Curious George. May I, Mommy?"

She looked into his pleading eyes as Miriam entered the room. "Please, Esther. I would love for him to have it."

Esther smiled. "Thank you," she whispered, then knelt before her son. David's smile spread into a huge yawn as he rubbed his eyes. "I think you have had a very busy day, young man. Do you think George is tired too?"

David held the monkey out to eye him. "I think he is, Mommy." He turned to Miriam. "Can he sleep with me?"

Miriam smiled. "I think he would be glad to." She looked at her watch and exclaimed, "My, I didn't realize how late it is. Are you hungry? I could have Libby bring you a snack. She is our part-time help. I believe that she is probably in the kitchen preparing dinner."

"I'm hungry, Mommy!" David's eyes brightened.

Esther laughed. "Well, if it isn't any trouble."

"No trouble at all." Miriam walked to the door and pushed a button that was on the wall next to a speaker.

"Yes, ma'am," came a voice.

"Libby, could you please send up a light snack for Esther and David?"

"Yes, ma'am," the voice from the wall answered.

Esther and David both stood spellbound. "Does she live in the wall?" David frightfully asked, his eyes wide in wonder.

Miriam turned, looking a bit confused until understanding dawned on her face. "Oh, no David. This is an intercommunication system. It's like a telephone in each room. Libby is down in the kitchen. Perhaps after dinner we will go and meet her. After you have a snack, I think it would be a good idea for all of you to rest," she said, seeing the fatigue on Esther's face.

"Thank you again, for all you have done for us, Miriam. Isaac was right about you."

The comment caught Miriam's attention, and surprise showed on her face. "Really?"

"Yes, he said you would make us feel welcome, and you have." Esther's face clouded. "But I don't want to cause any trouble with your husband." She spoke the words softly, not wanting David to hear. She needn't worry, for David was busy with his little monkey friend.

Miriam was positioning two chairs beside a table and pushing the vase of flowers aside to make room for the coming tray. She looked thoughtfully at Esther before speaking. "Time, Esther. Just give it some time. I have learned over the years that my husband's bark is worse than his bite."

At that moment, a young girl entered the room carrying a tray of food and drinks. Her shoulders were squared and her stance straight. She looked the picture of servanthood in her black dress and spotless white apron. Her beautiful blonde hair was pulled back in a bountiful ponytail, and her bright blue eyes sparkled as she smiled. Esther knew she couldn't be much younger than herself, although the freshness on her face and the liveliness in her step made her seem like a schoolgirl.

"Esther, this is Miss Libby Steinmeyer. She is new to this country as well," Miriam explained, "and she is a Godsend!"

She turned to the maid. "Libby, this is Esther and her son, David."

Esther noted the absence of any last name and felt that it would be best to yield to the desires of her hosts and remain somewhat anonymous. She knew who she was, and that was all that mattered.

"It's good to meet you, Mrs. Esther. And you too, David." Libby set the tray on the table and turned to Mrs. Hirsch. "Will there be anything else, ma'am?" she asked politely. Esther didn't miss the European accent. If she was not mistaken, it sounded German.

"No, thank you, Libby. I'm sure you are very busy with dinner preparations."

Libby nodded and left the room.

"Well, I'll leave you two alone. I have a few errands to run, but if you need anything, please feel free to ring Libby. Dinner will be served at five o'clock, if you would please be sure to be in the dining room at that hour."

"Again, thank you," Esther said as she moved toward Miriam. She embraced the woman, noting her surprise and stiffness. But as Esther held her for just a moment, she felt the tension leave and the hug was returned. They smiled their goodbyes, and Miriam was gone. Esther moved to quietly shut the door, sighing deeply.

"Mommy! Look at all the good food!" David exclaimed as he made his way to the table. Esther lifted the lid of the carafe to find ice-cold milk. Removing the napkin from a plate, she found little sandwiches made with different kinds of spreads. Several thick slices of Babka were set aside on another plate. Her mind whirled back to her mother spreading the dough with chocolate and twisting it into the traditional braided loaf. She hadn't thought of it or tasted it in years!

She looked over to see David watching her. "What's wrong, Mommy?"

"Oh, David, it just looks so good, and I was just thinking about how good God has been to us." She smiled as she placed Curious George beside the vase. "Let's thank Him for this wonderful food and for the Hirsches."

They bowed their heads and prayed, both hearts overflowing with joy. Everything tasted as wonderful as it looked. When they finished, Esther tucked David into her own bed beside her. "Aren't I going to sleep in my bed?" he asked as his eyes already drooped in sleep.

"Tonight, my little fellow. You and Curious George can have a whole bed to yourselves." But David was already asleep.

Esther slipped in between the satiny sheets and looked around the room one more time before sleep overtook her as well. She was startled awake by a sharp buzzing sound. She sat up in bed and frantically looked around. Again, the buzzer sounded. She realized that it was the intercom, and hurried to the wall unit, not certain what to do. Hesitatingly, she spoke, "Hello?"

"Excuse me, ma'am, but Mrs. Hirsch wanted me to ring and see if you needed anything before dinner."

Esther anxiously looked at the clock on the bureau. Four-thirty!

"Oh, no, I think I can manage, but thank you," she spoke haltingly at the speaker.

"Alright, ma'am." And the room was silent once again.

She turned to the bed and saw David was stirring. Walking to the side of the bed, she looked down into his cherub face, reaching down to stroke his cheek and push back the hair from his face. "David," she called softly, "it's time to wake up."

He stirred again and groaned a sleepy groan. Slowly his eyes slid open, and his ever-ready smile played on his lips. "Hi, Mommy," he said groggily. Then, as though shocked into action, he sat up, looking for Curious George. The little monkey had somehow worked his way under the pillow. "You curious little monkey! What are you looking for?" he asked as he pulled the toy into his arms.

Esther pulled him onto her lap and finger combed his hair. "Are you hungry?"

"No, but I—" He left the sentence dangle as he headed for the bathroom.

Esther followed, taking time to help him finish, then washed his face and hands and tucked in his shirt. It was a little wrinkled, but she knew the others in his bag would look no better. Peering into the mirror, she saw her hair and face needed some attention too. "Why don't you take George into your bedroom for a minute while Mommy freshens up?" There was no argument as he scampered to the nursery.

After retrieving a few of her toiletries from her luggage, Esther worked at making herself presentable. She felt as though they were both on trial and felt she needed to say as much to her son. Although he was a good little boy, a reminder to mind his manners certainly wouldn't hurt.

Finding him at the bookshelf looking at another Curious George book, she knelt beside him, turning him toward her and laying the book aside. "David, I need for you to be on your best behavior at dinner tonight."

"Yes, ma'am," he said obediently. He looked as though something was bothering him. He cocked his head to one side in his comical little way before asking, "Why did Mr. Hirsch seem so cranky? Doesn't he like us?"

She smiled at the boy's intuition. "Well, I don't think he's used to having strangers in his home."

"But Grandma Hirsch doesn't think we are strange," he stated.

"Yes, but we had all afternoon with Mrs. Hirsch. We only had the car ride with Mr. Hirsch, and it's very hard to drive in America." She knew it was not the exact truth, but the bare facts would be lost on his mind. "So you just be the sweet little boy you are and let Mr. Hirsch get to know you."

"Should I call him Grandpa?" The question was so innocent, but it nearly made Esther choke.

Suppressing her urge to laugh, she swallowed hard before replying. "No, we better call him Mr. Hirsch."

The timid duo headed out into the hallway and down the stairs. It had been a struggle for David to leave his new friend on his bed, but Esther was proud of his quick obedience. Not a squeak sounded from the majestic stairway. Truly, the house was silent as a tomb—the quiet unnerved her. She remembered seeing the dining room as they came in from the foyer, and as they turned at the bottom of the stairs, she could hear voices floating in from the dining room. Miriam was pleading with her husband. "Please, Solomon, won't you at least give them a chance?"

The answer was not so quiet. "That boy is the son of a German officer who killed our people, and that woman spurned your own nephew!"

"But—" It was all that Miriam had a chance to say.

"Silence!"

Esther was shocked at the ferocity with which the word was spoken. *How sad*, she thought. Her heart broke for the dear woman with an empty heart.

***

During dinner, Mr. Hirsch was cordial. Miriam tried to ease the tension with little success. David was an absolute angel, and Esther wanted to cry, never so glad for a meal to end. All she could think of was the verse she had read in Kurt's Bible. *"Better is a dinner of herbs where love is, than a stalled ox and hatred there with."* She wondered what Mr. Hirsch would think if he knew that a Bible was being sheltered under his roof as well.

That night, as she tucked David into the extravagantly carved bed under luxurious blankets and matching counterpane, she knew she could not stay in a place where she was not wanted, no matter how beautiful.

"Mommy, do we have to stay here?" he asked. "Grandma Hirsch is so nice, but I don't think Mr. Hirsch will ever like us."

Sadness etched her smile as she spoke, "No, David, I don't think he will."

"But why, Mommy?"

What could she tell her son? How many times would he ask the same question in the coming weeks? "I can't answer that David, but please know it has nothing to do with your behavior. You were a perfect angel at dinner, and Mommy is very proud of you!" She snuggled him close to her, enjoying the sweet childish scent of his hair. "You have a wonderful night's sleep." She kissed him and tucked Curious George a little closer under his arm. He smiled trustingly and murmured his good night.

That night, though tired and confused, Esther sat for a long time nestled in the window seat, staring out across the city. The streets were quiet except for an occasional pedestrian. Two lovers strolled along the sidewalk, arm in arm, making Esther ache inside. She felt so alone—so lost and abandoned. She buried her face into her hands and wept hot tears of rejection. *I thought it would be different here, Father*, she prayed. *Will my people ever accept me and my dear son?*

Will my people ever accept My dear Son? The thought came out of nowhere. *Is that how God feels?* She wondered. Her thoughts moved on to safer ground: her story—Esther, the queen. Was she ever a mother? Did she know the burden of a mother's heart? Certainly she carried the burden of her people in her heart, but was that the same as a child? She felt drawn to the book that was more and more her only source of comfort.

Tucking herself into bed, she started in the Psalms, feeling the peace and comfort wash over her as her heart opened to the words— God's words. She continued to read passage after passage from the prophets, the words strengthening her as she too felt as though she was in bondage.

One verse in Ezekiel seemed to give her the resolve she needed to continue to follow God's guidance: *"And they shall comfort you, when ye see their ways and their doings: and ye shall know that I have not done without cause all that I have done in it, saith the Lord GOD."* She closed the book and slid it deep under the covers. *Oh Father, I know you have led me here. Please continue to show me the way. Forgive my doubting spirit. Show me your way.*

Gladys was glad to be home. Her family surrounded her with love and laughter as they talked late into the night. They plied her with questions that she was glad to answer.

"So, tell us about your mysterious friend," her father asked, crossing his long legs and settling into a more comfortable position. The bowl of popcorn had long ago been depleted, and the soda bottles were just empty reminders of the evening treat.

"Oh, I wonder how dear Esther is fairing this evening?" The question bothered her. "I should have insisted that she come home with me."

"Is she Jewish?" her mother questioned.

Gladys related all that Esther had told her. They sat spellbound, often shaking their heads or nodding in understanding. She came to an end, the frustration edging her words, "And then to watch her trail off after that, that—"

"Gladys," her father reprimanded before she said something she would regret. "They are an austere people who have just suffered unbelievable atrocities at the hand of the Germans."

She started to form a rebuttal but his hand halted her. "You just need to continue to be a friend to her and help if and when you can. She may not want your help now that she is back with her people."

"But how can you say that?" Gladys asked incredulously.

"Their religion is their salvation, Gladys." The statement gripped Gladys' heart like an iron fist, and she was suddenly very tired. Her father spoke what all of them were thinking. "I'd say we've all had enough talk for one night."

Heads nodded in agreement as each picked up the debris of their evening snack, said their good nights, and headed to their rooms. John Porter put his arm around his daughter. "Keep praying, Gladys. And I think you should pay your friend a visit."

Gladys looked up into his loving face. "I missed you so!" She rested her head on his shoulder. "I just hope I can help her."

She gave him a hug and headed up the stairs to her long-awaited room. Pasha had already retired for the night right in the middle of the bed. "Hate to tell you, Pasha, but I'm home for good!"

The large gray cat stretched out as if to cover as much territory as possible. Gladys laughed as she pushed under the covers, causing Pasha obvious discomfort and disapproval. Disgustedly, the enormous feline moved to her old spot at the bottom corner of the bed.

Chapter Twenty-Five

"Trust in the Lord with all thine heart;
and lean not unto thine own understanding.
In all thy ways acknowledge him, and he shall direct thy paths."

Proverbs 3:5,6

Summer of 1950

A heavy fog had settled over the city during the early dawn. Esther's mind was in a fog as well, as she slowly surfaced from a deep sleep. Her night had been dreamless, and she had trouble understanding where she was.

As she slipped back into a restless morning sleep, her dreams took her back to Amsterdam. She was rushing from the house in fear of being late for school. Her dear friend Silla was with her, and they were running down the street. Suddenly, German soldiers seemed to appear from everywhere, surrounding them and threatening to arrest them for running in the streets. Clinging to each other, the girls shivered with fright, not knowing what would happen to them.

One officer broke through the cluster of uniforms, taking charge of the situation. It was Kurt. Esther gasped and ran to him. He held her in his arms protectively while Silla looked on in horror. Esther tried to explain to Silla who this SS officer was, but she just shrank away.

At the sound of approaching footsteps, they all turned to see Gabriel running toward them. Esther could feel her heart race. What would he think? Why was she in the arms of a German officer? As he drew near, Esther saw the look on his face turn from fear to hurt. He looked into her eyes, then up into the eyes of her husband, and turned away. A sob caught in her throat as she buried her face into Kurt's chest.

She awoke with a sob, holding her pillow tightly. It took a moment for her to realize it had been a dream. How strange! As she sifted back through the illusion, her heart sank at the recollection of all her losses and failures. Tears stung at her eyes, brought on by the hopelessness of her present situation. *Will there ever be a place for me,* she cried to God.

"*Thou art come to the kingdom for such a time as this.*" Esther nearly gasped at the solidity with which the statement had come. She repeated the words in her mind: *Thou art come to the kingdom for such a time as this.* America? Was God once again reaffirming His leading of her to America? Slowly but ever so surely, a wonderful peace of God settled upon her, and she was rebuked again for her lack of faith. She reached for the Bible and began to read.

David slept late that morning, giving Esther plenty of time to gather strength for the day from God's Word. She had spent a great deal of time in prayer and was up and dressed when a knock came to her door. She hesitatingly walked across the room and opened it. Libby stood there with a tray laden with food. "Mrs. Hirsch thought you might be hungry," the girl said with a smile.

Esther stepped back, allowing her to enter and place the tray on the table. "Thank you, Libby."

The maid turned and gave her a quick curtsy. "Is there anything else, you need?"

Yes, a home and a friend, Esther thought. "No, thank you though for asking."

Libby seemed to hesitate, wanting to say something. Her eyes were a sapphire blue, so like Kurt's, Esther thought. They sent forth a message of empathy and caring that tugged at Esther's heart. "I know what it is like to be in a strange country—not wanted because of who you are," the girl said. "If you ever need a listening ear, just press this." She walked over to the door and pointed to the little button, her eyes twinkling as she left the room.

How sweet, thought Esther. And for the first time since arriving at the Hirsch household, she felt like she had a friend who could truly understand her situation.

***

Gladys had allowed two days to pass before she decided it was time to visit Esther. She didn't want to be too forward, but the unknown and the stern image of the Hirsches drove her to action. She chose her clothing carefully—a dark skirt and plain white blouse. Somehow the outfit seemed less offensive than bright colors or slacks.

Hailing a cab, she gave the driver the address that Esther had given her on the ship. Again, Gladys marveled that God had placed Esther and David just a few blocks away from her home. She rarely visited the Jewish Quarter but was familiar with it, as she was with many of the Jewish ways. Having always been fascinated with God's chosen people, Gladys had taken several courses on Jewish culture and traditions—one reason for her recent visit to Israel. She marveled at the young Jewish girl's story, knowing that God's hand was directing her path.

She watched out the window as the scenery changed from Gentile to Jewish, awed at the stark contrast between the two ethnic groups. The cab stopped in front of an impressive row of townhouses. She paid the cabby, double checked the house number, and walked to the door.

"Libby!" Gladys blurted out as the young maid opened the door.

"Gladys! What are you doing here?" Libby asked, just as surprised. Her face brightened when Gladys explained her mission.

Gladys continued to speak, "You know I feel badly that you have been coming to our church now for several months and I never bothered to ask you about your work." Gladys smiled.

"I understand. You haven't been back very long. Did you have a nice trip?"

"Oh, yes! That's how I met Esther,"

"Oh that's wonderful." Libby lowered her voice, "She needs a friend." Her eyes spoke volumes before she resumed her servant demeanor. "Please come in. I'll show you the way."

Gladys followed the young woman as she led her into the foyer. The maid turned to her, and in a quiet tone said, "I believe Esther would rather your visit take place in her room."

She led her up the stairs and down the hallway. Gladys was impressed with the obvious wealth displayed at every turn. As they neared the rooms, she heard the familiar voices singing a childish song. David's laugh nearly brought tears to her eyes. How she loved the boy!

Libby knocked and waited for a reply, and a smiling Esther answered her, standing there with David in hand. As soon as David saw Gladys, he squealed her name and was in her arms. "Oh, Miss Gladys, I missed you," he said with childlike seriousness

"I missed you too, David," she replied as her eyes met Esther's, "and your mother."

Without any hesitation, David was dragging Gladys through Esther's room to show her his room. Libby smiled and quietly closed the door. She wondered at the sense of protection she felt for this woman and her son. She knew they would not be here long, having overheard last night's conversation between the Hirsches.

Mr. Hirsch's bitterness toward the little boy especially cut to the heart. She didn't know the circumstances behind his birth, but it surely wasn't his fault that his father was German—it probably wasn't his mother's fault either. Libby was ashamed of the atrocities that had taken place in her country. She had been a young innocent girl when she followed blindly the workings of the Third Reich, as did many of her people. Libby had fled to America not to avoid the difficulties her country now faced, but to minister to the Jewish population here in New York City. She longed to share the gospel with them, especially the children, which was one reason that she had sought work with a Jewish family. She wondered how fast Mr. Hirsch would have dismissed her if he knew that some of her relatives had been officers in Hitler's regime!

"Oh, Gladys," Esther cried as she pulled her into a fierce hug. "I have missed you so much."

Gladys did not miss the sob and pulled Esther back to look into her eyes. "Esther, what is wrong?"

Esther sighed deeply. "Isaac's uncle does not want us here. He hates the fact that David's father was a German officer."

The deep hurt that Gladys saw in Esther's eyes made pity well up within her. As the two women sat in the bedroom, Esther told of the events of the past few days.

"I'm so sorry. You don't have to stay here. Please, come with me. Mother and Dad have already said it would be fine with them. You could come today!"

"I hate to leave Miriam, but I know I cannot stay."

"You can always come and visit Mrs. Hirsch while Mr. Hirsch is at work."

Esther was quiet as she thought through her options. It didn't seem as though she had many. "I think, under the circumstances, that would be best." She looked into her dear friend's eyes continuing hesitantly. "I am Jewish, Gladys. I would like to live my heritage."

Gladys smiled broadly. "Did I ever tell you why I was in Israel?"

Esther thought for a moment. "I don't believe so."

Gladys' grin grew wider. "I was researching Jewish traditions and customs for one of my courses at the university. I have always been fascinated by your people, Esther."

Your people. Somehow the phrase had a hollow ring to it. Just exactly who were her people?

"Will you come with me?" Gladys was asking.

"I don't know what to do. I hate to just leave Miriam without saying goodbye."

"Is she here?"

"I don't think so." She went to the intercom and pushed the button. Gladys watched curiously.

"Yes, ma'am?" came the polite voice.

"Libby, is Mrs. Hirsch home?"

"No ma'am. I believe she is shopping."

Esther paused. "Thank you, Libby."

"Was there anything I can do for you?"

"No. I believe I will be leaving with my friend, but I will leave a note for Mrs. Hirsch."

"We will miss you, ma'am."

"Thank you, Libby. And thanks again for all you've done for me. I'll be back to visit."

"That will be nice, ma'am. Goodbye and Godspeed."

"Goodbye, Libby." Esther heard a click, which ended the conversation. She looked up at Gladys, the emotions swirling across her face. "It will take me a minute to write a note. Would you mind packing David's belongings?"

"Sure, take your time." Gladys moved to the nursery to give Esther time to think.

Esther found paper and pens in the drawer of the end table. She took them to the table and sat down to write. What should she say? She tried to express her gratitude for all that they both had done for her and David. She also included Gladys' address and telephone number, asking Miriam to call her if she wanted them to visit. After a short note of thanks from David, she went and got the little boy and had him 'sign' his name. It was a bit scribbled, but you could make out a *D* on either end.

It only took a moment for Esther to pack the few belongings of her own. With a backwards look at the beautiful room, she took David's free hand, Curious George in the other, and followed Gladys to the street.

Although Esther had lived at Auschwitz with a Gentile husband, somehow this situation was different. She had had no choice about her living status before; this time it was her decision, and it bothered her. However, Gladys' family could not have been more supportive.

"We have a small apartment above the garage. Father thought it would be perfect for you," Gladys explained.

"But don't they rent it?"

"No. Actually, it is what our church calls a 'prophet's chamber.'"

The sound of it put Esther on edge. It sounded like holy ground.

Gladys laughed when she saw the horror in Esther's face. "Not to worry. Do you remember the story of the Shunamite woman whose son Elisha raised from the dead?"

Esther nodded.

"The family decided to add on a room for Elisha so that when he was in the area, he would have a place to stay. Some churches have made places available in which visiting missionaries and their families can stay. My dad is a great supporter of missions and decided to make the room above our garage into such a place. It's furnished and ready for use."

By the end of Gladys' explanation, they had reached the door that led upstairs. She unlocked it and led the way. They walked up an enclosed stairwell, which would have been dark had it not been for the three square windows spaced along the outside wall. At the top of the stairs was a beautiful stained glass window. Esther was instantly drawn to it.

"What a beautiful window!"

"Yes. I wish it were in our house. Dad thought that it would be a blessing to the folks who stayed here; some of them are pretty worn out from all the traveling they do."

Esther wanted to ask more—none of it made any sense to her—but Gladys had unlocked the door and was motioning her into the apartment.

The room was hot and stuffy, and Gladys immediately went to the windows and threw them open. "If we had known you were coming, we would have freshened up the room a bit."

Esther's doubts resurfaced. "Are you sure this isn't too much trouble?"

Gladys turned abruptly. "Not in the least! I'm sure you don't mind helping me to clean the place up."

"I'd be happy to."

"Me too," David echoed, not wanting to be left out.

The women laughed, and Esther gave him a quick hug. "You certainly may, my little man."

Gladys scanned the room. A combination of kitchen and living room, it was open and spacious. A cool breeze floated in from the window over the sink. Esther went to it and looked out on a small garden. Mrs. Porter was hanging cloths on a line that ran across the backyard. A wave of homesickness flooded her, but she quickly pushed it away. She didn't want Gladys to ever think that she was not eternally grateful for making a place for her.

"Here, I'll give you the grand tour," Gladys said, putting on her official tour guide air. She cleared her throat and walked to a door off the living room area. "Here we have the spacious master bedroom." She opened the door to a pleasant room, homey and comfortable. She smiled. "I realize it's not anything fancy like the accommodations you are used to ..."

Esther couldn't help smiling either.

Again, Gladys cleared her throat and proceeded with the tour. The middle door was the bathroom, and the door off of the kitchen was another bedroom. It certainly was not the beautiful nursery David had enjoyed for their short stay at the Hirsch residence, but it was already more like home to her. Gladys went to the closet and pulled down a box from the top shelf.

"I believe these need someone to play with them," Gladys remarked, her eyes twinkling at David. The little boy stared with delight. Gladys placed the box on the floor and watched with amusement as David opened it.

"Everything is perfect, Gladys!" Esther exclaimed.

"Not yet," Gladys spoke with mock sternness. "It will be perfect after we do some cleaning."

For the rest of the morning, the girls cleaned and chattered. It felt so normal and right to Esther to be here—Gentile or not. Little David was such a good helper. His dedication to his tasks made them both smile, aching to laugh, but not wanting to crush his enthusiasm. The place was sparkling by lunchtime.

"I'm hungry," David complained as they finished shaking the last rug.

Gladys came over to him and knelt before him. "How would you like a nice hot bowl of Jewish Penicillin and a peanut butter and jelly sandwich made with Challah Bread?"

David was furiously nodding his head while Esther just stared in wonder. "But ... how?"

Gladys laughed. "I told you it wasn't going to be that hard. Our favorite bakery is Swartz Bakery. It just happens to be Jewish."

"Can we eat now, Mommy?" David's pleading eyes brought a smile to Esther's face.

"Yes my little *arbiter*," she said, slipping into Yiddish.

"'Worker,' right?" Gladys exclaimed excitedly.

Esther smiled. "Sometimes I think you are as Jewish as I am."

***

Linda Porter had enjoyed the morning. Spring had always been her favorite season, and May was her favorite month. She had gotten a lot done: the laundry was all hung out to dry, supper was in the oven, and a nice pot of chicken soup was simmering on the back burner.

When Gladys had returned with Esther and David, Linda was thrilled. While Gladys had no special young man in whom she was interested, Linda was more than ready for grandchildren, and she was thrilled to play Grandma to that precious little boy. When she thought of all he and his mother had been through, it nearly broke her heart.

All three came bustling into the kitchen, ready for lunch. Almost simultaneously, she heard the front door open as John headed for the kitchen too.

"Mmm, what smells so good?" he exclaimed as he made his way first to her for an embrace and kiss, and then to the pot on the stove. "My favorite!" he exclaimed as he bent down to smell the delicious aroma.

He looked over at the threesome who had been watching him. "Well, hello," he commented, smiling first at Gladys and then Esther. His kind eyes went to David. "Are you hungry too?"

The little boy's face brightened, drawn to the man who looked like a giant to him. He nodded, his eyes wide with wonder.

"Well, Mother, let's eat," John said, and they all went to action. Esther and David were ushered into the dining room, where every-day dishes awaited them. Gladys poured the water and brought in the sandwiches. Esther noticed that the plate contained two different kinds: the offered peanut butter and jelly, and some other sort of spread.

Linda brought several other bowls of food. Some, Esther did not recognize. As if on cue, Linda explained, "These are potato chips, Esther. They are potatoes sliced thin and fried. I doubt that they are kosher, though," she said with a frown. There was also a bowl of applesauce and some sort of relish dish.

"And this," Gladys put in, "is mom's famous cabbage slaw. I think everything in this would be kosher, don't you, Mom?"

Linda agreed. Esther didn't have the heart to tell them all the restrictions about cooking utensils. The food certainly was kosher, but only if the utensils were as well.

"Shall we ask the Lord's blessing?" Mr. Porter spoke. "Our gracious Heavenly Father, we are grateful for Your many blessings. Thank You for a beautiful spring day to enjoy. Thank you for family and friends that can gather at this table today. We thank You for the food and ask You to bless it to our bodies. We pray in Jesus' name, amen."

David's eyes were already trained on the sandwiches as Mrs. Porter ladled the soup. John passed the dish to Esther, and she placed a sandwich on both her and David's plates. The boy ate as though he hadn't eaten all week. "David, slow down and mind your manners," Esther chided.

David looked sheepish. "Sorry, Mother. But it tasted so good!"

Everyone laughed. "It tastes so good because you worked up such an appetite," Gladys put in. "You should see the apartment, Mother. I don't think the furniture has ever shined so!"

David's faced beamed. "I dusted," he explained around mouthfuls of peanut butter.

"I have a great idea," John put in. "Why don't you give Esther and David a little tour of the store before someone gets too sleepy?"

"I have an even better idea," Linda said. "Why don't you leave David here with me, and you two girls can tour as much as you want?"

"Are you sure you don't mind?" Esther asked.

"Not at all. I think we can find something to keep us busy." Her smile was infectious, and David smiled back. Esther knew that he would be in good hands.

Chapter Twenty-Six

"Hope deferred maketh the heart sick:
but when the desire cometh, it is a tree of life."

Proverbs 13:12

"Our first stop is the famous Service Hardware—the pride of the neighborhood," Gladys announced. Her father, who was walking beside her, snorted at the comment.

"I think you have an overinflated opinion of the place. It's just a hardware store."

"But it's run by the best entrepreneur in the country."

John laughed and put his arm around Gladys. "Another exaggeration."

The act of love sent Esther's mind back to Israel, back to her father. John, the expert sleuth, reached over and put his other arm around Esther.

"All I know is that I get to show my wonderful store to the two prettiest ladies in town."

Esther and Gladys both looked at each other and smiled. It was the sweetest act of kindness that Esther had felt since arriving in America, and it gave her hope for the first time.

Service Hardware was something to behold for a woman from Amsterdam. They certainly had hardware stores there, but nothing like this. Long aisles sported everything from nails to draperies. Gladys chattered on and on as they perused the store. "My favorite section is the household goods. I've always loved looking at all the pots and pans and utensils."

As they neared the end of the aisle, they could hear a very irate customer on a tirade with some poor clerk. "I wonder who's in trouble now," Gladys commented as she changed direction and started heading toward the noise.

"This incompetent man has messed up my paint order *again*!" the woman was shouting. "Is it asking too much to have the paint that *you* sold to me match the drapery that *you* ordered for me?"

242

As they approached from one end of the store, John Porter came from the other. "Well, good afternoon, Mrs. Goldstein." His face was beaming.

"Don't 'good afternoon' me, John. Why do you hire such incompetence? This young man doesn't know blue from green. I do believe he is color blind!"

John had to agree with the woman. Johnny McAllen had just arrived in New York City and was desperate for work. John's soft heart had overtaken reason. He thought the boy could handle the paint charts, but this was the third complaint this month. Sam Goodall was the best paint mixer in town, but at the age of seventy-two, he was more than ready to retire; John had hated to let him go.

"We'll mix you another order of paint, Mrs. Goldstein."

"Can't you just fix this? You know how I hate waste," Mrs. Goldstein complained. She lifted the can of paint onto the counter. "I have the paint and the swatch of drapery right here."

"I'm sorry, ma'am. It's very difficult to remix colors," John said as she handed him the swatch. He held the material up to the splash of paint on top of the pan. The clash almost set his teeth on edge. He cast a woeful look at Johnny, who was pathetically trying to blend into the paintbrush display.

"I believe it just needs a little more cyan and maybe a touch of black," Esther said as she studied the colors.

Mr. Porter looked at her incredulously. "Do you know about mixing paint?"

"Not paint as much as glass," Esther explained. "My father owned a stained glass factory, and I often went with him. I always had an eye for colors," she finished rather sheepishly when she noticed that everyone was staring in her direction.

"Well, I'm just going to throw it out. Why don't you give it a try?" John urged.

He showed her back to the paint section. He knew most of the workings of his store, but this had been out of his realm—it had always seemed a bit magical the way Sam could come up with any shade of color under the sun. He watched with fascination as Esther pried open the can and placed it under the various color dispensers. She picked up a stir stick and methodically stirred, adding more pigment as needed.

Mr. Porter looked in wonder as the paint took on the exact shade to match the draperies—a perfect match. "You have yourself a job, Mrs. Gerstein," he nearly shouted. "That is, if you want one."

"Are you serious? I do need a job. I've been wondering how I would ever find one, and if I did, how I would get to work."

"That means I get to walk to work every day with one of the prettiest gals in town!" John smiled and held out his hand. "Shake?"

Esther beamed and took the man's hand.

"Good. You can start on Monday. That will give you the rest of the week to get situated and enjoy Gladys' company."

Esther's face clouded. "But what about David? What will I do with him?"

Mr. Porter smiled a wry smile. "Well, since I know for a fact that Gladys adores him and that my dear wife is aching for grandchildren—which doesn't look to be a reality in the near future— I'd say that between the two of them, they would be glad to watch David for you, at least until school starts."

After the paint incident, the girls finished their tour, which was now more of an orientation than just a friendly tour. Esther was fascinated and overjoyed at the prospect of working for Mr. Porter. She couldn't contain her excitement.

"Oh, Gladys, Jehovah has prospered my way when I had no hope."

"Praise God!" Gladys exclaimed. "Oh, this is going to be so fun! I can't believe that you will be living with us and working for Dad. He really likes you and David; and Mom, well, she's in seventh heaven."

"Seventh heaven?"

Gladys laughed at Esther's puzzled look and hugged her. "It's just a saying. It just means that she is really, really happy. Hey, I've got a great idea! Let's celebrate!"

She left Esther and ran to her father. Esther could see her talking animatedly. He smiled, looked as though he was mockingly reprimanding her, then opened his wallet and handed her some money. She counted it, looked at him in surprise, and then hugged him fiercely. She looked like a child who had just received her favorite candy.

"Alright, Mrs. Soon-to-be-working girl, you are about to have the time of your life!" Gladys linked her arm with Esther's and headed for the door.

The day became a blur to Esther. They hailed more taxis than she could remember. Gladys was completely undaunted by the task of maneuvering about this great city. They did everything.

"You haven't lived until you've eaten at Childs," Gladys explained.

The buildings and people, the sights and sounds—everything was so fascinating. They window shopped and walked through the newly restored Central Park. Bailey's Fountain made Esther feel as though she were back in Amsterdam. Their final stop was the Brooklyn Botanical Gardens inside Prospect Park, just a few blocks from the Porters' neighborhood. The spring flowers were absolutely beautiful.

"When I left Amsterdam, I never thought I would see such beauty anywhere, but this is beyond anything I have ever seen."

Gladys smiled, so full of peace and contentment she felt she would burst. "We'll have to bring David here—he'd love it."

"Oh, would you? I must admit that when we first pulled into the New York harbor and I saw such a big city, I was afraid that he would forget what trees and flowers looked like."

Gladys laughed. "You're not alone. When I told some of the other students in Israel that I lived in New York City, they just stared at me as if I was from another planet. They had so many questions." She chuckled as she remembered. "One girl asked me how I liked the trees and grass around the Hebrew University, as if I had never seen any before."

As they walked past the Japanese Hill-and-Pond Garden, Esther felt like she was in another world. The Japanese Cherry Blossoms were beautiful. The oriental ornaments and little arched bridge combined man's creation with the crowning beauty of the Creator, making a breathtaking sight. She turned to face her friend, her eyes glistening with unshed tears. "Oh, Gladys, I will always cherish this day."

The two strolled arm in arm, no words necessary as they drank in the beauty around them. Their bond of friendship tightened its grip, almost enabling Gladys to forget that their worlds were so very far apart. As they strolled, Gladys prayed, *Lord, help me to share the beauty of salvation with her. May she someday see the truth as clearly as she sees Your hand in all this.*

***

245

Life quickly took on a comfortable routine. Esther would breakfast in their apartment and then bring David to the Porter house, where they were always greeted with delight. David's love for Grandma and Grandpa Porter, as they were called, sometimes tugged at Esther's heart. How quickly they had replaced her own father in her son's mind.

She had written to Isaac, Etka, and her father, explaining where they were and all the events that had led them to this place. Isaac's letter was short and rather impersonal, but she could hardly blame him. How could she expect him to understand? Her life seemed to be slowly swirling away from all that had once been so comfortable and familiar. She knew none of them except Papa would understand how she could leave the home of one of her people and instead live with Gentiles. It was unheard of in Amsterdam and Israel, but this was America. Oh, how different America was from anything she had ever known!

After breakfast, Mr. Porter always read the Bible to his family. The scene took her back to her own childhood. Images of her mother and father, Ad and Daan all seated around a much different table but reading the Holy Scriptures together danced across her mind. How strange, yet how familiar.

On one particular morning, as Mr. Porter read, a loud noise exploded in front of the house. They all jumped in surprise, and then began to laugh.

"Mr. Hester must be taking his old jalopy out for a drive," Mr. Porter explained amidst the peals of laughter.

But all were suddenly still as they looked upon a much different reaction from Esther. She was shaking and trying desperately not to cry out with fright. Gladys was out of her seat and holding her friend in an instant.

"Oh, Esther, did the noise frighten you?" she asked as though speaking to a child, yet with no hint of condescension.

How could she explain? Must she explain? As she looked into all the faces around the table, including her son's, their pity and compassion overwhelmed her. The tears flowed uncontrollably.

Gladys looked to her father, resting Esther's sobbing frame upon her shoulder. She knew this was more than just a startled reaction. "What is it, Esther?"

Esther pulled back, reaching for the tissue in her pocket. She looked out the window at the trees swaying with a gentle morning breeze. She glanced in the direction of the stairway, where, in her home, there would have been a stained glass window. She sighed deeply, not quite knowing how to word her thoughts but feeling an urgency to explain and perhaps promote the healing that already had begun to take place in her heart.

"We—my family in Amsterdam—would read the Holy Scriptures much the same way you start every day. The day we were all taken, Papa was reading from the Ketuvim. We had just sat down to breakfast when a stone came crashing through the stained glass window into the dining room."

The memory made the tears flow, but she went on. "The soldiers pounded at the door and came crashing into our home, demanding that we follow quickly. We did as we were told." Her voice choked, but she swallowed, desperate to finish. "As we left the house, Mama—Mama shouted at the soldiers, and one of them just shot her."

Tears and sniffles echoed around the room. "I'm so sorry Esther," Gladys spoke as she wiped her own tears.

Esther felt a bit embarrassed. "I'm sorry, but the setting here and the sound just brought it all back."

"Are you okay, Mommy? I can go to work for you if you want." David's little face revealed such earnestness that it gave her strength and a smile. The storm had passed.

"No, Little David, I'll be alright."

Mr. Porter was staring at her with an expression of awe and wonder. "You are a brave young lady, Esther, and I marvel that God was so gracious to allow us to be a part of your life."

She smiled her gratitude. After a beautiful prayer of thanks and petition on her behalf, the meal continued a bit more subdued than usual, and then she and Mr. Porter were off to the hardware store. She could sense that Mr. Porter had something on his mind as they walked, and she didn't have to wait long to find out what it was.

"Esther, do you think it would help you to heal from all the tragedy you have faced to write it down?"

She looked up into his sensitive eyes. "You mean, like a journal?"

"Yes." He said with guarded animation, "Sometimes it helps to put the past behind us as we see it on the written page."

She was quiet as the idea settled over her. A journal? Could she write her thoughts? Did she really want to, or would it be better to push them all away as she had done in the past? "I don't know," she answered in hardly a whisper.

"Well, it's something to think about. We have some nice journals in the stationery department. Why don't you look them over and pick one out? I'd like you to have one—free of charge," he finished with his usual flourish.

Esther took him up on his offer and perused the books during her morning break. She found a nice one with a dark blue cover. The edges of the pages were buffed, giving the book an antique look. As she headed to the front of the store, she heard a familiar voice. She smiled as she saw Libby sharing some papers with Mr. Porter. She drew closer, waiting for them to finish, when Libby caught a glimpse of Esther, her face brightening.

"Mrs. Esther!" Libby said with surprise. "I didn't think I'd see you again." Her eyes radiated warmth and caring that drew Esther to her.

"You know each other?" Mr. Porter asked in surprise.

Both girls turned to look at him and smiled. Libby was first to speak. "Yes, I work for the family that Esther stayed with for a few days."

Understanding dawned on Mr. Porter's face. "Oh, yes—the Hirsches. I had forgotten that you worked there. What a small world."

Now it was Esther's turn to be confused. "But how do you know Libby?"

The two smiled, and Libby explained, "We attend the same church. I was just asking Mr. Porter if I could place a stack of these fliers on the counter."

Esther eyed the papers curiously.

"Here," Libby said. "You may have one."

Her smile mirrored the joy in the young girl's heart that Esther admired. She looked at the paper as Libby explained, "Mr. Porter allows me to use one of the empty office rooms for my Children's Club. I teach children Bible stories every Tuesday afternoon here, at four o'clock." Her face brightened. "Do you think David could come? He is such a bright little fellow."

Something in Esther's mind told her that she should not even be considering such a thing. She was Jewish, and David was Jewish. But Kurt's face flashed before her. David was only half Jewish, and the other half was Christian—very Christian.

Libby silently prayed for wisdom. "Mrs. Esther, we do start in the Old Testament. Later in the year, we will also have lessons from the New Testament. I have designed the classes for Jewish children. You could stop coming if it gets too uncomfortable."

"I think the lessons would be good for my son."

Libby smiled, trying not to look too surprised. "Oh, that is wonderful. It will also be a way for him to meet some children his own age." She turned back to Mr. Porter. "Thanks again. I'll see you next Tuesday." Smiling, she turned to go, leaving the two of them alone.

Mr. Porter looked at the fliers and then to Esther. "You are a very dedicated mother, Esther. I know you want to do what is best for David but aren't always sure what that means."

Esther shook her head in amazement. "Sometimes I think you read minds."

He smiled. "Let's just say, as Mr. Sherlock Holmes would say, I see details that most people overlook. Exposing David to our family would have been frowned upon in your country, right?"

Esther sighed. "Yes, you are correct."

"Do you think he has been harmed in any way because of it?"

She hesitated, not wanting to offend this gentle man who had come to mean so much to her. "Well, I know that my people would say yes. I have exposed him to another religion—a very dangerous religion. But your family reminds me more of my family than the Hirsches do. You love the same God that I do, and it shows in your caring ways." She looked up into his compassionate gaze. "I don't know what to believe anymore."

"Esther, keep searching after God, and He will show you the way."

At that moment, Mr. Porter was called away. Esther stood there a moment looking at the paper in her hand. *Oh, Papa! I wish you were here!*

"I will never leave thee, nor forsake thee." She had read these verses several days ago, and they seemed to be continually on her mind. *Thank you, Heavenly Father. I am truly grateful.* Her step was lighter, and a song was in her heart as she headed back to the paints to mix an order.

***

The day had been long and busy. Mr. Porter had joked with Esther, saying, "It's amazing how many of the contractors seem to migrate back to the paint section. I've sold more paint since you took over that department." Catching the alarming look in her eyes, he immediately regretted his words. "Oh, I was only teasing."

Seeing that his explanation was not repairing the damage, he came over to her, placing a fatherly hand upon her shoulder and praying for the right words to say. "I'm sure you know that you are a very attractive young woman. That is not a bad thing."

"Yes, I know, Mr. Porter. At first I hated my looks—they seemed to draw attention that I did not wish for. I saw that God used my attractiveness to lead me to Kurt and spare my life, but I don't want to cause you any trouble by ..."

Mr. Porter looked chagrined. "I have totally misled you by my teasing. The young men may be happy to gaze upon your beauty, but they are truly coming because of the wonderful job you are doing. Add to that the fact that you are always pleasant and go out of your way to please the customer, and that description fits someone who deserves a raise," he exclaimed, as though the thought had just come to him.

"You don't need to do that. I should be paying your wife for keeping David all day."

Mr. Porter hesitated, not certain he should share the tidbit of information that was on the tip of his tongue.

Esther read his expression and asked, "What is it that you are not telling me?"

He smiled. "Do you know what they call you?"

She looked at him doubtfully and shook her head.

"They call you the Merry Mixer, and it is meant as a compliment."

She rolled her eyes and smiled, then shook her head. No words would come to her mind. What could she say? She loved her job and enjoyed the challenge of mixing the colors to match the samples that the contractors brought in. She suddenly felt very tired.

Mr. Porter could sense her feeling—he had that uncanny ability—and acted accordingly. "Listen, you have been working so hard and have done such a great job. Why don't you take the rest of the afternoon off?"

She looked up in surprise. "Mr. Porter, you don't have to do that. I'm alright."

"I insist," he exclaimed in his usual bantering way as he lifted his arm to escort her to the door. He reached into his pocket and pulled out his wallet.

"You don't need to—"

"Tut, tut, my dear. You are getting a bonus today." He placed several bills into her hand and folded it shut, a look of tenderness flooding his face. "I should be paying you for allowing you and your son to bring us so much joy. David has become the highlight of my wife's days. He has filled a gap in her life. We think of you as our daughter." He gave her a quick hug and sent her out the door.

Esther stood there for a moment, not quite sure what to do with her new-found freedom. Her mind went back to the day with Gladys. The park! She would go to the park. As if she were a born and bred New Yorker, she hailed a cab and asked him to take her to Prospect Park. As she sat back in the seat, a thought came to her. Should she? She wrestled with the thought for only a moment and then impulsively leaned forward.

"Sir, would you happen to know where 681 Elm Street is?"
The man smiled. "Why sure, missy. It's right on our way. Would you like to go there?"

Esther's heart raced. "Could we just stop there for a moment, and then go to the park?"

"Absolutely," the man chimed.

He went several more blocks and then took a right-hand turn. Esther felt her heart jump into her throat as she read the street sign. She watched the numbers roll by. The houses were bigger than anything she had seen in Brooklyn. *Mr. Bachman must be even richer than the Hirsches*, she thought. She wasn't sure what she was expecting to find. Certainly Gabriel would be on his own by now. For all she knew, he could be back in Amsterdam.

"Do you want me to park here at the curb, ma'am?"

"Yes, that would be fine," she answered.

As if on cue, Gabriel came out of the front door, just as the cab pulled to the side of the street. Esther gasped. He was carrying a little girl, probably about two years old, and was talking to an older woman whom Esther guessed was his aunt.

Time froze as she took in the sight. There he was, as handsome as ever. His hair was cut slightly shorter, but the effect was becoming. He looked the part of a successful New York business man. All the

251

feelings that had been trampled and dampened, ignored, and pushed to the recesses of her mind came flooding to the forefront. She watched as he said goodbye and turned to leave.

"Let's go, Daddy," the little girl piped.

"Please, pull away," she nearly screamed, but not soon enough. As she looked back out the window, her eyes locked with Gabriel's. She tried to tear herself from the window but seemed mesmerized by his stare. He was there. And then the taxi was pulling away. She just stared ahead, her heart racing.

"To the park, miss?" the cabby asked, his voice quiet. He could see that she was shaken by the whole encounter. He loved his job—it provided him with an income and a lot of drama, but at times like these, he hated the unsolved mysteries it left in his overactive imagination.

"Yes," Esther choked. She willed herself to be still, but when the taxi was once again stopped, it was with a shaking hand that she paid the driver.

She walked blindly through the park, her thoughts whirling. What did it all mean? He was carrying a child—his child. He was married and living here in New York City. The tears blurred her vision.

"Oh, Gabriel," she sobbed in her heart. Her mind raced back to Amsterdam. He was standing there, looking at her with eyes so full of love. *I'll wait for you if it takes forever, Esther.* Had that been real? His letters. They too had been filled with love and longing, but that had been six years ago. She had lost him. No, the war had stolen her away.

Gabriel looked as though he was seeing a ghost, she thought. *He probably thinks that I am dead. Why would he think any differently?* She thought back to the letter that she had written, explaining all that had happened to her. Had he read it? Did he not want her to be alive? He probably wished that she was dead.

Esther found a bench far back from the path and sat alone with her thoughts. Something inside of her died the moment she saw him there with the child. He wasn't her Gabriel any longer, and the thought nearly crushed her. She now realized that much of her reasoning for coming to America was to find him. Her hopes had clung to the idea that maybe, just maybe, he would still be waiting for her, but it was not true. He belonged to another woman—the mother of his child.

Little David's sweet face played before her, and another image was not far behind: Kurt Gerstein, her husband. She too had a son and a husband—well, she had had a husband. She wanted to curl up and die, but she couldn't—she wouldn't. David needed her. *Oh, Father, my heart wants to be bitter. I can taste it! I want to hate You and Gabriel and Kurt for leaving me. Why did You lead me here? I should have stayed with Isaac.*

But you did not love Isaac, the thought came to her like a cold Arctic wind.

You are right, Lord. I did not love him, but I could learn to love him. Am I to return to Israel? The thought left her anxious and cold.

She continued her walk, losing all track of time; she only half saw the beauty before her. Even the splendor of the gardens seemed to have lost their appeal. The colors all washed together into a faded gray.

As the sky darkened, a resolve came to her. She would build a new life for herself and David. She would work hard, save the money, and wait upon God to lead. Perhaps they could move farther into the country—see a little bit of America. She had read several books about America, and the South fascinated her. What would it be like to never be cold?

At that moment, the thought was very appealing. She shivered and noticed that the day was far spent. In near panic, she rushed to the street, hailed a cab, and headed for home. Home! Little David was there waiting for her. The Porters were probably worried sick. Well, it would be a good distraction. She would forget this day, forget Gabriel, forget it all, and start living.

***

"Daddy sad?" Debby's little voice sounded frightened.

Gabriel looked over at her from behind the wheel. "Oh, nothing, Debby. I was just thinking about something."

"'Bout what?"

He should have thought before he spoke. At age two and a half, Debby was the most inquisitive child he knew. She wanted an answer about everything.

"I was thinking about all that Aunt Judith had said. She told me that you were a very good little girl today." He smiled, hoping that the little lie would be forgiven.

253

This time, it worked. Debby chattered on about her day with Auntie Jee, as she affectionately called her great aunt. Gabriel managed to nod an answer at the right time as his mind continued to race back to the face in the taxi—Esther's face.

He had to be mistaken. She was dead. But how could he ever forget that face? It couldn't be her, but it had to be her. He had seen the note from the authorities at Auschwitz saying his family had died and that the Raul family had been taken too. He tried to remember the exact wording of the letter. It had said something about David Raul surviving and then being taken somewhere. Had it mentioned her name? He couldn't remember. What if she was really alive? But why would she be in America? The thoughts continued to play over and over in his mind.

Chapter Twenty-Seven

*"But he knoweth the way that I take: when he hath tried me,
I shall come forth as gold."*

Job 23:10

"Let us sing the books of Moses, of Moses, of Moses. Let us sing the books of Moses, for He wrote the law."
Esther looked on with delight from the back of the room, watching David thoroughly throw himself into the song. She had been a bit skeptical about allowing David to come to Libby's Children's Club, but as she watched him sing with such enthusiasm, she was sure she had made the right decision.

Esther had been surprised at how many of the children were Jewish. She recognized them from the synagogue she was attending, and she couldn't help but wonder if some of the other young mothers were searching just like she was. America was different in so many ways, and the worship service was no exception. Perhaps it was just the newness of it, but Esther felt an emptiness she hadn't experienced in Amsterdam. Their synagogue at home had always lifted her spirit as they sang the songs of Zion and listened to their beloved rabbi share from the Word of God. Here, there was a lack of enthusiasm—it just seemed to be a required ritual instead of a time to worship God.

She thrilled at the lessons Libby taught of Moses, Daniel, and Gideon—all her heroes. The young woman was a born teacher. She made each lesson come alive, and Esther often found herself on the edge of her seat, holding on to every word. Libby's German accent somehow brought a sense of comfort, as if Kurt was very near, and at times her mind would wander back to those few precious days that they had had together. Oh, how he had wanted her to become a Christian. She didn't know what the future held—she only wanted the truth, and she knew being here with Libby was the right thing for her to do.

They had been coming for several weeks now, and Libby had warned her that she would soon be moving to the New Testament. Esther had to admit, she was anxious to hear what Libby would say.

***

"I'd like you to check over these invoices. Something is not adding up right." Mr. Bachman's voice trailed off as he looked at his nephew. "Gabriel?"

Gabriel started, "Yes? I'm sorry, sir. I—I didn't hear what you said."

Mr. Bachman was not a patient man, especially at the office. He was known for barking his orders, particularly when numbers did not fall into orderly little columns. But his heart was soft toward Gabriel. This young man had suffered so much loss and yet had shown himself to be made out of tougher stuff than Jacob had thought.

"What's bothering you?"

Gabriel looked into his uncle's softened gaze. Should he tell him? He'd probably think he was losing his mind. Somehow, he had to take that chance.

"The other week, when I was picking up Debby from Aunt Judith, I saw …"

"Yes?" Jacob said, a little too impatiently.

Gabriel's eyes went to his lap, where his fingers dug into the palms of his hands, then back to his uncle's face. "I saw a woman in a taxi."

Silence.

"And?" Jacob prompted, hoping that perhaps Gabriel's heart had started to heal and that he was showing interest in women again. He knew any of the single ladies at the office would have gladly comforted this young widower.

The silence was unnerving, but Gabriel plunged forward. "She looked like Esther," he finished lamely.

Jacob Bachman's face became a stone as his heart dropped to the bottom of his stomach. He was thankful that lunch had been several hours ago, or else he would have been sick. "Esther?" he asked with doubt lacing his voice, trying not to show any emotion.

Gabriel had left his chair and was pacing back and forth. "I know it sounds crazy, Uncle Jacob, but if you knew Esther, you would know. I mean that face ... her eyes ..."

Jacob tried to stall for time as his mind raced forward. "But it has been six years since you saw her. How do you even know what she would look like?"

"That's just it." Gabriel was gesturing frantically with his hands. "She wasn't a sixteen-year-old Esther. She looked to be about twenty-one, but it was Esther's face. And those eyes. Those eyes have haunted my sleep ever since then."

"But the papers from Auschwitz, they said—"

"They said that my family had not survived, and that David Raul had survived. What if Esther had survived too? Uncle Jacob, what if she is alive?"

Jacob's mind whirled to the letter they had burned. His thoughts raced faster than his heart. Should he tell him? Would it only mean more hurt? And why would she be here?

Gabriel caught the look in his uncle's eyes and questioned him.

"Do you know something more, Uncle Jacob?"

Jacob turned to the window. "Sit down, Gabriel."

The young man willed himself to be calm and sit quietly in the chair. He could hear his own breathing as he waited. Waited for what?

Jacob Bachman slowly turned and sat in his chair. How many difficult decisions had he made from this chair—decisions that changed the lives of men? But those all paled in light of this one. He stared into the face of the one whom he loved more than his own son. "Gabriel, please hear me out. I will tell you everything."

As Gabriel listened to the reasoning for burning Esther's letter, his whole body shook. Yes, he understood that he was married to Deborah when the letter had arrived. Yes, he knew that they had only his best interests at heart, but this was too much.

"What do you mean you burned the letter?" Gabriel shouted. "How could you? I am a man! I can make my own decisions!"

"Gabriel, you didn't read the letter. She was widowed, had a child to a German!" He spat out the word. "You were in no position to make any decisions, and what about Deborah? Would you have broken her heart?"

"And what about Esther? Do you realize what you have done? She was looking for me." Tears stung his eyes. "After all she had been

257

through. What do you think she thought when she never heard from me?" The thought nearly drove him crazy.

"You were in love with another woman. She was carrying your child!" Jacob shouted.

"I have never been in love with anyone but Esther!"

Even as he shouted the words, he knew they were not true. Deborah had been there for him. He did love her for all that she did and all that she was. Another thought broke into his thoughts like a lightning bolt, nearly buckling his knees.

The tears streamed down his cheeks, his face contorted. "She may still be alive if she had not married me."

"Don't be ridiculous. You have no way of knowing that." Gabriel looked like a wild animal, and it frightened Jacob, who worked to control his own feelings. "Gabriel, you need to calm down."

"You! Always playing God in everyone's lives. I—"

But he never finished. He had to get away. The cold, hard look in his eyes melted before Jacob, nearly breaking the older man's heart. Without another word, he was gone. Clerks watched as he ran to the stairs and stumbled out the door like a blind man.

The cold evening air hit him like a brick, but he forged down the darkening streets. He didn't know where he was going, nor did he care. Esther was alive. It could have been her. Oh, how would he ever find her? He would search the whole city if he had to.

As his feet carried him across busy streets, he continued to replay his conversation with Jacob. What was it that his uncle had said? She was a widow? Had a child? His steps slowed as the realization of her situation hit him. To a German? Poor Esther. What had she gone through?

Another thought came to him as he headed across another street. What name was she using? He would never find her. Maybe she didn't want to be found. Oh, how could he stand it if she was with another man? But if it had been Esther, she had seen him carrying Debby. What had she thought? That he was a happily married man, forgetting all about his Esther, his queen?

Gabriel's thoughts and blind steps had taken him to a park in an unfamiliar part of the city. As he looked around, he realized he had no idea where he was. Music floated across the air and seemed to draw him toward it. People were singing, singing about God. The thought made him curious. It was an unknown tune, but the words were now clear:

> *There is a place of quiet rest,*
> *Near to the heart of God,*
> *A place where sin cannot molest,*
> *Near to the heart of God.*

The words and sweet melody were like a balm on his tortured soul. He looked into the faces of each singer. Such a sweet peace and joy lingered on each brow. Every eye was earnest with the belief that was being sung. Then he heard it—

> *O Jesus, blest Redeemer,*
> *Sent from the heart of God,*
> *Hold us who wait before Thee*
> *Near to the heart of God.*

The forbidden name! He nearly turned and ran, but the words held him in his place.

> *There is a place of comfort sweet,*
> *Near to the heart of God,*
> *A place where we our Savior meet,*
> *Near to the heart of God.*

> *There is a place of full release,*
> *Near to the heart of God,*
> *A place where all is joy and peace,*
> *Near to the heart of God.*

The words "joy and peace" seemed to echo in his brain. When was the last time he had joy or peace? The thought was bitter to him. As his thoughts tumbled around in his mind, the group finished and was starting to mill about in the crowd that had formed. Gabriel turned to leave and found he was looking up into the face of a young man not much older than himself. "You look like you need a friend."

Gabriel stared into two pools of compassion. "I've just received some shocking news," he spoke, but it didn't sound like his voice, and he wondered if he had truly said anything.

The young man held out his hand. "Jason Himmel."

Gabriel looked at the offered hand, shook it, and said, "Gabriel Bachman."

"Would you like to talk?" The question was posed with no threat, no urgency, just friendship, and Gabriel could only nod.

They walked a bit as Jason began the conversation. He simply told Gabriel a little about himself, then posed questions that had Gabriel pouring out his whole story. Jason was a good listener—many had told him so—but this young man's story tore at his heart, giving him a deep love for his new friend.

"I watched you as we sang. I thought you were going to leave." Jason looked at him from his end of the bench where they had settled.

"I'm Jewish. The name," he couldn't say it. "It is a hated name to us."

Jason chose his words wisely. "He has many names. Did you know that the angels at His birth told His human father to name Him Emmanuel?"

Gabriel looked up in surprise. He had never heard such a thing.

Jason continued, "Emmanuel means 'God with us.' " He paused to let the thought sink into Gabriel's mind.

"God with us? I don't understand."

Starting with the Old Testament, Jason began to show Gabriel the words of Moses, Isaiah, Daniel and many of the prophets that foretold the Messiah's coming.

Gabriel was familiar with many of the prophecies. "I understand all that. I too am looking for the Messiah," Gabriel said softly.

Jason paused for a moment, looking deep into Gabriel's eyes. "He has come, Gabriel. He is the one we sang about. He is our source of joy and peace. Does your religion bring you joy and peace?"

Joy? Peace? Gabriel wondered if he even remembered what the words meant. He shook his head sadly.

"Gabriel, you have a form of godliness, but you deny the power of God."

It was true. Gabriel thought of the emptiness that he often felt in his heart. He had thought it was only because of losing Esther, and then Deborah, but it went past that. He thought that after his graduation from the university and his security in a good job, then he would have the contentment for which he longed.

When he had married, there was a sense of peace, and certainly there were happy moments. And when little Deborah had been born, he had felt an awesomeness at the thought that she was his. But his wife's death had made it impossible for him to have any real peace or joy. He realized for the first time that nothing had ever filled the void in his heart.

"God calls to each of us, Gabriel, no matter our religion. He says, '*I am the way, the truth and the life. No man cometh unto the father, but by me.'* "

Jason continued talking about his precious Savior as Gabriel listened with rapt attention. He turned back and forth, from one Old Testament prophecy to its fulfillment in the New Testament, amazing Gabriel that a man so young would know so much about the book he held in his hands.

"I understand all you are saying, and I am familiar with much of the Scripture that you have shared. I do believe in the Messiah, just as Abraham did. I am just still looking forward to His coming."

Jason looked at Gabriel with such earnestness, it nearly made Gabriel blush. "May I read you another passage?"

Gabriel nodded. Silently, Jason prayed for his friend, and he knew others were praying too. He began to read, "*Behold, thou art called a Jew, and restest in the law, and makest thy boast of God, And knowest his will, and approvest the things that are more excellent, being instructed out of the law.*"

"Your Bible talks about my people," he stated with astonishment.

"Yes. All the writers of the Bible were Jewish." He paused, seeing that the thought had never occurred to Gabriel. "And Jesus was a Jew as well."

Gabriel shot him a glance, then looked away, pondering all he was hearing. Why was he sitting here listening to this man? He should go, but he felt drawn to know more.

"Listen to these verses: '*For he is not a Jew, which is one outwardly; neither is that circumcision, which is outward in the flesh: But he is a Jew, which is one inwardly; and circumcision is that of the heart, in the spirit, and not in the letter; whose praise is not of men, but of God.'* "

Jason's eyes met Gabriel's. "God sees your heart. God, the Father, who called Abraham to birth His chosen people, has already sent His Son, who perfectly fulfilled all the prophecies of His first coming."

Again, Gabriel was taken aback. "You mean He is coming again?"

"Yes. Unfortunately, the Jews of Jesus' day were looking for a Conquering King, not a Sacrificing Servant. The prophecies both point to Jesus: He has come as a Suffering Servant and is yet to come as the Conquering King. When He comes again, your people will recognize Him then, and many will believe. But for you, today is your time to make a decision. Can you believe that Jesus is exactly who He said He was—the Son of God?"

"I believe what you have shown me to be true," Gabriel said quietly, but with deep conviction.

"Then will you receive His forgiveness? Will you believe that He came and died that day on the cross, and did rise from the dead, not to cover sins but to take away the sins of the world?"

Gabriel's bruised and weary soul thirsted for all that this man offered—no, all that God was offering. Why had he never seen this before? Why were his people so blind? It was all there. He could see why it was a hated book—it held the truth that destroyed their religion. No, it held the truth that *fulfilled* his religion! There was no need to wait any longer.

Jason sat quietly watching the war rage across Gabriel's face. He prayed for victory in the heart of this young Jewish man. He knew it was a lot to grasp in one night, but he also knew that God had prepared Gabriel's heart through all the trials and disappointments that had overwhelmed him.

Gabriel clenched and unclenched his fists. His heart was racing, and he felt as though he would be torn in two, when a gentle hand reached over and took his.

"Let me pray for you."

He could only nod; his throat was so constricted with emotion.

"Oh Father, God of the universe. We come to Thee with hearts broken and bruised. Oh, how we need Thy help, Father. Please, send the Comforter tonight, Thy Holy Spirit, to calm Gabriel's heart and make all things clear. Satan would like to have him, Lord, but I praise Thee that Thou art the Victor in this battle!"

Jason's voice carried such authority. He spoke to God like no other man Gabriel knew. He could hold the tears no longer. His voice broke into sobs, and Jason's arm reached out to hold him. He cried like a baby until there were no more tears left.

"Gabriel, He wants to hear you. He's ready to hear you, and He will wait as long as you need."

"But what do I say?"

"Talk to Him as a Father—a Father who loved you so much that He sent His only Son, Jesus, to die for you. Tell Him that you believe that Jesus died for your sins and that you take Him into your heart as your Savior."

Jason held his breath, not knowing if he should have used Jesus' name, but also knowing that Gabriel needed to understand that Jesus was his Messiah.

After what seemed an eternity, Gabriel began in a still small voice, like that of a child—not more than a whisper, "Father in heaven, Thou art my God. I have always believed in You. You have been my strength and shield, but"—he began to weep—"I didn't know, Father. I didn't know that—" A long pause passed before he continued. "I did not believe that Jesus was the Messiah. Oh, Father, forgive my unbelief. It's all there, in that book—your book. Father, I believe. Please cleanse me with the blood of Your Son, Jesus."

Jason waited a moment before he began to pray. "Oh, Father. Thou art the great and mighty God, the God of Abraham, and Isaac, and Jacob. Your chosen child has called upon Thee this night, and I thank Thee. Fill him with Thy love—and joy—and a peace that passes all understanding. May he grow as a mighty branch. May his life touch the lives of many with the truth of Your precious Word. In Jesus' name, amen."

Both men sat in silence, each enveloped in his own thoughts—each communing with God in his own way.

"Gabriel, you are a child of God. Your life is now His."

"But now what do I do?" Gabriel felt like a fresh washed lamb. The peace in his heart was nearly overwhelming—the stormy struggle was over. But it had been worth it for the calm that now rested upon him. He spoke quietly, as though to himself. "I can't go back to the synagogue. There's nothing there, and yet I don't know where else to go."

"Where do you live?" Jason asked. Gabriel gave him his address, and Jason scribbled it down. "Would you like me to pick you up this Sunday and take you to church with me?"

Gabriel looked incredulous. "Why would you do that? You don't even know me."

Jason smiled. "Oh yes I do. If we are both children of God, we're brothers."

Jason's smile spread from ear to ear. Gabriel just shook his head in wonder. "Alright, what time?"

"I'll be there at nine-fifteen."

"Should I bring anything?"

Jason looked down at his Bible and handed the precious book to Gabriel. "Yes, this."

"I can't take this," Gabriel protested.

"It's a gift, just like salvation." Jason looked at his watch. "Hey, have you eaten supper yet?"

Gabriel looked at his own watch and gasped. "Debby! I've got to go get my little girl. Thanks, but I must run."

As they shook hands, Jason held on to Gabriel's with his, placing the other on his shoulder as he spoke. "Gabriel, your family will probably not be too excited about your decision tonight. Don't get discouraged at their blindness. God may want to use you to open their eyes. Just be careful. Sometimes our zeal can do more harm than good." The clouded look on Jason's face made Gabriel wonder if his new friend was speaking from his own experience. "Be patient with them and just shine in your newfound faith."

"Thank you, Jason," Gabriel said with such earnestness that Jason had to swallow back the tears.

"The pleasure has been all mine. I think I'll just go home and praise God a bit!"

The statement surprised Gabriel, but his mind was already on Debby.

***

It was a long walk back to the office, but Gabriel needed the time to think about all that had happened in the last few hours. He picked up something to eat from one of the vendors along the street and ate as he walked, Jason's words replaying over and over in his mind—especially his last few words: *Your family will not be happy about your decision.*

No kidding, Gabriel thought. When he thought about his uncle's reaction to his decision, Gabriel knew he should be shaking in his shoes; in fact, his decision would possibly cost him his job. But the peace that had entered his heart stayed firmly in place, becoming more galvanized with each step he took.

He hurried his pace, driven by the excitement that was in his heart, even though he felt drained emotionally and physically. His plan was to pick up Debby, apologize to his aunt for his lateness and to his uncle for his rudeness at the office, and leave as quickly as possible. He knew he was in no condition to explain anything.

As he rounded the corner of 64th and Elm, it seemed as though every light in the beautiful mansion was lit. He could see his aunt sitting in the front room with Debby on her lap reading her a story while casting frequent glances at the clock.

Gabriel quietly opened the front door and headed for the parlor. Both faces came up quickly, and Debby was out of Judith's lap and into her daddy's embrace instantly. "Daddy!" came the joyful cry. Gabriel pulled her close just as Jacob came through the door.

Before he could speak, Gabriel turned to Judith and said, "I'm sorry for being so late, Aunt Judith. Thank you for keeping Debby occupied."

Judith smiled, wanted to know more but keeping her questions to herself.

Gabriel turned to face his uncle. Their eyes locked like two bucks sizing up each other. "Uncle Jacob, I'm sorry for my rudeness at the office. Please forgive me."

"It's forgotten, Gabriel, but we would like an explanation of where you have been. We've been worried sick."

Gabriel couldn't read his uncle's emotions. Was he angry, disgusted, or just worried? "I'm sorry, I just can't explain it right now. Debby needs to get home, and I'm really tired."

He looked pleadingly into their faces. His aunt was genuinely sympathetic, but he could see and feel his uncle's annoyance at being put off this way.

Jacob let out a long sigh. "Alright. I'll see you tomorrow."

Gabriel smiled wearily as he turned to get Debby's coat from the front closet, absently setting the Bible on the small table by the door. As he closed the closet door and knelt to help Debby into the jacket, his uncle exploded, "What is that?"

265

Gabriel jerked his head up to his uncle's eyes and then followed his gaze, half expecting to see a spitting cobra by the door. He pressed his eyes shut and rubbed his forehead to try to stop the pounding headache that had started since he had arrived. He stood and reached for the Bible. "It's just something someone gave me in the park."

Jacob was instantly in his face. His breathing was hard, and he stood so close to Gabriel that he could feel his breath on his face. "What have you done, Gabriel?"

The question drove forward like a knife attempting to cut him down, but Gabriel stood his ground. He was tempted to spit the words in his uncle's face, but Jason's warning held his tongue and cooled his temper.

His countenance softened as he spoke. "Uncle, I do not think that now is the time." He cast a look at Debby and then at his aunt. He turned his attention back to his uncle, hoping he would be considerate, and turned to leave.

"Be in my office, first thing in the morning."

Gabriel nodded and pushed open the door. For the second time this evening, the cool night air refreshed him. Debby was unusually quiet, for which he was thankful, but as he deposited her into the car, she looked up at him with big brown eyes and said, "Uncle's mad."

"Oh Debby, he wasn't mad at you," Gabriel said consolingly.

"Mad at you, Daddy?" Her precious little face was in a pucker.

"It's alright. Uncle Jacob still loves us. Big people just disagree sometimes."

He loved the way she always looked at him as though she understood every word he said. She smiled, and he smiled back as she began a sing-song tune.

That evening, after Debby was put to bed, Gabriel found the Bible and took it to his room. He started in the beginning and was amazed that it paralleled the Torah so closely. He skimmed through the Old Testament, feeling a comfort that this book held the teachings of his people.

Turning to the New Testament, he began to read. He was amazed at the genealogy of Christ and its accuracy. He stopped to consider a verse in the book called Matthew: *"So all the generations from Abraham to David are fourteen generations; and from David until* the carrying away into Babylon are fourteen generations; and from the carrying away into Babylon unto Christ are fourteen generations." It fascinated him.

He continued to read the account of the angel meeting with Jesus' father, Joseph, and again was amazed. *"Behold, a virgin shall be with child, and shall bring forth a son, and they shall call his name Emmanuel, which being interpreted is, God with us."* This was one of the verses that Jason had referred to.

As he continued to read, questions swarmed his thoughts, and he couldn't wait to see Jason. He then realized that he knew nothing about Jason except his name. *What if he forgets me on Sunday?* Somehow, he knew that would not happen.

Chapter Twenty-Eight

*"And ye shall seek me, and find me,
when ye shall search for me with all your heart."*

Jeremiah 29:13

"You did what?"

The words seemed to bounce off the walls and echo down the hallway. Gabriel knew he had to tell his boss and uncle about his decision. He had thought about it a lot during the night, trying to come up with a plan, but the only plan that came to his mind was to trust God.

"Uncle, I know it all sounds far-fetched to you, but—"

"Far-fetched is putting it mildly, don't you think?" The anger and sarcasm in Jacob's voice pounced on Gabriel as if he were a child. "Blasphemy is more like it. You have rejected the teachings of your father and mother."

The words stung Gabriel, but he would not back down. "No, Jacob you are wrong." He had never used his uncle's first name, but he did so now not to show disrespect, but to emphasize that fact that they were both grown men. "I have not rejected their beliefs. I have accepted the fulfillment of them."

Jacob was speechless. How could this have happened? It was all because of that Esther girl. How he wished she had died. His blazing eyes bore into Gabriel's. "If you were not my nephew, you would be out on the streets."

Gabriel knew this would be his reaction and spoke thoughtfully. "Uncle Jacob, I will resign if you think that I will be a detriment to your company."

Gabriel's sincerity always deflated Jacob. *Oh why couldn't you be here, brother?* Daniel Bachman had always been the one who took his religion seriously. If he were here, this blessed son of his wouldn't have gone off the deep end.

He sighed. "No Gabriel that will not be necessary." He stood for a moment looking at the young man before him, so promising. He had plans of grooming Gabriel to take over the business someday, but now ... How could he do such a thing if Gabriel had left their beliefs for the religion of an impostor? When he finally spoke, his words were clipped. "But do not utter one word of this to anyone here. Do you understand?"

"Yes, sir," Gabriel said.

"And you will continue to attend the synagogue." It was a command, not a question.

Gabriel hesitated. He supposed that he could. He usually spent Sundays with Debby, often taking her to the Bachmans, but he could still do that. It was usually afternoon before they got there anyway.

"Yes, sir," Gabriel responded without any emotion.

They both stood eyeing each other, Gabriel wondering why his uncle was so blinded, and Jacob wondering what the ramifications of this decision would be. Maybe it was just an emotional reaction to yesterday's conflict. The thought brightened Jacob. *Perhaps I've been too hasty in my judgment,* he thought. He wore a bit of a smile as he spoke. "Well then, let's get busy. Sit down Gabriel, and we'll pick up where we left off yesterday."

It was as though Gabriel could read his uncle's mind and would have refuted his thoughts, but again Jason's words came to mind: *Be patient with them and just shine in your new-found faith.*

***

The day was bright but cold, and everyone seemed to need paint. Esther was so tired by the end of the day that she decided that she would miss the Children's Club that afternoon. But when Gladys came through the door with Little David laughing and sharing some special secret, her feet suddenly didn't feel so tired. *Besides, all you do is sit and listen—Libby does all the work*, she thought.

David was still giggling when Esther gave him a hug. "And what is so funny, young man?" she asked in mock sternness.

David saw the twinkle in her eye. "Aunt Gladys was just telling me about the time she—"

"Now hold on, partner," Gladys said with a cowboy twang that had David in stitches. "Are you going to tell my secret?"

269

David beamed. He adored Gladys almost as much as she adored him. "Well ..." he said as if considering his answer.

Gladys pounced on him, tickling his sides. "You better not, or I'll tickle you to death!"

David was nearly rolling on the floor with laughter when Mr. Porter came over. "What's going on here?" He played the part of a disgruntled adult, but the sparkle in his eyes gave him away.

"My partner here was just about to tell this woman our secret," Gladys said, pointing an accusing finger at the little traitor.

"Ah," her father exclaimed, "a serious offence." He looked down his nose at David and then bent down to talk to him face to face. "You know, we are nearing the time when secrets will be on every one's mind."

David looked curious. "What do you mean, Grandpa John?"

Mr. Porter leaned a little closer and whispered in the little boy's ear, "Christmas."

David's curiosity turned to confusion. "What's Christmas?"

For all of Mr. Porter's intuition, he completely forgot that David was Jewish. He looked up at Gladys, who was smirking at him, and Esther, whose eyebrows were lifted, and sputtered on. "Well son, Christmas is a very special time of the year when everyone gives presents." He longed to tell the boy the whole story, but he knew it was not his place.

"But why?" came the innocent response.

Gladys' eyes softened, and Esther came to the poor man's rescue. "David, we will talk about that soon, but don't you think we had better get to our Children's Club?"

As if on cue, Libby came sweeping into the building, flannel board in tow.

The usual crowd of youngsters began to arrive with a couple of new faces that Libby introduced as children from her Sunday school class. For some reason, the statement tugged on Esther's heart, and she pictured Little David sitting among the men at the synagogue looking totally lost.

After the usual attendance, Libby flew into the memory verse with her usual flair. "Could one of you older boys find Galatians 4:4 and read it for me?"

Several of the students furiously looked into their Bibles to be the first one to find it. A tall, red haired boy's hand shot up in the air.

"Danny, you read it, please."

The boy cleared his throat and read with a heavy brogue accent. "*'But when the fullness of the time was come, God sent forth his Son, made of a woman, made under the law.'* " He looked up and smiled.

Libby obviously received much affection from these children—they adored her. "Thank you, Danny. Now we have been learning a lot about the Old Testament, but today we are going to look at the New Testament. In fact, we are going to talk about heaven, and I have something very special I want to show you."

The excitement buzzed around the room. Libby often used objects to help the students have a visual picture with which to remember the lesson.

She went on to explain the verse, stating that all the Old Testament pointed to the time when God would send His Son to earth, made of a woman. "Who can tell me what holiday we celebrate that speaks of this wonderful event?"

Hands shot up, and one girl answered excitedly, "Christmas!"

David looked back at his mother with wonder, his face shining.

Esther would never forget the way that Libby spoke of the coming of the Messiah that day. She made everything so plain that for the first time, Esther began to understand.

"God told us exactly when, where, how, and why He sent us His Son." Using each adverb as an outline, Libby swiftly moved through many of the Old Testament verses that they had studied, and then read verses from the New Testament where they had been fulfilled.

"Can anyone tell my why God sent Jesus?"

Again, hands were raised, and another girl answered, "So we could go to heaven."

Libby smiled. "Yes, Patricia. And that's what we will be talking about in the next few weeks."

Her eyes were shining, and the children knew it was time for her surprise object.

"Do you remember the beautiful stones that God used to decorate Aaron's robe?"

Heads nodded. The students had especially enjoyed the lessons about Moses, the tabernacle, and the high priest's garments.

Libby turned to Revelation. "In the very last book of the Bible, God gives us a description of heaven. It also has twelve of something—

271

twelve foundations—and they are not made out of just ordinary, ugly cinder blocks like our houses are here. They are made of beautiful gems, just like Aaron's robe—jasper, sapphire, emeralds, and topaz, just to name a few. God used every color imaginable to make these foundations."

Her excitement swelled as she spoke of her favorite topic. "Just imagine! Each foundation will sparkle and shine in twelve glorious colors. And God used pearls to make the gates and gold—pure gold for the streets. God wants us all to be in heaven with Him forever. Don't ever forget that."

Her eyes twinkled as she turned around to take something from her bag. She put it into her hands so that no one could see it. "Can you guess what is in my hands?"

Several gave answers, but each time her reply was, "No."

Libby's face grew serious, even wistful. "Someone very special gave this to me, and every time I see it, it makes me think of heaven— partly because of the twelve smooth stones, but mostly because the one who gave it to me is there right now." She opened her hand and held out a locket with deep etchings and twelve colorful stones around its oval shape. It was a beautiful locket—it was Esther's locket.

Esther's heart raced. How could this be? It had to be a mistake, but she knew even as she looked on that it was her locket. There was never a locket like it. Her breath came in short gasps. She felt as though all the air had been squeezed out of her lungs. The room was tilting—she had to get out. Quickly, Esther turned for the door and burst out, tears stinging her eyes and blurring her vision. She stumbled down the hallway and through the door leading to the store, thankful that it was after store hours. Pushing the door open, she ran straight into the arms of Mr. Porter.

He held her, fearing that she might collapse, her sobs increasing as she rested her face against him.

"Esther, what is it?"

No answer. He held her and prayed for wisdom, waiting for the sobs to quiet before he led her to his office.

Libby had seen Esther's face and wondered what was wrong. Was she sick, or was she upset about the lesson? She quickly finished the lesson, placed the locket around her neck, and allowed the children to get a closer look.

Gladys had also seen the look on Esther's face and had wanted to go to her, but she knew she needed to stay with David. He seemed to have missed the whole scene; he was so engrossed in the lesson.

When most of the children were gone, Gladys went to Libby and suggested, "Why don't you go and see Esther while I stay with the children."

Libby smiled her thanks and rushed from the room. She followed the sound of voices and knocked on the office door, wondering what she would find there. As Libby entered the room, Mr. Porter looked up and nodded for her to come and sit beside Esther.

"Esther," Libby spoke softly.

Esther's face was in her hands. At the sound of Libby's voice, she looked up into her face, but her eyes immediately fell to the locket around Libby's neck. She reached out and touched it, bringing fresh tears.

Libby looked questioningly at Mr. Porter and then back to Esther. "What is it?"

Esther looked into Libby's eyes. "Where did you get this?"

Libby was a bit taken back, but she answered the question. "My uncle gave it to me."

Esther looked from the locket back to Libby's questioning face. How could this be? She thought about Kurt, and looked at Libby. Libby? Her face lightened as understanding dawned. "Elizabeth?"

Libby looked perplexed. She had not used her full name since she was twelve. "Yes, my name is Elizabeth."

Esther's hand flew to her mouth. "Kurt's niece?"

Shock strained every feature of Libby's face. "Yes. My uncle Kurt gave this to me. But how did you know?" she asked incredulously.

Again, Esther reached for the locket, but stopped. "May I see the locket?"

Libby only nodded, reaching behind her neck to unclasp the delicate chain. She laid it gently into Esther's hand.

Esther looked at it for several moments, running her fingers over the stones. She popped it open. The faces of her mother, father, and brothers all stared out at her. She looked up as the tears coursed down her face, bringing the locket to her lips and pressing a kiss on each photo.

"This is my mother and father," she said as she pointed to their faces. She looked down into the faces of her brothers, both gone.

273

Without looking back up, she explained, "This is Ad and Daan, my brothers. All of them, except my father died at Auschwitz."

Libby gasped. "You were at Auschwitz?"

Esther nodded.

"And you knew my uncle?"

Esther's face contorted. She swallowed the lump in her throat, but could only nod. Drawing strength from the locket she now held in her hand, she looked up and smiled weakly.

Libby and John looked on as Esther deftly removed the picture of her parents to reveal the letters *ERR*, holding it out for them to see. "My given name was Esther Ruth Raul. This locket belonged to my mother's family further back than I can remember. It had been a tradition in my family for the locket to be passed on to a daughter or granddaughter on her sixteenth birthday."

A faraway look came over her as she remembered the day. "That is when my mother gave it to me. When we got to Auschwitz, I tried to hide the locket, but it came unclasped and fell to the floor. The woman guard would have killed me and taken the locket if it had not been for your uncle."

Libby could only listen as Esther unraveled some the mysteries Libby longed to know. "I can't believe you knew Uncle Kurt."

Esther had composed herself enough to smile. "You know, you really should ask for more than just the first names of your students." She paused, "My name is Esther Ruth Gerstein. Kurt was my husband. Libby, David is your cousin."

They all looked at each other in shock, unable to grasp all the ramifications of what Esther had just told them. When Gladys and David came into the room, murmurs of exclamation filled the air. Everyone had so many questions, and Mr. Porter finally brought order to the room, filling Gladys in on all that had just happened. They seemed to have forgotten the little face that was looking on in utter confusion.

Amid the laughter and talk, David walked over to his mother, staring at the locket that now hung around her neck.

"Mommy, why are you wearing Miss Libby's necklace?" he asked, the wonder making his eyes twice their size.

Esther bent down before her son, holding the locket out for him to see. She pulled him close, placing a kiss on his cheek. "David, you never knew your father—he died before you got to meet him—but he was a wonderful man."

David nodded. His mother had talked about his father often.

Esther looked up at Libby, who was watching with misty eyes. "Miss Libby is your father's niece. Her mother was your father's sister."

Again, David nodded, casting a sideways glance at Libby.

Esther smiled and continued. "Do you know what that means?"

He shook his head slowly.

Esther's face glowed with the news she was about to tell him. "Miss Libby is your cousin."

For the first time since entering the room with all the talk and confusion, Little David understood one thing. "Do you mean Miss Libby and me is related?"

"Miss Libby and I," Esther corrected. "Yes, you are related to Miss Libby."

David smiled in her direction, still a little shy about the whole idea.

Again, Esther fingered the locket and looked at her son. She swallowed the tears, determined not to frighten him. "Do you remember Miss Libby saying that someone very special gave her this locket and that he is in heaven right now?"

David looked at her and nodded.

"She was talking about your father."

"But isn't the necklace Miss Libby's?"

"No, the necklace is mine. Your father was keeping it safe for me when I had to leave very quickly. I'm not sure how Miss Libby got it."

Libby took her cue and came to join their little circle. She bent down and spoke to David. "Your father came to visit me and my family when I was younger. He gave me this locket and told me that it belonged to a very special person," she looked at Esther, "and he was right."

She looked back at David. "You know, all my family is in Germany except you. Do you think I could give you a hug, since we are cousins?"

Libby didn't have to ask twice. David was in her arms immediately.

"I believe this calls for a celebration," Mr. Porter exclaimed. He looked around the room. "I know I have a lot of questions, and I'm sure you two have even more. If you don't mind sharing the whole story with us, Libby, why don't you come over for dinner tonight? That way we can all make some sense of all this."

***

When the meal was finished and all were settled into the living room, Esther felt shy, as everyone seemed to be waiting for her to ask the first question. It wasn't that she didn't want to know, but she had always hated being the center of attention. Libby came to her rescue.

"I'm sure you have just as many questions as I do, but I'd like to know how you got out of Auschwitz. I'm almost certain that Uncle Kurt thought that you were …" She looked over at David.

Linda saw the look and offered, "Why don't David and I head over to your place, Esther. I can get him tucked in while you all visit."

Esther nodded, but David balked. "I want to hear what Miss Libby has to say!" he pouted. "And I'm not sleepy." The protest was followed by a long yawn, bringing chuckles to all the adults.

"We'll just go over and read a little bit, David. Do you remember where we are in our story?"

That was all that needed to be said. He walked over to his mother and gave her a hug and kiss. Then he turned to Gladys and Mr. Porter for their hugs. Lastly, he looked over at Libby, still not sure it was all real. She smiled and beckoned to him. He came into her embrace. "You and I will have a long talk another day, okay?"

David nodded, kissing her on the cheek and running to Mrs. Porter.

Libby looked at Esther and continued. "I believe Kurt thought that you had died. No one ever escaped Auschwitz, and by the time he had returned, everything had changed—even the commander."

Esther's face clouded. "I was afraid that would happen."

She went on to explain how Herr Schindler had come and his girls had persuaded her to leave with them. "They were convinced that I would die if I stayed."

"I agree with them," Libby said.

"But perhaps if I had stayed—"

"Esther, after Uncle Kurt had visited us, everything fell apart for the Third Reich. Hitler was dead. It seemed like no one was in charge—so many died those last few days in the concentration camps.

276

The Germans were either moving the prisoners on death marches or killing them outright.

"I didn't know what my uncle did, except that he was my hero." Her eyes clouded. "He would always have nightmares when he stayed with us. His room was right next to mine, and I'd often be awakened in the night by his screams. But then he changed. Toward the end, we didn't see him as much, but when he was there, he seemed more at peace."

She smiled at Esther. "Perhaps you should pick up the story. I don't understand how he could have married you."

Esther brightened at the memory, but she hesitated before she spoke, not wanting anyone to think ill of her husband's actions. "Your uncle sought to save anyone that he could. He was in charge of a brothel." She paused. "He knew the girls would not survive the horrible conditions at the camp. It was not a life any of them would have chosen or understood, but it did save their lives."

She looked down at her locket, and then continued. "He chose me, but he kept me in his room. He was the most honorable, kind man I have ever met. He let me read his Bible, and we would often read it together at night.

"I knew it was getting hard for him to be so close to me and not be married. It was hard for me too. I had been there for several months when he asked me to marry him."

She smiled as she remembered the night. "Kurt disguised his pastor in an SS officer's uniform and brought him to our room. We were married that night."

Silence fell on the room as everyone thought through what she had said.

"Did Uncle Kurt know he was a father?" Libby asked.

Esther shook her head sadly. "I didn't even know until I left Auschwitz."

"How did you leave Auschwitz?" Mr. Porter asked.

"Yes, you mentioned Herr Schindler," Libby said. "Did you know him?"

"Yes, he came to Auschwitz to rescue a trainload of his women who had accidentally been shipped there. He was so commanding. Everyone just did what he said."

"He was on a wanted list by the government, but to the Jewish people, he was a hero," Libby explained.

Esther went on to explain how one of the girls had died and she took her place. She told how his girls nursed her back to health. "And when the war was over, he took me back to Auschwitz under a false name and helped me find my father." She looked at Libby with hope in her eyes. "Do you know what happened to Kurt?"

Libby shook her head. "He came to us after he had returned to Auschwitz. He must have been told that you had died, which makes sense by what you have said. He was so sad, but I couldn't understand why." Her countenance fell as she remembered. "The night he gave me the locket, I snuck down the stairs and listened to his conversation with my parents. He was so broken. He knew the war was over and that if the Germans found out what he had done, they would kill him. However, the allies would certainly arrest him as an SS officer."

She looked at Esther. "He fled to France and turned himself in, hoping that some of the outsiders that he had contacted during the war would come to his aid. We never knew what happened; only that he had died in prison. I'm sorry Esther."

The two sat beside each other on the sofa, where Libby leaned over to embrace her new aunt. "For a time, Kurt was so happy, and now I know it was because of you."

Esther began to cry softly, holding this one that so reminded her of Kurt. She looked at Libby, "You know, you always made me think of Kurt. I just thought it was your German accent. But I don't understand why you are here and how you were able to work for the Hirsches. You obviously saw Mr. Hirsch's reaction to my situation."

"After the war, I was devastated about what was discovered in the concentration camps. I had believed all the propaganda but had no idea what was really going on. My heart was broken for your people."

"You have the same heart as your uncle," Esther said.

"I wanted to help the Jews, but the situation was so volatile there in Germany. I decided that I would come to America with the hope of helping Jewish people to see the truth."

The truth shall set you free. Esther started as the words echoed in her heart. "What is the truth, Libby?"

Gladys and her father watched on, praying that God would use this special time to bring another of His children into the kingdom of God. Esther's pleading voice and searching eyes urged Libby forward.

"Jesus said, *'I am the way, the truth and the life. No man cometh unto the father but by me.'* The truth is that God chose to use

Abraham's family to bring forth His Son. All the lambs and other animals in the world could not pay the price of man's sin. Only the Son of God could completely wipe out our debt to God.

"As our memory verse said today, God's plan from the beginning of time was to send His Son to this earth to die. I'm sure you have seen all the prophecies before and are waiting for the Messiah."

Esther only nodded, engrossed with Libby's words. She looked over at Gladys, who smiled a knowing smile. How many times had they discussed the same thing, looking at all the Old Testament verses and comparing them to the New Testament fulfillments? She and Kurt had done the same.

There was a silence in the room. Every being, seen and unseen, seemed to be holding their breath, wondering what the outcome would be. With great earnestness and compassion, Libby continued. "Esther, can you believe that Jesus is the Son of God?"

The question hung in the air. Esther looked down at her locket. She thought of her last conversation with Kurt and then her final words with her father—one had such peace, while the other longed for the truth as she did.

The look in Esther's eyes slowly began to change as the truth entered her heart. Tears accompanied the gentle smile that formed on her lips as she softly spoke only one word. "Yes."

Chapter Twenty-Nine

"Call unto me, and I will answer thee, and shew thee great and mighty things, which thou knowest not."

Jeremiah 33:3

How the week had flown by for all in the Porter's extended family! Esther was like a sponge, and the family Bible time was alive with questions and answers long sought for. Esther couldn't read enough of the Word, nor could she get her answers fast enough.

"It's all so clear now," she often said as her adopted family smiled on. "I only wish Kurt knew."

"But he does, Esther," Mr. Porter interjected. Esther looked at him in surprise. He quickly leafed through his well-worn Bible. "Here in Luke 15:10 it says, '*Likewise, I say unto you, there is joy in the presence of the angels of God over one sinner that repenteth.*' Hebrews also talks about a cloud of witnesses. I believe your husband knows and is rejoicing, even more so knowing that the niece he loved led you to the truth."

Esther's heart was so full of joy, tears formed in the corners of her eyes. "I don't deserve to be so happy!" she exclaimed.

Another thought had haunted her all week as well—Gabriel. He was lost, and the thought broke her heart. She tossed the thoughts over and over in her mind. How could she just show up and tell him about Jesus? And what about his wife? What if he believed and she didn't? She went to bed every night exhausted—tormented by these thoughts.

Sunday dawned brisk and cool. Snow had fallen during the night, blanketing everything in a beautiful cover of pristine white. Esther stood at the kitchen window watching the glistening snow as a cardinal came to the backyard feeder. His brilliant red coat upon the diamonds of snow made Esther think about the blood of Jesus that had washed her white as snow.

She had just read John's account of the crucifixion that morning, and the image of all that Jesus had suffered nearly overwhelmed her. *Thank you, Father, for sending your Son. And thank you, Jesus, for suffering so much for me.* A tear slipped down her cheek.

"Mommy!"

David's excitement crowded out her thoughts and she quickly dried her face. She turned to him and scooped him up into her arms.

"Mommy! Did you see outside?" The wonder on his face always brought her such joy. "Can we play in the snow?"

She lifted him to the window so he could see the cardinal and his mate who had joined him. "Oh," he whispered, not wanting to frighten them.

"We don't have time to play in the snow right now, but maybe this afternoon we can."

She lowered him to the floor and led the way back into the bedroom to get dressed. "Do you remember where we are going today?" she asked, not certain what to expect.

The smile that broke across his face assured her that the idea of accompanying the Porters to church was a good one in his little mind. He had asked about going to the synagogue yesterday, but Esther had only said that they would be going with the Porters this morning. He looked at her oddly but didn't say any more. She hoped that someday he would understand.

***

As Mr. Porter dropped the family off in front of the church, Esther suddenly felt queasy. The only time she had been in a church was with her father after he had finished a stained glass window in one of the church sanctuaries in Amsterdam. She had been awed by the masterpiece of craftsmanship that her father had created. She remembered the figure of Christ kneeling by a huge stone and had asked her father about it. He had brushed her off, saying that it was not the person she needed to view, but the beautiful picture that the tiny pieces of glass had created.

Gladys sensed her hesitation and slipped her arm into Esther's, smiling a knowing smile. The beautiful stone building was inviting—the snow only adding to its beauty. Not many were there yet; the Porters were always early as Mr. Porter taught the Sunday school class for teen boys. Esther was surprised at the size of the building and the number of friendly faces she met.

After depositing David into Libby's class, she followed Mrs. Porter and Gladys to a women's class. "We don't always have separated classes, but right now we are studying the women of the Bible while the men are studying the men."

"That's fine. We never sat with the men anyway," Esther explained.

"Oh, that's right," Gladys said. "I had forgotten that."

Mrs. Becket, the pastor's wife, met them at the classroom door with a friendly smile. After Gladys' explanation of who Esther was, Mrs. Becket's face brightened. "It's so good to have you, Esther."

"Thank you," Esther replied shyly.

The Sunday school hour flew by, and Esther was enthralled as the lesson was about her namesake. Before she knew it, they were moving into one of the pews in front of the church. She let her eyes soak in the colors of the stained glass windows. Each seemed to tell a story, but her eyes were riveted to the one behind the choir loft of Jesus kneeling in the garden. It was almost exactly like the one she had seen with her father. Again, her mind went back to the morning's reading. *"Not my will, but thine be done." Yes, Lord,* she whispered in her heart. *May Your will always be done in my life.*

***

Jason arrived promptly at nine-fifteen, but the traffic was a nightmare and he hadn't realized how far Gabriel lived from the church. Debby jabbered happily from the back seat as Jason tried to maneuver through the tangle of cars.

"Have you always lived in the city?" Gabriel asked, amazed at the skill of Jason's driving. He had gotten his license after coming to America but still hated driving in the city.

Jason smiled right before he slammed on the brakes, just barely missing a stopped car. "Sorry about that," he offered as Debby giggled from the back seat, enjoying all the jostling. "Yes, I have. Can't you tell?"

"Just a bit," Gabriel offered with a smile.

"I'm sorry. We're going to be late. In fact, we've missed Sunday school. When we get there, I'll park as quickly as I can, and then we can take Debby to the nursery if you want."

"They have a nursery," Gabriel asked in surprise.

"Yes. In fact, they have a children's church too. They sing and tell Bible stories that the children can understand."

"That makes sense," Gabriel said, thinking about all the children that sat through the services at the synagogue.

"Do you think she'll be alright?" Jason asked.

Gabriel smiled. "Oh, yes. Debby has the female talk gene. She can make friends with a fence post." Both men laughed.

As the church came into view, Gabriel felt a sense of apprehension. *Am I doing the right thing, Father?* But even as the question lingered in his mind, the answer was already in his heart.

The two men quickly deposited Debby into a brightly painted room with lots of happy faces and toys and then slipped into the back pew. Gabriel recognized some of the faces in the choir as they sang an anthem. He let his gaze slide to the beautiful windows. The sun streamed from the eastern wall, sending splashes of color everywhere. Had he ever seen anything so beautiful?

With that thought came an image of long dark brown hair, the color of ebony, and two large brown eyes danced across his mind. Esther. What would she think if she saw him here in a Christian church? *Oh, Esther. Will you ever know the truth?* He said a quick prayer before rising to sing the final hymn preceding the pastor's message. To his surprise and thrill, it was the same hymn he had heard in the park. He looked over at Jason, who sported the same smile. Gabriel found the notes and sang with his whole heart.

He had just settled back into the pew when his gaze slid down from the pulpit to a family sitting in the second row from the front. A tall man and equally tall woman flanked a younger woman he presumed to be their daughter. But they weren't what held his attention—it was the woman on the end. He could only see the back of her head, but the wave in the hair, its color, her petite size ... *Stop it, Gabriel! You see Esther everywhere!* But then she turned and smiled at the woman next to her. Her profile! Her smile! *Esther! But how?*

Jason looked at his friend as he heard his sharp intake of breath. Gabriel's face was drained of all color. He felt concern and leaned toward him. "Are you okay?"

Gabriel shook from his stare and looked at his friend, then back to Esther, then back to Jason. "Esther is sitting up there." He nodded his head forward.

Jason looked in that direction. Sure enough, there was a visitor in the Porter pew, but how? He looked back at Gabriel and shrugged his shoulders. They both sat back and tried to concentrate on the sermon with little success.

It was the shortest half an hour that Esther had ever experienced and the longest that Gabriel had ever endured. Esther sat enthralled at every word Pastor Becket spoke as though he were an angel, and Gabriel heard nothing. He couldn't wait for the service to end, but then what? Should he just walk right up to her? She might faint, or slap him. He certainly didn't want to make a scene.

As the service was ending, Gabriel chose his plan. "Jason, is there some place where I can talk to Esther, alone?"

Jason's mind raced. "Yes, follow me."

Gabriel followed Jason to an empty classroom down the side hallway. As they entered the room, Jason spoke with commanding tones. "You stay here. I'll get Esther and bring her here."

Gabriel caught his arm. "But you don't understand. She may be married."

Jason frowned. "Well, you need to find out either way." He squeezed Gabriel's shoulder and left the room just as Gabriel heard the organ swell.

Esther was being introduced to several people when a tall young man came forward, looking at her with an odd expression. He turned to Mr. Porter. "John, would it be possible for me to steal this young lady away? There's someone who wants to meet her."

Mr. Porter looked first at Jason, then at Esther and Gladys, finally to his wife. She raised her eyebrows but nodded. "Certainly, Jason."

"Thank you. I know this sounds strange, but I promise to bring her back in one piece."

Esther looked at Gladys, who seemed to read her mind. "I'll get David," Gladys said and headed for the children's church.

Jason turned to Esther, trying to hide his emotions at the mention of a son. "Would you mind following me?"

Esther only nodded, giving a little wave and shrug to the Porters.

"What do you think that is all about?" Linda asked her husband.

"I don't know, but I do know that Jason would never do anything out of line." They both watched as the two disappeared around the corner.

Esther's mind was whirling. *Oh, Father. I don't want to meet some fellow who is taken with my looks. I'm just not ready for that.* She felt sick at the thought of this meeting. *Why did I say yes before asking more questions?*

But it was too late. Jason was standing beside the door of the woman's class room, allowing her to pass inside before he shut the door. Maybe Mrs. Becket wanted to talk to her. Certain that was who awaited her, Esther's heart calmed as she entered the room.

Across the room, looking out the window stood a young man. Something about him was strangely familiar.

Gabriel heard the door shut. Fearing to turn around, he remained still. What if he was wrong? He took a deep breath and slowly turned. There she stood, only a few feet away. Their eyes locked for what seemed an eternity before either spoke. "Esther."

Esther gasped, covering her mouth with her hands. It couldn't be! "Gabriel?"

Gabriel stayed himself, wanting to run to her and hold her forever, never letting her go, but he couldn't. "Esther, I—"

She stared at him, wondering why he was here.

"What are you—" They both started to speak at the same time.

Each smiled, and Gabriel suggested, "Why don't we sit down." He took his eyes off her for a moment and motioned to the table and chairs. Each moved forward, feeling the electricity in the air. He smiled weakly. "You begin."

She hesitated, knowing the first question she wanted to ask. Instead, she blurted out, "What are you doing here?"

"That's what I was going to ask you," he replied, staring at her with deep longing. "But first I need to know if someone is waiting for you after the service." He held his breath, waiting for her reply.

"Oh, just David, but Gladys is with him." Esther saw his countenance fall before her. She smiled at his wrong conclusion, dipping her head to hide it.

Gabriel looked hopeful, working to stay calm. "Is that your husband?"

"No, David is my son." She left the statement hang for what seemed like an eternity to both occupants of the room.

"And his father?"

Esther looked out the window, seeing nothing in particular. "He died in a prison in France."

"I'm so sorry," Gabriel said, and truly he was, but anyone could see the relief wash over his face.

"And you?" Esther asked, now sitting in the seat of hopeful anticipation.

Gabriel's gaze bore into her, "I have a daughter, Deborah, but her mother passed away in childbirth."

Seeing the shock on Esther's face, he changed the subject. "I thought I saw you in a taxi several weeks ago."

Esther's face warmed. She felt trapped, but knew she needed to explain. "Yes. I was heading for Prospect Park when I impulsively gave the driver your address. When he said it was on the way, I asked him to drive past. That's when I saw you with your daughter and just assumed ..."

Gabriel's face brightened. "I knew it was you! I thought you were dead, though."

Esther looked at him in surprise. "Then you never got the letter I sent from Israel?"

Gabriel's eyes clouded. "No, my uncle and aunt didn't tell me about it until a couple days ago. It had come after I was already married, and Deborah was expecting our child."

He felt hot, as though the statement had slapped her in the face, and he rushed on to explain. "I was frantic with worry during the war, and then your letters stopped—all the letters stopped. I feared the worst had happened to you. After the war, my uncle helped contact some authorities in Amsterdam. A letter came stating that all my family had died at Auschwitz, and that all of your family was gone too except your father."

He looked over at her. She was as beautiful as ever. She had changed—how could she not have changed for all she had been through? But the changes only served to enhance her beauty. The question that echoed in his mind was of her love for him. He continued, hoping that she could understand. "I thought you were dead, Esther, and Deborah ..." How could he explain? "She was there to pick up the broken pieces of my life."

286

He looked down at her small hands resting on the table and tentatively reached over, taking them both into his own. He looked up, fighting the tears that stung his eyes. "I loved Deborah. We had become friends at the university and at work, but I never stopped loving you, Esther, and she accepted that."

Gabriel didn't know how to read what he saw in her eyes. "I just found out this week from my uncle about your letter. I thought I'd go crazy. I was sure I'd seen you, so I knew you were here, but I didn't know your married name or if you even would want me. I knew you had seen me with Debby, and I could see how you would think that I was a happily married man who had forgotten you. I never stopped loving you, Esther, but I knew I had to go on with my life."

Esther's heart was racing. From the moment that he had taken her hands into his own, time stood still, and all the past had washed away. But it hadn't washed away—he had just laid his heart at her feet, and she suddenly felt so unworthy.

"So much has happened, Gabriel. Perhaps you won't feel the way you do after you've heard my story."

Gabriel wanted to deny it, but he held his tongue.

"As soon as we arrived at Auschwitz, I was taken by an SS officer who ran a brothel." The horror and pity which rose in Gabriel was unmistakable. "But it's not what you think. Kurt, the officer, was a Christian who loved our people and took the girls as a way to rescue them from the certain death that would have followed."

"But—" Gabriel's protest cut short as Esther pulled away and went to the window. She couldn't face him.

"I know it sounds strange, but his heart was good. He took me to his room and protected me there. He was always completely honorable. He allowed me to read his Bible, and we often read it together. At first I read just the Old Testament. It was such a comfort to have the Word." Esther took a deep breath and willed herself to continue. "It was very difficult for him to be in such close company with me, and I knew that he was falling in love with me. After several months, we were married."

Relief washed over Gabriel. He rose to his feet and went to her, gently turning her around. "Oh, Esther, I thought—all I knew was that you had a child to a German officer." He stared at her in wonder. "Even at Auschwitz, God had His protecting hand on you. Oh, my queen, my Esther."

287

He pulled her close and just held her as she broke into sobs. "I can't believe this is happening."

Esther pulled away, knowing she needed to tell him more. "But Gabriel," she said as she looked up into his eyes—those eyes that always melted her heart. *I must tell him everything!* The picture of their lives together stood like a sentinel warning her not to tell him. But even as the war raged within her—even though she wanted him more than life itself—she had to be true to her newly found Savior.

"I'm a Christian now," she whispered.

Gabriel stared at her in wonder. "When?"

"Just last week." Esther felt a flush rise on her face as a tear slipped down her cheek. Certainly this would mean the end. She bowed her head and cried. So close, yet forever separated.

Gabriel tipped her face to meet his. Instead of seeing scorn, she only saw love. "Me too," he whispered, leaning forward to kiss her hair.

"Are you serious?" she asked incredulously. "You are a Christian?"

"Yes. The young man that brought you here told me the truth about Jesus."

"I can't believe this." Her face glowed with the truth.

Gabriel laughed a laugh that came straight from the bottom of his heart. It felt so good! It had been so long since he had felt like laughing. "Here we are in a Christian church, both newly saved. Oh, Esther. Jehovah be praised!"

He could hold himself no longer. He tipped her head upward, drinking in the joy and love that he read in her eyes. He kissed her softly and cradled her in his arms. His kiss took her back to another place, another time, another man. Somehow she felt disloyal to Kurt. He had loved her, protected her, and had given her a son. Yet as she rested in Gabriel's tight hold, a peace came over her. She did not hear a voice, yet somewhere deep within she heard it—she felt it. *It's okay, Esther. You were mine when I needed you most.* She gasped and began to sob against Gabriel's strong shoulder.

"It's okay, Esther. You are here, and I'll never let you go." Gabriel stroked her hair and held her close.

"I know. I just can't believe it." She pulled away, taking the offered handkerchief and dabbing the tears from her eyes. "God is so good. He gave me Kurt when I was so lost, and then a son to keep his memory alive. And He did the same for you."

"Esther, I don't want to wait. Will you marry me? Soon?"

Esther laughed and studied the serious face before her. She couldn't answer for the catch in her throat but simply nodded.

Relief washed over Gabriel. He sighed, thinking yet again how God had brought them both into this church, on this Sunday, *for such a time as this.*

As a knock came to the door, Gabriel looked at his watch. He looked at Esther. "Are you okay?"

She nodded and smiled weakly as Gabriel went to the door.

Epilogue

*"O the depth of the riches both of the wisdom and knowledge of God!
how unsearchable are his judgments, and his ways past finding out!"*
Romans 11:33

May, 2018

Gabriel listened as the commencement speaker read his opening text. *"Only fear the* LORD, *and serve him in truth with all your heart: for consider how great things he hath done for you."* As he continued on, eloquently yet passionately urging the graduates to remember all that the Lord had done for them, Gabriel turned to find Esther staring at him with a knowing smile. *Oh, what great things our God has done for us!* The message seemed to travel from one heart to the other without a word.

His mind wandered back to just a few weeks ago when the family celebrated Esther's ninetieth birthday and their sixty-seventh wedding anniversary. He thought back on her statement those many years ago, when they had decided to marry on her birthday. "My two greatest earthly treasures I received on my birthday: my fortress and love, and my twelve smooth stones."

Sixty-seven years, he thought. It seemed like just yesterday that they had rediscovered each other. He looked down the row at David, now a grandfather himself. He had to smile at the blond heads that were sprinkled among his mostly dark-headed brood of forty-two. How he had loved that boy just as much as Esther had loved Deborah.

Forty-two! Oh Father, how You have blessed me! They all know You and love You, and many are serving You as missionaries to Your people! A tear choked his throat. He didn't often think of his own mother and father. He couldn't bear to think that they were possibly suffering for rejecting God's Son. *Thank you, Father, for showing me the truth.*

He redirected his thoughts to the platform and listened intently to the rest of the address. He couldn't help but let his eyes wander to his grandson, sitting on the platform with the rest of the honorary doctorate recipients. His heart raced as he heard the name.

"Mr. David Kurtis Gerstein Jr.," the announcer proclaimed.

Esther reached for Gabriel's hand, unknowingly holding her breath. David came forward and stood before the president of the university as the man spoke.

"David Gerstein graduated from this university in 1991 with a bachelor's degree in Missions. He earned his master's degree with a Biblical Languages concentration. David and his wife, Lydia, also a 1991 Mission's graduate, were then called to the Netherlands, where they have labored as missionaries for twenty-three years, mainly to the Jewish population.

"David has planted three thriving churches in Amsterdam and other smaller villages. In 2000, he began the Amsterdam Christian Academy, which has grown to include a Bible Institute as well, where David teaches and mentors future pastors and missionaries."

The man looked at David. "David Gerstein, please come forward."

David took the few steps closer to the announcer and faced the president.

"Dr. David Kurtis Gerstein Jr., I present you with this honorary doctorate and confer to you all the rights and privileges pertaining thereto."

David turned forward as the dean placed the colored hood over his head. He turned to shake the president's hand. Words were exchanged, and David went to the podium.

He looked around the audience, letting his gaze rest on his family before speaking. "Mr. President, faculty, graduates, friends, and family: It is a great honor to stand here today. I stand in awe at the mighty power of the Almighty Jehovah God. He has blessed our ministry, and we have had the privilege of working with some of the finest Christians I know.

"I'd like to take a moment and tell you about a wonderful lady." His eyes connected with Esther's, whose tears were running freely. "She grew up in Amsterdam in the Jewish quarter in the 1930s. At the age of sixteen, she was taken from her home, witnessing the death of her mother by the bullet of a German Nazi.

"She survived Auschwitz with the aid of my grandfather and later migrated to Israel. It was there that my father was born. From the beginning, my grandmother, Esther Ruth, loved her God and waited earnestly for her Messiah. She moved to New York, not knowing why, but sensing the Lord's leading. It was there that she found her high school sweetheart, my stepfather, only a week after both of them had found Jesus Christ to be the long awaited Messiah.

"I praise God for the love I saw in my family, especially the love for God's chosen people. I was raised to love them, and it is no wonder that my heart felt a call to go to them with the Gospel.

"Thank you, Grandma, for surviving, and striving to live and love your Lord. Is it possible that you were spared *for such a time as this?* God only knows how many are in His kingdom because you chose to believe."

As he walked from the podium, Esther's heart was overwhelmed with love for her dear family and an even greater love for her Lord. She didn't hear much of the rest of the service. Before she knew it, the graduates were marching out, and her family was hovering about her like a protective wall. She suddenly felt very tired.

"Are you alright, Esther?" Gabriel asked with concern in his voice.

She smiled up at him. "Yes, just a little tired. It's been a long day."

"It's been a long life," David Jr. said as he came up behind her. He gathered her in his arms, his own family mulling about.

"You didn't need to say all that, David," Esther chided.

David bent to look into those eyes he adored. "I did need to say them, Grandma. You are my heroine."

The sincerity Esther read on his face made the tears clog her throat. "David, you are so much like your father and grandfather."

She reached up to stroke his face—something that she often did with all her grandchildren. She looked around at all the faces she loved so much. Esther, her oldest great-granddaughter, stood beside her father, looking fondly into her great-grandmother's eyes. Esther's hand went to the locket she wore around her neck. She held it momentarily before reaching back to unclasp it.

She reached for Esther and pulled her close. "I know I should wait until your sixteenth birthday, but with everyone here and, well, at my age, who knows if I'll make it to September!"

Chuckles and protests rose at that statement. When all quieted down, she reached up and put the locket around Esther's neck. She could feel Gabriel's strong hands on her shoulders, as though signaling his approval. With the locket in place, she reached for it and opened it. A faded picture of her parents and brothers still graced its opening. She kissed each one and closed the locket. She bowed her head, and as if by a silent signal, Gabriel began to pray.

"Dear Heavenly Father. We are truly overflowing with praise for You today. It is a day of great rejoicing. You have blessed us and honored Your name this day. We pray a special prayer for our Esther Ruth Gerstein. She bears the names of many great people: her great-grandmother, her father, and her grandfather. We praise You that she now wears this treasure. May it always remind her of Your people as well as Your Son and His heavenly kingdom. Use her, Father. Use us all to bring many into the kingdom, where we may one day dwell among those twelve beautiful foundations. We pray in Jesus name, amen."

Fact and Fiction

Any historical fiction includes real places and people as well as fictional characters. *Twelve Smooth Stones* is no exception. The following gives the distinction between the two:

Spanish Jews in Amsterdam

Many of the Jewish descendants living in Amsterdam had come from Spain and were called *Maarssen Sephardim*. This group did produce the first rabbi in the New World, and they were instrumental in founding New Amsterdam, or New York City.

Kurt Gerstein

Kurt Gerstein was an SS officer of the Third Reich who did not approve of Hitler's final solution to annihilate the Jewish population in Europe. He spent time in a concentration camp to rethink his loyalties, but he came out galvanized against Hitler's ideals. The atrocities he saw firsthand nearly drove him mad. After he told the secretary to the Swedish legation in Berlin, Baron Göran von Otter, of what was happening, the secretary thought that Gerstein was crazy. Only later would he find out it was all too true.

Although brothels did exist at some of the concentration camps, Kurt Gerstein was never in charge of such a diabolical reward system. As a chemist, he was in charge of acquiring the canisters of Zyklon B—the gas used in the gas chambers. He destroyed one shipment of canisters by burying them.

Herr Schindler's Visit to Auschwitz

A little known fact about Oscar Schindler is that he did nearly lose about 300 of his female workers when they were accidentally shipped to Auschwitz. Upon hearing of the mistake, Herr Schindler personally secured their release—the only Jews to ever leave Auschwitz other than by escape.

The name Anita Agorazo is fictitious; however, it carries a special meaning. *Agorazo* is a Greek word translated as "redemption." The idea is "to purchase in the market." How fitting considering the heroic effort of Oscar Schindler, whose entire fortune was spent to "hire" his Jewish workers, hence saving them from destruction.

Sonderkommando

A group of Jewish prisoners called the *Sonderkommando* did manage to destroy Crematorium IV with explosives.

Jason Himmel

Although Jason is a fictional character, his name carries a meaning and a memory. The name Jason means "God is my salvation or healer"; the name Himmel means "heaven." Through his efforts, Jason leads Gabriel to a saving knowledge of Jesus Christ, assuring him a home in heaven. Himmel is in honor of my parents: Jim and Martha Hummel, whose faithfulness in taking me to church as a child paved the way to a tender heart toward the things of God.

Beriha

Thanks to the *Beriha*, an organization formed by Jews who had survived the war, many Jewish survivors made the journey Esther and her father took through the Alps and into Italy—on foot.

Childs

Childs, the restaurant that Gladys takes Esther to visit on her tour of New York City, was a popular luncheon chain that began in the 1920s by Samuel and William Childs. The popular eatery expanded to over 120 restaurants all over the eastern coast, and the massive building that once housed the restaurant at Coney Island still stands today.

19418245R00170

Made in the USA
Middletown, DE
18 April 2015